Naughty Games
LENA MATTHEWS

Ellora's Cave
Romantica Publishing

SEVEN MINUTES IN HEAVEN

Naughty Games, Book One

In honor of her friend's birthday, Bev Navarro does something she swore never to do again, enter Holden Lancaster's home. At one time the two had been part of a close-knit group of friends, but that all changed thanks to one game of Seven Minutes in Heaven.

Holden can't understand why Bev is avoiding him. He can only hope tonight's festivities will give them the time needed to mend old wounds. But one look at her face tells him he's in for a night of disappointments.

The birthday surprise is on them though, because they're receiving a gift neither will ever forget. The stopwatch is going, and the only question is, will they make the same mistake the second time around?

I NEVER

Naughty Games, Book Two.

Thanks to his friend's thirtieth birthday, Tripp Kowlaski is forced to face the two people he's been avoiding for the last year—Skylar Daveigh and Gideon Foley. At one time the three of them had been part of a close-knit group of friends, but that all changed thanks to one game of I Never.

Some things can't be forgiven or forgotten. Unfortunately for Tripp, Gideon isn't in the mood to do either. He and Skylar are happy now together. The last thing either of them needs is to be reminded of what they can't have.

Skylar is conflicted. She's in love with two men who can't move past their anger or fear to admit their love for one another. All she wants is the three of them to be happy, together, but some wishes aren't meant to come true. The birthday surprise is on them though, because they're receiving a gift none of them will ever forget. The only question is, will they make the same mistake the second time around?

DOUBLE DARE

Naughty Games, Book Three

Paige Reyes is going to kill Shane Oxley if it's the last thing she does. Not only did the cold-hearted blackmailer force her to attend his thirtieth birthday party, he used her love for her brother to do it, giving her just one more reason to dislike him. Not that she needed it.

No matter how justified Paige's reasons are for avoiding him, Shane refuses to be without her for another second. Thanks to a risky game of Double Dare three years ago, Shane made the biggest mistake of his life and lost Paige in the process. Now all he wants is an opportunity to make it right again.

The birthday surprise is on Paige though. If Shane only has one chance with her, then he's going to do everything he can to change her heart. The gloves are off and everything is fair game.

An Ellora's Cave Romantica Publication

www.ellorascave.com

Naughty Games

ISBN 9781419960987
ALL RIGHTS RESERVED.
Seven Minutes in Heaven Copyright © 2008 Lena Matthews
I Never Copyright © 2008 Lena Matthews
Double Dare Copyright © 2009 Lena Matthews
Edited by Mary Moran.
Photography and cover art by Les Byerley.

This book printed in the U.S.A. by Jasmine-Jade Enterprises, LLC.

Trade paperback publication May 2010

The terms Romantica® and Quickies® are registered trademarks of Ellora's Cave Publishing.

With the exception of quotes used in reviews, this book may not be reproduced or used in whole or in part by any means existing without written permission from the publisher, Ellora's Cave Publishing, Inc.® 1056 Home Avenue, Akron OH 44310-3502.

Warning: The unauthorized reproduction or distribution of this copyrighted work is illegal. Criminal copyright infringement, including infringement without monetary gain, is investigated by the FBI and is punishable by up to 5 years in federal prison and a fine of $250,000.
(http://www.fbi.gov/ipr/)

This book is a work of fiction and any resemblance to persons, living or dead, or places, events or locales is purely coincidental. The characters are productions of the author's imagination and used fictitiously.

NAUGHTY GAMES
Lena Matthews

ಬ

SEVEN MINUTES IN HEAVEN
~9~

I NEVER
~93~

DOUBLE DARE
~239~

SEVEN MINUTES IN HEAVEN
ఴ

Acknowledgement

To Liz, my wonderwall. No tag backs! And to my girl Beverly Havlir who inspires me, impresses me and makes me laugh.

Trademarks Acknowledgement

The author acknowledges the trademarked status and trademark owners of the following wordmarks mentioned in this work of fiction:

Aerosmith: Rag Doll Merchandising, Inc.

Hallmark: Hallmark Licensing, Inc.

Jerry Springer: Multimedia Entertainment, Inc.

Martha Stewart: Martha Stewart Living Omnimedia, Inc.

Quantum Leap: NBC, Universal, Inc.

Chapter One

There were no two ways about it. Bev Navarro was a freak. Nothing else could explain why she was standing outside a closet door, coat in hand, getting wet. Nothing except the truth. The last time she'd felt any hint of real passion was when she was locked in there with Holden Lancaster.

Damn it. Closing her eyes, Bev cursed herself for her blunder. She had tried hard in the last years not to think his name, let alone say it. She was hoping she could continue the grand tradition of pretending Holden didn't exist. Although how she thought she was going to get through the night with that theory intact was beyond her. This was his house.

His house, their friends and Shane Oxley's birthday, and for that reason alone she was going to act civil and pretend as if she were happy to be there. Shane was worth it even if Holden wasn't.

Tonight they were all merging to celebrate their self-proclaimed ringleader Shane's thirtieth birthday. He was the first one to hit the big three-o and in his self-assuming way he demanded one night together. Just the old group—like old times. No dates. No excuses.

It was even rumored he'd personally flown the newly moved Paige Reyes in from Baltimore because she couldn't afford the trip. She was putting her brother through medical school and had very little extra cash to spend. Although Bev was willing to bet if Paige had refused the offer of aid, Shane would have driven the six-hundred-mile trip to pick her up himself.

Shane was never one to let anything stand in his way once he made up his mind. It was one of the things she most admired about him. Not only was he a go-getter, he was also the reason any of them knew one another.

He was the impetus behind them all and the glue that held them together, even after all these years. Distance and time didn't matter, which was, of course, why she was here now, despite not wanting to run into Holden.

Shane had said come and she did. Just like old times. Bev couldn't resist aiming to please him, forever grateful he'd been willing to give a bookworm like her a place to belong. Instead of disappearing in a sea of faces at college as she could have, Bev became part of a mixed crowd of jocks, artists and brains who inspired her to become the successful actuary she was today.

A successful woman, who was hiding in the hallway to gather her nerves. Bev had only been at the party for five minutes and she was already flustered. Just seeing Holden behind the bar when she walked into the living room had been enough to send her scurrying for cover with the excuse of having to hang up her coat.

"What's behind the Mona Lisa smile?"

Without turning around, Bev knew exactly who was behind her. She hadn't seen Holden in over a year, but she still recognized his voice as if it were yesterday. The sexy seductive pitch served him well career-wise as a radio personality. Smooth as a fine whiskey, his voice could charm birds from trees. "Dare I hope it's because of where you're staring and the memories it brings back?"

"Disgust wouldn't make me smile. Hello, Holden." With her resolve in place, Bev turned around and eyed him coolly. It took the strength of the gods to keep her face stoic and not reveal in any way, even after the pain he'd caused her, her body's reaction to him.

Not that she could really blame herself. The man was gorgeous. As disgustingly sickening as it was, all four of the men in their group were devastatingly handsome. It had been a running joke between Paige, Skylar and herself that in order for them all to go out together as a group the men had to agree not to shave and to wear wrinkled clothes. No women wanted to be around men who looked better than they did. Yet despite how handsome Shane, Gideon and Tripp were, to Bev, the line started behind Holden.

He had a wealth of thick black hair, compelling green eyes and a wide mouth that curved at the corner, which made Holden seem as if he were always on the cusp of laughing. He towered over her five-foot-six frame by at least eight inches with a dominating presence, thanks largely to his muscular body. In a word, Holden was yummy.

"Fair Bev, you wound me." Holden slapped a hand across his chest and took a few teasing steps back as if he were stumbling under the weight of her words. Her lips quivered in amusement.

Damn him! Even though she had a right to her anger and pain, Bev found it difficult to harden her heart against Holden. No matter how much she really wanted to. "Regrettably it's not mortal."

He winced at her words and held his hands in the air in a defenseless manner. "I surrender. Please lay down your arms at the door."

"You're safe...for now." Bev turned away before she did something stupid such as jumping into his arms, and instead opened the closet door. Ignoring the tug of her heartstrings, she stepped forward and reached for a hanger. Unfortunately, Holden followed.

She sensed more than heard him move, stilling as he reached over her and took down a hanger. His mere presence so close made Bev dizzy. *How in the world am I ever going to survive the night?*

"I wasn't worried. I'm more than sure I can take you."

Take you could have been interpreted in so many different ways. Especially the way he said it, as if it were more of a promise than a threat.

"I don't underestimate you at all, Holden." Her words sounded cool and collected, a vast contrast to the fire burning inside her. With surprisingly steady hands, Bev took the hanger from Holden and muttered a soft "thank you" in the process. Swiftly she hung up her jacket then turned around. As Bev suspected, Holden hadn't moved. He filled the doorway, blocking her exit.

The teasing tone was no longer present in his stance or his words. "How long has it been, Bev?"

"Since?" The word barely squeaked past her lips. *So much for cool and collected.*

"Since you've allowed yourself to be in the same room with me."

"I've seen you around."

"Around, huh?"

"Yes."

Holden crossed his arms over his broad chest and cocked his head to the side. His body language spoke more than his simple words had. Holden was gearing up for a battle of wills with Bev ringing in as his worthy adversary. "Like when?"

Bev didn't have to think to answer the question. She knew to the second when they'd last met. "Tripp's barbeque on the Fourth of July."

"*A year ago* at Tripp's barbeque." Holden stressed "a year" as if it may have somehow slipped Bev's mind how long ago the event had been.

"It's nothing personal, Holden. I've just been really busy."

"Not too busy to see the others, and don't bother to deny it. I've asked. You've even been to visit Paige recently."

"Checking up on me?" Although her words were flippant, she couldn't help but feel slightly pleased he'd been asking about her. Of course it was most likely just common courtesy. They had been friends after all—once. But it was impossible to steady her erratic pulse, just as it was beyond her control the way her nipples tightened beneath her blouse.

Holden bypassed her question as was his way when he was cornered. After ten years of friendship, it was easy to recognize one another's signs. "I noticed you greeted everyone else with a warm smile and a hug. Everyone but me, that is."

"You were behind the bar," Bev reasoned, even though she knew it was a lie. "Can we continue this conversation in the hallway?"

"So you can run? As usual."

"I don't run."

"Prove it. Come here and give me what you willingly gave everyone else." Holden dropped his arms to his side and waited. His words were spoken quietly, but the order could not be missed…or denied.

"Gladly." Bev wasn't a coward, but she wasn't stupid either. "But out there."

"Why not in here?" Holden glanced around as if noticing their surroundings for the first time. "I think it's fitting, don't you? This is where we shared our first kiss."

"Stop it, Holden." Bev didn't want to remember.

"This is the place where I had my first taste of your sweet nectar."

Bev held her hand out as if her palm could stop his damning words.

"The first place you came for me."

"Damn you." Quickly stepping forward, Bev tried to cover his mouth, but Holden grabbed her wrist and, using it as leverage, spun her around, slamming her back against his chest.

Lowering his mouth to her ear, Holden angrily continued. "No. Damn you, Bev, for walking away from me."

* * * * *

Two Years Ago

Holden glanced around at everyone in his house and shook his head in wonderment. People had actually shown up, some of whom he wasn't sure he even knew. Maybe there was something to this etiquette thing after all.

In honor of his first house, the girls decided to throw him a housewarming party. Though he'd appreciated the gesture, the idea of inviting people over just so they could give him stuff seemed a bit messed up. Besides, he didn't need much. He was a guy. It didn't really matter to him if his glasses matched his plates or if he had forks in two different sizes.

All he required of his new home was a tax shelter, a place to plug in his television and a pantry full of toilet paper. After sharing an apartment with Shane and Tripp, Holden was looking forward to being able to go to the bathroom with peace of mind.

Of course his take on things wasn't good enough for Skylar and Paige, or even Bev, who unsurprisingly took their side. And when all three of them batted their pretty eyes his way, he caved. As usual.

To their amusement, Holden simply reached in his back pocket and extracted his wallet. Closing his eyes, he held it open and told them to take what they needed but leave him enough money for lunch. Amidst giggles, Holden was robbed in the sweetest way, receiving parting kisses from each of them as they exited his house with his cash.

For his selfless act, he received kitchen supplies, enough towels and sheets to make Martha Stewart proud and from his Bev, a hundred rolls of TP. Shaking his head, Holden eyed his guests with amusement. He wasn't sure he knew everyone, but no one had walked into his house empty-handed and thanks to Bev, come Monday morning, a thank-you card would be mailed off from him, penned by her, to express his gratitude.

Bev. "His Bev" as he had grown to think of her. Holden picked up his lukewarm beer and took a deep drink as he watched her dance with a cane-wielding Shane in the living room. The up-tempo song kept her moving much to Shane's delight and her apparent amusement.

Bev was tipsy. Not drunk, but she was definitely feeling no pain. Tonight was one of the first times since he'd known her Holden had seen her have more than a couple of sips of hard alcohol. In college she had been a serious student. Her scholarship would require nothing else. It took an act of God to get her to leave her room during the week for anything short of an emergency. On those rare occasions they managed to whisk her away she always had a great time. Even after school she maintained a serious disposition. When they'd go out to dinner or whatnot, she'd occasionally have a glass of wine, but even that was rare.

Bev wasn't the life of the party, but she always made a room brighter just because she was there. Now Holden had come to the conclusion he wanted to see if she had the same effect in a bedroom. His bedroom to be precise. This wasn't a fly-by-night fancy, but something Holden had wanted for some time. Yet knowing how important her education was to her, he'd held back, waiting until she no longer had the pressures of school or starting a new career to worry about. Now it was years later and they were both settled. It was time for him to make her his.

"Who's ready for a blast from the past?" Skylar Daveigh walked into the room, holding a black baseball cap above her head.

The pretty blonde was the princess of the group. She was used to her good looks making her the center of attention, but anyone who knew her knew Skylar's lovely appearance wasn't the best thing about her. She had the biggest heart of anyone he knew. Something a bit uncommon in a woman with her beauty. It didn't mean Skylar was a pushover by any means. But she tended to lead with her heart, which resulted in a few breaks over the years.

"What's on your mind, Skylar?" Gideon Foley was splayed back on the couch, watching the pretty woman as usual.

He and their other friend Tripp Kowlaski had been vying for her attention for years, but Skylar was either oblivious to it or taking her sweet time with making up her mind. Lucky for Gideon, Tripp was on the road with his team. He'd been drafted directly from college with the Chicago Blackhawks, and with him gone this weekend, this was a perfect time for Gideon to make his move.

"Dirty, dirty things." Skylar slipped her hand into her pocket and pulled out her watch, wiggling it about in the air. "Anybody want to play Seven Minutes in Heaven?"

Some chick gasped, much to Holden's amusement.

"Aren't we a little too old for that?" Paige questioned.

"I haven't played it since high school." Then Shane grinned, the evil little grin that made Holden want to leave right now and head to an ATM for bail money. "I'm in."

"Of course you are," Paige muttered as she stood. "I'm out."

"Chicken," Shane taunted, walking over to the dark beauty. Out of everyone in their group, Paige was the one person who didn't always follow Shane's lead. Over the years, Holden had witnessed how it annoyed and intrigued his friend all at the same time.

Instead of rising to the bait, Paige shrugged her shoulders and walked around him as if he weren't even there. "And I haven't heard that since high school." Rising to her tiptoes, Paige brushed her full, soft lips against Holden's cheek before giving him a quick hug. He returned her embrace, glancing up at Shane as he did. From the scowl on his friend's face, Shane wasn't happy.

"I'll talk to you later."

"Thanks again, sweetie. It was fun."

"From the looks of things, I'm thinking it's going to get a lot more fun," Paige teased. Bev made her way over to them and was waiting with a hug of her own for Paige.

"You staying, girl?" Paige asked.

"I was…" a faint blush drifted over her cheeks, "thinking about staying for a bit more."

Well, well, well. Holden hadn't been expecting her to stay. He quickly raised his beer to hide his pleasure. Things were going to get a whole lot more interesting.

Paige grinned. "You go, girl. Call me tomorrow and let me know all the juicy details."

Paige wasn't the only person who decided to call it a night, and once everyone who was leaving finally vacated, Skylar handed out pens and little slips of papers for the women to write their names on. "We outnumber the guys a bit here tonight, girls, which means two lucky bastards get to go twice."

The women booed as a few men hooted and hollered.

"I'm going to pass the hat around and I want all you lovely ladies to put your name in here and then pass it to the next person." Skylar dropped her name in and handed the hat off. "Let the fun begin."

"This didn't happen at the last housewarming party I went to," Bev softly said as she dropped her name in the hat. As she went to hand the hat to the next woman, she suddenly stopped and shot her gaze up to Holden's. "This is a bad idea. I should have left with Paige."

"No, you shouldn't have." Before she could dive into the hat and search for her name, Holden snatched it out of her hand and passed it on. The last thing he wanted was for Bev to leave. "It's just a game, Bev."

"I know, but…" Bev lowered her voice. "What if no one picks me?"

"You'll get picked. You heard Skylar, a couple of guys will go twice."

"But what if no one wants to pick me?" Even though she spoke softly, Holden heard every word she said.

For the life of him, Holden would never understand how a woman could be as lovely as Bev and not know it. She might not have been the stereotypical stunner Skylar was, but she was definitely beautiful. The truth of the matter was, in his eyes, Bev was far lovelier.

She was an exotic beauty. Her Filipino heritage was ever-present in her lovely caramel-colored skin and flowing brown hair. She was willowy thin with full pouty lips, amazing dimples and the most mesmerizing chocolate eyes he'd ever seen. Bev had the type of body that made a man want to weep for joy. Yet she was apparently the only one who didn't know it.

"I assure you—"

"All right, partygoers, let's begin." Skylar walked to the center of the room, waving the hat in front of her. "Here are the rules. The lucky man will draw a woman's name from the hat and disappear into yonder closet for seven minutes of heaven—"

"I only need five, baby," Shane teased, revving his brows, much to everyone's amusement.

"After seven minutes I'll knock on the door and then the hat gets passed to the next lucky fellow."

"Aren't you supposed to fess up about what happened in the closet?" questioned one of the women. "Isn't that how a winner is chosen?"

"Look at them, honey, and look at us. Do you really think any of us are going to walk out of here not a winner?"

"Duly noted."

After the laughter subsided, Skylar began to slowly turn around in a circle. "The first contestant in our naughty game is…Holden."

"Good luck." Bev offered a smile.

"You too." In the midst of the hooting and catcalls, Holden walked to the center of the room and stopped in front of Skylar, who was holding the hat toward him.

"Choose wisely."

"I plan to." Without taking his eyes off Skylar, Holden dropped his hand into the hat and pulled out a piece of paper. He smiled when he saw the name on the slip then turned to Bev and crooked his finger in a "come here" gesture and lied. "I pulled Bev."

Chapter Two

Oh my God. She was going to die from embarrassment. Literally combust into flames from the heat scorching her cheeks.

As she stood woodenly in front of the closet door, Bev wondered if it would be too late to bail out now. She was sure Holden wouldn't mind. It wasn't as if he were dying to get her alone anyway.

"Okay, you two." Skylar opened the closet door and gestured for them to enter. "In you go."

Holden placed his hand on the center of Bev's back and tried to propel her forward but she held her legs stiff and refused to budge. "Wait."

"Yes." Skylar, damn her twisted soul, was grinning from ear to ear. She of all people should have known why Bev was hesitant to go in there with Holden. Skylar and Paige were the only two souls who knew Bev had a crush on Holden. Leave it to her friend to milk the situation for all it was worth. "How will we know when our time is up?"

"I'll come and knock on the door. Now get in."

"That's what I'm saying." Holden stepped around Bev into the closet and tugged on her hand.

"Come…" Panicked, Bev grabbed onto the doorframe and held on for dear life. She knew she looked idiotic but she didn't care. "You're not going to stay out here and wait."

"Hell no."

"But—"

"But nothing. I'll be back in about seven minutes or so."

"About!" With a strong tug, Holden pulled her into the room and wrapped his arm around her waist, holding her taut to him.

"Yes, I'm thinking you might need a few extra minutes to warm up." And with a wink, Skylar shut the door, sealing Bev alone in the dark with Holden.

The sounds of Skylar's laughter rang throughout the closet as Bev stood frozen in Holden's arms. Even though she'd dreamt of being with him in so many different ways, Bev couldn't seem to turn around.

"This is so mortifying," Bev whispered. She had never been so grateful for darkness in her life. She knew when she agreed to play she would end up in the closet with someone, but she never expected it to be Holden.

In fact, she'd prayed it wouldn't be him. Any other person she could have giggled her way through some heavy petting, a fumbled kiss or two, and walked out of the closet with her heart intact. Instinctively Bev knew escaping unscathed after seven minutes with Holden was highly unlikely.

"Why?" Holden loosened his hold but didn't release her. Instead he began to move his hand in slow circular motions against her abdomen as if he were trying to calm her.

"Because of who you are and who I am."

"That should make this easier not harder."

"I didn't say it was hard. Nothing is hard about this, just embarrassing."

"I wouldn't say *nothing*." Holden's dry words didn't penetrate her mind until she felt him move his pelvis against her back. Something was hard all right and it was growing harder by the second.

"Oh my…"

"You can say that again." Holden slid his free hand into her hair and turned her face up toward his own. "Or better yet, say nothing at all. The clock is ticking and I want to enjoy every minute I have you in my arms."

As Holden bent his head toward her, Bev's heart felt as if it were pounding out her chest. Despite the room being pitch black, Holden had no trouble finding her mouth. When his lips touched her own, she parted them willingly, allowing his tongue to sweep inside and dance around hers.

At her capitulation, Holden growled and deepened the kiss hungrily. If it hadn't been for his strong hold on her, Bev would have melted into a puddle at his feet. His kiss was as potent as the man himself and just as overwhelming.

Bev's arms crept up, clasping around his neck as she held on to the one anchor in the storm of desire. Holden ended the kiss, leaving Bev panting for more. She could have happily drank from him for hours, losing herself in the touch of his lips, intoxicated on the pleasure of his tongue.

Releasing her hair, Holden moved his hand under her arm until it was resting against the full swell of her breast. Bev's ragged breathing made her breasts rise and fall under his steady touch. Her head was swimming from his kiss, yet Holden seemed as steady and calm as ever.

Was it possible he wasn't as affected by her as she was by him? Worried, Bev released her death grip from his neck and moved it down to his hand to push him away.

"I don't think so." Holden tugged her T-shirt from her jean skirt and pulled it over her breasts.

"We don't have to take this further."

"The hell we don't." Holden cupped her breast, squeezing her erect nipple through her lace-covered bra. "Look what you've been hiding under your clothes all these years, Bev. What a lush handful. Do they taste as good as they feel?"

If he could be cool, so could she. "I wouldn't know."

"Then I'll just have to let you know."

This didn't mean anything. It was a simple game. Bev wanted to keep that thought front and center in her mind.

This wasn't a declaration of love. Holden was just playing and Bev could be like all the rest of the girls and play too. As long as she didn't let her body's reactions take over. Of course Holden wasn't making it easy on her.

Holden slipped his hand beneath her skirt and her panties, all without missing a beat. Raising his head, he chuckled lightly. "My, my, my. Now isn't this a surprise." Bev blushed as Holden ran his fingers over her hairless lips. "I would have never pictured you this way."

"I doubt you've pictured me any way at all." Bev closed her eyes as she surrendered to the pleasure of his touch. More than likely this was going to be the one and only time she'd be with Holden this way so Bev was going to do something very unlike her. She was going to enjoy it all with no thought of what ifs and no plans for regrets.

"You don't know anything." Holden's fingers delved past her lips and into her hot core. He sank knuckle-deep into her wet pussy, plunging his fingers deeper and deeper with each thrust. "Look how wet you are for me, Bev. Wet and tight. Damn tight. When was the last time you were fucked?"

Moaning, Bev didn't answer. She was too lost in his touch to think back that far. But apparently Holden took her refusal to answer a different way. Releasing her breast, he once again circled his arm around her and pulled Bev to him.

"You're right." His voice sounded thick and tense, and his grip around her waist tightened painfully. "It's best we don't talk about past lovers. I want the only cock you think about to be mine."

"Speaking of cocks…" Bev leaned in to him, happy to rely on his strength for support. "When do I get to touch you?"

Holden pressed his palm against her swollen bud in lieu of answering and pushed against her clit as he added another finger inside her. When she cried out in pleasure, he chuckled roughly and undulated his palm against her, harder and faster than before.

Fireworks exploded behind her closed eyes as Bev's body trembled under his talented hand. Rocking down on his finger, Bev fucked herself much to Holden's obvious delight. "That's right, Bev, fuck my hand with your sweet pussy."

"Holden!" she cried, pumping her hips faster.

"No time for pleasantries. The clock is ticking and I want you to come." Holden pressed harder against her ass and sped up the rhythm of his thrusting fingers. "Fuck my hand, baby, fuck it like you'd fuck me."

His words trigged her climax as Bev imagined his cock plunging into her instead of merely his fingers.

"That's right, Bev. Come for me now," he demanded as her body rocked and flooded his hand with her juices.

"God…" she cried instantly, biting her bottom lip to stifle her moans of pleasure. It was bad enough she let Holden finger her to release in his hall closet; she didn't need to let everyone at the party know too.

"You're so fucking beautiful," Holden murmured against her neck as he showered her with light little kisses. "So damn responsive."

Holden slipped his fingers from her and pulled his hand from beneath her skirt. Much to Bev's embarrassment, she heard him lick his fingers clean. "And tasty."

With a shaky breath, Bev stepped away from him, too tired to think, let alone respond. She reached for the door handle but was stopped by Holden's hand on her waist. "Where are you going?"

"I'm sure it's been more than seven minutes."

"And…" Holden grabbed her hand and placed it on the bulge protruding from his slacks. "I think we have a bit more time."

Bev instinctively tightened her hand on his erection. A man wouldn't be this hard if he hadn't been into it just a little bit. Bev turned around. "Is it finally my turn to play?"

"You can have as many turns as you like."

Smiling, Bev released his cock and began to unbutton his pants. "One will do."

"For now." Holden groaned as her hand slid inside his boxers and touched his rigid length. A sense of power filled her as she began to stroke him, loving the way his cock swelled even further under her hand. "We should have done this years ago."

Bev couldn't have agreed more. "Lucky for us you pulled my name."

"Luck had nothing to do with it."

"What do you mean?"

"I didn't pull your name."

Bev froze. "What?"

"What's wrong?" Holden placed his hand on top of hers, trying to get her to stroke him once more.

"Whose name did you pull?"

"I don't know."

Moving her hand from under his, Bev stepped back until she was leaning against the door. "Why did you say it was mine?"

"Lots of reasons."

"Such as?" A sense of dread filled her.

"I don't know, you were worried no one would pick you and I've always—"

"You felt sorry for me?"

"That's not what I said."

"You didn't have to." Bev grabbed the doorknob and turned it, flooding the dark room with light.

"Damn it, Bev, that's not what I said."

Bev refused to listen. She couldn't. Her head was spinning in disbelief. How could he? She was such an idiot.

Holden didn't care about her, not in the way she cared for him. He was just protecting her as he always had.

The bastard!

"You've said enough." Stepping out, Bev ran smack-dab into Skylar, who took one look at her face and frowned.

"What's wrong?" Skylar asked worriedly.

"Time's up. I'm going home."

Holden stepped out after her, buttoning his slacks as he did. "Not until we clear this up."

Spinning around, Bev forced a smile on her lips. She would never let him know how much he hurt her. She wouldn't give him power over her. "Nothing to clear up. Game over."

"Bev," Holden growled, and stepped over to her. His face was a mask of fury.

But it made no difference. There was nothing he could say to change her mind now. "Looks like Seven Minutes in Heaven was seven minutes too long."

* * * * *

Present Day

Even though Holden had played the crucial moments of the evening over and over in his head, he still couldn't see what went wrong. Lord knew he tried to get her to explain, but after that night, Bev pulled a Houdini. If it weren't from others mentioning her, and the sound of her voice on her answering machine, Holden would have thought Bev had dropped off the face of the earth.

He'd dropped by, he'd left more messages than he could count, but to no avail. Short of kidnapping Bev and tying her cute little ass to a chair to force her to listen to reason, Holden had done all he could.

Enough was enough already. He'd given her time. He'd given her space. Now the only thing left to give her was the flat of his hand across her sexy ass. There would be no more running.

Not from him.

Ever again.

"Let me go, Holden."

"After you explain."

"I don't owe you an explanation."

"The hell you don't," he growled, turning her back around. "Two years is two too many. Either tell me what went wrong or move on. I've put up with enough of your pouting. It's high time you come back to where you belong."

"Which is?"

"In my arms."

Holden could feel her stiffen under his hands. "I don't belong to you."

"I disagree." Frustrated beyond belief, Holden moved his head down to kiss her but was waylaid by a voice from behind him.

"There you two are." Skylar's cheerfulness sounded forced at best, cementing the belief Holden had that Bev's rebellion wasn't a one-man act. He was willing to bet Skylar had been her accomplice, helping her stay one step ahead and away from him. "Everyone was wondering where you two had wandered off to."

"Everyone or just you?"

"Whatever do you mean, Holden?"

"Right." Holden released Bev, grimacing in annoyance when she scuttled past him. Regardless of what Bev thought, this was merely an intermission, not the final curtain call. Before she could slip into the other room, Holden called out, "We'll pick this up later, Bev."

Bev paused and looked over her shoulder at him, meeting his icy gaze straight on. "I seriously doubt it."

"I don't." From the contemptuous look on Bev's face, his warning wasn't lost on her.

Holden waited until the two women rounded the corner before he slammed the closet door shut with a curse. This evening wasn't going exactly as planned. He'd envisioned everyone coming over, eating cake, bullshitting for a few hours and then getting the hell out so he could talk to Bev alone.

In the alternate reality he'd contrived, Bev would be apologetic for her behavior over the last two years, and they would quickly make up then out. Yeah…something told him his fantasy just wasn't going to happen.

But just because it wasn't going to happen the way he'd hoped didn't mean Holden wasn't planning on getting his way on the matter. It just meant he was going to have to use a bit more finesse than he'd originally planned. Even if it took all night or all month, Bev and he were going to have it out. Whether she liked it or not.

With a new sense of purpose, Holden followed Skylar and Bev into the living room and smiled. Damn, it was good to see everyone again.

The six people in the room meant more to him than most members of his own family. They'd been through everything together. First loves, a broken engagement for Paige, a pregnancy scare for Tripp and his ex-girlfriend Candace, graduations, job highs and lows and more hangovers and barhopping than a Navy fleet, but throughout it all they'd all managed to stay friends.

The only difference between hanging out then and now was the undercurrent of tension in the room. Everyone was kind of grouped up instead of sprawled about as they would have been in the past.

Since Bev was now safe from his evil clutches, Skylar had made her way over to Gideon and was sitting next to him on the loveseat with her hand resting on his khaki-covered thigh. Their body language spoke of an intimacy far greater than friendship, which explained why Tripp was staring in their direction with a mixture of anguish and annoyance. An odd combination to be sure.

There was definitely something going on with those three, and Holden had a pretty good idea what it was, but he knew it wasn't his place to interfere or judge. Far be it from him to offer love advice to anyone. He was too busy trying to get Bev into the closet to worry if the three of them were going to come out of it.

Shane and Bev were laughing over the many candles she was shoving into his cake. Thirty years old. It was a milestone, which for a while there Holden wasn't sure Shane was going to see. Four years ago, Shane had been involved in a terrible car accident that had left him on the brink of death. It had been a slow recovery they all had seen him through and not only had he beaten the odds and lived, he'd also proved the doctors wrong by walking again.

Shane was an inspiration to them all and the best friend Holden ever had.

"You got busted, huh?" Paige slipped her hand through the crook in his arm, interlocking them together. She was no bigger than a minute and even with help from her spiked sable hair, cut in a short, funky style, she didn't come to his chin.

"You could have warned a brother." Holden's mouth quirked with humor. Leave it to Paige to pull him from his self-imposed funk.

"Not likely. You know we girls have to stick together."

"Then give me a heads-up." He glanced into the face of the pretty black woman and raised a brow. There was no doubt in Holden's mind Paige had the inside info on what was going on with Bev. "Just tell me what went wrong and I'll fix it."

"Oh no, that's between you and Bev. I'm staying out of it."

"Right." As if any of them had ever been able to mind their own business. "That's why you came over here to instigate—because you're so impartial."

"I'm impartial when it comes to sides, but when the shit hits the fan, I want to be front and center with a big bag of popcorn watching the final round. You know I love a good fight."

"You're such a bitch," he teased.

"I'm not a bitch, I'm *the* bitch. Get it right, baby."

"Oh baby, you know I adore it when you talk dirty."

Paige's husky laughter drew Shane's glance their way, and from the hungry look his friend leveled on her, Holden knew there was more there than met the eye.

Everyone in the group had somehow become involved with one another over the years, although not very smoothly. It was more than obvious there was something going on between Tripp, Skylar and Gideon. Holden and Bev had their own issues to deal with, and apparently so did Paige and Shane.

Evidently they all had their little secrets. How interesting.

Chapter Three

"Happy birthday to youuu…" The last note was sung higher, louder and a whole lot more off-key than the rest of the song had been, but that was half the fun.

Shane waited until the very last note had rung before leaning forward and blowing out his candles. Amidst applause and wolf whistles, Shane nodded his head regally, all the while gesturing with his hand for more.

Bev laughed as she watched him ham it up. His behavior was highly uncharacteristic, but a person only turned thirty once. After the noise died out, Bev joined Shane at the head of the table to assist with serving. It was either help him or sit next to Holden, who in his high-handed manner had bullied his way onto the chair next to hers.

Abandoned by Paige and Skylar, who despite pointed looks refused to intervene, Bev turned into Helpful Hannah in her attempt to avoid sitting next to him for as long as possible. From the heated look in Holden's eyes, he was onto her plan and knowing him as well as she did, Bev was willing to bet Holden had every intention of waiting her out.

After cutting the cake, Shane relinquished the knife and took his seat. It took only a minute for Bev to dish up the seven servings and pass them around. Once the chore was done, Holden sat back in his chair smugly and rested his hand on the back of hers.

Bastard.

"Here you go." Holden pushed the chair back so she could sit down.

Bev plopped on the chair with a mutinous expression. She may have to sit here, but she didn't have to like it. Taking a bite of her cake, she closed her eyes as she let the heavenly confection melt in her mouth. Unfortunately it also meant her mouth was full and she was unable to protest when Holden's hand landed on her knee.

Her eyes popped open and she had to grab for her glass to wash down the cake she began choking on.

"Bev, are you okay?" Skylar's concerned look had her nodding.

Bev shot Holden a venomous look, but he didn't move his hand. Carefully placing her glass back on the table, she attempted to push his hand off her knee to no avail. Instead of removing his hand, Holden slipped it under her dress, traveling up the length of her thigh. Bev tried to squeeze her legs together to halt his movements, but all she accomplished was trapping his hand between her thighs.

When Bev realized what she had done, she quickly opened her legs and grabbed hold of his hand. She bent his fingers back as discreetly but as roughly as she could until she heard him hiss then release. To her delight, Holden moved his hand, but shot her an injured look.

"So." The word came out more like a squeak than an actual word. Everyone turned to look at her, much to Bev's dismay. The questioning looks she could have handled, but it was the knowing looks from Tripp and Shane that had her seeing red. *Was everyone plotting against her*? "What did you wish for?"

"Bev." His fingers were back. Ever-so lightly Holden brushed his fingers across her knee, toying with the hem of her dress. "If he tells us what he wished for, he won't get it."

"You're going to wish you sat somewhere else if you don't move your hand." Bev elbowed him to everyone's amusement and tried to scoot her chair over. Tried being the key word because Holden gripped her chair back tight and wouldn't let it budge.

"Where you going?"

"Let go, you big bully."

"Actually," Shane interrupted, "my wish was for all of us."

Gideon rubbed his hands together enthusiastically. "I hope it was for us to the win the lotto."

"Not exactly." Shane's dry tone was almost as amusing as the crestfallen expression that crossed Gideon's face.

"Damn." Gideon sighed.

"Then what did you wish for?" Bev asked again as she once more attempted to scoot over.

Like before, thanks to Holden's hold, her attempt was in vain. *Fine*. Releasing her seat, Bev brought her hands from under the table and crossed her arms over her breasts, and of course, as soon as Bev gave up on moving, Holden released his death grip and grinned. He was so freaking childish. *Brat*, she mouthed.

Holden blew a kiss in lieu of responding but left his hand on the back of her chair.

"In time all things will be answered." Shane rose from his seat. "I'll be right back. I have to go get the presents."

"Presents!" Paige's voice was full of accusations. Her sharp tone froze Shane in his tracks. "I thought you weren't accepting gifts this year. If you told me I didn't have to bring a present as some lame attempt to salvage my poor dignity or to preserve my pride, you needn't have bothered."

"The presents aren't for me, Paige. I bought them for everyone else." Shane's smile was cold as ice as he leaned down and brought his face in kissing—or from the look of anger on Paige's face, striking—distance. "And I assure you, little one, no one knows more about your pride than I."

Paige met his heated look stare for stare, but didn't say a word. It was a smart move on her part because her silence antagonized Shane more than any words she might have uttered. With a muttered curse Shane rose and stomped out of the dining room.

"Pipe down, Paige," Skylar chided from across the table. "It's the boy's birthday, for goodness' sake. Retract the claws and cut him a little slack."

"That's what's wrong with him now. Shane is so used to people treating him as if he were the crowned heir he doesn't know what to do when someone stands up to him."

Bev secretly agreed. It wasn't as if she didn't love Shane to pieces, but he was used to getting his own way. His attitude was one of the reasons Bev always believed Paige was the perfect woman for him. Yet Paige, much like Bev, had leapt without looking with a member of their group only in the end to have it bite her in the ass.

"Are you willing to test your theory?" Shane questioned as he entered the room with three gift bags of various colors and sizes.

"I should have never come." As far as Bev was concerned, Paige and she were on the same wavelength with that sentiment.

"As if you had a choice. My threat wasn't an idle one."

"Don't think I didn't realize that."

"So…" Tripp interrupted. "Should we all leave and come back at a better time?"

"No way. If we leave, I won't get my present," Skylar teased.

"And it's all about you, isn't it, dollface?" Although Tripp's tone was light, Bev couldn't help but think there was something hidden behind his words. *What a twisted little group they were.*

With a snotty little grin, Skylar tossed her hair over her shoulder in a dramatized way. "Of course it is. Now gimme."

"Don't be greedy. You have to share." Shane handed a long, rectangular orange bag with peach tissue paper sticking out the top to Skylar, who took it with childlike glee.

"Who am I sharing it with?" Her big blue eyes were alight with pleasure and she practically vibrated in her chair with uncensored pleasure.

"You're sharing with Tripp and Gideon." Skylar's smile instantly dimmed as she cast a not-so-discreet glance between the two men with whom she had to share her present. Neither of them looked any happier than she did.

With a reserved sigh, Gideon rose from the table with his glass in hand and headed straight for the bottle of wine on the table in the corner. After filling his glass, he turned and faced the room again as if nothing were the matter. His expressive eyes were hidden behind his wire-framed glasses, but nothing could hide the rigidness of his posture. "Shall we take this into the living room?"

"What a wonderful idea." Bev would agree to anything if there was a slight chance it would keep her away from Holden. Rising from her chair, Bev hustled into the living room and quickly made her way to his recliner. It was the only single seat in the living room and Bev was willing to fight to the death to posses it.

Lucky for her—and everyone else—no one tried to stop her. Her flee to freedom was met with a loud guffaw of laughter from Holden, who casually sat diagonally across from her on the arm of his loveseat. His amusement rankled her.

"On with the present-giving." Shane handed Bev a small, square, lemon-colored bag with light butter tissue paper. Bev smiled in delight. The bag was almost too pretty to open. *Almost.* "You'll be sharing your present with Holden."

Damn. Bev glanced from the bag to Holden's smiling face and estimated the distance between the two of them. If she threw it really hard, she might be able to hit him in the head with it.

"And last but not least." Shane walked across the room, stopping at the far wall where Paige was standing. "For you, little one. You're sharing with..." Glancing around, Shane made a show of counting everyone. "Well, with me."

"Note the surprise on my face." Paige made no move to take the small violet sack. "I'll pass."

"I think not." Shane's stance brooked no argument. "Take the bag, Paige."

"There are over a thousand nerves in the human body, Shane." Paige snatched the bag from his hand. "And you are on every last one of mine."

Bev couldn't help but smile. Misery definitely loved company.

Shane walked to the center of the room. "Everybody gather around with the co-owner or owners of your bags. It's time to play a little game."

A game. Bev glanced over to Holden once more and grimaced in dismay. She didn't think she could handle playing another game with him. He was way out of her league.

Holden didn't know where Shane was going with this, but he sure liked the direction he was heading. Feeling all kinds of cocky, Holden stood and made his way over to Bev. She'd been so cute earlier when she hightailed it across the room. Holden wasn't sure what amused him the most; Bev thinking she could escape him in his own house or thinking if she picked the one-man seat, he wouldn't be able to sit next to her.

Silly lady. As he had on the loveseat, Holden made himself comfortable on the arm of the chair. "So it seats two after all."

"Bite me."

"Oh, I plan on it."

Bev glanced at him from the corner of her eye before looking away once more. From the faint hue of pink glowing lightly on her cheeks, she hadn't intended her words to be an offer.

Pity.

Amused now, Holden glanced around the quiet room. Gideon and Skylar once more occupied the couch, but this time Tripp joined them. He looked uncomfortable yet not out of place with the two of them. There was something about their positions with Skylar between them that just seemed right.

Shane had also moved and he was standing next to Paige, who was peering into her small bag as if expecting something to leap out at her any moment.

"Now that everyone is in their place, feel free to open the bags."

"Yay!" Skylar opened hers and pulled out a bottle of tequila. From the confused expression on her face, Holden thought it was safe to assume she hadn't been expecting booze. "Exactly what type of game were you thinking of playing, Shane dear?"

"Yes." Paige dangled a set of keys off her index finger. "What's going on here?"

"Hold up." Tripp gestured over to Paige. "How come Paige has keys and all we have is booze. I don't want booze. I want keys too."

"What did you guys get?" Gideon asked.

Bev had waited until everyone else unwrapped their presents before she opened her own, and when she pulled it out, her face was a mask of confusion. "It's a stopwatch. I don't get it."

"Join the club," Skylar said.

As everyone turned puzzled looks each other's way, Holden just sat back and relaxed. They might not get what was going on, but he sure did. From the moment Shane had suggested this little birthday rendezvous, Holden had been curious behind his friend's motive. Shane was not only their leader but he was also the person everyone talked to.

When Bev had begun to avoid him, Shane was the first person Holden confided in. Okay, maybe confided was a bit strong. They didn't talk, per se. More like they got piss-roaring drunk and Holden had ended up spilling his guts. He also knew a few months ago Tripp had the same cathartic alcoholic-induced male-bonding moment with Shane. Holden hadn't been there for the Hallmark moment, but he definitely was there the next day when Tripp was praying to the porcelain god.

Unlike Bev, Holden understood what the stopwatch represented, but the keys and tequila were beyond his abilities of deduction. He didn't see how they fit into the puzzle pieces of his friends' love lives, but there wasn't a doubt in his mind they did somehow.

"You all wanted to know what I wished for this year. Well, the answer lies within your hands."

"You wished for tequila?" Skylar questioned, confused.

"No, I wished for a do over." Shane paused to look at Paige for a moment. "A do over for us all."

"What do you mean?" Gideon asked. "Why do you think we need a do over?"

"Because you're all unhappy. Let me rephrase that, *we're* all unhappy and some of us are eaten up by guilt and regret."

"You? Guilt?" Paige's snorted. "I don't believe it."

"Believe it." Shane looked around the room at everyone. "And I'm not the only one, am I?"

Leave it to Shane to pull a *Quantum Leap* and try to right what once went wrong. Unlike the television show though, going back in time wasn't an option. Surprisingly, even if Holden could go back, he wouldn't. He wasn't the type of man who ran from his mistakes. He learned from them, just as he planned to learn from this one. And what he wanted to learn the most was what went wrong and how to correct it.

"I'm not," Gideon said, apparently still confused.

"No, you may not be." Shane nodded his head to Tripp, who was no longer wearing his easygoing smile. "But he is. Filled with it."

Skylar's gaze cut to Tripp's. "What is he talking about?"

"I don't know." Tripp's words of denial rang false. "I need another drink."

As he rose, Shane said, "Why don't you play another game of quarters while you're at it? Maybe this time you won't chicken out."

Skylar's gasp of shock was almost as palpable as Tripp's grimace of annoyance. "What I told you was spoken in confidence."

"You told him?" Gideon asked, standing as well. "You wouldn't talk to us about it, but you would discuss it with him?"

"There was nothing to talk about."

"No?" Gideon's fist clenched and unclenched by his side. After a few seconds of pained silence, he spoke again. "You're right, Tripp. There is nothing to talk about. Now or ever again."

"Gideon?" Upset, Skylar reached her hand out to him. "You don't mean that."

"Yes, Skylar, I think I do."

Holden had absolutely no idea what was going on and it was killing him. Tripp was facing the dining room with his back toward Skylar and Gideon and his spine stiff as steel. "You don't, Gideon. No more so than I meant what I said a year ago."

"You don't know dick, Tripp."

"Which was part of the problem, wasn't it, ol' buddy?"

"Go to hell."

"I've been there all year." Tripp turned to face them again and the toll he'd been under for the last year was etched into his wounded eyes. "I could use a do over. I'd be willing to play. What about you, Skylar?"

Skylar bit into her bottom lip and cast her gaze around the room nervously. When no one spoke or uttered a single sound, she set the bottle on the floor and stood. "I would love a do over. I'm more than willing to try again."

"Then goody for the both of you because I'm sure as hell not." Gideon's retreat was stopped by Tripp, who walked in front of the other man, blocking his exit. "Get out of my way, Tripp. You should be real good at that after the last several months."

"I don't want out of your way." His confession sounded raw.

"This time it isn't about you." Gideon brushed past Tripp and out of the room. The sound of the front door slamming shut rang out into the silent room.

What the hell had he missed? Holden felt as if he'd been watching a Spanish soap opera. He could tell something was going on, he just couldn't understand what they were talking about.

Holden always thought Gideon was a little *sweet*, but he never would have thought Tripp, Mr. All-American Jock, was too. Honestly, Holden had been under the impression the tension between the trio was because both men were interested in Skylar, who was sleeping with the two of them. Apparently, they wanted to spread the love all the way around.

"It's not too late." Shane finally spoke, breaking the silence. "If you want to fix this, go after him and make it right. You only get one 'Do Over', Tripp, don't mess it up this time."

Tripp took a deep breath in, closing his eyes for a second as if he were centering himself. When he opened them again, he sadly smiled. "What do you think, dollface?"

"The same thing I thought a year ago. My feelings for the two of you haven't changed. I love you both, and I want to be with both of you."

Whoa. There was some kinky shit going on with them.

"Think we can change his mind?"

"I think we just might be able to." Skylar picked up the bottle and joined hands with Tripp. "For courage."

"For you, me or Gideon?"

"All three." With Tripp in tow, Skylar made her way over to Shane and pulled him in for a hug. She whispered something in his ear before pulling back and waving goodbye to everyone. Tripp, on the other hand, didn't utter a word.

Holden didn't blame him. He didn't think he'd have much to say either if he was going over to his male friend's house to do the nasty.

"And then there were two couples," Shane said. "Shall we move on to—"

Paige raised her hand as if to block his words and shook her head. "I don't think so. They may not mind you putting their business all in the street, but I do."

"Then come with me. You know what the key unlocks."

"Heartbreak and headaches, and thanks to you, I've already had plenty of both." Paige dropped the bag, keys and all and walked over to the coffee table where she had left her purse. "The only regret I have, Shane, is coming to your stupid party."

"Good." After picking up the keys, Shane stormed over to her. "That means you don't think the night in my cabin was a mistake. A night too good to be forgotten or regretted."

What night? Holden looked at Bev, who was watching their friends with a slack-jaw expression. *Good.* At least he wasn't the only one in the dark.

"Goodbye, Shane."

"Think again, little one."

Paige didn't even bother to say goodbye to Bev or Holden. She just turned and stormed from the room with Shane hot on her trail.

"Wow." Bev's voice was as mystified as Holden felt.

"You can say that again." Then it hit him. They were completely alone. There was no one left for her to hide behind.

Chapter Four

The house was eerily quiet. A large contrast to the dramatized production of *My Friends and I*, which had just taken place front and center in the living room. Crazy was the only word that could describe the hodgepodge of emotions that had filled the now-silent room.

Bev was amazed by some of the revelations her friends had just made. There were a few things she knew about. Skylar being in love with both Tripp and Gideon was old news. Paige's trouble with Shane was no surprise either, but the bi thing and Paige actually having had sex with Shane was completely new to her.

"I feel so out of the loop." Bev couldn't keep the hint of disgust she felt from her voice. *Am I the only person who doesn't keep secrets?* Next time she had a chance to be alone with Paige and Skylar, she was going to wring some necks. How could they keep her in the dark like that?

"There's out of the loop and then there's this Jerry Springer I'm-my-own-grandpa mumbo jumbo we just became a party to. And you thought we had issues."

Bev nodded her head in agreement. "Would you have ever thought our little seven minutes in the closet was the most normal relationship out of our group?"

"Doesn't seem so bad now, does it?"

"I didn't say that." Bev glanced at the stopwatch in her hand. The representation of the gift was now as clear to her as Gideon's sexuality. "I guess there's no need to ask if you told Shane about our little adventure."

"He was here the night of the party. Besides, I didn't think it was a secret. Was I wrong?"

She put the stopwatch in the bag as she thought about what he said. The desire to rail against him as if she were the injured party seemed a bit ridiculous. It wasn't as if Bev hadn't confided in Paige and Skylar. "Not for telling Shane."

"Then what for? I really want to know, Bev."

"Just let it go." Bev set the bag on the floor and stood. For the first time in two years, Bev didn't feel angry with Holden. It wasn't as if she'd forgiven him, but their little high-schoolesque drama didn't seem nearly as important as it had an hour ago. "It's over. Forgiven and forgotten. Let's just move on."

There had been way too much excitement for one night. The need to rehash their own wasn't appealing in the least. Besides, the longer she stayed in his company, the harder it was for Bev to remain hardened in his presence. As pathetic as it was, no matter how angry she was, she couldn't resist him. It was one of the main reasons she'd avoided him all this time. And her weakening resolve was a sure sign it was time to go. "Goodbye, Holden."

"Wait."

"What?" Bev paused, cursing herself for not being able to take the next step.

"You can't leave me here alone."

"I can't?"

"No." Holden tucked his hands in his jeans pockets and smiled sheepishly at her. It was the same little smile he used when he wanted to get his own way. "Those ingrates left a huge mess in their quest to get their groove on. Can you find it in your heart to forgive me for say an hour and help me clean up a bit?"

"Clean up." Bev couldn't believe his audacity. "Are you kidding?"

"Not at all. You're the one who said you wanted to squash things."

"So."

"So if things are cool now, what's the problem?" he asked. "Before the whole closet thing, you wouldn't have thought twice about helping."

"I'm not the same girl I was back then."

"Pity." His smile faded. "I really liked her."

"You liked her to help you with your papers when we were in school."

"Right..." he drawled slowly. "I used you for your brains."

The sarcasm in his voice rang out loud and clear. "I didn't say use."

"But you implied it. Strongly." Instead of being upset as she would have been, Holden seemed amused. "According to your *il*logic because you consider yourself the brainiac one of the group, it goes to figure the only reason I wanted you around back then was to mooch off your smarts."

"I didn't go that far."

"With your theory in mind," Holden continued on as if she hadn't spoken, "then I guess it stands to reason you used me then for...what...my good looks?"

"Dream on."

"Well, if we're going to stereotype each other, let's go all out." Holden withdrew his hands from his pockets and crossed his arms over his chest. "If you're the smart one, Skylar is the princess, Shane's the rich one, Tripp's the jock, Gideon is the misunderstood artist, Paige is the token black, which leaves me to be the hot one. Am I just another pretty boy for you to toy with, Bev?"

He was blowing what she said way out of proportion and trying to make a joke out of everything as usual. "Back then, whether you want to admit it or not, we all found ourselves together because we fit into neat little boxes," she said.

"What do you mean?"

"We weren't competing against each other to fill the jock role or the nerd role. There was a place for everyone. Of course things changed once we graduated, we grew up. On the other hand, in many ways they stayed the same."

"Did they now?"

"Well, yes. It's not like you still need me to write thank-you cards for you or help you cram for a test."

"But I still need you."

"Yes. To clean." She pointed out. "You didn't ask anyone else. Just me. The one who never says no to you."

"I remember you saying no on a certain occasion."

"That time was different."

Holden narrowed his eyes and glared at her in mock anger. "I get it now."

"Get what?"

"The whole closet thing. You got me alone in there and took sweet advantage of me."

I took advantage of him? What the hell!

"After I give you an orgasm, you totally bailed, leaving me vulnerable."

"Yeah right." *Holden vulnerable. That would be the day.* She was willing to bet he didn't even know the meaning of the word.

"I'm telling you, woman, you left me devastated. You obliterated my pride."

His mocking attitude of their very defining moment had her seeing red. "By walking away first?"

"No, by treating me as if I were a whore."

Bev gasped. "I did not."

"You might as well have left money on my bedside table."

"Better a whore than a charity case."

Holden's expression went from wicked amusement to cold fury in a matter of seconds. "What does that mean?"

"Nothing. I'm out of here." Resentful of the situation she allowed herself to get in, Bev silently chastised herself as she moved toward the hall closet.

"Fuck nothing." Holden caught hold of her arm to hold her in place. His green eyes darkened and his lips thinned with irritation. "You need to explain yourself and you need to do it now."

"Or what?" she retorted in cold sarcasm.

"Or I'm going to give you a reason to be pissed off."

"A reason stronger than the one I already have?"

"Try me."

"Already did, and I have no desire to go back for seconds."

"Your anger is as mind-numbing as your stubbornness. I've been trying to talk to you for the last two years." His voice betrayed his frustration. "Yet you run. You hide. You avoid me at all cost and it's driving me mad not knowing why."

"Holden…"

"No. Tell me," he ordered. "Was I too rough with you? Did you not enjoy it?"

Bev couldn't lie to save her life so instead she chose to avoid answering him. "I don't want to talk about this."

"Too fucking bad. I do."

"Stop this."

"No. You stop it. Stop pushing me away. Tell me why you've kept us apart. How can you just pretend my touch didn't burn you alive?"

"Conceited much?" she sneered.

"I'm just speaking from my own experience. I haven't been able to get the taste of you from my mind since that night. The little earthy sounds you made when you came have haunted me. No matter how many women I've been with since then, it's you I still crave—"

"Lucky me." The last thing she wanted to hear about was him sleeping with other women.

"It's your face I imagine." Unrelenting, Holden pressed on. "It's your name I have to bite back from uttering as I come. You, Bev. You."

"Damn you." She didn't want to know this. She had to keep herself aloof and immune to his charms.

"You've damned me, baby, and now I need you to save me." Holden crushed his mouth upon Bev's, stealing her breath, her reason and her desire to resist all in one move.

His tongue slid through her parted lips, teasing her own with his featherlike strokes and, despite her better judgment, Bev began to respond to his kiss. Sheer willpower alone was no match against his kissing dexterity. Holden was a very talented man.

Her lips weren't the only part of her body that responded to Holden's kisses. Bev's nipples tightened against the lacy confines of her bra and her pussy, now damp, ached to be filled with his hard, long flesh.

Everything inside was crying out for her to give into his touch, to put her body out of its misery and surrender to him. All she had to do was reach down and unzip his pants. One simple move and he'd be hers. Maybe not forever, but for tonight. But still she resisted. Resisted herself. Resisted him. Bev wouldn't yield so easily. No matter how much she wanted to. To tangle with Holden once more would be foolish. Especially since she'd be risking not just her body to his fiery touch but her heart as well.

Bev wedged her hands between them and shoved with all her might, separating them. "I will not be a pity fuck again."

"I've never pitied you." His breathing was harsh and shallow, and his eyes were filled with need. "Look at me, Bev, and see for yourself how much I want you. You."

She didn't have to lower her eyes to see the evidence of his desire. It was written all over his face. "You lied to me."

"Never," he denied, vehemently.

"Yes, that day. You didn't really pick me."

"I told you I didn't."

"A fact you should have kept to yourself."

"Why?"

"Because I could have gone my whole life not knowing the only reason we were together in the closet was because you felt sorry for me." The words came out fast and angry before Bev could stop them and she instantly regretted it.

No good would come from dredging up the past, and she wasn't in the mood to listen to his sorry excuses, which was a good thing, because none came barreling forth.

Instead, Holden stiffened as though she had struck him, and his face flamed with anger. "What the hell are you talking about?"

Words alone couldn't express the rage coursing through his body, not just at the insult she leveled on him, but the one she delivered to herself as well.

Sorry. For her. If memory served, it was he who had suffered from the lack of relief that night. If anyone should have incurred sympathy, it should have been him.

"Don't pretend with me."

"No worries there, Bev. I'm not pretending."

She lifted her chin, meeting his icy gaze straight on. "Let's be honest, shall we?"

"Yes. Let's give it a shot." His blood boiled at her accusations, but Holden continued feeding her rope, waiting for the moment when she'd undoubtedly hang herself.

"I've thought about this long and hard, and although I appreciate the *noble gesture*," she said the words as if they were vile, "and the sacrifice you had to endure in honor of preserving my pride, I despise the way you went about it."

"*Noble gesture.* Is that what you call fingering your sweet pussy?" Holden tilted his head to the side and mockingly tapped his finger on his chin as if in deep thought. "Sure, it was a gesture. Finger moving to and fro inside you—"

"Holden!"

"But I wouldn't call it noble. Although the fact I let you scurry away like a coward while I was left hard and aching, now that might have been noble of me, baby. Fingering, though, was pure pleasure. For both of us. Arguably you more so than me, but still it was about mutual pleasure."

"You are an animal."

"And you are an idiot."

"For ever going in the closet with you."

"No," he shouted. "For thinking I could ever pity you. Damn it, Bev, I should take you over my lap for even suggesting such a thing."

"I'd love to see you try."

His spanking threat wasn't an idle one, or one he wouldn't love to dish out. Bev was long due for swift justice and he was just the horny man to hand down her sentence. Even as upset as he was now, thinking about warming her cheeks with the flat of his hand had his cock stirring. "Great then, apparently we're of like minds when it comes to bedroom games."

"Ah…" She took a quick, sharp breath, unable to rally quickly enough to come up with a snappy comment.

"Just shut up. The next words to come out of your mouth better be an apology or else."

"Or. Else. What?" she asked with a heavy dose of sarcasm in her voice. She was trying him.

His eyes narrowed as he took a step closer to her. His hands, clenched at his sides, tingled to reach out and deliver the first of many spankings to come. "Apologize, Bev."

"I don't owe you a thing."

"The hell you don't. You insulted me, woman, and you know you did."

"How did I insult you?"

"By implying I was in the closet with you because I felt sorry for you."

"If it wasn't for pity, then why did you say you picked my name?" Her dark eyes were filled with angst-ridden skepticism. It was almost enough to make him curb back his anger. Almost.

"For such a smart person, you can be really dumb." Although he was angry, Holden knew what he said now would determine his future, one way or the other. "The one and only reason I said I picked your name was because I was looking for any excuse to get my hands on you."

"Your hands?"

"My hands. My mouth." He ran his hands through his cropped locks and let out a frustrated breath. "I've wanted you for so long I can't remember a time when I didn't. The stupid parlor game was just a means to an end, it wasn't supposed to be the beginning of it."

"But..." She took a step back, momentarily rebuffed.

"No buts, Bev. I know you wanted me. You can't deny your response."

"Stop, this is happening too fast."

Was she mad? "Two years is too fast for you?"

"You know what I'm saying."

"No." He laughed, shaking his head in disbelief. "I have no idea what you're saying."

"Holden, I have to go."

This time his laughter came out boisterous and loud.

"What's so funny?"

"You are if you think I'm going to let you walk out of here."

"I'll leave if I want."

"You're such a child." As amusing as their interplay was, it was getting them nowhere. Holden was tired of fighting. He was tired of being mad. The time for hurt feelings was a thing of the past. They were going to finish this silliness, and they were going to finish it tonight.

"And you're a bully."

"Maybe," he agreed readily. "But I'm not a fool and I'll be damned if I'll let you leave. I'm tired of letting you decide our relationship. And if you deny we have a relationship, I won't be responsible for my actions. We've been friends, sometimes more than friends and lately it seems as if we were enemies, but I want you as a lover and I think you want that too. Stop denying me, stop denying yourself, stop denying us."

"I'm not denying anything."

"Fine. You wanted honesty. Let's be honest." Holden crossed his arms over his chest. "Do you want me?"

He knew the answer, he just wanted her to admit to the truth.

"I..."

"It's a simple yes or no question, Bev. Do you want me?"

Bev couldn't mask the emotions dancing across her face. Uncertainty and fear were the leaders, but courage won out. "Yes."

Finally. As much as he wanted to shout *yes* to the heavens, Holden knew there was much more they had to work out. She needed to know his feelings for her and vice versa if they were ever going to make a go of this.

To Holden, this wasn't just about sex. Yes, he wanted to fuck her, but he also wanted to make love with her, hold her, sleep through the night with her in his arms. All the mushy stuff men dreaded he wanted to experience with Bev.

It might have taken them two years to get to this point, but if it all ended as he hoped it would, it was well worth the wait.

"Do you believe me about the night of the party?"

Bev paused for a moment before answering, and when she did, her voice was very hesitant. "It's hard to believe."

"The only person who makes it hard is you, Bev. Think back. Think to that night and how right you felt in my arms. I can't forget it or the raging hard-on I had because of you. One of many I'd like to add."

Bev turned away from, averting her face from his penetrating stare. Yet it wasn't enough to dissuade him from his course. "God, I wanted you, just as I have so many nights before and after. The taste of you, the feel of you has stayed with me. Driving me slowly insane. You're like a drug I can't resist. Tell me this is one-sided. Tell me the way you came so violently against my hand was an anomaly and I'll let you walk away."

"You will?" she questioned with a faint hint of hope in her voice.

Her reply had him seeing red. There was no way in hell Holden would make the same mistake twice. Not when it cost him so dearly the last time. "No. I can't. I won't. Not again."

Bev turned to him and bit her bottom lip, whether because of nervousness or indecisiveness, he wasn't sure. Then she smiled softly and Holden knew she was his for the taking. "Good. I don't think I could stand to walk away again."

"Don't worry, Bev. I'm not going to give you the opportunity to try." Holden closed the distance between them. Bringing his hand up, he gently rubbed it against her bottom lip before tilting her head up to his. "There's no going back now. You're mine."

Chapter Five

A misunderstanding. All of the misery, anger and loneliness she'd been dealing with the last two years was because of a misunderstanding. Her stupid pride had kept her apart from the man she loved—pride and fear of rejection.

Once upon a time Bev had refused to look deep into Holden's eyes from fear of what she might read in the green depths. Now she freely gazed into them and read, of all things, love shining down at her. The words may not have been spoken yet but the feeling was clearly there, just as she knew it was there in her own eyes.

The weight of the bitterness that had burdened her soul for so long slipped away, leaving Bev feeling happy for the first time in two years. Now the only question was what to do first. Make love or talk more.

Wait, it wasn't a question. They could talk later.

"I want to hear you say it, Bev."

"Say what?"

"Say you belong to me. You know it as well as I do."

"Do I now?" Bev stood on her tiptoes and gently brushed her lips against his teasingly.

"Don't play with me, woman," he growled, wrapping his hands around her waist and dragging her body close against his. "This hide-and-seek bullshit you've been doing for two years has been a horrible form of foreplay."

Then in a surprising move, Holden bent down and scooped her into his arms. Bev let out a loud screech as she wrapped her arms around his neck. She held on tight, not for fear of falling, but because she could.

"I would have never pegged you as the gallant type. Are you going to read me a poem next?"

"No, Gideon's the poet. I'm just the man dying to bed you."

And he said he wasn't a poet. "So romantic."

"I'll sweet-talk you later, I promise, but right now we have something we need to discuss...with our clothes off."

"You can skip the sweet talk altogether and go straight to the dirty."

"A woman after my own heart."

"I have been for years," she admitted softly. This wasn't the time to hold back. Not when she was so close to having what her heart had desired for so long.

"Counting the two we spent apart."

"Just because I didn't like you didn't mean I didn't want you," she teased.

"You liked me then and you like me now, admit it."

"Maybe."

Holden's expression changed from teasing to serious. "I want you to know this is more than a sex thing."

His words were nice and all but... "We're still going to have sex, right?"

"A few times." He laughed.

"Just a few? Pity."

"Keep it up, brat." Holden turned and, with her in his arms, carried her from the living room and through his house, stopping only when they entered his bedroom.

After depositing her on her feet near the bed, Holden dimmed the overhead light, illuminating the room in a soft, ethereal glow. With a determined expression on his face, he joined her at the bed. The laughing, joking man from only a few minutes ago was no longer.

"Bev, would you agree it's your fault we've been apart all this time?" His silky voice held a challenge.

"I think fault is a strong word." Her reply was shakier than she would have preferred but the intense way he watched her made Bev feel a bit apprehensive.

"I don't."

"It was a mistake at best," she hedged, still not willing to accept full blame for the situation.

"It was your fault."

Bev hated to admit there might be a smidgen of truth in his words, especially aloud to Holden, but she couldn't see a way around it. Awkwardly she cleared her throat and tried to depict an air of confidence she didn't feel as she searched for a plausible explanation. "I'm willing to concede at most the problem lay with both of us, but with me being the one who…might have accelerated the situation to a proportion that was…maybe…not as critical as I thought it might have been."

He seemed to enjoy her struggle to form an answer. "So you were wrong."

"Wrong-ish," she tried with a straight face.

"Right…well, wrong-ish behavior has consequences."

"Such as?"

"A punishment."

"Punishment?"

"Yes." Holden raised a brow and waited for her to respond.

"You're kidding, right?"

"Do I look as if I'm kidding?"

No, he looked stern and completely serious. For some odd reason it was working for her. Thinking fast on her feet, Bev blurted out, "Don't you think the time apart was punishment enough?"

"Hardly." Holden crossed his arms over his chest, showing no signs of relenting. "Besides, punishment is the only way I can assure myself you'll never make the same mistake of leaving me again."

"What will it consist of?" She tried to conquer her involuntary reaction to his domineering command, but her body had a mind of its own. Her nipples hardened under her mauve blouse, giving away her anticipation for what was to come.

"Complete and utter surrender in the bedroom."

Well, when he put it like that… "Okay."

"Whatever I want, whatever I say goes," he continued.

"Okay."

"No matter what."

"I said okay." The more he talked the wetter she became. "I'll gladly take my punishment."

"And you'll never leave me again," he ordered fiercely. "Say it."

"And I'll never leave you again."

"Good. Undress." Holden sat on the bed. Stretching his long legs out in front of him, he rested his back on the headboard and entwined his fingers together over his abdomen. "Slowly."

The beginning of a smile tipped the corners of her mouth until Bev realized Holden wasn't joking. Her amusement swiftly died as the gravity of his command hit home. "You're serious."

"Very."

"Should I do a little dance?" Holden turned his head to the side as if he were pondering her question. The fact he didn't just laugh her off pushed her into action. "Never mind."

Bev was glad the lights were dimmed. Hopefully the duskiness would hide her thighs and her embarrassment.

Closing her eyes, she stepped out of her sandals and began to unbutton her shirt.

"Open your eyes." Quickly obeying, Bev fought hard to keep her blush at bay. She tried to avert her eyes, but that was a no-go as well. "No, Bev. I want you to focus on me."

"Why?" she whispered.

"Because I said so."

"Bastard." With the last button undone, Bev let her shirt shimmy off her shoulders and fall to the floor. After unbuttoning her skirt, she slid it past her thighs until it too puddled at her feet. She stepped away from the pooled clothing and faced him clad only in her bra and panties.

"Now the bra."

The front latch was easy to undo and in a few seconds her breasts, round and firm, were on display. Her nipples were hard and aching. Bev had to resist the unfettered urge she had to reach up and cup them in her hands.

"Lovely." Slow and seductive, his gaze slid lower. "Turn around."

Without questioning him, Bev slowly turned.

"I want you to take off your underwear and bend over."

Jesus. Heat filled her cheeks as she meekly did as he bade. When Bev moved to step out of her panties, Holden stopped her. "Don't. Spread your feet as far as they can possibly go with them around your ankles."

What was he up to? Even though she silently questioned him, she obeyed, wanting to know where he would take her next.

"Now reach behind you and spread your ass cheeks apart."

Oh God! She was going to die. Drop dead on the floor before him. Her body trembled as she hesitantly reached back, gripped her ass and slowly pulled her cheeks apart. Bev waited for shame to fill her, but it never came. Instead she was overcome with an unquenchable need to please him more.

She was exposed. Lewdly on display for his perverted viewing pleasure and she loved it. Loved the way it made her feel. Slutty, wanton and sexy as all get out, so unlike she'd ever felt before.

"Your pussy is glistening, baby. Shining with excitement for me. I bet I could just step right behind you and slid my cock balls-deep into you right now and you'd come for me. Just from one thrust into your wet little hole."

That was a bet Bev wasn't willing to take. Blood rushed to her head and she felt dizzy, both from the position and the intense pleasure coursing through her body.

She heard the springs in the bed creak as Holden stood. She tensed, waiting for his touch. Waiting for him.

"So fucking pretty." She sensed his stroke seconds before she actually felt it, but when she did, it was electric. Bev stumbled forward, saved from doing a face plant into the ground by Holden's grip on her waist.

"Careful, baby." After steadying her, Holden moved his hands back between her legs, lightly brushing them along the lips of her sex before venturing forth inside her wet depths. "Your hot pussy is sucking my fingers in."

Holden pulled his fingers out and transported her sweet, sticky essence to her clit. He rubbed her heated button with his fingertip in firm, sure circles before gliding them back to her slick sex. Once again he plunged inside her heated opening, finger-fucking her for a few deep strokes before pulling out and tormenting her aroused clit once more.

"You like that, nasty girl? Bending over, showing me your asshole as I finger your pussy."

Like wasn't the word. "Yes."

"How does it make you feel?" His fingers slid back and forth inside her. The sounds of her arousal were quite evident by the gushy noise coming from between her thighs.

"Good." Bev arched her back and moaned with pleasure.

His laughter was rough and ragged. "I know that, nasty girl. I have the evidence of it dripping from my hand. Your pussy is sopping wet. You're making enough honey for me to do this with ease."

Holden took his wet fingers from her pussy to her asshole and speared the tip of his digit into her rosette, causing Bev to gasp at the unexpected invasion.

"You're getting close, aren't you?"

"Yes…" she muttered, rocking her hips to and fro, trying to take as much of his thrusting as she could. Her pulse pounded in her ears and the sensitive nerves in her ass throbbed. Bev had never felt so decadent before. If this was his idea of punishment, she was going to have be bad more often. She felt herself escalating toward orgasm with every thrust of his probing fingers. "Please…I need to…"

"Beg me sweetly, baby, and I'll give you everything you need."

God, she hoped so. "Make me come, Holden. Please, make me come."

"I will, but don't let go of your ass. I want to watch your asshole and your pussy as you come for me." His guttural words were filled with need. She wasn't the only one on the edge, but she was the only one about to come.

"Holden…" The weak sound of his name on her lips spurred him on. He increased his rhythm, thrusting faster and harder into her waiting body.

She flung her head back and held on to her cheeks with all her might. Her nails dug into her skin but the pinching sensation was an added thrill.

She screamed when the orgasm hit her. A torrent of fluids poured from between her legs as she cried out his name. Her legs convulsed, giving out under her release. If it weren't for Holden's quick actions, she would have crumpled at his feet. He held her until the trembles subsided and helped her stand.

She was dizzy and leaned back upon his chest to gather herself. He waited a few moments before speaking. "Are you okay?"

"Yes."

"Are you sure?"

"Yes."

"Good." Holden pushed her away from him and turned her around until she was facing him. "Drop to your knees and suck my cock."

Holden brought his damp fingers to his nose and inhaled deeply before bringing them to his mouth and sucking off her sweet essence.

Damn, she was a sexy little thing. Not just in looks but in taste and smell as well.

"Now, Bev."

She complied without saying a word, dropping to the floor in front of him happily. Her obvious desire to pleasure him forced Holden to stifle a groan. Bev was in full bloom sexually.

Sad to say, watching his fingers disappear inside her tight sheath was better than some sex he'd had. He had to force himself not to undress there and then and stuff her full of his cock. He was so hard he hurt, but he knew she was worth the wait. Watching her come undone in front of him was a memory he'd take to his grave. Never would he have thought she'd be so responsive, so involved and alive.

Holden stepped a few feet away from her and began to slowly undress. He was going to savor her mouth on him and then fuck her until his back was permanently indented with her fingernails. Once he was completely nude, he beckoned her to come closer.

Bev edged nearer on her knees. "That's a good girl. I loved watching you come for me, baby. I loved watching the sweet way your pussy devoured my hand." Holden took his shaft in his hands and lined it up with her sexy mouth. "Now I want to watch you suck my cock. Open up wide, little one, and let me come in."

With a greedy moan, Bev opened her full, pouty lips and took him deep within her warm, wet mouth. Holden groaned and pushed forward, watching her expressive face as he slid his cock back and forth. From the glazed look in her eyes, sucking his cock wasn't a chore at all.

When Bev moved her hand to the base of his shaft and began to stroke him, Holden intervened. He wound his hands in her chocolate locks and pulled out of her mouth.

Licking her lips, Bev eyed his cock regretfully. "What...what's wrong?"

"If I wanted a hand job, I'd ask for one," Holden stated firmly. He took his cock in hand and stroked himself while he talked. "I want to feel only your lips and tongue against my cock. No hands. Whatsoever. Do you understand?"

"I...I understand."

"Good." He stepped forward and rubbed the crown against her lips. "Now open up, baby, and suck me good."

Bev slowly parted her lips and engulfed the head of his cock in the warmth of her mouth. Holden knew she wouldn't be able to go as fast without the use of her hands, and that was just fine with him. He wanted to savor the feel of her tongue against his cock. And savor he did.

Bev tightened her lips around his shaft and took him as deep into her mouth as she could without gagging, and then pulling back, she let him slide slowly out until just the crown remained. She swirled her tongue around the tip before plunging forward once more.

She alternated between deep plunges and shallow sucking, keeping Holden on edge with her oral skills. "God, baby. Hmmm. So good."

Bev raked her teeth gently over the head of his cock. The rough sensation shot lightning bolts of pleasure down his spine, making his entire body jerk in response.

"Ahh..." Holden wrapped his hand in her hair as he powered into her mouth, using the dark strands to control her rhythm. "That's right, Bev, suck me."

She was driving him to the brink of insanity with pleasure. And as much as he wanted to come splashing in her mouth, he wanted to fuck her even more. There would be time for the other later.

"Enough," he panted, taking a step away. "Get on your back on the bed."

"Wait." Bev reached out to him. "I wasn't done."

"Oh yes you were." He chuckled shakily. "I don't think I could have lasted much longer in your mouth."

"Why do you get to call the shots?"

"Because you're the one in trouble," Holden reminded her as he walked to his nightstand. Opening the drawer, he withdrew a condom and set it on top of the bed. "Now do as I said and no one gets hurt."

"We'll see about that. You're taking this punishment thing too far, Holden," she grumbled as she rose to her feet. "If you think I'm going to let you keep bossing me around—"

Holden pulled her to him and spun her around until her back was flush with his chest. He slipped his hand to her sopping pussy and fingered her. Just as he thought, she was even wetter than before. His nasty little girl was all talk. "Then I'm completely right."

"Says who?" she moaned. Laying her head back against his chest, she widened her stance, giving his diddling fingers better access to her pleasure center.

"Says this." Holden pulled his hand away and delivered a smart smack to her erect clit. Bev gasped, cursing his name, but she didn't try to close her legs. "And that." He laughed. "Just admit it, Bev. You love it."

"Bastard."

"And then some." Holden removed his hand and nudged her toward the bed. "Don't make me tell you again."

With a sexy little pout, Bev climbed on the bed and sat with her feet flat on the quilt and her knees drawn together. Her hands were braced behind her back. The position forced her mouthwatering breasts to jut forward, which in turned caused Holden's cock to jerk.

"Damn, you're sexy."

"You're just a little horny," she teased as she lay back and gestured with her index finger for him to join her.

With a leering grin, Holden climbed on the bed, settled himself above her and slipped between her parted thighs. "Trust me, baby, little doesn't have anything to do with it."

With his cock in hand, he strummed himself against her hot pussy. The first stroke against her moist flesh had him gripping his cock harder, fighting his need to just plunge straight in, but he didn't press forward. Instead he moved his hand and his attention to Bev's full breasts.

"Look what you've been hiding all these years." Holden gently brushed his fingers against her nipples.

"You just didn't notice them before."

"I'm noticing now." The dark buds pebbled under his soft touch. Bev arched up and closed her eyes. He had barely touched the beaded tips yet she reacted as if he'd taken them in his mouth. Watching her carefully, Holden cupped her breast in his hand, and took one of her nipples between his teeth.

"Hmm…" Bev's thighs tightened around his waist.

"Your breasts are so sensitive, aren't they, baby?"

"Yes," she moaned, pressing them toward him more.

"I bet you can come from me sucking on them alone." Holden ran his thumb over the responsive nubs, twisting and tugging them as she moved wantonly beneath him.

"Maybe...I don't know."

"Then we'll have to try and see." Holden tightened his grip and watched in delight as she damn near came straight off the bed. "Yes...we will."

"Holden, please..."

"Please what?" Bending his head, Holden took the entire nipple into his mouth, sucking and laving the hardened point roughly as she cried out.

"Please..."

Holden raised his head and blew his cool breath over her nipples, chuckling when she jerked in reaction. "Please what, Bev?"

"Fuck me. Please fuck me." Bev sounded as if she were holding on to a thin thread, a state Holden was very familiar with.

"If you insist," he teased. Releasing her breasts, Holden sheathed himself for their protection then pressed the head of his cock against the slick opening of her sex and pushed forward. He clenched his teeth at the intense rush of pleasure that took hold of him.

Bev was hotter and tighter than he would have ever imagined. Sinking into her wet depths felt as if he were coming home. Holden was finally where he belonged. It was as if her body were made especially for his and he was going to do everything he could to lay his claim to her, now and forever.

Staring down into the black pools of her eyes, Holden began to pump slowly inside her. Flushed, Bev locked her gaze with his and wrapped her legs around his waist. He knew the need swimming in her eyes was a direct echo of his own.

"I dreamed of this moment for so long."

"As have I," Holden admitted. "I'll endeavor to make this everything you ever dreamt of."

"It already is."

"Bev..." Holden covered her mouth with his and kissed her passionately as he continued to thrust inside her. Bev was no wallflower. She gave as good as she got, slipping her tongue between his parted lips, kissing him as wildly as he kissed her, taking his punishing strokes as if they were a gift from God.

Spurred on by her fanatical response, Holden drove within her, trying with all his might to bury his cock as deep inside her as he could.

Her legs gripped his hips tighter as she met him thrust for thrust. Bev dug her nails into his side and tore her mouth away from his. Free of her tempting lips, Holden reared up and held himself above her with the strength of his arms.

Seeing Bev under him, feeling her body clasping him tight and knowing she wanted him as much as he wanted her made Holden want to shout out loud. Bev's eyes were glazed with desire and she had captured her bottom lip with her teeth, as if she were holding back her own words of delight.

"Tell me what you need, Bev."

"More," she begged as she undulated beneath him. "Don't stop."

She whimpered, she moaned, she rotated her hips wildly as they fucked. Her heated responses had him on the edge. She was a sexy, responsive little thing and it killed Holden to think of how they could have been together this way all the while.

Her pussy pulsated around his cock and her choppy moans grew louder and louder. Holden knew Bev was only moments away from coming, from flooding his dick with her sweet essence.

"So. Close."

Her and him both. "You want to come for me, Bev?"

"Yes...Holden...Holden."

"Then come for me. Come for daddy."

Her orgasm hit instantly. She screamed when she came, scoring his back with her nails as he plowed deeper. Her pussy, her sweet pussy, milked him, squeezing his cock like a fist. A wet, tight fist.

"Damn…" The pleasure of her body was too much to resist. Holden dropped his head back and ground himself into her, crying her name as he came.

It took all of his remaining strength to move off her trembling body and to the bed next to her. Panting, Holden tried to gather himself but it was a hard feat to accomplish. He was fucking exhausted. Exhausted from fucking. Too tired even to get up and make a trip to the bathroom.

Reaching blindly on the floor, Holden grabbed the first thing he touched and used it to remove the evidence of their lovemaking from his overheated body. Grimacing, he made a mental note to bring some tissue or a towel in the room before they went at it again so he could spare the rest of his shirts this sodden mess.

"Do you…?" Holden offered Bev, who was watching him with an amused look on her sweat-dampened face.

"Thanks but no." She held up her hand to ward him away. "I'll get up in a second."

"You want your shirt?"

"No. I'm good. Really." There was a trace of laughter in her voice.

"Okay, don't say I didn't offer." Holden dropped the shirt on the ground and pulled Bev over to him until she was resting her head on his shoulder. His hand stroked lightly over her shoulder as she snuggled closer.

"This is nice." Her voice was soft, as if sleep were slowly overtaking her.

Holden silently agreed with her. The feel of her in his arms, resplendent from their loving, was the nicest place to be. "Are you going to sleep?"

"Maybe for a second or two."

"You can lie on top of me if you want, you know, so you don't have to sleep in the wet spot."

Bev broke out laughing, just as he intended. "Baby, you say the sweetest things."

Smiling, Holden listened to her laughter. His heart filled from the sound of her joy as peace and happiness filled his soul. This was how it was meant to be. The two of them together. Happy. Always. "That's because I'm all about the romance."

"Yes, you are." She chuckled as she snuggled in close to him.

"I've got nothing but love for you, baby." Even though he said it teasingly, Holden was completely serious. He loved Bev and he knew she loved him. Now all he had to do was get her to admit it.

Chapter Six

"You're awfully quiet." Holden set a plate piled high with pancakes in front of Bev. She wasn't a big breakfast eater, but after last night's debauchery, she knew she had to consume as many calories as she could because they would be burning them off later.

"Am I? Sorry."

"Morning-after regrets?"

"Of course not." If she lived to be a hundred and five, she'd never regret last night.

"Then why so quiet?" Shirtless and dressed only in jeans, Holden strolled back to the stainless steel stove to fix his own plate. The muscles in his lean back flexed as he moved, drawing her attention away from her plate time and time again.

Watching him work in the kitchen brought a small smile to her face as well as a flood of memories to her mind. Bev and the rest of the gang had spent many weekends together and cooking breakfast had always been Holden's responsibility. Then, like now, pancakes had been his food of choice.

It was funny how some things never changed. His cooking and his kitchen were prime examples of the adage. The masculine room was exactly how it looked the last time she'd seen it, all white and stainless steel with no hint of warmth or color. In two years he hadn't made one update. In fact, she'd bet her bottom dollar he still had the same pot and pan, singular, he had when he moved in. Holden was such a *guy*.

Holden caught her smile and quirked a brow. "What?"

"Nothing," she said, vanquishing the nostalgia and amusement away with a small shake of her head. It would serve no purpose for her to get all sentimental now. Bev added butter and syrup to her plate as she thought back to the question at hand. "I'm a little worried is all."

"About us?"

"No." Bev was tempted to ask him what "us" meant to him, but she was afraid to know his answer. Sure, last night he'd seemed all into her. He'd been angry she'd pushed him away, but today, well, today he was back to his old big-brother ways. Minus of course his command she only wear one of his dress shirts. His order, as nipple-tightening as it was, was the only sexual-like move he'd made toward her all day.

While she showered, he'd changed the sheets and made the bed. He even left the room to let her get dressed so he could start on breakfast. It wasn't exactly how Bev imagined starting the morning. "About the others."

"What about them?"

"I tried to call Paige this morning, but she didn't answer her cell."

Holden let out a deep masculine laugh as he sat across from her, plate in hand. "I'm not surprised at all."

"Why?"

"Did you see the look on Shane's face when he tore after her? I'm willing to bet a billion dollars he has her spirited away far from a phone, a computer and anything or anyone who could interfere with his plans."

"And doesn't that bother you?"

"No." Holden regarded her solemnly. "Shane would no more hurt Paige than I would hurt you. In fact, if I had to worry about either of them, it would be him. Paige is a wiry little thing."

"She seemed really upset." More upset than Bev had ever seen her. The story, previously untold, now explained a lot about her friends' behavior in the last few years. Shane did something to hurt her, and knowing Paige as she did, Bev knew the grudge-holding woman wouldn't forgive him any time soon. "I wonder what happened."

"You know what I wonder?" Holden said as he took a big bite. He waited until he finished what was in his mouth before he continued. "What the heck is going on with Skylar, Gideon and Tripp?"

"Apparently a lot." Their announcement had thrown her for a loop to say the least.

"Did you know about them?"

"No!" she denied. "Did you? I mean, you did live with Tripp for four years."

Holden held up his hands as if to ward off her speculation. "Oh no. He was all about the pussy when he lived with us."

"As far as you knew," she teased. "Besides, if I understand correctly, he still is, he just happens to enjoy a little cock as well."

"You said little cock." Holden stared at her for a moment then burst out laughing.

"Shut up. I didn't mean little as in little." Bev could feel her cheeks heating in embarrassment. "Besides, Gideon is huge. I sincerely—"

Holden's laughter stopped cold. "What do you mean Gideon's huge?"

"That's not what I meant either." Bev rolled her eyes at the jealous tone entering his voice. "Your mind is in the gutter."

"Have you seen him naked?"

"Oh my goodness."

"Have you?"

"No." Bev took a sip from her orange juice, secretly pleased by his reaction. She wasn't the type of woman who brought out strong emotions in men normally, so it was a real boost to her ego to have Holden acting like a bonehead.

"Okay then," he said, seemingly pacified by her answer. The big baby.

"How do you feel about it?"

"About what?"

"The fact two of your male best friends might be lovers."

"I don't know." Holden took a drink from his coffee and pondered the question for a moment. "You know, I've always thought Gideon might be a bit bi. He's a poet, for Pete's sake."

Bev bit back a smile at his male-like deduction. "Being a poet has nothing to do with a person's sexual preference. Gideon also happens to run his father's construction business at the same time."

"Well, that's his girl-liking side. The poet is the guy-liking side."

"And Tripp?" she asked, amused at his reasoning. "He's a forward for the Blackhawks. You don't get more masculine than hockey. They go around bashing people with sticks."

"Yes." Holden pointed his fork at her as he nodded his head. "But they do it on skates. See, feminine."

"You are so stupid." She laughed.

"It's a gift."

"Seriously though, does it bother you?"

"No, it's odd, but it's whatever, you know. If they want to go at each other, it's their business. It's not my ass. They're still my boys, even if they're each other's boy," he wiggled his brow suggestively, "at the same time."

"You're the king of craziness, you know?" Bev shook her head in amusement as she cut into her food. Only Holden would see things so black and white. Shane too possibly. He hadn't appeared shaken up either. "Our whole group is crazy."

"I don't think we're crazy."

"No?"

"No." Holden pushed his plate away from him and leaned back in his chair. "I think on the whole we all care for each other, care deeply, and the problem is some of us are willing to open ourselves up to the 'what might be' and the other half of us are held back by the 'what might be'."

Bev set her fork down and mimicked his actions. "And which are you, Holden, part of the willing or part of the will not?"

"What do you think?"

"You know something, I'm not sure."

"Even after last night?"

"Especially after last night," she admitted.

"Why do you say that?"

She glanced away from him, thinking about the last two years and everything she'd been through without him by her side. She had survived, but she hadn't been happy, all because she was afraid to talk to him about that night. Here she was again, afraid to ask him how he felt about her, but this time she wasn't going to wait two years to get an answer. "Tell me, Holden, were we playing last night or was it something more?"

After everything, Holden still couldn't believe Bev didn't know how much he cared. For an instant anger reared its ugly little head then reason weighed in. Of course she didn't know how much he cared. He had yet to admit it aloud. He could simply say "I love you" and be done with it, but Holden had never taken the easy way in his life, why would he start now?

Besides, it wasn't enough to just say the words. There was more he had to share with her to make her understand just how deeply his feelings for her went. The only problem was he didn't know where to start.

"Never mind." Bev falsely smiled and rose from her seat. "It's not important."

Moving quickly, she made her way around the table and nearly past his chair before Holden grabbed onto her wrist and pulled her into his lap.

Silly girl, does she really think I'm going to let her get away that easily? "Slow your roll, speedy. I'm not letting you run away this time."

"I wasn't running."

"Right," he drawled, amused at her blatant lie. "Lord knows you'd never do anything as crazy as running from me for no good reason. Straddle me."

"Fine," she grumbled as she stood again and moved one leg on either side of his lap before sitting facing him. The position, as intimate as it was, allowed them to be face-to-face, able to view and talk to one another with no barriers or distractions, well, at least no distractions other than each other. All he had to do now was try to forget under the blue button-down work-shirt she was wearing was nothing but soft curves and opportunity. "Now what?"

Right, wrong or indifferent, she was a fighter all the way to the end. Damn, he loved this woman. "Bev, you are a walking, talking headache."

"And you're a pain in the ass."

"Not yet, but it can be arranged." His cock twitched from the mere thought alone.

"Pervert."

"You're damn skippy, but that's nothing new." She would probably be shocked to know just how perverted he could be, and he'd be only too happy to demonstrate whenever she was interested. But sex wasn't the only thing drawing him to her. "And neither is my desire to be with you. That's been around for a while as well."

"You never said anything." Even though she still sounded put out, he had her full attention. It was a good start.

"It never seemed as if it were the right time. Then of course we both know what happened when I finally did try to leap."

"It wasn't all my fault."

He wasn't about to go into fault again. As far as Holden was concerned, he was ready to put the matter to rest once and for all. "Fault no longer matters to me. Everything up to the part when you stormed off and left me with the hard-on from hell was wonderful."

"Which, according to you, you appeased with any and every woman in your path for the last two years."

"No, Bev. Not true." Holden encircled her waist with his hands and interlocked his fingers together behind her. He refused for there to be any more misunderstandings between them again. "I've slept with two women since that night."

"Only two." Her facial expression was an endearing mixture of amusement and annoyance. "Am I supposed to feel better now?"

"God, I hope not. Because it didn't make me feel better. I tried to purge you from my soul. You wouldn't talk to me. You wouldn't see me. I was crazy. And it was bad."

Her big brown eyes widened as she mockingly offered him a sympathetic look. "Poor you."

"Yeah, I can tell you're hurting for me, brat."

"Why should I? It's not as if I slept with two guys," she countered self-righteously.

"For which I'm eternally grateful." Holden couldn't help the immense sense of relief he felt. Sure, it was a double standard, but he didn't care. The idea of Bev making love with any other man just didn't sit right with him.

"Just like a guy."

"But if you had, I wouldn't hold it against you, just as I'm hoping you won't hold it against me." Even though Holden knew talking about his past lovers with his present one was a big no-no, it was important for the future of their relationship for Bev to understand this part of him. "It happened. I'm not proud or happy about it, but there's nothing I can do to change it. If it's any consolation, it was over a year ago. The last time was before the Fourth of July party at Tripp's. After seeing you again, I knew no one, nowhere could ever replace you or make me feel the way you have."

Her expression stilled and grew serious. "You're saying you haven't slept with anyone else in all this time?"

"If I couldn't have you, I didn't want anyone else."

"And how long was this self-imposed vow of celibacy going to last?"

His voice was firm and final as he spoke, looking directly into her eyes so there would be absolutely no misunderstanding. Of this he was completely serious. "As long as it took you to realize with me is where you belonged."

"And if that day had never occurred?"

Holden couldn't even think of the possibility of her scenario. "I knew it would."

"Because you think you're so irresistible."

"No, because you are," he said with absolute clarity and truth. "You're it for me, Bev. I love you. I think I always have."

"You think?"

"Loving you is such a permanent part of me, I can't honestly recognize when it began. It's not romantic, I know, but it's the truth."

"I don't think anything could possibly be more romantic." Bev leaned forward and covered his mouth with her own. With a rough, guttural growl, Holden took over the kiss, overpowering her sweet offering by winding his hand in her hair and plunging his tongue past her soft lips into her welcoming mouth.

Sinking into her embrace, Holden explored the softness of her mouth, plundered the depths. She met his every foray, responding so sweetly she took his breath away.

After breaking the kiss, Holden nipped gently at her bottom lip before pulling back and taking a deep breath. It was amazing how she moved him. No other woman had ever affected him so intensely or so profoundly before. Just kissing her made his cock rock-hard.

From the heavy way Bev was breathing, Holden was willing to bet their proximity was having the same effect on her it was so evidently having on him. Her eyes were glazed over with passion, and the way she was wiggling her hips on his lap made him wonder how much longer it was going to take to get her to admit what he already knew so he could do what they both so clearly wanted him to. All he needed first were the words.

"Well..." Holden moved his hands between their bodies and began to unbutton the shirt, secretly congratulating himself for a genius of an idea. Bev in next to nothing was up there with the microwave oven as far as he was concerned.

"Well, what?" she asked huskily.

Holden undid the last button and pulled the shirt aside. Her full, beautiful breasts were almost enough of a distraction, but not quite. "Aren't you going to say something, woman?"

"Such as?"

"Don't toy with me, Bev. I'm a man out on a ledge here."

"From the feel of it," Bev wiggled her hips, causing her pussy to press against his hardened cock, "I'd say I'm the one on the ledge."

"You just want me to spank your ass, don't you?"

"Maybe."

"If it's what it takes." Holden wrapped his hands around her waist and held on tight as he stood. "Either way, baby, you'll tell me what I want to hear."

"Wait." Laughing, Bev grabbed hold of his neck. "How about I show you instead?"

Chapter Seven

&

"Nope, no more teasing, young lady, I want those words."

Knowing she could kid and joke with him again, just like old times, made her giddy. It was better than old times though, because they had the added benefit of now being lovers. *Lovers.* It sounded strange, but love was truly the basis of her emotions.

"You don't want me to show you…stuff?"

"How about I show you something?" Picking her up as if she were as light as a feather, Holden sat her on the end of the table, pushing the dishes out of the way. The loud clattering of the plates hitting the floor barely registered to Bev, who simply raised a brow at his caveman-like antics.

Placing her hands palm down behind her, Bev leaned back and regarded him with amusement. Holden was so cute when he played the macho man. "Do you think you can?"

"I know I can."

"Hmmm." Things were getting good now. "Like wh—"

Silencing her, Holden moved in and covered her mouth with his own. Bev moaned as his tongue swiped through her open lips, flooding her senses with the sweet, lingering taste of vanilla coffee. He loved her. There was nothing better than that.

Bev leaned away from Holden, breaking away from his tempting mouth. The man was way too talented with his lips. *Way.*

"Do you think this strongman tactic of yours is going to get me to talk?" Because if he didn't, she surely did.

"I'm past trying to get you to talk." Holden took hold of her legs and pried them open. He moved until he was standing in the apex of her thighs and his hard bulge was pressed against her soft opening.

"Really." Bev tried hard to bite back the girly gasp, which rose to her lips. She concentrated hard on sounding controlled even though her tummy was all aflutter with wanton need. The feel of him so thick and hard was enough to have her juices revving once more. She had never considered herself an overtly sexual person before, but now, just the mere hint of his arousal was all it took to have her primed and ready to go.

"Yes." Holden moved his hand between their bodies and brushed his fingers against her damp folds.

Bev closed her eyes and leaned back on her hands, arching her hips toward his teasing digits. "Mmm..."

He didn't tease for long. Holden slipped his fingers between her swollen lips and plunged two deep within her heated depths. Bev gasped aloud at the surprising move and all but melted on the spot, much to Holden's obvious amusement. His deep chuckle rolled over her body like a lover's caress as he leaned forward and spoke softly in her ear. "Now I'm going for a scream."

If any man could do it, he was definitely the one. The way he played her pussy like a grand piano was proof of that. Never before had Bev come so close to orgasming so fast from mere fingering alone. "Hmmm, Holden."

"Tell me, baby, do you want me to stop?"

"No. God, no." Was he mad? She didn't want him to ever stop. With her weight resting on her hands, Bev pumped her pussy on his hand, grinding herself for all she was worth. Her gasp bled into barely audible whimpers as he strummed her clit with his thumb and thrust his fingers into her hot channel. "Good. So good."

"Good enough to scream for it?"

"Not fair." She wanted to stay strong, but Bev could barely breathe, let alone concentrate on their teasing little dare.

"All's fair in love and war, baby."

"Are we...at war?" she panted as she rocked her hips forward, fucking herself against his thrusting fingers.

"Never, baby. And I'll prove it." With a twist of his wrist, Holden turned his fingers over inside her until his palm was facing skyward and his fingers were pressed deep. The tips brushed across her G-spot and caressed her sensitive nub, sending lightning bolts of pleasure crashing into her. The pleasure was so intense it was almost painful and unbelievably good.

Bev could barely contain her hips or the orgasm washing over. "Ohh..."

"That's right, baby, fuck my hand." The once-silent room was filled with her reverberating cries of pleasures as she did her own version of a lap dance on his fingers.

"That was a scream all right, just not the one I was looking for." Holden barely let her come down from her orgasm high before he removed his fingers from between her legs and placed his hands on her hips. He pulled her toward him until she was sitting on the edge of table then snagged his chair from behind him and sat as if he were prepared to dine. "I guess I'll just have to try harder this time."

"Wait." Bev dropped back on the table, gasping for breath. She wasn't ready for round two yet. "Let me catch my breath."

"Breathing is so overrated." Holden grabbed the table and pulled it toward him, much to her amusement. He took hold of her feet and placed them separately onto the armrests of his chair. "Now this is the breakfast of champions."

Bev's body shivered in the aftermath of her release. She dragged in a tortured breath and then another until she was once again breathing rhythmically. She tried to raise her head so she could talk to him, but it, like the rest of her, felt too heavy to move. "Holden."

"Don't 'Holden' me. I have a scream to wring from you and two years to make up for."

"You don't have to do it all this weekend." If he kept up this pace, she would never survive the day, let alone the weekend.

"Says you," he said with a grin in his voice. He spread her lips apart and sighed like a contented man. "Damn, baby, you're beautiful. I could look at your pussy all day."

"Just look?"

"Look, taste…fuck." His lips soon followed his words as Holden leaned forward and pressed a sweet kiss against her aroused clit. His gentleness made Bev smile, which quickly turned to a moan when his kisses morphed into more.

A whole lot more.

Holden put the "O" back in orgasm by letting himself loose between her legs. He lapped, teased and tormented her pussy with his skillful tongue. Bev thrashed her head back and forth on the breakfast table as she undulated her hips, fucking his mouth with her pussy.

After the intense release only moments before, she hadn't believed she could peak again so soon. Apparently she was wrong, or her pussy had a mind of its own. Acting wanton and taking the pleasure he gave unapologetically, she reveled in the delight of his mouth.

But it wasn't just her pussy he tasted.

"Oh Holden…what…" With a shocked gasp, Bev cried out his name as he swiped his tongue across her rosette. Bev shivered from the forbidden pleasure. Nothing so naughty had ever felt so good. She moaned and squeezed her nipples between her fingers as Holden pressed his tongue into her rosette. The unbridled pleasure was mind-numbing and unbelievably good.

Bringing his fingers back into the action, Holden plunged them once more into her overheated depths while he feasted on her back door. When Bev thought she just couldn't take a second more, Holden slid his fingers back out and pressed them against her nether hole.

His finger gently slid deep within her puckered entrance, much to Bev's surprise. "Holden, I...never..."

Holden began to softly rotate his finger around as if trying to open her farther. "Relax, baby. We'll start off slow."

"How slow?"

"One finger. Then two."

"Then?"

"My cock when you're ready."

"Ready?" Bev didn't know if she'd ever be ready.

"Just relax." Clenching her cheeks together, she tried to do as he asked, but she couldn't help the instinctive reaction to tighten around his finger and push out. Yet the more she pushed out, the more he pushed in until she felt a second finger join the first. The shocking part was how pleasurable it felt. To be filled so intimately.

"There you go, baby." He began to move his fingers in a circular come-here motion, which dragged a moan of satisfaction from Bev's reluctant mouth. "Just sit back and enjoy."

"I don't know if I can. It's too much."

"Too much is never enough." Then, with a wicked little laugh, Holden moved his mouth back to her throbbing pussy and dove into her abyss. He glided his tongue over and around her erect clit, licking and teasing her as he continued fingering her ass.

"Holden..." she cried out. "Yes...don't stop...God..."

She had never felt so wild and out of control before. Holden had pushed past her limits, past all the barriers she'd erected, and took her, took all of her as only he could. The combined sensations of naughty and nice once again forced her over the precipice of pleasure.

Moaning with contentment, she squeezed her nipples hard between her fingers, plucking at the erect peaks and pushing her pussy into Holden's waiting mouth, coming harder than she had ever come in her life.

Holden needed a condom and he needed one now. With a reluctant groan, he pulled his fingers from her tight ass and moved away from her tempting pussy. Although he enjoyed tasting the sweet delicacy that lay between her legs, he needed to bury his cock inside her before he came like a schoolboy in his pants.

"Not hardly," Holden said as he stood. "I'll be right back. Don't move."

"As if I could."

"Words to warm a man's heart." Holden spun around and rushed from the kitchen, his mind on only one thing. The short distance between his kitchen and bedroom seemed to take hours rather than seconds to travel, but it was to be expected when all he could think of was fucking Bev.

Hurrying to his bedroom, he made his way over to his nightstand and retrieved a condom. If their sexual relationship kept up at this pace, he was going to have to seriously think about stashing condoms all over the house because running with a hard-on was for the birds.

After unbuttoning and unzipping his pants, he shoved them down his hips and onto the floor. As he walked briskly back into the kitchen, he ripped into the condom wrapper, tossing the black foil onto the floor mid-stride. Entering the kitchen, he caught sight of Bev lying on the table in the exact position he'd left her, legs spread and feet dangling toward the ground, and he smiled. Damn, she was sexy.

"Miss me?" As Holden put the condom on, he slipped between her splayed thighs and looked at his exotic beauty with pride. Her face was flushed with desire. Her hair was tousled and lay about her head like a halo, and her tawny skin was damp from exertion. Never before had she looked lovelier.

"More than you know." Her voice was husky and filled with need, a need Holden was all-too familiar with.

"You'll never have to miss me again." Taking his condom-covered cock in his hand, he centered the head of his erection on her moist opening and surged forward. A loud collective groan filtered up from the both of them as he buried himself inside her balls deep.

"Jeezeee..." Bev whimpered a sexy little noise that made the hair on his arms stand up. She arched her back as if trying to force him deeper within her as he held tightly to her legs. "Please..."

There was nothing he wanted to do more than please her, but Holden knew he needed to wait a few seconds for Bev to adjust to him. She was so tight it barely felt as if there were room enough in her body to accommodate him in the first place.

"Holden, please. Fuck me. Please."

Good intentions be damned. Holden pulled out and plunged forth once more, giving them both what they needed. "So good."

Her sweet pussy, tight and wet, engulfed his cock with a searing heat that almost took his breath away. Sex had never been this good before, pussy never as tight. The only difference he could fathom was the women beneath him.

The closeness he had with Bev was different than anything he felt with any other woman. This is what love was—this wanting, all-encompassing need. The need to possess her body and soul. He wanted her to have their time together burned into her memory so she never would consider leaving him again.

"I could fuck you forever."

"And I...could let you," she panted, meeting him thrust for thrust.

"Or I could let you." Now that sounded like a plan to him. "I want you to ride me."

"My pleasure."

"Oh no, it'll be all mine." Still buried to the hilt inside her hot box, Holden picked her up by her hips and stepped back, seating himself onto his chair. He had to move until his ass was damn near hanging off the chair so her legs could hang on the side of his, but the bit of discomfort was worth the effort just to have Bev ride him.

"Fuck, you're so tight." With his hands on her hips, he raised her up and pulled her down firmly, thrusting his cock into her molten center. "You feel so good."

Bev's head fell back and she let out a cock-hardening moan. Her breasts, her beautiful breasts with their chocolate-colored nipples were thrust sky-high as she arched her back and undulated on his lap. Unable to resist the siren-like call of her twin peaks, Holden raised his hands to her lower back and pulled her forward until her nipples were brushing against his waiting mouth.

Opening his lips, he tugged her erect nipple between his teeth, squeezing it with the added pressure he learned she loved last night. To his delight, Bev groaned and buried her fingers in his hair, holding him tighter to her breast.

"God, yes," she answered as she started to move on top of him. She began to pick up speed, forcing his lips away from her breast. Not to be denied, Holden replaced his mouth with his hands, stroking and teasing her full mounds as she rode him as if he were a thoroughbred.

"That's it, ride me, take all of me." Holden pushed up inside her, gritting his teeth as her body contracted around his cock. Her pussy was akin to a silk glove, milking his cock inch by inch.

His hands and hips were working overtime as he moved her up and down his shaft. His pelvis bumped against her ass as their pace quickened. Bev trembled as her breathing became a ragged clatter of noise.

"Ohhh…Holden…" Her low, husky cries filled his ears as she dug her nails into his shoulders, squeezing him with godlike strength as she came. "Yes. Yes. Yes."

"Christ!" He was right behind her, thanks to her contracting pussy, which pulled him over the edge of reason. With a bone-crushing hug, Holden buried himself deep inside her and held on for dear life as he came.

Bev's body collapsed onto his, her legs limply hanging to the sides as her head fell to his shoulder.

"I love you. God, I love you," she whimpered as she clung to him.

It wasn't a scream, but it would do.

* * * * *

"I can't believe we left the house this dirty all weekend long."

Holden stood next to Bev in the dining room entryway, afraid to take another step into the room. She was right. The room was a disaster. "We had more pressing issues on our minds this weekend."

"True, but it doesn't justify this room."

"It's not so bad," Holden lied. Walking to the table, he picked up a saucer, which was still encrusted with cake and grimaced. "Now we know what the smell was. I say let's just throw it away."

"What?"

"The dishes."

"They're not paper."

"So?"

Laughing, Bev shook her head and took the plate from his hand. "I'll take care of the dishes and you take care of the trash."

"No, that's not fair to you," he said halfheartedly. Holden had been completely serious about trashing everything. Cleaning up two-day-old chocolate wasn't exactly how he relished spending a faux sick day. "I think I'm beginning to really feel sick."

"Laziness isn't a sickness," she teased as she zipped out the door and headed to the kitchen.

"No, it's a disease." Despite his protesting, Holden wasn't too upset about the mess. It had enabled him to twist Bev's arm and get her to not only stay one more night but call into work as well. Since Friday's love fest, they hadn't left each other's side. And apparently, from the looks of the dining and living room, they hadn't left the kitchen or bedroom either.

Food, sex and the woman he loved. Life just didn't get much better than this. In fact, the only way things could possibly get better was if he could convince Bev to move in with him. They had already spent the last two years apart, and it just didn't make any sense to him for them to continue to remain apart.

His mind was made up about her. She was his. Forever.

"Stop woolgathering, boy, and get to work. The sooner we get this mess taken care of the sooner we can get back to bed."

"Sleepy?" he teased.

"Exhausted." She winked as she leaned over the table and gathered up the remaining flatware.

The black Aerosmith T-shirt she wore, like all of her weekend clothes, was the only piece she had on. The edge of the shirt hung just below her ass, teasing him with a mouthwatering glimpse of sexy flesh as she bent over. The image alone was enough to get him started because as she said, the sooner they began, the sooner he could have her out of it and riding his cock.

With the dirty image in his mind, Holden busied himself rounding up the trash in the dining room then he headed for the living room. Thankfully it wasn't half as bad as the other room had been. The only items he had to take care of were the wineglasses and a stray napkin here or there.

He was halfway out the door with the last glass when he spotted a small yellow bag on the floor. Grinning, he walked over to it and stooped to pick up the gift bag.

"Hurry up, slowpoke, so I can start the dishwasher." Bev strolled out from the kitchen to find him with the gift bag still in hand. "Is that what I think it is?"

She took the bag from his hands and dug around inside, pulling out the stopwatch. A broad smile crossed her face as she swung the watch around on the thin nylon cord. "Shane probably had no idea how his gift would affect our weekend."

He wasn't so sure about that. Shane never did anything without a reason or a plan, and Holden was willing to bet somehow Shane had known or hoped for this outcome. He could only wish Shane's gift to Paige and his gift for Tripp, Gideon and Skylar went over just as well. "I'm just damn glad he decided to take matters into his own hands and give gifts this year."

"You and me both…" Then with a devilish little grin Bev took the empty wineglass from his hands and set it on the end table. "Speaking of gifts, come with me."

With the stopwatch in hand, she pulled him into the hallway toward the infamous closet. Opening the door, she gestured for Holden to enter. "After you."

Holden grinned. The watch combined with a hallway closet could only mean one thing for him. *Playtime.*

Without a word of protest, Holden stepped inside. It was a bit more crowded since the last time they were in there, but he was willing to adapt. "You know I have a perfectly good bed just down the hall."

"So true." Bev stepped in and shut the door partially behind them. "But I think I have a bit of making up to do."

"Do tell?"

Bev began to set the stopwatch as she spoke. "The last time we were in here, I was taken to heaven and you were left out in the cold. I think it's past time for you to get your seven minutes."

"Only seven minutes?"

Bev grinned and tossed the watch out the door before shutting them inside. "For you, Holden, I have all the time in the world."

I NEVER
ಸಿ

Acknowledgement

☙

Dedicated to Steven and what might have been if I had been a male or you had been attracted to females. I love you, man!

Trademarks Acknowledgement

☙

The author acknowledges the trademarked status and trademark owners of the following wordmarks mentioned in this work of fiction:

Barbie: Mattel, Inc.
Betty Boop: Fleischer Studios
Brokeback Mountain: Focus Features
Chicago Blackhawks: Chicago Blackhawk Hockey Team, Inc.
ESPN: ESPN, Inc.
Friends: Warner Bros. Entertainment Inc.
Mr. Clean: The Procter & Gamble Company
NHL: National Hockey League
Parcheesi: Hasbro, Inc.
Patrón: St. Maarten Spirits, Ltd.
Plexiglas: Rohm and Haas Company Corporation
Scooby Doo: Hanna-Barbera Productions, Inc.
Superman: DC Comics Inc.
Wheaties: General Mills, Inc.
Zamboni: Frank J. Zamboni & Co., Inc.

I Never

Chapter One
☙

Tripp Kowlaski was a glutton for pain, and not in the hot, sexy way either. Whatever made him think he could survive a night in the company of the two people he was in love with and not walk away singed was beyond him.

If there ever was a time he felt less in the mood to celebrate, it was now. Unfortunately for him though, he was at a birthday party and celebrating was mandatory. The worst part was he wasn't the only person who was there for the bash. So were the two people he had hoped to avoid for a just a bit longer. Skylar Daveigh and Gideon Foley. The two banes of his existence also happened to be the two people he couldn't erase from his mind.

To be honest, part of him had hoped they wouldn't attend. To add insult to injury they came as a couple. It was official. His lovers for one night were now lovers without him.

What the fuck was that about?

In the midst of his ruminating, the birthday boy and guest of honor Shane Oxley sidled up beside him and slapped his hand down on Tripp's shoulder. "You're going to have to work on your poker face, pal, if you're going to try to pretend it doesn't hurt you to see Skylar and Gideon together."

"I have no idea what you're talking about." Tripp pulled away from Shane and leaned his shoulder against the wall in a small yet nevertheless stupid show of indifference.

It didn't work of course. It only caused Shane to laugh at his blatant lie. A lie that was as pointless as the countless women he'd bedded in the last year to prove to himself he was completely straight.

"Sure you don't."

"'Nough about me." Tripp changed the subject as he had done every time Shane tried to turn the conversation to anything remotely involving Skylar and Gideon. Shane was the one person outside the trio who knew the messy details of their one night together. And damn his black soul to hell, he wouldn't stop trying to intervene and help out. "Let's talk about you, old man. The big three-oh. How does it feel?"

"Surprisingly the same as the big two-nine and the big two-eight before it," he said in a dry tone, as was his way.

"You never did say what you wanted for your birthday."

Shane nodded absently as he glanced away to the busy living room. "That's because I have everything I could ever want here tonight."

"What's that?"

"Everybody back together again."

Tripp followed his gaze and couldn't help but smile. With the exception of Bev Navarro, who had yet to arrive, the old college gang had all turned out, as decreed by their self-appointed ringleader, for his birthday. Out of the seven of them, Shane was the first one to turn thirty and in lieu of a present, he requested everyone gather together for one night.

Of course Shane being Shane added a stipulation to his own gift. He wanted the night to consist of just the old group—like old times. No dates. No excuses.

According to Holden Lancaster, host of this little shindig, Shane had even gone as far as to fly in Paige Reyes from Baltimore. She had recently moved there for a new job, and since she was putting her brother through medical school, she was short on funds. Although knowing Shane and the secret liaison that bound him to Paige, Tripp was willing to bet Shane hadn't exactly given her the option of missing the party.

Shane was never one to let anything stand in his way once he set his mind to something. It was a characteristic Tripp admired, especially since he lacked it in himself. "It's been a while, hasn't it?"

"Yes, it has." Somehow after college they'd all managed to stay close friends. Even if they didn't get together as often as they would have preferred, they still managed to see each other in one fashion or another as their schedules permitted. Although in the last couple of years it seemed as if one or more of them, for whatever reason, was absent from their group get-togethers. Paige had been the missing one last year at the barbeque. Thoughts of what had happened that night were subsequently squashed as soon as they flitted into his brain. He wouldn't go back there again. He couldn't.

"I noticed Skylar and Gideon arrived together."

"Oh, did they?" The words sounded false even to his own ears.

Thankfully Shane didn't point it out. "Yes. Have you talked to the either of them yet?"

"Sure."

"What did you say?"

"Hi mainly." To which they replied the same then nothing. For a split second it looked as if Skylar were going to say more, but then Gideon had turned and walked away, leaving the two of them staring after the other man in silence. For three people who used to spend hours just wasting time talking, they remarkably had nothing to say to one another. Or rather nothing any of them was willing to say.

"Yes, that's going to fix it," Shane said dryly.

"Hey, man, nothing needs fixing."

"Really?"

"Yes. We're all fine." Or as fine as they ever were going to be. Lord knew, Tripp wanted to change things, but for the life of him he just couldn't figure out how. It was easy to admit to himself he was in love with both a man and a woman all at the same time, but admitting it aloud was a whole new ballgame.

"Fine, huh? That's why they're sitting close enough to need only one cushion and you're over here all by your lonesome."

Ignoring Shane's unspoken question, Tripp glanced at the couple and a feeling of longing overwhelmed him. The way Skylar was absentmindedly caressing Gideon's sable hair as she talked to Paige displayed a familiarity Tripp just couldn't handle. If he hadn't recognized before this moment they had continued being lovers in his absence, he would have known now.

It had been over six months since he'd seen Skylar in person, but nothing about her had changed. If anything, she looked even more appealing than before.

She was a classic beauty with jutting breasts, a small, trim waist and legs that went on for days. Her generous, tempting lips seemed always upturned in a smile, which until their fall out, was usually aimed in his general direction. Her crowning glory was the thick ash blonde hair that swung past her shoulders.

She was as beautiful on the outside as she was on the inside, and he missed talking to her on a daily basis almost as much as he missed the way he felt buried deep inside her. Now the pleasure belonged to someone else, someone he could scarcely look at without facing his own inner demons.

As if sensing his intent look, Gideon turned his smoky gray gaze toward him. The wire-framed glasses did nothing to hide his unflinching stare. Peering at him now made Tripp wonder how he could have ever thought the other guy soft.

Other than Gideon's preference for poetry, they weren't so different. Where Tripp earned his scars on the ice, battling for the puck and glory, Gideon had earned his out on sites, building suburbia one cookie-cutter house at a time. Out of all the guys, Gideon had been the one he talked to most. They shared a love for hockey, fast food, fast cars and Skylar. It was funny, but what had once kept them joined at the hip through college now separated them years later.

Tripp was loath to admit it, but it almost hurt to look at Gideon. There was a vast difference from the person Gideon was last year and the person he appeared to be now. The earnest man he'd known for years looked almost hardened and contemptuous, but maybe it was only when Gideon looked his way. Tripp was having a hard time meeting his eyes. Hell, he was having a hard time meeting his own eyes in the mirror these days.

Living with regret was no way to live at all.

Shane cleared his throat, garnering his attention once more. "Holden says Gideon asked him to go shopping with him next weekend."

"Gideon's asking Holden for fashion hints?" The thought made him chuckle. Before he knew of Gideon's sexual orientation he'd constantly teased the other man for his neat and orderly appearance. Of the four men, Gideon was always the one who looked as if he had stepped from a store window.

It wasn't as if he dressed flashy, it was just that he always looked…nice. His pants had creases, his shoes were always dirt-free—and that was saying a lot seeing how he worked construction. During college he'd slaved away part-time at his father's company, and now that he had his bachelor's in business, he was slowly taking over the reins.

"No, it wasn't for clothing."

"Then what?" Tripp asked with confusion.

Shane raised his beer bottle and took a swig. "Holden didn't say, but I got the distinct impression it might be a jeweler."

"Jeweler—" Tripp cut his gaze to the pair lounging on the sofa, taking in their closeness. Even he had admitted to himself they were a couple. That much was obvious. But marriage? He couldn't believe they'd go so far. The pain he felt from being excluded was unbearable. Which didn't make sense since he'd been the one to push the two of them away.

The ringing doorbell cut off any remark Shane might have made on the subject. "Looks as if Bev finally made it. Time for the fun to begin."

* * * * *

Skylar had never been one for playing games. She didn't cheat. She tried not to lie and she never purposely hurt anyone. Until today. Tripp was hurt. She could tell no matter how many times he shot her a false smile or laughed out loud at some lame joke.

He was faking it. He was good at pretending he felt one way when he really felt another. His displeasure was very obvious, at least to her. She had always been able to read him like an open book. The way he stood, isolated, even surrounded by friends, broke her heart. Unfortunately there was nothing she could do she hadn't already attempted.

To be fair though, she wasn't trying to hurt Tripp. However, she could tell she was merely by being there with Gideon instead of him. Not that he'd ever come straight out and said he wanted her with him. Though if he had, she would have probably turned him down.

It wasn't that she didn't love him because she did. It was because she loved him and Gideon both—equally—with every fiber of her being. Gideon accepted that. Hell, he'd be hard-pressed not to seeing how he was in love with her and Tripp himself. Regrettably they were the only ones willing to be honest with their feelings. Maybe things would have been different if Tripp could have been more truthful, at least to himself if no one else.

Just seeing him again tonight had her aching to go to him once more. The last six months had been good to him. He was handsome in the stereotypical all-American way with blond hair and blue eyes, and thanks to his career as a forward for the Chicago Blackhawks, he was very, very fit. Skylar distinctly remembered the feel of his muscular pecs under her fingers and the way he looked nude when he—

"So are you going to tell me what's going on, or am I going to have to guess?"

Skylar glanced from the unwanted chip she'd been drowning in dip for the last five minutes into the knowing eyes of her friend Paige Reyes. The petite African-American woman was watching her intently, making Skylar wonder how long she'd been there. "What are you talking about?"

"You know what I'm talking about." Paige glanced behind Skylar and looked pointedly at Tripp then at Gideon before returning her gaze to Skylar. "I thought once you hooked up with Gideon the ongoing *Friends* saga of Rachel, Joey and Ross would come to a close. I mean, you picked Gideon, why aren't you happy?"

If only things were so simple. Skylar knew what her friends thought—good and bad—about her feelings for the two men. During the course of their ten-year friendship jokes had been made, wagers placed, all at the expense of her heart. But it wasn't a joke. There was nothing funny about loving two men. Nothing at all. "Gideon does make me happy."

"But you're not happy."

"I am happy. I could just be happier."

"If...?"

"If," Skylar turned her back on the two men who both held a piece of her heart, "they both weren't so stubborn."

"Stubborn?" Paige furrowed her brow in confusion. "What are you talking about?"

How could she explain without sharing more than either man probably wanted her to? "You know how they are. Babies, both of them."

"I do, and knowing them as I do, I would assume you picking one didn't please the other."

If only picking one over the other was their only issue. The problem was she wanted both of them. "Seems to me as if you're tap dancing around something here, Paige. So unlike you." Her sarcasm seeped into the words.

"I'm not dancing."

"Say what's on your mind."

"Girl, you know I love you, but you're breaking up the band, Yoko."

Skylar stiffened at the accusation. "Right, because we were all so harmonious before."

"Fine, we didn't always play on the same key, but look around at us." Paige swept her arm around the room. "Gideon is pretending Tripp doesn't exist. Tripp is pretending he doesn't care. Holden is casing Bev as if she were his prey and she's avoiding him as if he has the clap."

"Let's not forget our band's backup singers, you and Shane. You haven't said boo to him since you arrived and it's his birthday." Skylar was willing to give just as good as she received. Paige had no right to blame her for everything.

"With good reason," Paige fired back. Skylar didn't know specifically what happened between the two of them, but it was more than apparent something had. Unfortunately Paige had been very close-mouthed about the entire incident, leaving Skylar to draw her own sordid conclusions.

"I'm sure we all have good reasons, Paige." An unwelcome tension sidled up between them, forcing the two women into an old-fashioned stare down.

Yes, maybe Tripp and Gideon would still have been friends if she had gone home with the rest of the guests after the Fourth of July barbeque, but that didn't mean they'd be happier. Even if they never spoke again, the night the three of them came together would remain with them forever. Good and bad.

"I hate the way things are between all of us now," Paige finally said, breaking the silence.

"I do too." Skylar placed her arm around the other woman's shoulder and leaned her head against Paige's. "But we can't go back."

"Lord knows I've wished we could a time or two."

I Never

"You're not the only one." "If only..." had become her new mantra. She couldn't even count the number of times in the last year she'd wished things had gone differently that night.

"How in the world did we ever get ourselves in this mess?"

"We're stupid."

"You can say that again."

"Okay, we're stupid."

"Uh-oh..." Paige nudged Skylar and gestured to Holden, who was following Bev from the room. "I think one of us should go rescue her before he does something stupid."

Skylar sighed, taking her arm down. Bev had made Paige and Skylar promise not to leave her alone with Holden. "You mean again."

"Yes again." Paige held her closed fist out. "Rock, paper, scissors?"

"No, I'll go." She needed a break. "But if I'm not back in five minutes, send reinforcements."

"In the form of whom? Gideon or Tripp?"

"Maybe I'll just kamikaze it."

"Good choice."

Skylar quickly made her way from the living room into the hallway where she spotted Holden holding on tight to the pretty Filipino woman. From the looks of things she was just in time. Two years ago she had made the costly mistake of suggesting a little game of Seven Minutes in Heaven at Holden's housewarming party. Holden pulled Bev's name from the hat, or so he told everyone.

Come to find out he'd lied and Bev never forgave him for what she had perceived as pity. Skylar always believed he had done it for less lofty means than compassion, but Bev wouldn't be persuaded. She held on to a grudge almost as tight as Paige did.

"There you two are," she said as cheerfully as she could. "Everyone was wondering where you two had wandered off to."

"Everyone," Holden asked, "or just you and Paige?"

Skylar batted her eyes at him, secretly laughing inside. He was such a goner. If Bev thought this little interlude was going to help her in the long run, she was sadly mistaken. "Whatever do you mean, Holden?"

"Right." Holden released Bev, grimacing in annoyance when she scuttled past him.

"Thank you," Bev mouthed when she neared Skylar.

But Holden refused to let her go so easily. "We'll pick this up later, Bev."

Bev paused and looked over her shoulder at him, apparently more confident now that Skylar had arrived. At least she was good for something. "I seriously doubt it."

"I don't." Skylar shivered at the underlying threat in his words. Bev was in some serious trouble, and from the way her friend paled, she knew it.

* * * * *

This was easier than Gideon thought. And in a few short hours he and Skylar could blow this pop stand unscathed. He was actually surprised how smoothly the night was going. Although to be honest, he probably shouldn't have been. Tripp was the king of denial. Gideon should have known Tripp wasn't going to make a scene. If he did, then he'd have to admit their night together happened, and Gideon was more than positive the other man didn't want to do that.

"You don't look like a man who's having a good time." Skylar came up beside him and slipped her arm around his waist.

Gideon smiled in the dark. She'd found him. He'd thought he'd made a clean break when he slipped out the kitchen door so he could have a few minutes to himself. But he should have known better. Skylar had never allowed him to escape into himself. In college she and Paige, the two social butterflies of the group, had dragged him kicking and screaming out of his introverted ways and into polite society.

It was thanks to their efforts he began to open up and show the other side of his personality. To people who didn't know him he came off as determined and somewhat standoffish, but it was only when he was around this group he was able to joke and kid.

The seven of them had complemented one another. It was as if he'd found in each of them just what he needed. And in Skylar and Tripp he'd found even more. Together the two of them completed him—although it had been just for one night.

"I'm having fun."

"Liar," she teased. "I think you're forgetting, mister. I know exactly the face you make when you're having a good time."

"This party would have to get a hell of a lot kinkier for me to break out my 'O' face."

"Let me see what I can arrange."

Gideon caught Skylar's hand as she took a step away from him in a mocking attempt to leave and pulled her back firmly against him. "I don't think so, princess."

"Awww, spoilsport."

He snorted. "We've had enough group sex to last a lifetime."

"Speak for yourself."

"Then you're braver than me."

"I'm an incurable optimist."

She said that as if it were a good thing. "Hmmm…"

She might be an optimist, but he was a realist. Life didn't always go the way he wanted, and wishing for things to be different didn't make a damn bit of difference. Instead, he had learned to accept things for the way they were and move on. Or at least he tried to. It was becoming increasingly obvious from his reaction to seeing Tripp tonight he hadn't quite moved on.

The rush of resentment that filled him at the sight of his old friend shocked even Gideon. The thing that bothered him most though, was knowing if he didn't care about Tripp at all he wouldn't feel so strongly about him. Why couldn't Gideon just walk away from him as Tripp had obviously walked away from them?

"How long are you going to be angry with him?"

Now that was the question of the millennium. One with no right answer, at least not one that would please Skylar. She didn't believe him when he said he wasn't angry, and if he said he was, she'd want to talk about it. He was done talking.

In the last year they had talked enough for a hundred people. His feelings, her feelings, their perception of Tripp's feelings, it was enough to make a grown man cry.

"Well?"

Even though he knew it wouldn't work, he tried anyway. "I'm not angry at him. I just don't want to talk to him anytime soon."

"Define soon."

"This lifetime."

"Gid—"

"Stop, baby. He made his choice, he made it abundantly clear. He doesn't want anything to do with us." No, that wasn't entirely true. As much as it pained him to admit, he had to speak the truth. "With me. He'd slay a slew of mythical beasts for just one more kiss from you though."

"I'm with you now, Gideon."

"Yes, but I know you still love him."

"As do you." She lifted her chin and met his stare with a challenging gaze of her own. "We both love him, and he loves us. Whether he wants to admit it or not."

The likelihood of Tripp admitting that was small to nil. After hours of arguing, he would barely concede he willingly had sex with Gideon. Tripp was hell-bent on blaming the alcohol for his foray into the dark side—the alcohol and Gideon.

According to Tripp, if Gideon hadn't instigated it, they would never have made love. Gideon was willing to concede that—for the first time. But it was hard as hell to believe he was the catalyst to the entire night of debauchery when at one point in the night he'd woken up to Tripp stroking his cock.

Tripp had backpedaled faster than the speed of light once morning came, sputtering lies and accusations left and right. At first Gideon tried to understand. It had taken him a good portion of his adulthood to come to grips with his own dual sexuality, so of course he didn't think Tripp was going to jump on the bisexual bandwagon with no qualms.

Not that Gideon was asking him to wave a rainbow flag or march in a parade. All he wanted was for Tripp to acknowledge their feelings for one another. He didn't think he was asking too much.

Apparently Tripp did though.

The only good thing from that night was the woman standing by his side.

"It makes more sense for you to be with him instead of me."

"How do you figure?"

"You know it would be easier. One man, one woman. The way the world says it should be."

"If I were the type of girl who could live happily in a one-man, one-woman world, it would be easier. But I'm not." He was proud of her. It was an admission she never could have made in college, but she'd grown a lot since then. Hell, it had taken her eight years to admit she wanted to be with both of them. He didn't begrudge her the time it took though, because he'd eventually ended up with what he wanted. Almost anyway. "I'm not ashamed to admit I love the feel of two strapping men making love to me."

"Skylar."

"I'm not afraid, Gideon." She turned and leaned against him, pressing her hand against his clothes-covered cock. "I loved having you buried in my pussy while I sucked him off. I loved seeing you jerk off as you watched Tripp fuck me."

His shaft grew under her stroking hand, thanks in part to her words. But he wasn't the only one turned-on by her trip down memory lane. He could feel her hardened nipples pressing against his chest.

"And do you know what I loved most of all?"

"No." The word sounded harsh even to his own ears. "Tell me, baby."

"I loved watching you suck—"

"Am I interrupting anything?" An amused tone broke the two of them apart. Irritated, Gideon stepped away from Skylar and turned to see the guest of honor lounging casually against the kitchen doorframe. From the way Shane was grinning from ear to ear he'd heard a least part of her declaration.

"Yes, you were. I was in the midst of talking dirty to my boyfriend." Skylar's snappy comeback surprised him. Gideon thought she might be a bit embarrassed to be caught speaking so bluntly about their sex life, but boy was he wrong. Although she might look like the stereotypical Barbie doll, she had a spine of steel and was more than willing to speak her mind.

"Don't let me interrupt you."

"Pervert." Skylar shook her head in amusement.

"Apparently I'm not the only one."

"You have no idea," Gideon replied.

I Never

"So I see." Shane watched them speculatively for a second before gesturing toward the open kitchen door. "We're about to fire up the cake."

"We don't want to miss this," Skylar said.

"No, you don't."

Shane waggled his brows before turning around and heading back into the kitchen.

When Skylar stepped to follow him, Gideon held her back with a hand on her arm. "Why do I have the feeling he's up to something?"

"Because he's Shane. And whenever he has that look on his face, the fit is going to hit the shan."

"Be afraid."

She nodded ruefully. "Be very afraid."

Hand in hand they followed Shane into the house to the dining room where everyone else was gathering around the table. Unfortunately, since they were the last two to arrive, there were only two seats left—right next to Tripp. Skylar stopped in the doorway, seemingly reluctant to move toward the two open chairs, but Gideon wasn't going to show any weakness. Not now when the night was almost over. His hand at the small of her back, he propelled her forward and pulled out the chair closest to Tripp.

"Your seat, milady."

Tripp had turned to stare at them and the look of longing and regret on his face was almost priceless. Unfortunately for him, Gideon wasn't in a forgiving mood. He smiled at Skylar as she sat then joined her in the last chair, leaning over and draping an arm over her shoulders. He could put forth an air of complete ease with no problem. It was time to wish his friend a happy thirtieth.

In a loud hammy chorus they sang to Shane, who stood regally at the head of the table until the very last note. Amongst laughter and small talk he cut the cake and then sat, allowing Bev, who was forced to sit next to Holden, to pass it around. From the way she took her time placing each piece neatly on the saucer, she was apparently in no hurry to resume her seat. Unfortunately for her, there were only seven people at the table and the job was done in no time.

With a begrudged look, she took her seat next to a grinning Holden and began to ignore the other man all over again. "So." Her words came out desperate rush. "What did you wish for?"

"Bev." Holden leaned toward her, eating up the space she managed to create for herself. "If he tells us what he wished for, he won't get it."

"You're going to wish you sat somewhere else if you don't move your hand."

Gideon choked on his laughter as Bev tried, and once again failed, to move away from Holden. Was everyone fucking someone else in the group?

"Where you going?" Holden asked innocently.

"Let go, you big bully."

"Actually," Shane said, interrupting the arguing duo's bantering, "my wish was for all of us."

Now that was Gideon's kind of wish. "I hope it was for us to the win the lotto."

"Not exactly."

"Damn." Gideon frowned mockingly.

"Then what did you wish for?" Bev asked.

"In time all things will be answered." Shane rose from his seat. "I'll be right back. I have to go get the presents."

"Presents!" Paige's cry of outrage stopped Shane in his tracks. "I thought you weren't accepting gifts this year. If you told me I didn't have to bring a present as some lame attempt to salvage my poor dignity or to preserve my pride, you needn't have bothered."

Ruh roh! Gideon's inner Scooby Doo could sense trouble in the making. No matter in what direction he looked there was an underlining sense of impending doom closing in on their once tight-knit group. They were coming apart at the seams, and in the process they were going to rip their friendship to smithereens.

"The presents aren't for me, Paige. I brought them for everyone else." Shane's smile was bitter and cruel, and directed straight at Paige. "And I assure you, little one, no one knows more about your pride than I."

Paige tilted her chin and met his icy gaze head-on. She was just as stubborn as Shane. There was no doubt in Gideon's mind she would sit there all night without saying a word, waiting for Shane to break, and Shane, being the obstinate fool he was, would wait her out. To his surprise it didn't come to that. With a muttered curse Shane turned and stormed out of the dining room, leaving everyone staring after him in his wake.

Maybe Shane was becoming wiser in his old age.

"Pipe down, Paige," Skylar scolded softly. "It's the boy's birthday for goodness' sake. Retract the claws and cut him a little slack."

"That's what's wrong with him now. Shane is so used to people treating him as if he were the crowned heir he doesn't know what to do when someone stands up to him."

"Are you willing to test your theory?" Shane questioned as he entered the room with three gift bags of various colors and sizes.

"I should have never come."

"As if you had a choice. My threat wasn't an idle one."

Or maybe he just learned how to pick his battles.

"Don't think I didn't realize that." Paige's sullen statement made Gideon wonder, and not for the first time, what was really going on between the two of them.

"So…" Tripp interrupted. "Should we all leave and come back at a better time?"

"No way. If we leave, I won't get my present," Skylar teased.

"And it's all about you, isn't it, dollface?" Tripp's lighthearted tone didn't fool Gideon for a second, and it took everything in him to refrain from responding with his fist.

His irritation didn't go unnoticed by Skylar, who gripped his leg under the table, silently telling him to be good as she joked with Tripp as if she didn't have a care in the world. "Of course it is. Now gimme."

"Don't be greedy." Shane teased as he handed her a long orange bag. "You have to share."

"Who am I sharing it with?"

"You're sharing with Tripp and Gideon."

Tripp and Gideon glanced at one another in stunned silence. Well, didn't that just fucking figure.

Chapter Two

෩

Well, damn. Tripp hadn't been expecting that and from the looks of his fellow gift holders, they hadn't either. Flabbergasted, he glanced over at Shane and wondered what the hell his friend—no, possible former friend—was thinking.

Gideon on the other hand wasn't as speechless. The other man stood, glass in hand and made a beeline for the wine bottle on the corner table. After filling his glass, he turned and faced the silent room with a fake smile spread across his face. "Shall we take this into the living room?"

"What a wonderful idea." Bev quickly rose from her seat and fled the dining room.

"This is going to be fun," Tripp said to Skylar, who had yet to rise.

"Do you know what this is all about?"

"I haven't a clue."

"Don't you just love surprises?" The sarcasm dripped from every word.

Tripp knew just what she meant. Surprises such as these never ended well. Before he could reply to her, Gideon came up behind them and pulled out her chair. "Shall we...?"

"Always the gentleman," Tripp scoffed. He didn't know why, but he felt the urge to antagonize the other man. Gideon's unfailing grace was getting a little old.

Tripp wanted him to respond, be it with fist or words. Something. Anything to show Gideon acknowledged his presence. But he waited in vain. Without sparing him a glance, Gideon held out his hand to Skylar and pulled her to her feet, all without uttering a simple word to Tripp.

Irritated, Tripp rose and followed them from the room. As stupid as it was, he refused to be ignored. Yes, he was the one who had pushed Gideon away. And yes, he was the one who'd avoided him for the last year, but that was then and this was now. And for some unexplainable reason he wanted Gideon to recognize the fact he was not some aberration the other man neatly avoided.

"On with the present-giving." Shane handed Bev a small yellow bag. "You'll be sharing your present with Holden."

From the stunned look on her face, she was about as happy as Tripp at the turn of events.

"And last but not least." Shane walked across the room, stopping at the far wall where Paige was standing. "For you, little one. You're sharing with…" Glancing around, Shane made a show of counting everyone. "Well, with me."

"Note the surprise on my face." Paige crossed her arms over her breasts in lieu of taking the bag. "I'll pass."

"I think not." Shane didn't budge. "Take the bag, Paige."

"There are over a thousand nerves in the human body, Shane." Paige dropped her arms and snatched the bag from his hand. "And you are on every last one of mine."

Shane walked to the center of the room. "Everybody gather around with the co-owner or -owners of your bags. It's time to play a little game."

Shane moved until he was standing next to a disgruntled Paige again. "Now that everyone is in their place, feel free to open the bags."

"Yay!" Skylar opened theirs and pulled out a bottle of tequila. "Exactly what type of game were you thinking of playing, Shane dear?"

"Yes." Paige dangled a set of keys off her index finger. "What's going on here?"

"Hold up." Tripp glanced from their gift to Paige's. "How come Paige has keys and all we have is booze. I don't want booze. I want keys too."

"What did you guys get?" Gideon asked Holden and Bev.

Bev slowly reached inside the bag and pulled out their gift. "It's a stopwatch. I don't get it."

"Join the club," Skylar said.

Their confusion seemed to be just what Shane was looking for. "You all wanted to know what I wished for this year. Well, the answer lies within your hands."

"You wished for tequila?" Skylar questioned, confused.

"No, I wished for a do-over." Shane paused to look at Paige for a moment. "A do-over for us all."

"What do you mean?" Gideon asked. "Why do you think we need a do-over?"

"Because you're all unhappy. Let me rephrase that, we're all unhappy and some of us are eaten by guilt and regret."

Tripp sat back against the couch, not liking where this was going at all. If it was the last thing he did, he was going to kick Shane's ass. Not just a little ass kicking either. There was going to be blood spilling and bones breaking. Gory stuff horror movies were made of.

"You? Guilt?" Paige's snorted. "I don't believe it."

"Believe it." Shane looked around the room at everyone. "And I'm not the only one, am I?"

"I'm not," Gideon said, apparently still confused.

"No, you may not be." Don't say it. Don't say it. Shane turned knowing eyes Tripp's way. "But he is. Filled with it."

He said it.

Damn it, Tripp silently cursed as he plotted where and how to dispose of Shane's limp and comatose body.

Before he could utter a word in his defense, Skylar turned her attention full blast on him. From the angry tilt of her chin, she was far from happy. "What is he talking about?"

"I don't know." Tripp had to try, even if the only person he was fooling was himself. "I need another drink."

As he rose, Shane said, "Why don't you play another game of quarters while you're at it? Maybe this time you won't chicken out."

Skylar's gasp of shock was almost as palpable as Tripp's grimace of annoyance. Not only was Shane spilling his secret, he was getting it wrong to boot. Tripp closed his eyes, thankful his back was toward the group, and he was able to hide his expression from their knowing eyes. "What I told you was spoken in confidence."

"You told him?" Gideon asked, standing as well. "You wouldn't talk to us about it, but you discussed it with him?"

Now Gideon had something to say to him. "There was nothing to talk about."

"No?" Gideon's voice held a nuance of cold contempt. "You're right, Tripp. There is nothing to talk about. Now or ever again."

Hearing Gideon say that was akin to having a bucket of icy-cold water dumped on him. A cold knot formed in the pit of his stomach. Tripp knew without a doubt if Gideon walked out the door now, feeling as he did, Tripp would never see him again. It was not an option he was willing to take.

He might still have lingering misgivings about the night the three of them spent together, but try as he might, he could no longer pretend he didn't enjoy being with the other man.

"Gideon?" Skylar's voice was shaky and filled with despair. "You don't mean that."

"Yes, Skylar, I think I do."

Tripp flinched at the finality of his words. "You don't, Gideon. No more so than I meant what I said a year ago."

"You don't know dick, Tripp."

"Which was part of the problem, wasn't it, ol' buddy?" he replied with heavy irony.

"Go to hell."

I Never

"I've been there all year." Tripp turned to face them again. Now that he'd started down this road, he wasn't going to chickenshit his way off it. The last year had been the longest and loneliest of his life. "I could use a do-over. I'd be willing to play. What about you, Skylar?"

Tripp asked her first because he knew how she felt. Out of the three of them she'd been the only one willing to work things out this year. In the first few months after their night together, she would call him and damn near beg him to talk to Gideon. He could only hope she was willing to change the relationship the two of them apparently had now to include him.

Skylar nervously glanced around the room at their silent but attentive audience for a second before setting the bottle on the floor and standing. With her head held high, she met his stare head-on and smiled shyly. "I would love a do-over. I'm more than willing to try again."

Gideon stiffened as if she'd slapped him and took a step toward the hallway. "Then goody for the both of you because I'm sure as hell not." The disappointed look that flashed across Skylar's face was nothing compared to how Tripp felt. Moving quickly, he stepped in front of Gideon, stopping the other man cold.

Tripp watched Gideon's fist clench and unclench by his side, and wondered if the other man would give in to his rage and strike. Part of Tripp wanted him to. Then he'd finally feel something besides regret. After a few seconds of pained silence, Gideon finally spoke. "Get out of my way, Tripp. You should be real good at that after the last several months."

"I don't want out of your way." Tripp's confession sounded raw even to his own ears. But it was the truth, and he knew now the truth was the only way he was going to get anywhere with Gideon.

"This time it isn't about you." Gideon brushed past Tripp and stormed from the room.

One Year Ago

"You're looking very patriotic in that bikini, princess."

Skylar pushed her sunglasses higher on the bridge of her nose and smiled at Gideon who was peering at her as she lounged on her chair by the pool. She smiled when she saw the handsome brunette. It was like looking back in time. Dressed in tan cargo shorts and a white T-shirt, his casual attire made him appear as if he were still a college student instead of seven years past graduation.

Tripp's Fourth of July party had started a few hours ago and was now in full swing. The partygoers were milling around in small groups, some by the pool and others just inside the house, but everyone was drinking and having a good time. Even she had an icy margarita close at hand, not that she planned to get tipsy just yet. That, she would save for later when it was just the three of them and she'd need the alcohol to do what she desperately wanted to.

Most of their old college friends were there, although Paige hadn't been able to make it, claiming low funds after her move halfway across the country. Tripp had also invited some of his teammates, and others he'd met through his hockey connections. There were quite a few women there, groupies— all of them—looking for their fifteen minutes of fame for nabbing a player.

Women like that disgusted her, especially when the player in their sights was Tripp. She had grown tired of sending death threats via her squinting eyes and eventually removed herself to the lounge chairs in hopes it would help her resist the temptation to get catty and rip their hair out. Besides, being separated from the pack was in some ways the best mechanism for drawing attention. It certainly had brought Gideon to her side.

"This old thing? It's just a little something I picked up in Key West last summer."

"I'd say little aptly describes it."

As did she. Her breasts were almost spilling out the red-and-white-striped bra top and her ass wasn't faring much better in the blue bottoms covered with white stars.

Of course it wasn't an accident the bathing suit fit as it did. She'd bought it that way—with Gideon and Tripp in mind—and from the hungry look on his lean face, she'd accomplished part of her goal. Now all she had to do was get Tripp to salivate before she burned beyond recognition. Skin as fair as hers wasn't meant to wear so little in the blistering sun.

"You're getting red. You need to put on some more sunscreen."

Skylar sat up and reached for the white hemp bag on the ground. She set it on her lap and dug around inside until she came across the item she was searching for. "Would you do the honors?"

Before Gideon could say yes, she handed him the lotion and dropped the bag back on the ground. With a wicked little grin she rolled over onto her stomach, giving him the back view of her bathing suit. If he thought there was little to the front, he wasn't going to be all that impressed with the T-back thong.

"Jesus," he hissed, causing her to smile into her towel. Operation Bring Gideon to His Knees was coming along very nicely. "What are you wearing?"

"It's called a thong, Daddy."

"You're lucky I'm not your father because if I were, I'd tan your ass and send you inside the house to change."

His words had her salivating at the image. "You don't like my bathing suit?"

"I like it too much. As does every other man out here." Gideon sat beside her on the lounge. "Tell me, princess, are you trying to get someone killed?"

"Of course not." Her goal was to capture the attentions of the two most eligible men there tonight.

"Then I would roll over real quick if I were you. Tripp almost speared a goalie with his skewer for making a comment about your ass earlier, and that was when you were wearing clothes."

"I'm sure the big, bad goalie can take care of himself, unlike me. I need you." She pushed herself up and peered over her shoulder at him. With his sunglasses on she couldn't read his eyes, only hope she was getting through to him. "You don't want me to burn, do you?"

"No."

"Then touch me."

She stayed upright until Gideon squirted the lotion on his hand and rubbed them together. Lying back down, she rested her head on her folded arms and sighed in delight when his strong hands began to spread the cool cream onto her warm skin. "Hmm...that feels good."

"You were beginning to turn pink. A few minutes longer and you would have burned."

"But now you're here to take care of me."

"As usual. Move your hair?" When she complied, he moved his hands up her back to her shoulders where he began to expertly knead her muscles. His actions brought back fond memories of late-night study sessions when the only thing that sustained her through the night was extra-strong coffee and Gideon's shoulder massages.

"Am I really such a pest?" Skylar knew he really didn't mind, but she asked just to hear him protest her innocence.

"You know you're not."

As he ran his fingers along her back she moaned in appreciation. His touch was firm and sure, but her back wasn't the only place she wanted to feel his hands. This was a long time in the making and she wanted to enjoy every single second of it. Trying to act nonchalant, she shifted on the lounge and spread her legs a bit. "Don't forget my legs."

"As if I could," he muttered under his breath, much to her delight. It was wonderful to see he hadn't grown immune to her. During college she'd flirted with practically every man she'd come into contact with. Gideon had fallen under her charms early and they'd remained friends through school and beyond.

"Didn't you forget something?" she asked as he pulled away, leaving her rear lotion-free.

Instead of taking her blatant hint, Gideon recapped the lotion and tossed it on the chair next to her. Startled at the abrupt change in his demeanor, Skylar rolled onto her side until she was facing his taut frame. "What?"

"What are you doing, Skylar?"

"Sunbathing, what does it look like?" she replied flippantly, unsure of how to react to his cool detachment.

"Right." He wiped his hands on his arms and made a move to rise, but she stopped him by placing her hand on his tense arm.

"Wait, why are you mad?"

"I'm not a boy to be toyed with, princess."

"Who's toying?"

Instead of answering, he asked a question of his own, one that went straight to the heart of the matter. "Finally stopped running, princess?"

"Yes."

"So you've made your choice then."

"I have."

"And Cord?" he asked, referring to her as-of-last-week ex-boyfriend.

"Out of the picture."

"For good?"

"Yes." Cord had been the shield she kept in place for the better part of three years to keep her unnatural desires at bay. It hadn't worked of course. All it managed to do was to put off the inevitable and hurt a good man in the process. Skylar wasn't pleased with herself for the way she'd strung him along all these years. When he began to speak of buying a house and the possibility of marriage, she knew right then and there she had to call a halt to things.

"For sure this time?"

She nodded her head in lieu of answering. Deep inside she was sure Gideon and Tripp were tired of her indecision, but truth be told, she'd been more confused than confident since she met the two of them.

Skylar had never wanted for anything a day in her life. She wasn't proud to admit it, but it was true. She was the only child of a high-society couple who bred because it was expected of them. She was their crowning heir. Good looks, good fortune and a good life were all hers for the taking.

Everything she'd ever wanted she'd been given. Even now, though she was a college graduate with a degree in art history, she'd never worked a day in her life. It wasn't expected of her. She went to school not only to learn, but to fall in love with a suitable lawyer, doctor or MBA-type man and continue with the tradition of money marrying money.

Only things hadn't quite happened that way. She fell in love, all right, but with two men instead of one. And her life hadn't been the same since. It had taken her a while to figure out how to get what she wanted without losing everything she'd worked hard to build with the two of them. Now that the time was upon her she felt a bit unprepared for it, but that didn't mean she was going to back down.

"And…"

"Hang around after the party and you'll find out."

"Just like that?" He laughed harshly. "After eight years of indecision you've made up your mind?"

"I'm a slow learner."

"Tell me something I don't know." Gideon glanced across the backyard toward Tripp who stood by the barbeque laughing with Holden.

Skylar watched him, wondering what he was thinking, but too afraid to ask. Had she waited too long to come to her senses? Would she lose her chance to be with them now that she had finally worked up the nerve to ask for what she truly wanted? When the silence became too heavy to bear, she nervously licked her lips and spoke Gideon's name softly. He picked up the lotion and glanced at her. "Lie back down."

She didn't hesitate, instantly obeying his sharp command. When she first set out to seduce Gideon, she'd mistakenly thought she would be the one in charge. From the steel in his tone, she quickly realized maybe she didn't know him as well as she thought she did.

Silently he began to rub the lotion into her upturned cheeks, taking his time, touching every available inch of her. His thumb brushed against the thin fabric between her legs, sending bolts of pleasure ricocheting throughout her body. Without volition her legs fell open to accept his questing touch, wondering if he would dare go further. She didn't have to wonder for long. He slipped his finger under her suit and into the dark cavern of her sex, chuckling low when he discovered the moist evidence of her desire.

Embarrassed now, she shut her legs firmly, or at least she tried. Gideon didn't move his hand, nor did he stop caressing her, in fact, the bastard added another finger to his wicked play.

"Stop it," she said in a broken whisper.

"I guess I'm not the only one turned-on by the suit."

"It's not the suit." Her body was pulsing with desire despite the fact they were surrounded by people. He was going to make her come. Right here in front of God and country, and there wasn't a damn thing she could do about it. "It's you."

"Me, huh. It's about damn time." Instead of being satisfied by her answer and stopping as she thought he would, Gideon continued to delve his fingers into her wet sex, fucking her with his hand as she lay helpless before him.

To be honest, Skylar didn't know what part of this she loved more. The fact Gideon was fingering her, or that he was doing it in a very domineering, controlling way. It was as if her safe, fun-loving friend had morphed into a sex maniac, and she loved every second of it.

She did her best to suppress a moan of pleasure when the tip of his fingers brushed across her G-spot, but it was like trying to hold back a flood with a single sheet of paper. "Gideon—"

"This looks friendly."

Skylar jumped at the sound of Tripp's voice and quickly rolled over. Thankfully Gideon moved as swiftly and removed his hand before she twisted in her effort to look presentable.

"Our Skylar's a friendly girl," Gideon said boldly. He didn't seem the least bit embarrassed to be caught with his hand in the proverbial cookie jar, unlike Skylar. In contrast, she was mortified and could do nothing else but stare at the two of them, tongue-tied. She was sure her cheeks were ruby red and this time it had nothing to do with the sun.

"I can't believe I'm missing all the fun, and at my own party even." Although Tripp smiled when he spoke, his voice was absolutely emotionless. She couldn't decide if he was angry or amused, but she could tell by the bulge in his Hawaiian-print shorts he was interested. Very interested. "Can I play too?"

Gideon wasn't quite sure what Skylar was up to, but he was intrigued by her abrupt change in behavior. Maybe abrupt was a bit strong. She'd always been a flirt, hell, it was one of the things he loved about her, but for some reason she was turning up her sex appeal wattage to full blast.

The thing that shocked him most was the timing of her little change of heart. Eight years was a long time to say yes with your eyes but no with your mouth. In college she toyed around with both him and Tripp. Things never became physical, but she let it be known she was more than interested in both of them. But letting them know was as far as it ever went.

She'd dated countless men in college, which was okay with him. It wasn't as if he'd stayed at home, dick in hand, pining away for her. He'd been laid more than Italian tile over the course of their friendship, but no matter how many women he was with, there was a part of his heart he reserved for her alone. The other part belonged to the man staring down and watching them intently.

Tripp's expressive eyes were filled with questions. Questions Gideon didn't yet have the answers to, but there was no doubt in his mind he soon would. No matter how he felt about Skylar, he wasn't going to allow her to play him for a fool. He loved her to pieces, but he'd take her over his lap and paddle her sweet ass beet red before he'd allow that to happen.

"Here," Gideon stood and took a step away from the tempting enigma lounging like a sacrificial rite before them. She was lethal, and until he understood the rules of the game a bit more, he was going to sit out a few hands. "You can take my turn."

"Gee, buddy, thanks," Tripp said sarcastically as he slapped Gideon heartily on the back. "You're a real giver."

He was such a smartass. "Don't mention it."

"Wait," Skylar cried out as she pushed herself up into a sitting position. "Where are you going?"

"I have to go see a man about a horse."

"Oh."

"Hey, before you leave, Nash Boone wanted me to let you know he was looking for you." Although Tripp didn't word it as such, Gideon heard the question in his tone. Tripp was damn curious as to why his teammate would want to talk to his college friend, but Gideon didn't plan to enlighten him.

Gideon sent Tripp a distracted nod, too intent on delving to the bottom of Skylar's antics to think about much else.

Apparently though, the nod wasn't good enough for Tripp. "So what does he want?"

"Who?"

"Nash."

"I don't know. I haven't spoken to him yet."

"I didn't know you two were friends."

Gideon wouldn't have necessarily put Tripp's teammate in the friend category. They had met up after one of the games and chatted about a few things, but it wasn't worth mentioning. The fact of the matter was Tripp, as usual, didn't want Gideon to be friends with anyone outside their little group. It was almost as if the other man were afraid Gideon was going to like someone better than him. "Is that a problem?"

"No." Tripp frowned, obviously lying.

"Don't think so hard. It'll make your brain explode."

"Kiss my ass."

"Bare it and share it."

"You wish," he said, giving Gideon a little shove toward the house. Instead of responding with a sarcastic comeback or a juvenile physical response, Gideon smiled and walked away. Normally he would have snapped off a smartass retort without even thinking, but there was no retort for the truth.

I Never

Because, even though Tripp didn't know it, he was right. Gideon did wish he could kiss his ass.

It didn't get more clichéd than falling in love with your straight male friend, but as trite as it was, he had. Fallen so hard he hadn't been able to shake the feeling, no matter how many men he was with. Lucky for Gideon, he had his obsession with Skylar to balance it out. The two of them were his kryptonite.

Skylar with her fair-haired beauty and Tripp in all his macho glory were his alpha and omega, his beginning and end. The problem with being in love with the two of them was hell. Skylar didn't know what she wanted, and Tripp knew exactly what he wanted—pussy—one thing Gideon didn't possess. His love life was a big old ball of confusion and it was no one's fault but his own.

After handling business in the bathroom, Gideon wandered back out to the party but made sure to stay clear of Tripp and Skylar. Instead, he hunkered down with Shane and Holden near the basketball hoop and kicked back with his boys until the fireworks began.

* * * * *

It was close to the end of the evening, after most of the guests had gone, when Tripp cornered him in the kitchen. Nash, who apparently had a better gaydar tracking system than Gideon did, had made him an offer he was still pondering whether or not to refuse.

Although his immediate family knew of his bisexuality, Gideon had yet to come out to his friends, and dating Tripp's teammate wasn't exactly the way he wanted to do it.

"Where you been all night?" Tripp's question sounded almost accusatory.

"I've been around." *Avoiding the two of you*, he added silently to himself as he leaned back against the gray granite counter. Leaning was about all he could do because the room was trashed. It was going to take a small army to clean the place, which was a shame, because out of every room in Tripp's house, the kitchen was Gideon's favorite.

The dark-painted room brimmed with chrome and granite. He'd often heard others in the gang refer to the room as cold and unwelcoming, whereas he saw the great outdoors brought inside. It reminded him of the trip to Colorado he and the guys took one summer to go whitewater rafting. He wondered if that was where Tripp drew his inspiration from. Knowing Tripp though, he probably just asked his decorator to fill the room with easy-to-clean appliances.

"So."

"So..." Gideon echoed back, wondering what was on the other man's mind.

"I ran into Nash on his way out. You two talk?"

"Yep." Would have kissed too if it was up to Nash.

"And?"

"And what?"

"What did he want?"

"None of your business." Gideon found a perverse pleasure in denying Tripp the information.

Tripp narrowed his eyes. "You holding back on me?"

If he only knew. "Fine, if you must know, we're planning a surprise birthday party for you."

"My birthday isn't for another three months."

"Surprise!"

"Be an asshole then." Tripp paused for a moment as if waiting to see if Gideon would change his mind. He must have finally decided Gideon was going to stand firm in his silence and abruptly changed the subject. "I had a very interesting conversation with Skylar."

"Did you now?" Gideon was suddenly intrigued.

"Yeah." Tripp took a sip of his beer before setting the brown bottle down on the counter next to Gideon. "She told me she and Cord split up."

"I know." Gideon picked up the bottle and took a long drink of the cool ale. It wasn't that he was thirsty. He just wanted to press his mouth on the same spot Tripp had. It was as intimate as he could be with the other man without arousing suspicion.

"She also said she wanted to talk to the two of us after everyone left."

"Why?"

"She wouldn't say."

"What do you think it's about?" He offered the bottle to Tripp, who took it from him. Gideon watched in fascination as he turned the bottle to place his lips over the same spot yet again. He wondered if it was just coincidence and then figured it could be nothing else.

"I don't know, man. We've all been dancing around this for so damn long it doesn't even make sense anymore."

"You can always bow out."

"Or you can."

That was very true. He could, parts of him wanted him to, but not the part that mattered most. "No can do, buddy."

Tripp sighed heavy, warily shook his head. "I was afraid you were going to say that. Now I'm going to have to kill you."

"You could try," Gideon smirked.

"I'm not seeing anyone. Are you?" Tripp asked hopefully, as if that would matter if Skylar choose Gideon.

"Nope."

"Fuck."

"Yep." That aptly described their predicament, all right. Fucked.

Chapter Three

✽

"If I give you fifty bucks, will you take off?"

Gideon paused in the midst of picking up a half-empty paper plate in the living room and peered over at him. "If I recall correctly, didn't you just sign a seven-figure deal with the Blackhawks?"

"Yeah."

"And all you're going to offer me is fifty bucks? Cheapo."

"Fine, seventy-five dollars then." Tripp didn't bust his ass out on the ice to give his well-earned money away to a greedy interloper, even though Skylar was worth every cent he had.

"Hell no."

"Haven't you heard the old saying 'two's company and three's a crowd'?"

"Yeah, so maybe you should take off."

What the fuck! "This is my place."

"I promise to lock up after we're done."

"Gee thanks."

Tripp watched as Gideon tied the ends of the black trash bag together and dropped it on the floor next to the other two. The living room actually appeared livable again. Despite the fact he had a cleaning crew coming in tomorrow, Skylar had insisted the three of them pick up the place a bit before they had their talk.

Personally, Tripp thought she was just trying to buy time and he was going to allow it—for now. Besides with just the right incentive, he could turn the semi-straightened living room into a seduction palace fit for two. In order for that to happen one of the three of them would have to leave, and he was quite positive just who he wanted gone.

Short of throwing the other man out though, there wasn't much he could do to make him leave, and as annoying as Gideon was, Tripp couldn't just kick him out. Bastard or not, he was one of his best friends.

Speaking of friends... "I cornered Nash on his way out."

"Good Lord, man, give it a rest."

"What?"

"You know what."

He did know, and yet still he pushed on. "I wouldn't have to browbeat the man if you'd just tell me what's going on."

"What's the big deal?"

"The big deal is you're acting all secretive and it's annoying."

"Right." Gideon let the word linger in the air with enough sarcasm dripping from it to start a flood. "I'm being annoying. Me. Not you."

"Yes, you." Tripp's exasperation grew in the face of Gideon's silence. "Nash isn't the kind of guy you should hang around with."

"Yes, Mother," Gideon drawled with barely contained mockery, and pushed his glasses back up.

"Seriously. I've heard some things about him."

"Like what?"

"Just things, accusations." Things he didn't want to mention to Gideon. The NHL was similar to the armed services with the very loud unspoken rule of "Don't ask, don't tell". With some people though, there wasn't a need to ask and they didn't have to tell. Nash was one of them.

"I'm a big boy. I think I can handle myself."

"Fine. Don't say I didn't warn you."

"Noted. Duly warned."

"Fine." Things were so not fine. And he was not pleased. Not at all. Tripp couldn't stand it when Gideon acted this way. From time to time the other man, who normally was an open book, would simply shut down and become almost secretive. The most irritating part was, for the life of Tripp, he couldn't figure out why it agitated him so much.

There was no secret about it—Tripp was a very domineering person. His attitude didn't necessarily win him friends and influence people, but he refused to change. He liked being in charge, which was one of the reasons Gideon and he sometimes bumped heads. Neither one of them wanted to be the one to back down first, and there were times—literally—when Tripp had to refrain from enforcing his will on the other man. Like now.

Tripp would have enjoyed nothing more than grabbing him by the scruff of the neck and shaking him until Gideon answered him. The need was so strong Tripp actually had to shove his hands in his pockets to resist giving in to the urge.

He didn't want Gideon hanging out with Nash and what he wanted he usually got.

With a heavy sigh, Tripp glanced across the room at Gideon, who was on his hands and knees picking up an overturned ashtray.

Amused, he shook his head. Fucking neat-freak. Gideon's obsession with orderliness was one of the reasons he refused to live off-campus with Holden, Shane and him. "Freak."

"You'll thank me later."

"Doubt it." Trying to shake his thoughts from Gideon, he returned to the reason they were both still here—Skylar. "Look, man, don't you think we've been pussyfooting around this issue long enough? You know I'm into Skylar."

"As am I."

"But only one of us can have her."

"She's not the last bottle of beer."

"Yes, but I bet she comes with good head."

Gideon sat back up on his knees and glanced over his shoulder at Tripp with a disapproving look on his face. "I can't believe you just said that."

Neither could he. "Yeah, let's just pretend I didn't." Working with testosterone-overloaded meatheads day in and day out was showing on him. Weary, he rubbed his hand over his eyes. "Man, I'm tired."

"Me too."

Tripp opened his eyes in time to see Gideon bend back over to finish his task. As he stretched forward to retrieve something, the tan shorts pulled tight against his backside, bringing his well-shaped ass into plain view. Gideon had always been beefy. Years working construction had paid off for the other man, but this…this was different.

"You…uhh…been working out, man?"

"I've been trying. I hit the gym when I have a free minute or two."

"Yeah." His gaze roamed shamelessly over Gideon's bent figure. The shorts accentuated the curvy fullness of his bottom that by all rights no man should have. Where the hell did he get that ass?

"Yeah." Gideon coughed softly. The startling noise roused Tripp's attention, finally freeing his gaze from the Bermuda Triangle that held him captive. Unfortunately for Tripp, where his gaze landed next was far worse. Instead of staring at his friend's ass, he was staring into his eyes. Gideon was watching him just as intently as Tripp had been watching his butt.

Gideon didn't say a word, nor did he move. He merely watched Tripp, as if waiting for his next move. For the life of him, Tripp couldn't think of a thing to say or do to fill the awkward void. He'd been staring at his male friend's ass. And liking it. There was definitely something wrong here.

"I started the dishwasher. We're probably going to have to do a couple of loads before..." Skylar's voice trailed off as she glanced between the two men. "Should I come back later?"

"No." Tripp chuckled nervously, grateful for the interruption. "We're done in here as soon as Mr. Clean moves off his hands and knees."

"Just trying to help out." Gideon rose clumsily to his feet. "I'll be back. I'm going to go take the trash bags to the cans."

"Hurry back," Skylar urged.

"Why, you ready to talk?"

"Sort of." She pulled her hand from behind her back, revealing a bottle of Patrón and three shot glasses. "Lookie what I found. Anybody up for a game?"

"Of?" Tripp asked, intrigued.

"I Never."

"Arrgg." Gideon groaned good-naturedly. "I was always hated that game."

"That's right, you did." Tripp sized the other man up. "Why, too afraid someone's going to find out something you don't want them to know?"

"Maybe. Or maybe I realized some things are better left unspoken."

"Funny you mention that." Skylar made her way over to Tripp and handed him a shot glass. Once the sun went down she'd changed out of her bathing suit into a pair of cutoff denim shorts and a red spaghetti-strap tank top. Although it covered more than her tribute to the stars and stripes, it was still sexy.

Tripp's gaze ran hungrily over her bare legs, up to the full curve of her breasts that, from the looks of her erect nipples, weren't confined behind a bra. Once again, he found himself unable to stop his lustful thoughts from straying to one of his friends. And once again he was caught ogling by his object of lust. This time it was more acceptable though. Skylar was a she. A very sexy she.

"Eyes up here, big boy," she teased, waggling the glass out toward him. "As I was saying, I've been thinking about that a lot lately. Unspoken things."

"Why's that?" Instead of taking the shot glass, Tripp took the bottle and opened it, much to her delight. Grinning, she set the glasses down on the coffee table and took the now-open bottle back. She liberally poured the tequila to the brim of each glass and then set the bottle down.

"Because I wonder if my life would be different if only I had spoken up in college about what I really wanted."

"What did you want?" Gideon asked.

"If you want to find out, you'll play."

"Still trying to run the show, princess?"

"Could be." She picked up her shot glass and downed her drink in one fell swoop. She winced as she swallowed then coughed as the alcohol hit her system. Shaking her head, she added, "Or maybe I just need a bit of alcohol to loosen my lips."

"Loose lips. I'll drink to that," Tripp teased, saluting her with his drink before he downed it. Just when he thought he had her figured out, she changed her colors like the beautiful chameleon she was. Whatever prompted her to keep Gideon and him at arm's reach all these years seemed to have disappeared. "Count me in."

Skylar bent over and picked up the remaining shot and offered it to Gideon. "What about you? Are you in?"

"You should be careful what you wish for," he warned, accepting the glass. "Both of you."

"I think we can handle you." Satisfaction pursed her mouth.

"I guess we're about to find out." Gideon stared hard at both of them before downing his drink. "Don't start without me."

"Wouldn't dream of it," Skylar said as Gideon grabbed the bags and headed out of the living room.

Looked as if things were about to become interesting.

* * * * *

"Damn, I suck at this game," Tripp grumbled as he chugged down another gulp of tequila. Skylar had lost count of how long they'd been playing, but they were on the second bottle of booze and were no longer using shot glasses, so that was saying something.

Originally she'd started the game in hopes of building a bit of liquid-induced courage to spill her guts, but now she was enjoying playing for the simple pleasure of it all. She had missed this. Really missed being with the two of them like the good old days.

She had taken their affection for granted. Always assumed it would be there when she was ready to make her mind up. She could tell now though, although they still had feelings for her, she was in no way dealing with the young men she'd known in college. These two were a bit out of her league, but instead of worrying her, they only intrigued her more.

Although they were laughing almost as much as Tripp was drinking, there was still a thick undercurrent of sexual tension in the room. Even the way they were situated on the couch was a bit more intimate than they'd been able to be in the last few years. Skylar sat next to Tripp on the suede love seat, so close they'd brush against one another every now and then, with her legs folded to the side. Gideon was sitting on the floor, with his side to the couch, resting his head against her legs. They were both touching her as if they had a right to do so. And if she had her way, after tonight they both would.

"It wouldn't be so bad if you weren't such a whore," she ribbed.

"I'm not a whore." She tried to not laugh as Tripp slurred the words.

"Tripp." Her lips trembled with the need to smile. "You've had to drink after every single question that was the least bit sexual."

"That doesn't make me a whore."

"If that doesn't, I don't know what does," Gideon teased. Even he had begun to have a good time. His eyes, which were normally so guarded, were a bit glassy from the alcohol and lit with amusement. Gideon nuzzled her bare leg with the side of his head. His soft hair tickled and yet felt so good against her skin. "It's my turn, is it not?"

"Yes." She picked up a lock of his hair and toyed with it gently. She missed this too. The freedom to touch them how and when she wanted, free of the disapproving glares of their previous significant others.

"I never..." Gideon paused for a second then grinned. "I've never masturbated to a Betty Boop comic book."

"Fuck." Tripp flushed as he reached for the bottle once more, which in turn caused Skylar to roar with laughter. He'd taken so many shots she wasn't sure why he didn't just keep the damn thing on his lap. "I'll never tell you anything ever again."

"Tell me..." she was laughing so hard she could barely get the words out, "he's...joking."

"One time. One!" His protest fell on deaf ears.

For as long as she lived, Skylar was never going to let him live this down. "It's a comic book character."

"Betty Boop is not a comic," he argued. "She's an icon with a great set of ti—"

"Hey!" She slapped his arm, halting his words. There would be no talk of tits unless they were referring to hers.

"Sorry." Narrowing his gaze, she saw him fixate on Gideon. "You're setting me up."

"Just playing the game, buddy."

"No fair using inside knowledge against me."

Gideon quirked his eyebrow mischievously. "You do understand the concept of this game, don't you?"

"Asshole."

"It's not our fault we know you so well."

"So you think." Tripp snorted.

"Oh, but we do. I mean how many people know that your true name is?" Skylar and Gideon spoke his name simultaneously, a secretive smile dancing between them. "Korneli Kowalski, the third."

Tripp shoved the bottle to Gideon who was grinning wildly. "Oh, I can't believe you two went there."

Skylar knew he hated his given name with a passion. It was a family name. And even though his father had gone by Junior to avoid the horrific moniker, his mother had still stuck their only son with the family name. She was second-generation Polish and she took her heritage very seriously.

"Fine, it's on." Tripp's eyes glittered with revenge. "I've never made out with Paige."

Gasping, Skylar hit him again.

"What did I miss?" Gideon's eyes widened with unabashed delight as he passed Tripp the bottle back.

"It was a stupid dare." She waved her hand, not wanting to share the embarrassing details more than she had to. She'd learned a lesson that night. Never play truth and dare with Shane and Tripp. "And it was only for a few seconds."

"Fifteen, thank you very much." Tripp handed her the bottle with a very satisfied look on his face.

The disappointed look on Gideon's face was priceless. "I missed that. Damn."

"It was the hottest fifteen seconds of my life, man."

"I doubt that." She quickly downed her drink before immediately turning the tables on them. "I've never peed standing up."

"Stuff like that shouldn't count," Gideon grumbled, and took the bottle out of her hand.

"I don't make the rules, boy. I just play by them."

"Tell me something, princess." Tripp pushed stray tendrils of her hair off her cheek. The unexpected touch surprised and excited her. She wanted to lean into the caress and let her inhibitions fly away. "Are you trying to get me drunk so you can take sweet advantage of me?"

She licked her lips. The alcohol had definitely lowered her inhibitions. It wasn't too much to hope it would do the same for them. "Maybe."

"Thank you, God." His heated gaze was as soft as a caress and twice as addicting.

If there was ever any doubt in her mind Tripp still wanted her, it dissipated then and there. The knowledge they each wanted the other was there, if only they had the courage to reach out and take it. Their intimate moment seemed to last a lifetime, although she was sure it was only seconds before Gideon cleared his throat and broke their locked gazes.

"If that's your goal, I say the 'I never' statements should be far more interesting."

"Like what?" She had a feeling she knew where this was going and thankfully it was in the direction she'd hoped.

"Like…" Gideon pondered a moment before speaking. "I've never purchased a sex toy for my own personal use."

He handed her the bottle, but she smiled and shook her head. "Sorry, neither have I."

"Say it isn't so," Tripp said. "You don't own at least one vibrator?"

"No, Tripp. I own several. I've just never bought them."

"Hand me the bottle." Tripp held his hand out and gestured for Gideon to pass him the tequila. When he had it in hand, he held it up to the light and swirled the alcohol around. "There's enough for about two, maybe three more shots. Let's say we make this a good one."

"Go for it," she said boldly, more than ready to see where this was heading next.

"I've never..." Tripp paused dramatically. "Fantasized about making love with the other two people in the room."

"You need a better fantasy life then," she teased as she reached for the bottle. She took a long, slow drink, maintaining eye contact with Tripp the entire time. Skylar didn't want there to be a single doubt in his mind she was completely onboard with the way he was steering this ship. She wanted to make love with them—both of them—and from the lazy grin on his face, not only did he realize it, he was fine with it.

One down and one to go.

To her utter and complete surprise, the second she moved the bottle from her lips, Gideon swiped it out of her hand and raised it to his mouth.

Tripp chuckled and made a grab for the bottle. "No, man, you didn't understand, I meant both of the other people in the room."

"Yes, I knew exactly what you meant," Gideon clarified as soon as the bottle left his lips.

The surprise on Tripp's face most likely matched her own. She knew she wanted both men. Hell, she even knew both men wanted her. But Gideon wanted Tripp as well? This was a development she wasn't expecting, but surprisingly she wasn't turned off by it. Her feelings were the exact opposite. She could feel herself moisten at the thought of the two men together—with or without her. Although she'd planned to seduce them both to make love to her, this was a very interesting turn of events.

I Never

Gideon didn't break eye contact with Tripp, holding his shocked gaze with his own steady one. He supposed he should have eased into the big revelation, but hell, he never did do things the easy way. He could always blame the alcohol, but the truth was he wanted them to know. He was pretty sure Shane suspected, but he'd never revealed to anyone in their group his bisexual tendencies. It was one of those things he kept private.

He knew his habit kept Tripp on edge and it amused Gideon somewhat that the other man didn't realize he had his own issues. Gideon usually didn't mind Tripp's controlling personality in most aspects of his life, but he also enjoyed keeping the other man a bit off guard as well. He'd more than done his job tonight with his little announcement.

"Uhh..." Tripp shook his head as if trying to clear his mind of the troubled words. "If we're going to be sharing this much information, I'm going to need another drink." Tripp stumbled up from the couch and headed to the bar, muttering under his breath.

So Tripp was going to take a boat ride to the land of denial. That was one way of handling it. Amused and slightly irritated at Tripp's lack of response, Gideon turned his gaze to Skylar. He needed to know if she was packing her bag to join Tripp on the boat, or merely grossed out by his declaration. When he met her steady gaze, he was surprised at what he saw. Instead of revulsion or pity he found interest.

"Seems we're more alike than I realized." Skylar's softly spoken words resonated with him.

But just to be sure, he had to ask. "You're not disgusted?"

"Far from it." Licking her lips, she glanced from him to Tripp's rigid back with a look akin to hunger on her pretty face. "The idea of the two of you going at it is the hottest thing I could have ever imagined."

"I'm very happy to hear that." Gideon couldn't even begin to describe how pleased Skylar made him by admitting that. To know the woman of his dreams could not only accept that part of him but found it sexually exciting as well was a bigger turn-on than he'd ever believed possible.

Gideon closed his eyes and brushed his lips against her silky-smooth leg. In response, she tangled her hand in his hair and gave a soft tug that had his cock stiffening. Skylar had found his weakness. For him, sex wasn't completely satisfying if a little pain wasn't involved.

"Enough with honest." Tripp's voice boomed from above them. "Let's play another game."

Gideon opened his eyes and focused his lust-filled gaze on Tripp. "Are you sure you can handle another game?"

"Please." He snorted. "I can handle anything you dish out, boyo."

Everything that was in no way in relation to his confession, that was. Gideon felt as if he were walking a tightrope. On one hand, he wanted Tripp to acknowledge what he'd said—acknowledge and accept it—but on the other hand, he didn't want to push his friend. "Maybe I should go." Gideon rose unsteadily to his feet. The last thing he wanted to do tonight was alienate his best friend. He didn't want Tripp uncomfortable around him. He just wanted to be honest with him for once.

"No." Skylar grabbed on to his belt loop and pulled herself close to him, laying her head along the front of his hip. He could practically feel her breath over his cock as she spoke. "I don't want you to go. And neither does Tripp."

"He doesn't?" It wasn't good enough for Skylar to speak for Tripp. Gideon needed to hear the words from the man's lips himself.

"No, I don't," Tripp said fervently. "Dude, I don't care that you've fantasized about me. To tell the truth, I'm not even surprised."

"You're not?"

"No." Tripp grinned. "I'm smoking hot. Of course you want me. Everybody does."

"Asshole."

"Seriously, man, everybody has fantasies. Doesn't mean anything."

Sure it did, but if Tripp wanted to pretend otherwise, who was he to correct him. "Still, it's late. I should probably head on home."

"Home!"

"Dude, you're far too wasted to drive. Both of you are. You two are staying the night and that's final."

"Tyrant." Even though Gideon thought it best he leave, he knew Tripp was right about driving.

"Damn straight."

Skylar pulled back from Gideon and grinned at Tripp. "Since you have us here at your mercy, good sir, whatever shall you do with us?"

"Drink of course. How about another round?"

"God no." Skylar moaned, standing as well. "I'm beyond done."

Tripp jiggled the bottle enticingly. "Come on, peer pressure, peer pressure."

But Skylar held strong. "Unless you want this peer to hurl all over your newly installed hardwood floors, you'll set the bottle down and slowly back away."

"Spoilsport." Much to Gideon's amusement Tripp turned his attention his way. "What about you?"

Just the idea of taking another shot made his gut clench. He had just enough alcohol to ensure the wrath of the headache gods. He didn't want to test the vomit gods as well. "No, I'm too drunk to drive and way too drunk to drink."

Tripp looked at him, puzzled. "That doesn't make any sense."

"It doesn't have to. I'm drunk."

"Fine," Tripp grumbled, setting the bottle down on the table. "You guys suck."

Gideon wasn't sure how the other two were feeling, but the alcohol had hit him a few minutes after he stood. Unfortunately, the longer he attempted to stay upright, the worse he felt. And Skylar didn't look much better.

"I need to crash." Skylar swayed slightly as she reached out to hug Tripp. "Sorry I'm pooping out on you."

"Lightweight," he groused affectionately. "I'll go make up the guestroom for you. Gideon, you can crash on the couch in the office or on the couch out here."

"Or I can crash with Skylar."

"Or you can sleep in the office or out here," Tripp reiterated, shooting Gideon an icy glare.

"Who's the spoilsport now?" Gideon teased.

"I'm going to make the bed then I'll be back. Keep your hands to yourself if you know what's good for you." Tripp pointed two fingers at his own eyes before turning them outward toward Gideon in the universal signal for "I'm keeping an eye on you". After shooting the two of them one more evil look, he turned on his heel and strolled unsteadily out of the room.

Gideon watched, amused, as Tripp swayed a bit as he disappeared down the hallway. "Was he warning me or warning you?"

"Me, definitely." Skylar laughed, sitting back on the couch. "God, I'm wasted. Whose idea was it to play this stupid game to begin with?"

"Yours, my dear." Gideon was quickly losing his ability to stay vertical. In order not to disgrace himself any further tonight than he already had, he dropped down next to her on the couch, wincing a bit when everything in his line of sight doubled up. Tequila was the devil and the hangover he would surely have in the morning was hell. "So tell me…"

"Yes?"

"Did you get out of it what you were hoping for?"

"Not necessarily." She grinned lopsidedly. "But close."

Gideon laid his head back on the couch and closed his eyes. He was having a hard time focusing on what he wanted to say. The words were there, but they were jumbled about in his brains like alphabet soup. "What...did....you...want?"

"The two of you." Gideon opened his eyes and turned his head at her softly spoken admission. A flush of pink covered her cheeks, but she continued to speak despite her obvious embarrassment. "I started this game for one simple reason. To let you both know I wanted you — together."

"Together?"

"Yes. I always thought I had to pick, but I was never able to. I mean, how could I?"

Gideon could more than relate to that. "And now?"

"Now I'm going to be greedy and take what I want." She snaked her hand out and grabbed hold of his hand. "The two of you. Of course, that won't happen unless we're all sober."

"Speaking of sober." Gideon tried to focus on the clock hanging on the cobalt wall, but eventually gave up after the numbers began to do a synchronized backstroke in front of his eyes. "Shouldn't Tripp be back by now?"

"You'd think so, wouldn't you?"

"Come on, let's go check on him."

"Slowly. Slowly." After a few failed attempts, the two of them made their way upright. Laughing to himself, Gideon thought it must be amusing to see their struggles to rise. They probably looked like a couple of puppets with their strings in knots, using each other as balancing beams to stand.

"Thank you, God. Let's never sit again." Skylar frowned and took a timid step away from him.

Gideon would have nodded his head in agreement, but he was too afraid it might fall off. The way he was feeling he didn't want to ever move again, but of course that wasn't much of an option.

Moving at the speed of a hyped-up seahorse, they made their way down the hall to the guestroom, which was surprisingly empty. "Uh..." Skylar looked up at him, bewildered. "Did he mean the other guestroom?"

"Is there another guestroom?" He was way too gone for complicated questions.

"I don't think so."

"Hmm." Confused, he looked down the hallway and noticed the master bedroom door was open. "Maybe he's in there. Hey, Tripp?" he called out as they walked to the other room. The sight that met their eyes wasn't the one Gideon was expecting.

Tripp laid sprawled out, flat on his back with the top sheet clutched in his hand. His head was cushioned by a pillow, but his feet were hanging off the side of the bed.

"He must have passed out. Uhh...making his own bed?" Apparently Tripp was a hell of lot more drunk than Gideon originally thought.

"You think?" Skylar was giggling, the alcohol obviously making her a bit giddy.

"Help me get him situated." Gideon was really trying to hold it together although he looked at the bed longingly. He'd love to join Tripp. Not only for his nefarious sexual fantasies, but because he was really feeling the need to lie down.

Skylar tugged off Tripp's shoes then stood back up. "Do you think we should take off his shorts?"

Gideon eyed the orange Hawaiian-print shorts warily. He wanted to say yes, but knew he would be doing it for his own desires, not to make Tripp more comfortable. "No, he'll probably be all right."

"Okay." The longing in Skylar's voice matched the one inside his heart, but Gideon knew it was the right thing to do.

Trying his best to keep his mind on the project ahead of them, Gideon took Tripp's feet in his hands and swung them around until they landed on the bed.

Bad idea.

"Oh hell, that wasn't good." Gideon reached out and sat down hard.

"Are you going to be sick?"

"No, my head's going to explode."

"Maybe you better lie down."

He wanted to tell her no, but he was thinking she might be right. He needed to close his eyes to stop the room from spinning.

"Okay, just for a minute."

After taking his glasses off and laying them on the nightstand, Gideon laid back on the bed. The cool sheets felt good against his heated skin and he closed his eyes gratefully. He could feel Skylar at his feet, but he was reluctant to open his eyes to discover what she was doing.

"What—"

"I thought I better take off your shoes too." She proceeded to do just that.

"Thanks." Gideon reached out blindly and felt her tiny hand clasp his. He tugged lightly and she sat down next to him on the bed. "How are you feeling?"

"Uh, tired and kind of seasick."

"Why don't you join me just for a minute? Once we feel better we can..." He didn't really know what they would do then. He just knew he wanted her to be there with him. With a tortured groan, he scooted over, making room for Skylar in the middle. "Come on, princess. Make yourself at home."

"Okay." He could hear Skylar kicking off her own shoes before snuggling next to him on the bed. "Just for a little bit though." She yawned as she made herself comfortable.

"'Kay." A little bit, that sounded good to him. Just a few minutes and then he'd get up.

Chapter Four

ಐ

"Uggg..." As much as he dreaded moving, Tripp knew he had no other choice. His bladder was on fire, and if he didn't relieve himself, he was going to explode. Groaning, he rolled to his side and opened his eyes, jerking in surprise when he spotted Skylar's pale hair in the semi-dark room.

What the hell did I miss? He eased up in his bed and peered over at not one sleeping figure but two. Apparently the decision to buy a king-size bed had been the right one after all because not only had he slept with Skylar and not noticed, he'd also slept with Gideon. Before he could dwell on the ramifications of that discovery, the ache in his bladder reminded him once more he had more pressing issues to concern himself with.

Carefully he eased off the bed, made his way quietly into the bathroom, and softly shut the door. He felt along the wall until he found the light dimmer and slowly turned it on until the bathroom became filled with a muted glow. After emptying his bladder, he washed his hands. In need of a quick wake-up solution, he filled his hands with the cool water and splashed it onto his face. After dousing his head, he grabbed the hand towel off the towel bar and wiped his face dry.

He was beginning to feel like himself again. After toweling his damp hair, he mustered the courage to turn up the lighting. Big mistake. Staring at his reflection in the mirror, Tripp grimaced. He'd seen better days. It was luck, and luck only, that allowed him to keep the contents of his stomach inside where it belonged. After all the tequila they'd consumed, the only repercussion so far was a bit of a headache. That and the knowledge he could have gone his whole life not knowing.

Tripp wasn't a hundred percent sure how he felt about what Gideon admitted, but he was convinced, now more than ever, he was right about keeping Nash away from him. Gideon was confused, the last thing he needed was Nash pushing his twisted views on him.

Twisted. Maybe twisted was too strong a word, especially in context with Gideon. It wasn't as if Tripp hadn't had wayward thoughts a time or two that were less than PC.

He could still remember a day when he and Gideon had come across one of Holden's skin flicks the other man had left in the VCR. They had the apartment to themselves and no date in sight, so it seemed natural for them to rub one out as they watched the movie.

It was innocent of course with him on the recliner and Gideon sitting on the couch with enough room between the two of them to make the incident completely non-gay. Just two guys watching a movie, jerking off. They never spoke about the incident afterward. To this day, however, Tripp would still become aroused when he thought back on that evening, and it had nothing to do with the high caliber of the porno.

But that didn't make him gay or bi or whatever, and he was sure Gideon's little fantasy didn't mean he was either.

Convinced his world was right once more, Tripp opened the medicine cabinet and took out some aspirin. After filling his rinse cup with tepid water, he took two aspirin and brought the four remaining in his palm back into the bedroom along with the glass of water. Tripp was sure he wouldn't be the only one waking up with a headache.

Once back in the bedroom, all thoughts of pain immediately disappeared. While he had been in the bathroom they had rolled over. Skylar was now facing him, deep asleep, with Gideon spooning her from behind. They looked so peaceful, so comfortable in each other's arms that for a moment he felt like an interloper in his own home.

He had another room with a bed in it. It wouldn't take much for Tripp to just go lie down in there and leave the two of them asleep with one another. They looked right together. But he was a selfish man. One with many faults, and try as he might, he couldn't just walk away from them.

Quietly he walked over to the side of the bed Gideon was lying on and set two aspirin down on the nightstand. He also left the glass of water. If Skylar woke up first, he'd just get up and bring her a glass. When he moved to walk away, Gideon rolled over. Tripp froze, waiting to see if the other man would wake, but he didn't. He continued to sleep as peacefully as he had before Tripp came over. Satisfied everything was fine, Tripp returned to his side of the bed and climbed back in. He set the remaining pills down on his night table and lay down.

He rolled over onto his side, facing away from Skylar and willed sleep to come once more. Of course it didn't. He was far too conscious of the other two people in bed with him to just drift off again. So in essence he was stuck. He didn't want to leave the room, and yet he couldn't sleep while they were there.

Before he could muster the courage to just leave, the bed shifted and Skylar edged closer to him until he could feel not only the heat from her warm body, but the soft curves of her breast. Tripp lay very still, not wanting his restlessness to wake her. To his surprise though, she was already awake. She brought her hand up to his hair and lightly ran her fingers through his thick strands.

He closed his eyes for a moment, letting himself sink into the sensations of her hands caressing him. But it wasn't enough, he needed to see her. He pushed away from her for a moment to make enough room to roll over.

Her gaze, like her voice, was as soft as a caress. "Hey."

"How are you feeling?" he asked just as softly, wanting to keep this moment between the two of them.

"Surprisingly well. You?"

"Fine." At least he did now. Skylar hadn't made a single move to leave his bed, if anything, she was nudging closer to him.

"You finally have me in your bed."

"So I see."

They both lay there staring into each other's eyes for a moment, not speaking. There were so many things he wanted to say, but at the same time he just wanted to soak up the pleasure of her presence.

"So are you going to do anything about it?" Skylar taunted with a lilt in her voice. "Or do I have to get tough?"

"I'm definitely going to do something."

Gathering her in his arms, he held her against his taut body. His hand locked against her spine then slid lower, filling his grasp with her supple bottom. Skylar let out a soft gasp at his bold touch, but she didn't push him away.

Her soft curves molded to the hard contours of his body, accentuating all the things that made her a woman and leaving no doubt about all the things that made him a man. Tripp had waited for what seemed a lifetime for this moment, and he wasn't going to rush it by moving too fast.

Skylar wasn't willing for him to take that time however. She moved her leg up and hooked it over his hip, pressing her center against him. Knowing she was just as urgent for him as he was for her made him desire her all the more.

"You're playing with fire." His words were whispered, but no less intense.

"I'm ready to get burned." Her lips were opened slightly as if in invitation and he wasn't willing to pass on the opportunity. Bending his head, he took her mouth under his, parting her lips with his tongue. She welcomed him wholeheartedly, kissing him with a hunger that matched his own.

Lost in her flavor, he kissed her with reckless abandon. His tongue swept over her, caressing her, committing her taste to heart. He had to have her. All of her, and he wasn't going to wait a moment longer.

With a hungry growl, he swept his hand upward beneath her tank top to stroke at the silken skin there. There was nothing soft and gentle about his touch. Tripp had waited far too long to be gentlemanly now. The touch of her skin and her lips under his was everything he'd wanted and yet it wasn't enough. He needed more. He wanted to see her lying nude beneath him. He wanted to look into her eyes as he pushed himself into her body.

He broke their kiss and took a deep breath, trying to regain some control. "Lift your arms."

Without question she did as he bid, raising her arms above her head. Her gaze locked onto his and her desire for him was shining forth. He quickly stripped the red bit of cloth from her body and tossed it over his shoulder, exposing her supple breasts to his gaze.

He moved his hands up to cup her, marveling at how perfectly she fit him. Her skin was pale in contrast to the rest of her sun-kissed body, all except for the rosy tips. He grasped her nipples between his thumbs and fingers, tugging lightly on the engorged berries.

Skylar moaned and shuddered in his arms. She tightened her legs over his hips and pressed her pelvis up to rub against him. "Tripp."

Just one word, but it held a wealth of meaning to him. He could hear her desire and longing. She wanted him. His longing unleashed, Tripp covered her mouth with his once more. Digging his fingers into her denim-covered ass, he pulled her tighter against him, rocking his pelvis against her.

Suddenly the bed dipped and he felt Gideon roll over until he faced the two of them. Skylar must have felt it too because without breaking their kiss, she released her hold on him and reached behind herself to grab Gideon and pulled him flush against her back. Her bold movement caused Gideon's hardening cock to brush against Tripp's hand.

He froze, his entire body shutting down for a brief moment. This was wrong, very wrong. He should break off the kiss and demand Gideon leave the room, or at the very least, he should want Gideon to leave. Try as he might, he couldn't find a single feeling of revulsion or horror. He was kissing the woman he had wanted for too many years to count while at the same time he was in bed with his best friend and liking it. Something here just didn't compute.

Tripp angled his head to the side as he kissed Skylar and opened his eyes, locking his gaze firmly on Gideon's. Instead of reading anger in the other man's eyes, he saw hunger, and it excited it him. As did the feel of the other man's erection against the back of his hand.

He wanted to turn his hand around and touch the outline of Gideon's cock with his fingers, but he didn't possess the daring to do so.

Gideon, on the other hand, apparently didn't have the same problem. He moved his lower body even closer to Skylar, trapping Tripp's hand effectively between the two of them. He moved his face toward theirs, and for a moment Tripp thought Gideon was going to touch his lips against theirs, but he didn't. Instead, he brushed his mouth against Skylar's arms, kissing his way up to her shoulder.

Skylar turned her head away from Tripp, breaking their kiss, and whispered Gideon's name. He looked up at her and moved with lightning speed to cover her mouth with his own, grinding his erection against the back of Tripp's hand in the process.

Once again Tripp waited for the disgust to come, and once again he waited in vain. It never came. Neither did any doubt, confusion or worry. His newfound bravado might all be alcohol-related, but he didn't care. He was tired of second-guessing his desire. He was going to give in, if only for tonight.

Finally. After years of waiting and wanting, Skylar was where she belonged. Between the two men she loved more than life itself. She was so overcome by joy her eyes welled with tears, but she held the downpour back. Skylar didn't want to chance either Tripp or Gideon getting the wrong idea and stopping. Because there would be no stopping. And there would be no going back. This was what was meant to be. She was where she was meant to be. She was home.

As she lost herself in the pleasure of Gideon's taste, Tripp busied himself with her bare breasts. He pulled his hand from between their pressed bodies and moved a few inches down the bed until his mouth covered one of her erect tips.

He laved a nipple greedily, teasing and torturing the erect bud in the sweetest of ways, all the while Gideon devoured her mouth. Skylar's pleasure sensors were on overload. She'd never made love before to two men at once, never been consumed as completely as she was right now. In a word, it was wonderful.

Moaning, she tightened her fingers in Gideon's hair, kissing him with all the pent-up desire she'd felt for the both of them over the years. With a muted groan Gideon broke their kiss and pulled back. He moved a few inches away from her then pressed on her shoulder so she could move onto her back. Once there, he closed his lips over the tip of her free nipple, creating dual sensations that were beyond belief.

"We're...going to...ohh...mmm." It was hard to talk and be teased at the same time, but there were a few things Skylar needed to say. "We're going to...need two things...lights and condoms."

"Lots of condoms," Gideon agreed as he began to unbutton her shorts. His lips followed the open space his fingers made, sending shivers of desire throughout her body.

"God yes." Tripp rolled off the bed and walked around the foot of it as Gideon sat back on his heels and tugged on her shorts.

"Lift up, baby," he ordered as he pulled her shorts and panties off her hips. He tossed them over his shoulder at the exact same moment Tripp clicked a switch, filling the room with light. "You have no idea."

The hunger on Gideon's face made her heart swell. "About what?"

"How long I've waited to see you like this."

"The feeling is mutual." Skylar had waited a lifetime to be in their arms.

Tripp, who took a moment to undress, joined them on the bed once more. The two men moved until they were flanking her sides with her nude in the middle.

Although she expected they would immediately turn their attention to her, she was surprised when they lay there, not caressing her, but just looking at her.

"Tell me you want this. Tell me that you want us," Gideon insisted.

"Is there any doubt?"

"Say the words, Skylar," Tripp ordered.

Skylar looked from Tripp's heated gaze back to Gideon's and knew there was no going back. "I want this. I want to make love with both of you. Together. Tonight."

"Beautiful." Skylar couldn't tell who spoke, but it was a sentiment quickly echoed by the other.

Closing her eyes, she gave in to the mind-numbing, body-tingling sensations overtaking her body and surrendered to the men caressing her. Hands. Hands everywhere, touching, teasing, learning every inch of her frame kept her teetering on the edge. Never before had she felt so cherished or desired or thoroughly known. But she wanted more.

"Gideon." Skylar opened her eyes and looked down at the man who was kissing his way down her stomach. It wasn't that she wasn't enjoying where this was heading, she just wanted something else from him right now. "Get undressed. Now."

"You heard the lady." Tripp grinned wickedly. "I'll take over from here."

"Opportunistic bastard." Gideon swiftly moved off the bed and began to undress.

Tripp moved down the bed and knelt between her thighs, licking his lips as he stared between her spread legs. "Lucky bastard is more like it." And that was the last thing Tripp said because he quickly began to use his mouth in a much more meaningful way.

Skylar whimpered as Tripp found her with his mouth. The way he laved her clit made her eyes roll back in her head. Blindly she reached out and grasped his hair in her hand, tugging on the light strands.

"Hmm... God..." Skylar wasn't sure if she was trying to pull him away or push his tongue deeper inside her. All she knew was she needed to do something with her hand. Lucky for Tripp and his hair, Gideon climbed up on the bed once more and gave Skylar something far more interesting to do with it.

Skylar reached down and took hold of his hard shaft. She stroked him, learning the feel of his cock. He was hot and hard, and completely yummy. His erection throbbed under her fingers as she trailed them over his thick flesh. He was bigger and better than she ever imagined, and he was all hers.

While she learned the shape and feel of Gideon, Tripp was learning her. His mouth and tongue delved into her, driving her to the brink of madness from the talent of his kiss. She needed to come, but it was as if he were purposelessly holding back.

"Fuck, I can't take much more." Gideon pulled his cock from her questing fingers. She echoed his frantic need.

"Tripp, please." She pumped her hips toward him, her every word and motion begging for release.

"Is he eating your pussy good, baby?"

"Yes... God yes." Her hips rocked against the bed as she chased the release she so desperately needed. She was so close it was almost painful.

"Then show him. Fuck his mouth with your sweet pussy."

Skylar didn't know what sent her spinning out of control, Tripp's tongue or Gideon's words, but she didn't care. With a banshee-like cry, she gripped the sheet as hard as she could and came in a blinding storm of pleasure.

Before she could catch her breath Tripp stole up her body and kissed her senseless. The tangy flavor of her release filled her mouth as his tongue tangoed across her own. As he released her, he stared into her eyes for a moment and they shared the knowledge of what was to come.

"Damn, baby, that was good," Tripp murmured with a self-satisfied grin.

"You're telling me." Her body shook with the aftershock of her release, making it hard to breathe, let alone talk.

"My turn," Gideon said quietly from the sideline. While she'd been coming, he'd been busy sheathing his cock with one of the condoms Tripp had taken out earlier.

Part of Skylar expected Tripp to protest, but to her happy surprise he didn't. "Keep her on her back and fuck her long and deep. I want to watch."

"I think I can do that."

"No one comes until I say so." Tripp sent Gideon a leveled look. "No one."

"Says who?"

"Me," he replied firmly. "Is that understood?"

I Never

Skylar couldn't and wouldn't speak for Gideon, but Tripp's domineering tone had her pulse pounding and her pussy aching for more. Licking her lips, she answered, "Understood."

Tripp raised a brow as he waited for Gideon's acquiescence. He didn't have to wait long. "Fine." Then under his breath, Gideon added, "Tyrant."

His comment wasn't lost on anyone, neither was Tripp's arrogant grin. Working in tandem, the men quickly positioned themselves with Gideon moving between her splayed legs and Tripp moving to the side near her shoulders. From the sexy look of anticipation Tripp sent her way, he was going to enjoy this as much as she planned to.

With Gideon firmly seated between her thighs, he centered the crown of his cock against her sex. "No going back."

"Ever," she agreed, wrapping her legs around his waist.

"Ever." He took her mouth with his and drove his cock deep into her with one swift thrust.

Skylar arched toward him and dug her nails into his back. She held on for dear life as he found his rhythm, pumping over and over into her. He moaned as he pushed inside her. His thick shaft stretched and filled her in a way no other man had before, and she wasn't even sure if he was all the way in.

"Fuck, man, she's tight. So fucking tight. I don't know how long I'll last."

The crown of his cock brushed against the edge of her G-spot, forcing Skylar to cry out. The mingling sensation of pleasure and pain had her grasping for air and begging for more. "Please. Please."

But Tripp overrode her pleas. "You'll last as long as I say, no matter how good she feels."

"Easy for you to say," Gideon grunted.

"I know." Tripp grinned evilly. He wasn't fucking her but he was in control. That said more than any words ever could.

"Bastard." Gideon drew his cock out until only the tip remained then powered back in, sending her spine bowing under the intense plundering.

"Damn, baby," Tripp said, taking his cock in hand. "You look so sexy stuffed full of his cock."

At his words she glanced up at him. They were a twisted trio. She watched Tripp stroke himself as he watched Gideon sink his cock into her over and over. They were all in tune with one another, each staring intently at the others as if their pleasure belonged to one and all. It wasn't just two of them in bed, it was the three of them, and it felt right.

"Gideon...feels so good." Skylar had to take a moment and catch her breath before she could continue. It felt that damn good. "Does it look as good as it feels, Tripp?"

The aroused man turned his hungry gaze from Gideon's cock to her. "What do you think, princess?"

"You tell me." She wanted him to admit it. Admit that he enjoyed watching the other man fuck her. Maybe if they put it all out in the open things could go even further. Gideon's confession had fueled fantasies she'd dared not admit aloud until tonight. The idea of the two of them touching was just as arousing as them touching her, and if she had her way, tonight a lot of firsts would happen.

But instead of giving in to her, Tripp grinned and said, "She's a chatty little thing, isn't she, man? Maybe I should give her something to keep her mouth busy."

"That sounds like an excellent idea." Gideon punctuated his words with a thrust of his hips, sending his cock deeper inside her. "What do you think, baby?"

"Yes. Please." Skylar turned her head toward Tripp and reached out to grasp his thick cock. "Let me suck you."

"If you insist, princess." Tripp grinned at her obvious need, but she couldn't fault him for it.

Skylar's mouth watered as she stroked Tripp's cock. She couldn't wait to feel him slide past her lips. "Come here."

I Never

Tripp edged closer to her but gently batted her hand away. "Ah-ah-ah. I'll drive, baby, you just suck."

The command in his tone sent her pulse racing. Moaning, Skylar opened her mouth and engulfed his crown. She'd never given head this way, sans hands, but there wasn't much about this experience she was all that familiar with.

The thing was, she trusted Tripp not to hurt her. So she relaxed her jaw and let him control the motion and angle. Allowing him to be in charge freed her to be open with Gideon. They moved like the ebbing of the tide. They rocked, they rolled, they moved as one, all as Tripp fucked his cock in and out of her mouth.

The room was a symphony of erotic sounds. Moans and groans came from all directions, some even from deep inside her. Skylar was in an abyss of pleasure she never wanted to end.

As Tripp pulled back, Skylar turned her head to take a deep breath and her gaze connected with Gideon's. The desire she saw there took her breath away. He was staring hungrily at her moist lips, as if he wanted to devour them whole.

Smiling, Skylar slowly ran her tongue over her lips, watching in perverse pleasure as his eyes darkened with passion. His unspoken desire was beyond apparent to her. He wanted what she had, and lucky for him, she wasn't selfish. "If you ask me nicely, I'll share."

Her words paused him in mid-motion. "Wh-What?"

"Admit it. You want to taste his cock."

"Skylar…" Tripp's voice held a hoarse warning she refused to heed. His mouth may have said one thing but his face was taut with unveiled desire.

"Ask and you might receive." She dangled the offer in front of them both. "Say pretty, pretty please and maybe Tripp will let you suck his—"

Gideon drove his mouth down on hers, silencing her. But he wasn't just kissing her. His tongue stroked over every inch of her mouth that Tripp's cock had touched. In essence it seemed as if Gideon tasted Tripp's cock in the only way he probably thought he could.

But Skylar thought otherwise. She allowed Gideon his moment to plunder her lips, but then turned her head, breaking the kiss. She moved once more, her mouth taking Tripp's cock for a few strokes before releasing him to kiss Gideon once again.

He welcomed her kiss, devouring her mouth and cleansing it of all traces of Tripp's flavor before pulling back to allow her to suck Tripp again. Skylar went back to Gideon's mouth, replaying their wicked tango again and again until Tripp's control finally broke.

"Fuck," Tripp growled before butting his cock at the corner of their joined mouths. "Suck me...both of you."

That would never do. "Take him, Gideon. Suck his cock."

Needing no other encouragement, he did. And it was the sexiest thing she'd ever seen. Without losing a beat of his drumming inside her, Gideon wrapped his lips around Tripp's cock, swallowing the turgid length for all he was worth. At first Tripp seemed surprised by the turn of events, but it didn't last long. Muttering under his breath, he gripped Gideon's shoulder in his hand and used it as leverage to saw in and out of the other man's mouth.

If she hadn't been ordered not to come, she would have. Like many women, Skylar had often fantasized about watching two men make love. Seeing it up close and personal was better than she'd ever imagined.

Skylar refused to close her eyes; she didn't want to miss a single thrust or stroke of her men. The intense feeling of being filled by Gideon as his mouth engulfed Tripp's cock was beyond anything she'd ever experienced before. She felt wicked, wanton and loved. Utterly and completely loved even though neither man had spoken a word of devotion. But she didn't need words. It was there in their every look, their every caress, in their being.

"Fuck, I'm going to come." Tripp pulled out of Gideon's mouth and aimed his cock toward Skylar's lips. "Finish me, baby."

Gideon's glazed eyes focused on hers as he sped his thrusts. "You heard him. Swallow him good so he'll let us come."

As if she could possibly turn that down. Despite what Tripp had ordered earlier, Skylar moved her hand up and grasped his cock. She opened her lips wide and took him as deep into her mouth as she physically could. His answering groan was all the encouragement she needed.

She didn't have a clue how they did it, but somehow Tripp fucked her mouth at almost the exact same speed Gideon fucked her cunt. He pumped past her lips so rapidly she could barely keep his length in her hand. Despite his fervent rhythm he never went deeper inside her mouth than she could handle.

"That's it. I'm coming. I'm coming," Tripp cried. Skylar clamped her lips around his cock as he spurted his seed inside. "Fuck. Fuck…come, baby, come." He panted as he pulled his sated cock from her mouth.

Skylar wasn't sure which one of them he was referring to and she wasn't going to ask. Opening her mouth, she gasped for air, needing as much oxygen as she could to help her survive what she knew was coming next. She dug her nails into the sheet and held on for dear life. She was close, so fucking close she could taste it. Despite Tripp giving permission, Gideon fucked on.

He rode her like a champion steed, hard and fast, which was just the way she wanted it. And it wasn't long before the steady bumping of his pelvis against her aching clit sent her headlong into the abyss.

"Fuck me. Fuck me. Fuccck…" she cried as her orgasm ripped through her body, sped along by Gideon's frantic pounding into her pussy.

Her release triggered his, and with one final thrust, he came, shouting her name in a hoarse, guttural cry. Shivering, Skylar wrapped one arm around him as he collapsed onto her body and reached out with her other hand to Tripp. She needed to feel them all together at this moment so they all could share in the beauty they had made. Tonight had been better than she could have ever expected and better than she had ever dreamed.

* * * * *

Gideon woke to the feel of a hand lightly touching his cock. He opened his eyes and peered into the darkness at a sleeping Skylar who was softly snoring into the pillow, which only left one other person. Tripp. Somehow the sleeping arrangements had been changed from Skylar in the middle to Gideon in the middle with Tripp spooning him from behind, not that he was complaining. This was a hell of a way to wake up, surrounded by the people he loved.

Instead of immediately saying anything to let Tripp know he was awake, Gideon closed his eyes again and allowed the pleasure of the moment to sink in. He had wanted this for so long—to be with the both of them—like this. As pathetic as it sounded, he'd almost been afraid to fall asleep earlier, worried that when he woke he'd realize it had all been a dream. But it wasn't. It was reality. His reality. And he was in heaven.

"I know you're awake," Tripp whispered in his ear.

"No, I'm not," he teased softly. Reaching back he laid his hand on Tripp's hip, dug his fingers in the other man's skin and pulled him against him. "I'm completely asleep."

"I want to ask you a question."

Since his hand was on Gideon's cock, pumping him to life, as far as Gideon was concerned, right then and there,

Tripp could have asked him for the moon and he would have delivered it on a silver platter. "Ask."

"Was tonight the first time you sucked cock?"

The question brought a quick smile to his lips. "No."

"You do it often?"

Now that was a question that deserved a face-to-face answer. As much as it pained him, Gideon moved Tripp's hand off his stiffening erection and gently rolled over until he was facing the other man. "How often is often?"

"Every day and twice on Sunday." The sarcasm rang out loud and clear despite the low pitch of his voice.

He was such a smartass. "Not that often, but I've fooled around enough to know what I like."

"Which is?"

"Options."

"I see."

Gideon sniffed and wrinkled his nose. "You smell like tequila."

"I had another drink…or three. You want one?"

"No." Truth be told, Gideon didn't think he'd want one for quite a while.

"So was it anyone I know?"

"Was who anyone you knew?"

"The person you gave head to before."

"Maybe one of them."

"Who?" He frowned. "Not one of the other guys?"

The thought of making out with Holden or Shane made him chuckle. Sure, they were cute and all, but Gideon wasn't swayed by any pretty face. He was attracted to Tripp for more than his good looks. He was drawn to the man inside. "No. I think they're completely straight."

"Oh. Who then?" Tripp took Gideon's cock in hand once more and slowly began to stroke him. His movements were measured as if he were studying Gideon's cock, learning the grooves and curves of it.

Gideon was so lost in the pleasure of Tripp's touch it took the other man whispering "Who?" again to get him to respond, and when he did, it was with hesitation. "Oliver Corus."

"Oliver Corus!"

So much for being quiet. "Shh…you're going to wake Skylar."

"I don't think she'll mind too much." Okay, he had a point there. Their little princess had proven she was more than able to handle the both of them. "Olive Corus. I can't believe you messed around with him. I hated him."

"I know."

"He was always hanging around you. It used to annoy the shit out of me."

"Why?"

"Because I didn't like it," Tripp replied stubbornly.

"Why?" He had an idea, but he wanted to see if Tripp would admit something Gideon was beginning to suspect. With the exception of Shane and Holden, Tripp had always been very agitated when Gideon brought other guys around. He was very dog in the manger that way. Tripp could be buddies with anyone he chose to, but he did his best to run off anyone else with his rude, sarcastic behavior whenever Gideon showed the slightest bit of interest. At first he had thought Tripp was just being a spoiled asshole, but now he wonder if it wasn't something else. "There has to be more to it than that."

"Because he was an asshole and he was always there, as if he wanted to be part of the group." His expressive eyes held a hint of annoyance in them.

"And thanks to you, he never was."

"Me?" he scoffed. "None of the other guys liked him either."

I Never

"And for the life of me, I could never figure out why."

"It's simple math, man. Three girls, four guys. We would have exceeded the dick limit."

"It seems to me we were already one dick over, what harm could one more have been?"

"I would have harmed him, okay? He was always hanging on you, touching you." If it wasn't for the firm grip Tripp had on his cock, Gideon might have teased him about his jealous tone, but he was a huge fan of his cock and didn't want to tempt fate. "And laughing at your cheesy jokes. He was a regular poser."

"He was a nice 'nough guy. Gave good head."

"I still can't believe you let him suck you off."

Since they were being honest… "Among other things."

Tripp's hand stilled, causing Gideon to open his eyes and focus on him. "What, was that too much sharing?"

"You let him fuck you."

"I didn't say that."

"You didn't say you didn't."

"Does it really matter?" Gideon asked.

"Yes," Tripp fired back.

"Why?"

"Because I want to know if you like getting fucked, Gideon?"

Gideon had to lick his lips before answering. "I'm…more of a top than a bottom."

"What about for me?" Tripp challenged. "You'd bottom for me, wouldn't you? Let me sink my cock deep in your ass. Fuck you long and hard."

Gideon's mind screamed "Hell yes", but his mouth refused to submit so easily. "You think so, do you?"

"I'm pretty confident about it." Tripp released Gideon's cock and slid two fingers into his mouth. He lapped at them with his tongue until they were slippery wet. Without breaking eye contact he slowly pulled them out of his mouth and brought them down between Gideon's slightly spread thighs and up between his ass cheeks. "Spread your legs."

Tripp didn't ask, he told, which got him fast and obedient results. Gideon had never given it up so quickly before to anyone, but with Tripp, he hungered to obey.

"I like the way you do as you're told."

He liked the way Tripp ordered, but he would be damned if he admitted it. "Don't let it go to your head."

"I won't," Tripp retorted sarcastically before teasing at his hole.

Gideon sucked in his breath and held it as Tripp's questing finger slid knuckle-deep in him. It had been a while since he had been taken there by anyone other than his own vivid imagination. Tripp added a second finger into Gideon, pushing it in deeper as he primed him for his cock.

"Oh yeah, pretty damn confident."

Tripp pulled his fingers out of Gideon's ass and sat up on the side of the bed. He reached onto the nightstand and grabbed one of the few remaining condoms. "Roll over."

"No."

Tripp's luminous eyes widened a bit in astonishment. "What?"

Gideon sat up and grabbed Tripp's hand, condom and all. "If you're going to fuck me, we're going to be face-to-face. No pretending my ass belongs to someone else, male or female."

His heated words seem to surprise the other man. "I know very well who your ass belongs to."

"Really?"

"Yeah, me." Tripp pulled his hand back and lightly shoved Gideon back onto the bed. "Now where is that...?" He fumbled through the open drawer until he scrounged up a half-empty bottle of lube. After sheathing his cock, he opened

I Never

it. He squirted a drop of gel onto his palm and then greased his condom-covered cock. "A little dab will do it."

"Think again. There's no way in hell you're shoving that log up my ass with only a dab."

"Big baby."

"When it's your ass, then we'll see if a dab will do."

"I'll just have to take your word for it." Tripp grinned, adding more lubricant to his shaft. Once he was slicked to Gideon's satisfaction, Tripp climbed back on the bed between Gideon's legs.

Before centering his cock at Gideon's opening, Tripp put his hand back between Gideon's cheeks and began to stroke him again, adding the slick gel to his play. He pumped two fingers in Gideon, stretching the other man for his cock. Just when Gideon thought he'd go off from that pleasure alone, Tripp removed his fingers, centered his crown against Gideon's puckered back door and pushed slowly in.

Gideon hissed at the burning invasion and dug his heels into the mattress. The brief stab of pain took a second to become accustomed to. He hadn't been lying when he said it had been a while.

"Damn, you're tight." Tripp pulled back then pressed slowly forward, going in deeper this time, yet still not all the way. "Open up and let me in. Let me fuck you. Let me fuck you. Let me make it good for you."

He already did. Gideon tilted his hips and moaned in delight when Tripp's cock slid deeper into his tight channel. Tripp's thickness filled him as no other had done before. Common sense told him to just lie still and let his body adjust to Tripp's cock, but common sense and Gideon never really went hand in hand.

He wanted to move. He wanted to rock into Tripp and take him balls-deep inside him, but he needed something from the other man before he could do that. "Harder. Faster."

"It'll hurt you." Tripp's words sounded strained, as if it were killing him to go slower.

"Don't worry. Do it."

"You want me to hurt you?"

"A bit."

"Fuck." Tripp pulled back until only the head of his cock remained then pushed forward with all his might, sinking gloriously in to Gideon's depths.

"Damn, man," Tripp gasped as he hit rock bottom. "Fuck."

"Yes, fuck. Fuck me." Licking his lips, Gideon did something he swore he'd never do. He begged. "Fuck me please, Tripp."

"Ahh... Jes... God." Tripp took him at his word and fucked him hard and deep, his hips pistoning to and fro in a frenzied dance of desire. The longer he pumped the better it felt. Gideon's body was now accustomed to his thick girth and he was in paradise. The bed rocked under the furious lovemaking.

Tripp rested his weight on his hands as he powered into him, leaving plenty of room between the two of them for Gideon to take matters into his hand and fist his cock.

"Fuck, that's hot," Tripp grunted as he slowed to stare down at Gideon jerking off.

"No," Gideon begged. "Don't stop fucking me. Don't stop."

"I won't stop until I'm coming in your hot ass. So hot. So tight. Fuck!" Tripp's words must have had the same electrifyingly arousing effect as they did on Gideon because Tripp sped his thrusts, fucking him harder and deeper with each stroke. The head of his cock grazed his prostate, sending Gideon into a maelstrom of sensation.

He was so close his balls ached, and just when he thought he would die of unappeased arousal a low, feminine moan of satisfaction caused him to turn his head. He met the heat-filled gaze of Skylar, who was watching them intently as she pleasured herself with her own hand.

Knowing she was as into it as they were was the final catalyst to his release. He gripped his cock and jerked once then twice, groaning Tripp's name as he came in jets across his stomach and chest. His orgasm started the chain reaction in the others with Tripp following closely on his heels and Skylar bringing up the rear with her sweet, melodic cries.

The two men stared at one another, their breath harsh, gasping, and gazes locked before Tripp finally broke and turned his head. Gideon felt a disappointing sense of loss when Tripp eased from his ass and rolled to the side between him and Skylar, disposing of the condom. Gideon slowly lowered his legs and turned his head toward his two lovers.

"Damn, that was hot." She slid her hand from between her legs and brought it toward Tripp, who greedily lapped at her wet fingers. With a wicked grin, she pulled her hand back and edged closer to them. "My turn."

Chapter Five

With the muted light creeping through the curtains Tripp finally gave in and opened his eyes, almost immediately to close them again. It wasn't the light that caused him to want to remain in the dark. It was the sight that greeted him. Gideon's arm lay motionless across Tripp's midsection in a sleeping embrace. It was as hard to stomach as the memories that came crashing back.

They'd spent the night in a frenzy of fucking, running out of condoms before they ran out of hard-ons. Over the course of the night they'd had sex in almost every position three people could without penetrating Skylar anally. They'd ended the night with him buried in her doggy style. The fact that she was sucking Gideon while he did didn't diminish the experience, it only added to it. Unfortunately with the thought of the other man Tripp suddenly remembered everything else that had occurred last night.

Weighed down by guilt, he pushed Gideon's arm away and stumbled from the bed and into the bathroom, barely making it to the commode in time to lose his liquid dinner. Tripp had consumed a lot of booze last night, but there wasn't a doubt in his mind that his stomach pain had more to do with the sex than the tequila. What the hell was he thinking?

With a shaky hand he flushed the toilet and rose from the floor weak-kneed. Without turning on the light, he stumbled into the shower and turned the cold water on full blast. He needed the needle-sharp sensation to rouse him completely. Maybe if the water was icy enough, it would wake him from the nightmare he'd blindly walked into.

Disgust and shame went 'round and 'round in his head as he tried to wash away his sins, each fighting for the title of heavyweight champion of the world. How could he allow Gideon to suck his cock or have been stupid enough to be seduced into the idea of fucking him? If this got out, his career would be over. After his hefty new contract, the press was just looking for reasons to hang him on a cross. Everything he had worked for, dreamed of since he was a kid would be gone instantaneously. Everything.

He needed to talk to Gideon. To make him understand that last night was a big mistake, and maybe if he was lucky, he could preserve his sanity along with their friendship.

Nauseous once more, Tripp stepped out of the shower and dried off. He was numb and mentally exhausted from what he had done and from what he had yet to do. Quietly he opened the door, nearly colliding with Gideon who was standing in front of the bathroom holding a glass filled with red liquid.

Gideon toyed with the arm of his glasses and shot him a shy smile that made his gut clench. "Morning."

"Morning."

"I...uh...heard you throwing up so made this for you."

"Thanks." Tripp took the glass from Gideon's hand without touching him, or meeting his eyes. He couldn't. Hell, he could hardly meet his own eyes in the bathroom mirror.

Gideon's smile dimmed and he stepped back, eyeing Tripp warily. "No prob. I'm going to take a shower." He brushed past Tripp before he could get another word in edgewise, slamming the door behind him.

"Fuck," Tripp muttered. This was not going well.

Rather than confront the issue, Tripp took a big gulp of the Bloody Mary, grimacing as he swallowed the drink. He hated the way the hangover remedy tasted, but sometimes the cure was worse than the poison.

A sound from the bed had Tripp turning his attention to Skylar, who was lying on her side staring at him. Her face was wreathed with confusion and she looked as if she wanted to ask him something but didn't know what to say. He knew the feeling.

Instead of joining her on the bed as he wanted to do, he turned his back on her and headed to the dresser to pull out some clothes. He heard the shower shut off and quickly began dressing, avoiding looking at the bed or the bathroom door, which he feared would open any minute.

He knew his fear was irrational, but at the same time it was also very real. He didn't want to lose their friendship, but he couldn't do what they wanted. He wasn't stupid. Tripp knew both of them were pleased with the way things had gone last night. More than pleased. He was pretty sure they'd be satisfied to continue. But neither of them was being realistic.

It had happened, and even if he was unable to admit it aloud, he had wanted it to happen. Sure, he hadn't expected to have Gideon suck his cock or to later fuck the other man's ass. Hell, he had never thought of any man in that way. But with Gideon it had somehow seemed okay. But it was an anomaly, something never to be repeated.

Except he didn't think either of them would see it that way. And unfortunately it was going to be his job to convince them. Before he could make a grand exit from the bedroom, the bathroom door opened, sealing his fate. He could either flee or fight, and he wasn't much of a runner.

Taking a deep breath, he turned around and faced a semi-nude Gideon who was staring at him guardedly. The towel he wore low on his hips called out to Tripp and it took everything inside him not to reach out and tug it off the man. Good Lord, what was wrong with him? Shaking his head, he tried to erase the unwanted thought from his mind. This was not the direction he needed to go if he wanted to get this over and done with.

Tripp had experienced awkward morning afters before, but never to the extent of this. If Gideon had been a woman who walked in the room after a night of mind-blowing, soul-shattering sex, Tripp would have gathered her in his arms and kissed her senseless. Then again, if Gideon had been a woman, Tripp wouldn't be feeling this way now.

There were a million things going through his head, but he only uttered one. "What?"

"You tell me." Gideon crossed his arms over his bare chest and leaned back against the door.

"What's going on?" Skylar sat up in the bed and brought the sheet up to cover her breasts. Tripp was the only one dressed, but he felt the barest.

"That's what I want to know," Gideon said snidely.

"Nothing." His voice was absolutely emotionless. He couldn't afford to feel. It would make things easier.

"Nothing, huh?" Gideon dropped his arms to the side and took a step toward Tripp, who instinctively stepped back. His retreat stopped Gideon in his tracks. "Right, nothing."

"About last night—"

"What about last night?"

"It was a..." the word stuck in his throat, but he forced it out, "mistake."

"What?" Stricken, Skylar dropped the sheet and rose to her knees, modesty obviously forgotten.

"Better question, which part? Fucking Skylar or fucking me?"

"Look, we were drunk. Things happened."

"I wasn't drunk and neither were you."

Yes, yes, he was. It was the only thing that made any sense to the madness that was now his life. "Don't pretend you know me."

Gideon's voice was cold and lashing, and his words were dead-on. "I think I know you better than you know yourself."

"Can't you see, man, this was just an abnormality."

"Maybe for you, but not for me. I've known I liked both men and women for a long time."

Who was this man and where did he put Tripp's best friend? "I can't believe that." He wouldn't, because if he did, it would leave the door wide open for him to examine himself.

"You may be in denial about who you are, but I'm not."

"Fine, if you want to be a fag, that's on you, but I'm not gay."

"Neither am I."

"It certainly fucking sounds as if you are."

"And it certainly felt as if you weren't straight last night when you were balls-deep in my ass."

"Shut up," he spat. Tripp always knew he would need anger to make it through this and he drew upon that emotion, blocking all the others from his mind.

"Stop it, you two," Skylar demanded, jumping out of the bed. "Stop it before either of you says or does something you'll regret."

"I think we already did," Tripp fired off. "Look, man, if you can't accept that last night was a mistake—"

"It wasn't," Skylar insisted.

"It was. It was wrong and disgusting and—" Tripp ran out of lies and grasped for anything to fill the void.

"No, the only thing that's disgusting is the way you're acting now." Skylar's eyes filled with tears. "Tripp, what are you saying? Why are you acting this way?"

"Because he's a fucking coward." Gideon dropped the towel and pushed past Skylar to grab his shorts off the floor. "He's not worthy of your tears or your time."

"No, maybe you're not worthy of my time." Tripp had come this far, there would be no backing down. "If you can't see this for the mistake that it is, then maybe you need to take your blind ass out of my house and out of my life. For good."

"Tripp, no." Skylar grabbed on to his arm but he shook her way. This was between Gideon and him, and it would only be resolved if the other man did as he requested.

"Say it was a mistake." Tripp wanted to force the other man to do it so they could just pretend it never happened. "Say it, Gideon."

"It was a mistake, all right. One I'll regret for the rest of my life." Dressed now, Gideon turned to face him, his face filled with fury. "Now I understand."

"Understand what?"

"The drink you had before you woke me up. You needed it to give you the balls to touch me, didn't you?" Tripp wasn't going to answer that. It was too close to the truth. But Gideon didn't need him to say anything, he just kept on. "Maybe I should go grab another bottle and we can play quarters this time and the first person who misses has to fuck the other. Does that work better for you, Tripp? If we make it a stupid game. Will your courage return then? Maybe if you just pretend it didn't happen you can keep thinking you're straight, and no one will ever know the truth."

No one could ever know the truth either way. "What happened between the three of us stays between us."

"There is no us. We're not boys, we're not lovers, we're," Gideon gestured between the two of them bitterly, "nothing. You're dead to me."

And dead inside, but that was another matter altogether. Before Tripp could muster the courage to say another word, Gideon stormed past him and out of the room. He didn't stop for a sobbing Skylar or a regretful Tripp. The saddest part was Tripp didn't blame him because Gideon was right. Tripp was a coward. The worst type of fool there was.

* * * * *

Present Day

This was a bad idea. No, worse than bad, a horrific idea. She was losing her mind. Yes, that was it. Nothing else could explain her rapid turnaround. Well…one thing could. Love, and wasn't it a bitch?

With a heavy sigh, she followed Tripp down the hall and out the door into the dark, cold night. Then she stopped and looked at the empty spot in the driveway where until two minutes ago Gideon's SUV was parked. Unlike her, however, Tripp continued on, walking past the driveway toward the street where a red convertible sports car was parked.

Now what? Gideon was going to be beyond angry if she brought Tripp home with her, but it wasn't as if he left her with many options. She'd arrived with Gideon. Now that he'd stormed out like a pouting child, she was stuck without a ride home. Leaving her no choice but to allow Tripp to drive her.

Right.

No choice.

That was her story and she was sticking to it. Even when Gideon turned his molten gray gaze her way, she wouldn't falter. This was so not her fault. None of it was. It was the fault of the two men in her life because they wouldn't listen to reason, also known as her. She could have fixed things months ago, but *nooo*, no one would listen to her. Why would they? She was simply the third in their relationship. Apparently no one of consequence.

Forget that crap. Skylar refused to be a guest player in her own life. Stomping down the drive, she stopped directly behind the current source of her anger. "You are a colossal idiot."

Startled, Tripp turned around to look at her. "Okay...did I miss something between the living room and the front door?"

"No, not between there and here, but you did miss the last year." It was a lot cooler now than when they first arrived, but despite the chill in the air, she wouldn't be moved. They were going to have this out here and now. "A year, Tripp."

"I know."

"No, you don't know." If she didn't love him so much she'd hit him over the head with the tequila bottle until he bled a river at her feet. "You almost messed everything up."

"Almost?"

"Almost with me anyhow. I don't know about Gideon."

Tripp flipped the lapel of his coat up as a barrier against the chilly air. "Gideon and I will work it out."

Was he really that stupid?

"Don't you get it? There isn't a Gideon and you. There's Gideon, me," she pointed her finger in her chest before jabbing it in his, "and you. You guys aren't a couple. We're a triad. Three people in one relationship and you walked from it all. For what?"

"I..." Tripp's face was closed and guarded, and he was unable to meet her unflinching stare. "Let's take this in the car?"

Looking around the quiet neighborhood, she wondered who the hell he thought he was hiding from. Holden's house wasn't exactly a buzzing center of activity. Hell, she didn't even think anyone on the street was paying attention to them. And who cared if they were? She was done hiding. "Why? You don't want the world to hear?"

"No, Skylar, I don't." He ground the bitter words out through his teeth. "You think I don't understand, but I do. Trust me I do. I fucked up. Big time. I not only hurt you and Gideon, I hurt any chance I might have had of being with the two people who loved me almost as much as I loved them. I let my stupid fear ruin everything that could have been. Trust me when I say I completely understand."

Okay, maybe he did understand. "Still—"

"No, you're right to an extent. There is no Gideon and me, and it's all my fucking fault. I understand. But I have to believe he and I will work it out, because if we don't, there will never be an us. I hurt you, but you've always known I love you, so it's easier for you to forgive me. Gideon doesn't have that luxury to comfort himself with."

Mixed feelings surged through her. She wanted to be happy at his about-face, but Tripp had taught her to be wary. Just being with him once more roused old feelings of fear and uncertainty. He'd hurt her. Badly. And damn his soul to hell, he had the power to do it again, but only if she let him. This wasn't just her life she was toying with. It was Gideon's, and she needed to know Tripp was on the up-and-up before she risked her lover again. "Why now?"

"As opposed to before?"

"No, as opposed to at all. What's different today from yesterday, or the day before?"

"Honestly?" he asked, his voice tentative.

"Yes, that would be nice." Try as she might, Skylar couldn't keep the sarcasm from her words.

If he sensed it he didn't let it show. "Tonight was what was different."

"Why?"

His expression stilled and grew serious. "Because I saw, I finally saw what it was I didn't see before."

"Which was?"

"A life with the two of you." He shook his head regretfully. "Hockey has been my dream, my life since I was tall enough to hold a stick and lace my skates."

"What does hockey have to do with it?" If she sounded confused, it was because she was. As far as she was concerned, his job wasn't even on the radar of the whys and hows of the demise of their relationship.

"It has everything to do with it. I can either be straight and skate, or be bi and have the two of you. But that's all I'd have. No job. No endorsement deals. Nothing. I'll be just another washed-up has-been who tells stories of the good old days when I was on the box of Wheaties and hundreds of people use to scream my name."

"Don't you think you're blowing this out of proportion just a little bit?"

"No, I don't."

"Tripp, no one cares anymore who's fucking who!"

"Of course they do. It's don't ask, don't tell, not live and let live." Tripp ran his hand through his hair. "I know you probably think I'm seeing this very black and white, but in my world there's little room for gray. I call it like I see it."

"And what does that mean for us?"

"It means that in order to have everything I want, I risk losing everything I've worked so hard for."

"No one is asking you to give that up."

"Yes, you are. By being what you want me to be, I'd have to give up everything I held true. But I see now."

"What?"

"That's it abso-fucking-lutely worth it." The warmth of his smile echoed in his voice. "You're worth it. Gideon's worth it. We are worth it."

Skylar was caught off guard by the sincerity in his voice. "That hit you tonight?"

"I'm a slow learner."

"No shit." She paused for a moment as if thinking about what she wanted to say. "You do realize that what we do in the privacy of our bedroom isn't anyone's business, Tripp. The world doesn't need to know you and Gideon are lovers just because you and I are."

"Do you really think America will be more accepting of the three of us together if Gideon and I pretend we don't touch?"

"America doesn't have to know."

"So you'd have me deny Gideon and what I feel for him for the rest of our lives."

"No. I just..." Skylar's words trailed off as if the complexity of their situation finally hit her. "I guess I just don't know."

"Do you think it was easy when I made the decision I did?" Tripp questioned, frowning. "It wasn't, not at all. At the time, I thought it was better than the alternative. But there hasn't been a day gone by I haven't ached for the two of you. That I haven't regretted my actions, my words, my decision."

"You couldn't tell on our end."

"Maybe not, but anyone who's seen me in the last year will tell you I've been in hell. A hell of my own making, granted, but hell nevertheless."

She wasn't going to let him off that easy. "You weren't the only one."

"I know, princess, and I'm going to do everything in my power to rectify it."

"It won't be easy."

"It shouldn't be," he admitted. It was becoming more than apparent he understood the severity of the situation greater than she realized.

"At least we both can agree about that."

"I'm willing to do anything to make this work."

Hope filled her and chased away any and all doubt from her mind. Here was the man she'd fallen in love with so long ago. "Anything?"

"Yes. Crawl through glass, eat dirt, throw myself on the mercy of the court. Anything."

"If I were you, I wouldn't give Gideon any ideas," she warned. Gideon had been hurt more than he'd ever admit, and she knew he wouldn't forgive easily.

"I don't think I can suggest anything he hasn't already thought of." He smiled remorsefully.

"True."

"I know I have no right to ask this, but I'm selfish bastard so I'll ask anyway. Can you—will you—forgive me and give me another chance?"

"Don't make me regret this."

"Is that a yes?"

"It's not a no."

"I'll guess I'll have to work hard at making it a yes." Before she could say another word, Tripp pulled her into his arms and capture her mouth with his.

His kiss was urgent, exploring her mouth as he seemed intent to renew himself with her every nuance. Skylar knew she should protest. At best turn her mouth and pretend for a split second she didn't want to kiss him, but enough time had been wasted apart as it was, and who was she kidding. She wanted this almost as much as she wanted him.

Moaning, she sank into his embrace, surrendering herself to his kiss. Instantaneously the old feelings came flooding back as if the last months had never been. She loved him. Neither time nor anger had been able to erase the intense longing she had for him in her heart. Because he was half her heart, and the other half waited at home for them.

Tripp slowly ended the kiss, pulling away a second at a time until their lips no longer touched. He didn't release her though. He held tight to her, as if he were afraid she would disappear. "Is it still not a no?"

"It's definitely not a no."

"Then my work here is partially done." Tripp released his hold on her body but not her hand. He turned back toward the car and unlocked the door, holding it open for her as she entered. After shutting it, he quickly walked around to the driver's side and slid in. He started the car, turning on the heater for warmth. "Where to? Home?"

The phrase sounded better than any other. Home to Gideon. "Yes. I live with Gideon now, at his old place."

His smile dimmed a bit, but didn't completely fade away. "I did miss a lot."

She reached out and laid her hand on his thigh. She refused to think about what was to come, only enjoying this time now. "But not too much."

He put his hand on the stick shift, but didn't shift into gear. Instead he turned to her. "Can I ask you a question?"

"Yes."

"Did you know before that night Gideon was bisexual?"

"Don't you mean did I know that you and Gideon were bisexual?"

He shot her a quick smile as if amused by her question. "Yes, that's exactly what I meant."

Finally Tripp was admitting he was bisexual. That was a leap in the right direction. "No, I had no idea."

"But you didn't seem all that bothered by what occurred."

"I wasn't bothered. One might even say I enjoyed it." She grinned. "Greatly."

"That's what surprised me, I guess."

"Why? You didn't think only gay men went to see *Brokeback Mountain*, did you? There are women out there who love guy-on-guy action just as there are men out there who love girl on girl."

"I guess I never thought of it that way."

"Hmm, I guess there were a lot of things you never thought about before," she couldn't help but add.

"I've had plenty of time in the last year to think about a lot of things."

"I guess you did." Skylar could only hope Tripp's newfound revelations weren't in vain and Gideon would be as willing as she to open his heart and forgive. Somehow she didn't think it would be so easy.

* * * * *

As he walked toward the kitchen, Gideon could hear the muted sounds of people talking. Suddenly the red sports car parked out front made sense. Skylar and Tripp sat at the breakfast bar drinking coffee and speaking in hushed tones. They hadn't noticed him yet, but he could certainly see the writing on the wall.

He was fucked.

Gideon knew a setup when he saw one, and from the stubborn tilt of Skylar's chin when she noticed him, he'd just walked into one. One he wasn't in the mood to deal with. It was bad enough he'd been blindsided by Shane, but he'd be damned if he'd put up with it in his own house.

"Hmm…doesn't this look cozy?" Gideon watched in cynical amusement as Skylar took Tripp's hand in hers. Snorting, he set the brown bag on the counter and crossed his arms over his chest. "*Et tu, Brute.*"

"Nice of you to drive off and leave me at the party."

"I figured you could catch a ride home." Not the one she ended up catching though.

"I guess you figured right."

"Oh boy, this is going to be fun." Gideon turned toward the counter and scrunched the bag down around the bottle of bourbon.

"Is that necessary?" Tripp asked, speaking for the first time.

"Yeah, skater boy, it is." At this point he held down the anger simmering just under the surface instead displaying an icy demeanor. "But if I knew you were coming, I would have bought tequila instead."

"Funny," Skylar said, not looking amused at all. "I hope you're not planning on getting drunk."

"And miss the night's entertainment? Wouldn't dream of it." But having a drink didn't equal getting drunk. With a sardonic smile he twisted the cap off the bottle. It was as close as he came to the alcohol before Skylar yanked her hand away from Tripp, stormed over to him and snatched the bottle from Gideon's hand. "Hey, I was about to drink that."

"And now you're not." She walked to the sink and angrily tilted the bottle over, pouring the brown liquor down the drain.

"That was just mean," he grumbled. "And you owe me twenty bucks."

"Bill me."

So much for that. "There went my plan for the night. Parcheesi anyone?"

"Stop it." Skylar's expression was thunderous. "Stop acting this way."

He didn't want to. He was in a shitty mood, hurt and feeling just a tad bit betrayed by little Miss "We're In This Together". "Why is he here?"

"Why don't you ask me?"

"Fine." Gideon turned his heated glare from Skylar to Tripp. "What are doing here?"

"Trying talk to some sense into you."

"Yeah. Not going to happen. Feel free to leave now." Gideon went to move past him, but was stopped by Skylar's hand on his arm.

"Please."

"Please what?"

I Never

"Listen to him. Just for a few minutes. That's all I'm asking."

A few minutes. Even that was too much. He knew Skylar wasn't a pushover, so either Tripp had done some fine dancing or said something that really touched her. Then again, she was in love with the man so she was probably more forgiving than anyone else might have been in the situation. And definitely a hell of a lot more forgiving than he was feeling. "Whining to Shane didn't get you very far, so you went off and whined to Skylar. I knew you were pathetic, but hiding behind a woman's skirt, that's low even for you."

Instead of becoming upset as he expected, Tripp merely arched a brow. "Anything else you want to say?"

"What?"

"If it will make you feel better, let it all out." Tripp's sympathetic expression was pure mockery. And the rage inside Gideon began to bubble to the brim as the other man nodded his head compassionately and motioned with his hand for more. "I can take it. Then you can cry, we can have a big group hug and then maybe, just maybe, you'll get over yourself and stopping acting like an ass."

"Why? Because it's your role?"

"Precisely."

Irritated, Gideon shook Skylar's hand off his arm and took a menacing step toward Tripp. "You might have swayed Skylar with sweet words and kisses, but that shit isn't going to work with me."

"Then tell me what will and I'll do it," Tripp offered.

"There's nothing you can do." Gideon wasn't going to fall into his trap and continue listening to his bullshit. He'd given up on Tripp last year and any words now would be meaningless.

"I don't believe you."

"Excuse me?"

"You wouldn't be so pissed off if you didn't care so much."

Gideon hated that Tripp might be right. He thought he had severed the bond, but seeing Tripp, especially together again with Skylar, hurt more than he ever thought possible. But there was no way he'd admit to it. He'd deny, deny, deny until somebody started believing or he ran out of words. "You think you know me."

"Almost as good as you know me, which was pretty good by the way."

"Is that so? In my opinion I don't think I knew you at all." Gideon still could feel the hurt and anger from that night so many months ago. Tripp hadn't just been his lover—he'd been his friend for years. He never would have believed the other could have treated not just him but Skylar so callously. Speaking of Skylar, Gideon turned on his heel and pierced her with his steely gaze. "I can't believe you're so willing to forgive and forget."

"Why?"

Was everyone insane? "Because of the way he treated us...you."

"I love him, Gideon," she answered him thickly. "Just like I love you. I could no less turn my back on him than I could on you."

"Really, because I thought you did a damn fine imitation of someone who could do just that in the last few months."

"I didn't turn my back on him, Gideon. He turned his on me."

"Exactly."

"But I've forgiven him."

"That shit right there, that's what doesn't make any sense."

"Sometimes we all fall short of the glory," Tripp added quietly from behind him.

Angry, Gideon spun around and shoved the palms of his hands into the other man's chest. "I'm not talking to you."

Undaunted, Tripp pushed back. "Maybe you should be."

"Walk away, Tripp," he warned. "Walk away now before…"

Tripp didn't back down. Surprisingly, he did the exact opposite and got right in Gideon's face. "Before what?"

"This." Channeling all the rage, hurt, love and anger he'd felt over the last year, Gideon brought his arm back and slammed his fist into Tripp's jaw, sending the other man reeling back.

Damn, that felt good. So good he was going to do it again. Gideon raised his arm to do just that when Skylar cried out his name. "No. Don't."

When she moved to go to Tripp's aid, Tripp held up his hand to ward her back. "I'm fine."

"Then apparently I didn't hit you hard enough."

"Give it another shot then."

"Tripp—" Skylar took another step toward him but once again he stopped her.

"I think you should leave us alone for a bit." Even though Tripp's words were directed at her, his thunderous gaze never left Gideon's face.

Finally something Gideon could agree with. "Yeah. Why don't you?"

"Because you guys are going to do something stupid." She bristled with indignation and rage, feelings Gideon could more than relate to.

"That's pretty much the plan." Gideon was aching to get his hands on Tripp again, and he didn't want to chance Skylar being hurt in the scuffle. As calmly as he could, he took off his glasses and set them down on the counter. "It will be fine, babe."

"Don't 'babe' me. I think this is the stupidest idea I've ever heard, but if it enables you two cavemen to work it out, then fine. But if you guys kill each other, I'm going to be really pissed off," she warned, shooting them both a hostile look. "And I'm not going to clean up any messes either. Assholes."

Neither man took their gaze off the other as Skylar stormed from the room. The second Gideon heard the bedroom door slam though, it was on again. The space between them was eaten away in a heartbeat as Gideon flung himself at Tripp, tackling the man to the ground.

"Bastard," he grunted out as he slammed his fist into Tripp's face. Maybe if he made the man less attractive neither he nor Skylar would think about him so damn much.

Tripp wasn't a lightweight though. Years of fighting on the ice had given him skills of his own. And before Gideon could get another blow in, Tripp had him flipped onto his back, landing a strike to his midsection in the process.

The punch had Gideon ready for blood. Shoving Tripp away from him, he heard the other man grunt in pain as he landed against the edge of the island. Oh yeah, he was feeling better already.

Chapter Six

There was no doubt in Tripp's mind Gideon had a right to his anger. He might even deserve every punch Gideon threw, but that didn't mean he was going to just lie there and take it. He was remorseful, not stupid.

Groaning, he used the island for leverage and pulled himself to his feet, keeping his gaze locked on Gideon all the while. Normally he would say the two of them were pretty evenly matched, but Gideon had months of rage on his side to fuel him on, something Tripp lacked. Instead, Tripp was going to have to use cunning to come out on top, or he'd lose the battle and the war.

"Is that all you got?" he goaded. Pushing away from the island, he crouched down into a boxer's stance and gestured with his hands for Gideon to stand up. Tripp had to time this just right or he was going to be bruised and battered for a week.

"Fuck you."

"Only if you play your cards right, pretty boy," he added a wink just to infuriate the other man more.

It worked.

With a roar, Gideon charged. Acting swiftly, Tripp grabbed Gideon by his shirt and swung him around, slamming him into the wall.

A wooden plaque fell off its hook and the drywall cracked under their massive weight, but neither stopped the fight. Gideon landed an uppercut to Tripp's rib, causing him to grunt in pain and lose his grip on the other man's shirt.

"I can't say enough," he pushed Tripp back and slammed his fist into his eye, "about how much we missed you."

"It—" Tripp ducked the follow-up swing and slammed his shoulder into Gideon's stomach, slamming him back into the wall. Once he had him pinned again, he took hold of his shirt, anchoring him to the wall. "Shows."

"Fess…up, Tripp." Gideon's face was a road map of pain, but he didn't let up. "You're just back because you were in the mood for kinky sex."

Since Gideon didn't throw a punch, Tripp didn't. He had no reason. He was there to make up, not break bones. But he didn't release the man. He held him by his shirt, more for his own sake than Gideon's. Tripp was breathing hard, in pain, and strangely aroused, giving Gideon's words a bit of credence. But just a bit. He hadn't come back for the kinky sex. It was just an added bonus. "You have no idea what you're talking about."

"I think I do." To Tripp's surprise, Gideon reached between them and placed his hand against Tripp's denim-covered cock.

Although he was slightly embarrassed to be caught with an erection, he didn't release Gideon. Tripp wouldn't have put it past the other man to touch him in that manner just to make him to ease up. "It isn't about that."

"This is what it's always been about with you. Your cock. It thinks on your behalf and you act on its behalf."

"Not true."

"Liar."

"Really? Prove it."

Gideon released his hold on his Tripp's cock and moved his hands to the top of Tripp's pants.

"What…what are you doing?"

"Proving my point."

Okay, this was new. Tripp wasn't sure if he should protest or just release him. He did know he didn't want to go another round with his cock hanging out. "Stop it."

"Sure. In a second." Tripp didn't even get a second. Gideon's nimble fingers had Tripp's pants undone and his cock hanging out before he could even form a coherent thought.

If it wasn't bad enough he exposed him, Gideon had to take it a step further and fist Tripp's cock. "Tell me again it's not about the kinky sex."

"It...wasn't." With his dick hard as stone, he could see why Gideon didn't believe him. But still, the truth was the truth. "You're just trying to turn this around."

"No, this is me turning it around." Gideon released his cock and grabbed Tripp, spinning him until their positions were reversed. "Admit it. Admit you just want to fuck me and I'll let you. But then you go. Out of our lives for good."

"No." There was no way in hell he'd agree to an asinine deal like that. "I love Skylar. I love y—"

"Shut your lying mouth."

"I'm not lying. And I think you know it." Tripp grabbed hold of Gideon's hand and went to remove it from his shirt, but stopped when he noticed a very notable bulge in the other man's pants. He released his hold on Gideon's wrist and moved his hand down to Gideon's pants. There was an advantage to being in this position after all. "Looks as if kink isn't just my downfall."

"That doesn't mean anything," Gideon growled.

"I'd agree fully if I didn't think you were lying." Tripp didn't waste time trying to unbutton Gideon's pants. Instead he used one hand to pull on the waistband of his khakis and boxers, the other slipped inside and wrapped around Gideon's dick. It was a tight fit but it was workable. "It matters because I matter to you."

"You don't—"

"Now you shut up. Shut up and touch me."

"I hate you," Gideon muttered as he released Tripp. Instead of taking his cock in hand as Tripp would have hoped, Gideon moved his hands to his own pants and quickly undid them, pushing them down his hips.

Then to Tripp's vast relief Gideon grasped Tripp's cock, fisting him as rapidly as Tripp was stroking him. This was not the way Tripp imagined their first time back together, but it was a start in the right direction. "Hate me all you want. But later. Right now love me."

"Fuck," Gideon groaned, thrusting his hips hard against Tripp's hand. Gideon was rock-hard and dripping pre-come like a leaky faucet. His slick essence only aided Tripp in stroking his hard shaft, giving him the lube he needed to move with ease.

"This is a real good punishment you came up with for me." Tripp thrust into Gideon's hand as if it were the tightest of pussies, moaning his pleasure in tune with the other man's. How they managed to stay standing was a mystery to Tripp, but where there was a will, there was a way. And it was his will to feel Gideon splash his seed all over his cock.

"Just shut up and—"

"Stroke your cock?" Tripp asked, doing just that. "Is that what you want, Gideon? Is this what you like?"

"Yes. God, yes."

"Remember that night when I fucked you." Gideon moaned his acquiescence and sped his hand on Tripp's shaft. "No matter how it ended, it was still the best night of my life. There hasn't been a week gone by I haven't had a dream or jerked off to the image of you beneath me. And I will have it again."

"No." Gideon's denial didn't carry the same strength of his early words.

"Yes." Tripp tightened his grip on Gideon as if he could force his will through his hand and make the man his again. "I will have you and Skylar, and this time I won't let you go."

Gideon groaned and wrapped his other hand around Tripp's neck, bringing their bodies closer together. There was barely any room to move, but the new position enabled their cocks to rub against one another, which was a new sensation altogether.

Their breathing became stilted and rough, their movements more pronounced. Soon rubbing against one another wasn't enough and their hips got into the mix until they were humping and rubbing and stroking like high school kids in the backseat of a car.

They were moving so fast Tripp could hardly keep track of who was touching who where. All he knew was it felt too good to stop now. He didn't want to be the first one to come, but from the way Gideon was grinding against him, so fucking hot and sweet, he didn't see any way out of it.

Thankfully he wasn't the only one nearing release. "Tripp...I'm gonna...I..."

"Yes. Come for me, Gideon. Come." The words had barely left his mouth when Gideon shouted his name, coating their cocks with a torrent of warm semen.

The feel of those ropy strands on his cock became the impetus for Tripp's own release.

Crying out, he tightened his grip on Gideon, who returned the caress, damn near bringing Tripp to his knees. "Fuck. Fuck. Fuck."

His hips jerked uncontrollably as his balls tightened before his cock spurted his release. He came for what felt like ages. With every jet he felt closer, renewed, more alive. The only way this could have possibly been better was if Skylar had been involved. But that was just a formality. Soon she'd be back in his arms and—

"Let go." Until Gideon spoke Tripp hadn't realized he still had hold of him.

Reluctantly he released him and leaned back against the wall for support. He felt drained. Literal and figurative. Worse yet, Tripp wanted to kiss him, but he didn't know how to take the first step in that direction. Despite what they had just done with one another, he didn't see an opening to make the move. They might have rubbed one out together, but they were no closer in resolving their initial issue than they'd been fifteen minutes ago.

Still, he had to find hope in the darkest of places. This was a start. He could work from that.

* * * * *

Skylar hated men. Slamming the bedroom door behind her, she marched over to the stereo and turned it on full blast. She didn't want to hear them "work it out". Actually, the more Skylar thought about it, she wasn't so sure she wanted to ever hear from either of them again.

There was a time when all she wished for was the opportunity to have the two of them in the same room. She should have been more careful for what she wished. Although no sane person could have foreseen the two of them battling instead of talking it out. Because talking of course would make far too much sense, and sense was something apparently neither had in abundance.

One thing she did know was they'd better clean up the kitchen when they were done. Because if she walked in there tomorrow morning and saw any remnants from their fight, she was going to throw some punches of her own.

Stupid idiots.

Grumbling, she made her way into the bathroom and started a bath. Five months ago when she moved in, she had done her best to feminize the rooms a bit, starting with the master bathroom. She turned the once-taupe space into a spa-like haven, painting the walls ivy green and fitting it with matching towels and candles. In the end, the room had become one of her favorites in the house. For the first time though, the serene space had no effect on her. Not only were they messing up her night, they were also ruining her favorite place in the house.

"Bastards," she muttered as she took off her earrings. She resisted the urge to slam them down on the vanity, but only barely. If she did that, she couldn't hold the title of "adult" in the house.

Closing her eyes, she took a deep, calming breath then laid her earrings gently on the vanity. Once she was centered, she opened her eyes and stared at her reflection in the mirror. She could make it through tonight because tomorrow would be better.

It better be anyway.

After undressing, she piled and pinned her hair up so it wouldn't become too wet then turned off the water. She dimmed the lights but left the bathroom door open so she could hear the music as she soaked. After the type of day she'd had, she needed to relax.

Skylar stepped into the hot, bubble-filled tub and sank down. She desperately tried not to think about the two men in the other room and what injury they might be causing one another, but it was a doomed task. They were in her thoughts daily. What made her believe today of all days she would be able to dismiss them so easily?

She could only pray her decision to bring Tripp into the house wasn't going to come back and bite her in the ass. They needed to be able to work this out. Even though she loved Gideon, she knew there was no way their lives could continue as they had the last months. They were two-thirds of a whole, not meant to be a duo, but a trio, and they all knew it.

"Hey."

Skylar glanced over at Tripp, who was standing sheepishly in the doorway. Aside from his clothes being a bit disheveled he didn't look any worse for wear, hopefully her kitchen could boast the same. Satisfied that he was at least alive, she turned her head back around and closed her eyes. "I'm not talking to you."

"Understandable." She heard him move farther into the room but still didn't open her eyes. She'd forgiven him once today. She wasn't in the mood to do it twice. "I'm going to head out, but I wanted to see you before I left."

"You're seeing me."

"Yes, I am." The frank appreciation in his tone caused her to grin despite herself.

She didn't want to be pleased by his words, but of course she was. "Did you destroy my kitchen?"

"Destroy, no. Rearrange a few things, yes. But don't worry, Gideon is picking up."

"And you…?"

"I'm going to head home. I think we all need a little time to think, and you guys can't do that if I'm here."

Irritated, she opened her eyes and faced him. "Don't you think we've had enough alone time?"

He returned her look earnestly. "I'm not running, Skylar."

Although he seemed sincere, she had to wonder if he was trying to convince her or himself. "Seems that way to me."

"I can understand why you might think that's the case, but honestly it's not. This time the space isn't for me. It's for Gideon. He's still angry. Very angry."

"The punches didn't help?" she asked sarcastically.

He winced and rubbed his side. "They didn't help my ribs, that's for sure. But I think it helped him. And it…" a faint blush stained his cheeks and Skylar began to wonder what else might have occurred besides the fight, "wasn't all bad."

"Did you talk?"

"Umm...no."

She cocked her eyebrow. This sounded interesting. "Did you do something besides talk?"

"Umm, maybe you should talk to Gideon about that."

"Oh no, none of that." Skylar wasn't going to play that game. "I really don't like the idea of the boys ganging up against the girl here. Start as you mean to go, I always say, so spill it."

A rueful grin flashed quickly over his handsome face as he walked over to the tub and kneeled beside her. "We didn't exactly have a meeting of the minds. More like a meeting of hands wrapped around dicks."

Well, well, well. Now this was worth hearing more about. "Are you telling me that in a middle of a fight, you two stopped to jerk each other off?"

"Something like that." His gaze raked boldly over her as fingers slid sensuously across her upper arm, sending shivers racing along her spine. Despite the cover of the bubbles she felt wickedly exposed. Her beaded nipples played peekaboo with the suds, giving Tripp irrefutable evidence about how turned off she wasn't by his encounter with Gideon.

"You two blow my mind." Only men could turn a fistfight into a fist-fuck. And damn it to hell and back, she'd missed the show.

"I thought it was pretty mind-blowing." His voice had lost all traces of humor and in its place was unadulterated lust. Once again, Skylar cursed the fates that kept her from seeing her men caress one another. Just imaging the naughty scene in her mind was sending all sorts of warm, gooey feelings to her pussy.

"Did you at least break out the cell phones and take some pictures for me?"

"Sorry, baby. No time."

"There's always time for photos." The heat from his intense gaze made the water seem downright cold in compassion. From the way he was staring intently at her, Skylar was willing to bet Gideon wasn't the only person he wanted to get his hands on tonight.

"I'll keep that in mind for next time." Reaching out, he fingered a freed tendril of hair.

"Will there be a next time?"

"Most definitely, but with one tiny change."

"What's that?"

"Instead of filling our hands with cock, we'll fill you instead."

"I like the sound of that."

"I thought you might." He tangled his fingers in her hair and tilted her head back until she was looking deep into his eyes. His possessive grip didn't bother her. Quite the opposite. It thrilled her. Tripp's take-charge attitude had always been one of the things she found very attractive about him.

With deliberate slowness, he lowered his mouth onto hers and took her lips in a soul-singeing kiss. He took without asking, once more sealing her fate with his wicked touch. His tongue glossed over hers, forcing bittersweet memories to come rushing back. His kiss was just as sweet and tempting as she remembered. Kissing him was like coming home. It just felt right.

When Tripp lifted his head, she murmured an incomprehensible plea for more. She didn't want this to end ever again. He was the missing part of her soul. "Stay the night."

"How I wish I could," he whispered, brushing his lips across her once more. "I have a game Sunday afternoon. I would really like it if the two of you could make it. I can leave tickets for you at will call."

"A game? Isn't it off-season?"

"It's an exhibition game for charity."

"Sounds fun but I can't make any promises."

"Try, that's all I ask." He traced his thumb across her lower lip. "I love you."

He rose without saying another word and left before she could utter the words back. Skylar wondered if he left so quickly because he was afraid she wouldn't say them. If that was the case, he hurried in vain. Skylar had loved him from afar for years, a few months of estrangement wasn't going to bring that to an end.

* * * * *

"Come on, admit it." Skylar elbowed Gideon softly in the side to garner his attention. The arena was packed with people making their way to the parking lot. Neither one of them felt the need to "hurry up and wait" as the case would be in this packed crowd. So they ignored the evil looks people sent them as they tried to climb around the two of them still sitting in their seats.

Tripp could have procured them better seats in the players' box, but he knew Gideon preferred to sit near the ice. What was the point of going to a game if it had to be watched on a big screen? "You had a good time."

"It was all right." Even under threat of torture, abstinence or a chick-flick marathon, Gideon would never admit how much he'd enjoying watching Tripp play again.

Despite how much he loved the game, Gideon hadn't been able to watch one since his blowout with Tripp. He'd forgotten just how much he loved going. Short of Tripp and Tripp's parents, there wasn't a single soul who'd been more thrilled than Gideon when his friend was drafted. For Gideon, hockey was right up there with orgasms and ESPN. Being able to see his then-best friend on the ice only made the experience that much better.

"Just all right." He could feel her eyes boring into him and briefly turned to catch her incredulous stare.

"Yeah. Nothing special," he lied. Special wasn't the word. It had been a fan-fucking-tastic game. Both teams were equally matched and motivated. It was by luck and luck alone that the Blackhawks made the last goal. The puck had ricocheted off the goalie's blade, preventing overtime by mere seconds.

"Right, that's why you were screaming like a banshee when he was sent to the penalty box."

"Fucking ref is blind." Just thinking about the unjust call had him seeing red. Flying pucks weren't the only reason Plexiglas separated the fans from the ice. Calls like that could incite a spectator or two to shove a ref under the Zamboni.

"Blind?"

And no one could convince him differently. "If Kragger doesn't know how to stay upright on his blades, he shouldn't be out on the ice."

"What about when Tripp assisted with the goal?"

"What about it?"

"You were on your feet."

"As was everyone else in the stadium. Stop trying to make a big deal out of it. I love hockey. It has nothing to do with Tripp." He would have jumped out of his seat and screamed at the top of his lungs for anyone who made a goal.

It was the nature of the game to be loud and crazy. Hockey was a violent sport. It brought out the caveman in him. It had nothing to do with the sense of pride he felt when Tripp searched the stands until he found Gideon and pointed in a shared moment of victory. It was about the game and nothing more.

"You are so full of—"

"Mr. Foley...excuse me."

Thinking he heard his name, Gideon glanced over his shoulder in the direction from which the sound had come. All he could see was a sea of people making their way up the stairs.

"I'm not full of anything. It was a good game. Nothing more. Nothing—" Gideon was cut off in midstream as he once again heard his name being called. Confused, he stood to try to get a better look into the crowd.

"What was that?" Skylar asked, standing as well.

"I'm not sure." Just then, a glum-faced usher pushed his way past two teenagers and waved his hand wildly in the air.

"Do you know him?"

"No."

"Apparently he knows you."

"Mr. Foley. Ms. Daveigh." The usher fought his way through the throng of people and stumbled to their side. "There you are. I was afraid I missed you."

"What's going on?" Skylar asked.

Straightening himself, the young man pulled on the hem of his vest and stood up proudly. "Mr. Kowlaski asked me to come and find the two of you."

The way he said Mr. Kowlaski made Gideon want to laugh. Apparently hero-worshipping was part of the job description. "Why?"

"He wanted me to escort the two of you to the players' exit."

"Because..." Gideon questioned blankly, not at all understanding the purpose of the kid's errand.

"Mr. Kowlaski didn't say, sir."

Of course he didn't, and it wouldn't occur to Fan Boy to ask either. "Look, I'm not going to wait outside like some star-struck fan."

"No. No, sir. He wants me to take you inside. It's right outside the locker room, not outside the arena."

"I don't think—"

"We'd love to," Skylar interrupted.

Would they? Gideon looked over at Skylar, who appeared as if she were trying her best to hold back laughter.

"Don't be such a poor sport. If you're a good boy, I'll see if we can get some autographs for you."

Gideon snorted derisively. Thanks to Tripp, he knew most of the players already. He didn't need or want their autographs. But of course Skylar knew that. She was just being a brat as usual. "If I go, you'll owe me big time."

"Hmm...I can't wait."

They waited a few more minutes for the crowd to thin before trudging to the locker room. Halfway there Skylar's phone rang. She pulled it out of her jacket pocket and glanced down at the face. "It's Bev's number. Give me a sec."

She took a few steps away from him and began to speak quietly into the phone. The usher left them in the passage in front of the locker room with strict instructions not to venture out of the hallway.

Rolling his eyes, Gideon nodded his agreement and glanced around the busy corridor. Skylar and he weren't the only people waiting outside the locker room. He nodded to a few of the faces he recognized from parties and other player get-togethers, but didn't edge closer to talk to any of them. He knew them, but he didn't know them, and he wasn't in the mood to make small talk. Gideon had other important things on his mind, such as how he was going to make Skylar pay.

He lounged casually against the wall and briefly closed his eyes as he imagined her on her knees in front of him. Skylar was very good with her mouth. She knew how to tease and torment with just a flick of her tongue. Suddenly in his mind Tripp was there, standing next to him nude with his dick in hand.

Gideon quickly opened his eyes. That hadn't happened in a long while and it disorientated him. He shouldn't be surprised though. Tripp hadn't been far from his erotic thoughts since their tryst Friday night.

When Skylar came back to his side, she was frowning.

"What's wrong?"

"Bev wanted to know if we'd heard from Paige since Friday."

"What did you tell her?"

"I told her no." Her face was tense, worry creasing her brow. "Apparently she and Shane left right after Tripp and I did, and neither one has been heard from since."

"If she's with Shane, I'm sure she's fine."

"Like we are?"

This was as close as Skylar had come to asking him his feelings regarding Tripp. Surprisingly Tripp's name had only come up yesterday when she told Gideon of his request for them to attend the game. No talks of the past or what happened Friday night, although he knew she was aware of it. They had both wordlessly agreed to let it go for the moment. Apparently the moment was over.

He didn't want to fight. He didn't want to upset her, but he also didn't want to say everything was good to go when it wasn't. "Things aren't okay."

"But they could be."

Skylar was determined. He'd give her that. "I'm not going to jump into anything." Even as he said it, he knew Skylar was going to make him eat his words.

"Of course anything doesn't refer to hand jobs then, right?"

And there she was, ready to hand him a spoon. When he was right, he was right. Gideon shifted uneasily under Skylar's mocking glare. Fuck it. No need for backpedaling now. "Right."

"So does that mean I'm entitled to a hand job of my own from Tripp?"

Now that had merit. Besides, Gideon had already proven that when caught between the crosshairs of arousal and anger, arousal won every time. It was time to face facts. "Can I watch?"

"You didn't let me." She pouted prettily.

"To be fair I didn't exactly plan for it to end as it did."

"Just think what will happen when you do plan it."

He chuckled and leaned in to kiss her when he noticed something out of the corner of his eye. A reporter stood off to the side staring at the two of them and jotting something down in a notebook.

"Hey," he whispered out the side of his mouth. "That guy over there is press."

"And?"

"And I don't want to give him anything to write about. I'm going to go wait outside."

"Gideon, it's not that serious."

"Better to be safe than sorry." He dropped a quick kiss on her furrowed brow, and strolled down the hallway and out of the arena. The second the doors opened light bulbs flashed and people swarmed. "Sorry, I'm not a player, folks."

The distinct chorus of "Awws" made him grin.

"Gideon, is that you?" Gideon turned around and spotted Nash standing in the midst of autograph hounds, staring at him with a huge smile. "Wait up, man."

Gideon nodded his head in agreement and waited as Nash smiled for a few photos and signed a slew of autographs. After detangling himself from the hangers-on, Nash rushed to Gideon's side and slapped him heartily on the back. "Haven't seen you in a while. What have you been up to?"

"Not much."

"Good to see again." Nash moved his hand from Gideon's back to his shoulder, giving it a squeeze. "You waiting for Kowlaski?"

"Yes."

"I'll wait with you then. Let's go over to the parking lot where we'll have a few minutes of privacy. The owners finally gated it so there's no press or fans allowed," he said with a wink.

Nash's audacity amused Gideon to no end. Even if he weren't in a relationship with Skylar, he still wouldn't have been open to Nash's advances. They'd hung out a few times before the barbeque, but nothing had ever come from it.

Frankly Gideon wasn't interested. He hadn't been then and he wasn't now, but he also didn't feel up to waiting for Tripp to come out of the locker room. "Sure." Subtly, so not to offend the other man, Gideon nudged Nash's hand off his shoulder. "Good game by the way."

"Thanks." Nash took the rebuff good-naturedly, shooting Gideon a knowing smile as they walked toward the gated parking area. "So how come you never called me?"

"I didn't know I was supposed to."

"Yeah." Nash nodded at the security guard standing by the gate and gestured for Gideon to precede him. "I told Tripp to pass my number to you only a billion times."

"He didn't."

"He and I will have to have words."

Words. Hmm. Maybe he should have tried that instead of fighting, maybe they wouldn't have ended up coming all over the place. "Maybe it slipped his mind, or something came up."

Nash grabbed hold of his arm and pulled Gideon to a stop. "Or maybe he just wants you for himself."

"No. We're just friends." Gideon had no intention of outing Tripp to anyone, not even if they were of the same persuasion.

"Right." His mouth said one thing but his tone said something completely different.

Undaunted, Gideon tried to shrug it off. "What?"

"I have plenty of female friends and I don't cock block any of them." Nash's mouth twitched with suppressed amusement.

"Seriously. There's nothing between us," Gideon assured him. There hadn't been for a while and one night of misguided passion wasn't going to change all that.

"Great." Nash leaned forward as Gideon moved to step back. "Then he won't mind this."

"As usual, Nash, you're dead wrong." Tripp's furious words rang out over the parking lot.

Chapter Seven
ଛ

There were only two questions roaming through Tripp's mind. Should he hit first and then ask questions, or the other way around. Fury nearly choked the life from him when he saw Nash lean into Gideon to kiss him. The only pair of lips other than his own he wanted to see even remotely close to Gideon was Skylar's. And Nash was no Skylar.

With a heavy sigh, Nash took a step back and turned to face Tripp and Skylar, who had remained surprisingly quiet the entire time. "As usual, Kowlaski, your timing is off."

Instead of trading barbs with the other man, Tripp zeroed in on Gideon who was watching him with indifference, which only fueled his temper more.

He'd been riding high after the win, wanting nothing more to celebrate with Skylar and Gideon. When he walked out of the locker room and spotted Skylar standing alone in the hallway, his spirits had plummeted a bit. But only a bit. It was simply impossible not to be happy seeing her smiling at him once more. They'd walked out hand in hand only to spot Gideon walking with Nash into the parking lot. Knowing the lecherous man as he did, they followed only to stumble upon this bullshit.

"I told you to stay away from him, Nash," he reminded the other man, all the while his gaze was firmly locked on Gideon's. It was a good thing too, because if he'd glanced away, he wouldn't have seen Gideon's eyes widen in astonishment at Tripp's forceful, jealous words.

Tripp couldn't fathom why Gideon was surprised. He'd been possessive of Gideon's time and attention long before they became lovers. Now that they were, estranged as the case may be, he was twice as selfish and protective of what he considered his.

Nash snorted derisively. "And for the life of me I could never figure out why."

If he wanted a reason Tripp would give him one, in spades. "Here's why."

Pulling Gideon close, he bent his head to capture his lips in a passionate kiss. Although they'd fucked, they hadn't yet experienced this intimate embrace. Different than Skylar's soft lips, Gideon's mouth parted under his. Their tongues hesitantly explored one another for the first time, oblivious to all those around. His mind calculated the many differences that existed between kissing Gideon versus kissing Skylar. Yes, she was softer, which was oh-so nice, but Gideon used more force, and that was nice as well. As far as Tripp was concerned, there were no losers here, only winners. Damn, he was a lucky man.

Tripp angled his head and continued to revel in the experience of the kiss. It was only when Gideon pushed his shoulder did Tripp begrudgingly release his hold on the other man.

"Tripp," Gideon hissed, as he pulled back and looked nervously around. "It's the middle of the afternoon and this place is crawling with press."

"I don't care." And surprisingly he didn't. His hand reached out to caress Gideon's stubbly jaw before he leaned forward again to softly brush another kiss over Gideon's lips. He knew it was more than past time he stopped hiding his feelings and those whom he loved, no matter what might be written about him.

Instead of appearing the slightest bit apologetic, Nash seemed amused. "I didn't realize I was stepping on anyone's toes."

"Actually you're stepping on more than one set of toes," Skylar replied coolly.

Nash eyed her mockingly. "That's cozy."

"We think so." Skylar held her hand out to Gideon, who quickly pulled her into the mix of things. Using her as what Tripp could only describe as a human shield, Gideon moved her between the two of them and anchored his arms around her waist tight. Amusement shone like morning glories in Skylar's eyes, as did joy. Smiling, she leaned back into Gideon and brought her arms up and rested them on top of his. "Very cozy."

Pleased he at least had her blessing, Tripp turned his attention back to Nash. "Don't you think it's more than time you left?"

"Still the same controlling asshole, huh?" Nash sneered.

"Why wouldn't I be?"

"I don't know," Nash replied bitterly. "I thought maybe you finally coming out of the closet would mellow you out or something."

Tripp waited for Nash's words to send him into a tailspin, but it just wasn't there. The innuendos didn't bother him. He loved Gideon. He didn't know if it necessarily made him gay, or bi since he also loved Skylar. It wasn't as if he had ever been attracted to any other men. It had only ever been about Gideon.

"Go home, Nash, and leave what's mine alone."

Nash snorted and headed toward his car. Tripp turned around to see Gideon holding Skylar in his arms. The sight didn't evoke the bleak despair he'd felt at Shane's party. Instead there was a small ember of hope in his heart that he would now be included with them.

"Who said I'm yours?" Gideon's question, although softly spoken, held a world of weight behind it.

"I did." And he meant it. If Gideon wanted to push the point right now, Tripp was more than primed and ready to go.

"You damn sure aren't his." Skylar beckoned to the retreating man. "I can't believe he tried to kiss you. If he had been a she, I would have yanked him bald."

"He skates like a girl." Tripp scowled, irritated at Gideon's comment. "There's a small chance he might fight like one too."

"Hey." Skylar pulled away from Gideon and smacked Tripp on the arm. "Girl here. Hello."

"Sorry," he teased, pulling her into his arms. "If you want, you can pummel me later."

"I'm going to do something to you later, all right."

"Nice."

"I just have one question. What happened to keeping things on the down low?" Skylar asked.

The answer seemed obvious to him. "He was touching Gideon. I didn't like it."

"What about the cover of Wheaties?"

"Fuck 'em. Never did like the way they tasted anyway. Besides if that asshole can be open about who he is, I damn well can." Not everyone on the team knew Nash was gay, but the ones who did respected his privacy. Tripp could only hope the same curtsey would be extended toward him and the people he loved.

"We'll have you marching in a parade just yet," Skylar teased.

"If you two are through, we should leave. I think you made enough of a spectacle of yourself for one day, don't you think?" Gideon asked snidely.

Frustrated, Tripp released Skylar and took a menacing step toward Gideon. "I just can't win with you, can I?"

"No."

"Why won't you forgive me? What do I have to do?"

"There's nothing you can do," Gideon fired back.

Tripp shook his head in denial. "I refuse to accept that."

"And I refuse to accept you back in our lives."

"Hey, you two, this is no place for a fight-slash-jerk-off session." Skylar stepped between the two of them and held them apart by her hands.

"I'm already back in your lives." Tripp's words steamrolled right over Skylar's in his quest to be heard. "I love you, goddamn it, and I'm not going to let you go. Again." The last word he said softer than the first. "I love you."

Gideon swallowed hard, but he didn't relent. "I don't believe you."

"Oy," Skylar muttered angrily, moving from between the two of them. "Here we go again."

Tripp couldn't agree more. "You want me to come out to the entire world to prove it, because I will." Telling Nash was akin to making an announcement on ESPN, but if Gideon wanted more, he'd do it.

"That's never what I wanted," Gideon denied hotly. "Hell, I don't even want to come out to the entire world."

"Then what is it you do want?"

"I want you to wake up tomorrow and the day after and the day after that and face yourself in the mirror and not be ashamed of loving us."

Tripp met Gideon's accusing eyes without flinching. He wasn't afraid. "I've already done that, baby. I'm done being ashamed."

"It's easy for you to say it."

"The only way I can prove it to you is to make sure the first eyes you see every morning are mine. And once you see them filled with love and gratitude and not disgust or shame, maybe then you'll begin to believe in me."

"If my opinion means anything..." Skylar's words drew their attention away from their dispute and onto her. Tripp knew this was hard for her, having to watch the two of them fight, but if they didn't get this worked out and soon, none of them would be happy.

"Of course it does," he said softly, not wanting to upset the one person he had on his side.

"Then I suggest we take this battle of the wills back home."

Tripp opened his mouth to protest, only to have her hold up a hand. "Not because we're trying to hide anything, but because I think we'll be a hell of a lot more comfortable there."

The promise in Skylar's words as well as in her eyes was more than enough to change his mind. Although he still needed to make up with Gideon, knowing she was going to be there to soothe all their hurts when the fighting was over was a good reason to willingly give in. "Let's go."

* * * * *

Skylar hated to see her two men upset. She wanted this to end. Tonight. For good.

Silently she walked into the house with the men on her heels. It had been a long, silent ride for her and Gideon from the arena to the house they shared, but Skylar was okay with that. She needed time to think and plan.

Gideon was hurt. His words and actions told the story with the same amount of sincerity as Tripp had exuded with his apology.

There was just no easy way about this. She was going to have to step up and bring this whole sordid mess to a close. Neither of them would rest tonight until the three of them were back together.

After turning on the light, she waited until the two men entered the living room and gestured with her head to the couch. "Sit. Both of you."

Gideon and Tripp exchanged startled looks but didn't budge. Bad moves on both their parts. "I wasn't asking."

Tripp frowned. "When the hell did you become so bossy?"

"When I realized letting the two of you deal with this shit wasn't going to work."

She waited to see if they would call her bluff. She wasn't the type to take control, but this was the one time she was more than willing to try. But if they totally refused, she didn't really have a plan B. She only hoped they didn't realize it.

Gideon shrugged his shoulders at Tripp's look of disbelief and took a seat on the far end of the couch. With a muttered curse, Tripp followed suit, sitting on the other end.

"Thank you."

"This is never going to—" Gideon began, but Skylar was done listening to him.

She held up her hand to silence the onslaught of his words. "I've listened to the two of you go at it for two days now, and I'm done. It's my time to have the floor. I think I deserve it, don't you?"

Her comment sent off a flurry of "Of courses" and "Yeses" from the two men, which suited her just fine. "Good. Tripp, what you did was idiotic, cold and borderline cowardly. To sum up, your behavior sucked. Big time."

"Damn straight it did," Gideon muttered under his breath, but not low enough to go unheard or spare him a scathing look from Skylar.

Did he really think this was going to be all about Tripp? "And Gideon…"

"What?" The smug look of satisfaction slid from his face as he turned startled eyes her way.

"You're acting like a child. A big, pouting, woe-is-me child."

Wide-eyed, he pointed to Tripp who was grinning widely. "He's the one—"

"Yes, he is." Gideon didn't need to finish his sentence for Skylar to comprehend the gist of it. "But he's also the man who jerked you off not a good two days ago."

Tripp's snort of amusement earned him a level look, which caused his smile to drop instantaneously. At least one person was taking her serious.

Brows raised, she glanced back at Gideon, who was frowning now more than ever. "I know you, Gideon, and there's no way in hell you'd have let him do that if you didn't still care. Right?"

He crossed his arms, stubbornly refusing to answer, so she tried again. "Right?"

"Right," he admitted sullenly. "But caring isn't enough."

That's where he was wrong. Smiling, she sat down on his lap and brushed his hands aside. "Caring is always enough."

Now that she'd finally told them how she felt, she was ready to move on to Phase Two of her plan.

"Gideon, kiss me." For the first time since they'd been home, he smiled and did as she requested, no questions asked. Taking her face in his hands, he lightly brushed his mouth across hers before parting her lips with his tongue and exploring her mouth. His slow, drugging, addictive kiss sent her heart dancing in her chest.

With a shaky breath she pulled away and rested her forehead against his briefly before turning her attention to the other apple of her eye. Moving off Gideon's lap, she crawled the few inches toward Tripp, and whispered, "Tripp, kiss me."

Her lips, still warm and moist from kissing Gideon, were taken hungrily under Tripp's. Where Gideon had been soft and sweet like a light spring rain, Tripp's kiss was fierce and overwhelming like a wild thunderstorm. Both kisses had her pulse racing and her body aching for more.

She pulled back reluctantly and ran her tongue over her tingling lips. "Now kiss each other."

"Sky..."

She placed her finger over Gideon's mouth, silencing him. "Kiss him, Gideon. Not to prove a point. Not to win a fight. Kiss him for the same reason you kiss me. Because you love him."

Gideon stared at her hard for a moment then rose from the couch and turned his back to them. Disappointment filled her as she watched him close his eyes and breathe in deep and unsteady. She could see he was waging a battle inside, and it was anyone's guess as to who the victor would be.

For a few painfully long seconds she wondered if he was going to refuse her request. She prepared for heartbreak while hanging on to hope by a thin thread. Then to her utter delight, he spun around and walked toward Tripp. Reaching out, he grabbed the other's man arm, pulled him up and kissed him.

The fierceness of the act had her gasping as much as Tripp. The other man seemed shocked by Gideon's boldness, but Tripp wasn't as opposed as she thought he might be. To her delight, he allowed Gideon to control the movements as the other man plundered his mouth, displaying not only the love she'd insisted on, but also his hurt and anger.

There was nothing sexier than seeing the two of them being intimate. When Tripp kissed Gideon earlier today, Skylar had wanted to cheer, now she just wanted to moan. No longer able to just be a spectator in this show she dropped to her knees beside them. She had some kissing of her own to do.

Unfortunately her actions had them pulling apart in surprise. Smiling wickedly, she reached up between the two of them and stroked her hand over their zippers. "No, you two keep busy up there while I get busy down here."

Gideon needed no further encouragement and immediately returned his attention to Tripp. While they were otherwise occupied, she unfastened Tripp's trousers, pushed them down to his thighs and released his cock into her hands. His rapidly hardening erection responded quickly to her caresses and was soon standing at attention.

It was a sight that at one time she thought she'd never have the pleasure of seeing again. Unable to resist the call of her inner siren, she leaned forward and swiped her tongue over the crown, smiling when he groaned in reaction.

Although it almost killed her, she moved on to Gideon and she treated him to the same erotic handling. The power she felt was a heady experience. Sitting back on her haunches she started at the purely sexual visual before her. Two hard, long, eager cocks awaited her. What a lucky, lucky girl she was.

Licking her lips, she moved back to her knees and grasped their cocks, one in each hand, and began to slowly stroke them. Her mouth salivated at the smorgasbord of delectable treats at her very fingertips. The only problem was where to start first.

There just was no wrong choice here.

Acting on instinct, she leaned toward Tripp and opened her mouth, engulfing the head of his cock in one fell swoop. Skylar moaned as his familiar flavor permeated her senses once more and took him deep inside her mouth. His answering groan was all the thanks she needed to set her rhythm of hard, long thrusts. Not wanting to be an ungracious host, she slid her hand up and down Gideon's cock in tune to the same pace with which she sucked Tripp.

After a few key strokes of both her hand and her mouth, she switched, taking Gideon's cock between her lips as she worked Tripp over with her hand. Then she became inspired. If one cock was delicious, two would taste divine.

This had to be a new all-time record. Skylar had only been touching his cock for about a minute and he was ready to blow. Gideon wasn't sure if it was from the expert way she was sucking him, the way her hand felt squeezing the life from his stiff shaft, or Tripp's lips devouring his own. Either way, his balls were tight and ready to spill.

Try as he might, he could no longer deny he wanted Tripp back in their lives, but that didn't mean he wasn't skittish as a newborn colt. Still, life went on. He couldn't keep waiting for the bad to come. He might miss out on the good if he did. And this was good. Real good.

Her hot little mouth had him groaning at the intensity of it all. Breaking his kiss with Tripp, he glanced down to watch Skylar taking him deep in her mouth once more. She looked beyond sexy, her mouth stuffed with his dick and her hand caressing Tripp's. His dirty little princess, all sexy and sinful, and all theirs.

As if sensing his intense stare, Skylar pulled back and looked up at him, her mouth glistened in the sexiest of ways. "Closer. I need you two closer."

"Baby, I don't think we can move closer."

"Sure you can." She gently tugged on their dicks until they stepped together in the direction she wanted. If he thought they were close before, it was nothing compared to the way they were standing now, hip to hip, but facing at an angle toward one another.

"Be careful, honey," Tripp teased. "I have plans for them later."

"You can have them later, right now, they're mine."

The feral look in her eyes pleased Gideon to no end. It was about time she was able to stake her claim with the both of them. Ever since Tripp left, he had taken control of their relationship. And although he knew she enjoyed submitting to his every sexual whim, this side of her was sexy as hell. It delighted him almost as much as Tripp's look of astonishment at her action.

His laughter quickly turned into a groan when Skylar pressed the head of his cock against Tripp's. Amazingly, he somehow skipped this scenario in all the many ways he'd imagined the three of them together.

Hungrily he watched Skylar as she swiped her tongue across their touching crowns. Pressed together, they were far too thick to enter her mouth smoothly, but she gave it a hell of shot.

The combination of Tripp's cock rubbing against his own and Skylar's hot, wet mouth put him into sensation overload. The three of them together, pleasing and pleasuring each other was everything he'd once hoped they could have.

Groaning, Gideon wrapped his hand around Tripp's waist to steady himself. He was a mere mortal, he couldn't imagine how he was going to be able to come this close to paradise and live to tell about it.

"Fuck, Skylar, I don't know how much more I can take." Tripp's words echoed his own thoughts. If Gideon thought he'd been on the edge before, he was teetering on one foot at this point.

Skylar released the two men and sat back on her heels, staring up at them with a satisfied little grin. "This is my show, boys. It's time to adjourn to the bedroom."

Gideon had no arguments with her. After helping her to her feet, Tripp and he pulled their pants back up but left them undone. There was no point in buttoning something that was just going to be unbuttoned in a minute. Together they made their way down the hallway to the bedroom with Skylar walking in front of them, swishing her hips in the most provocative of ways.

As they neared the room, Tripp reached out and took Gideon's hand, a move that both surprised and pleased him. He glanced over at the other man, not sure what to make of Tripp's actions or the small smile on his face.

"So how long are we going to continue letting her think she's in charge?" Tripp asked in a mock whisper.

"Until we've all come at least twice."

"Sounds like a plan to me."

Right now anything sounded damn good to Gideon as long as he got to come. When they entered the bedroom, Skylar made a beeline for the stereo and turned on her favorite R&B mixed CD. Flashing them a come-hither look, she moved to the bed where she sat down and crossed her legs.

"Undress," she ordered, swaying slowly to the beat of the music pouring out of the speakers.

"All right." Gideon brought his hand to his shirt hem but was stopped cold by Skylar's next words.

"I meant each other."

Gideon was caught off guard by her order, but also intrigued.

"Wouldn't it be quicker if we just undressed ourselves?" Tripp asked.

"This isn't the arena, ice man. Not everything good is fast. Take your time, learn each other's bodies then come fill mine."

Damn, Gideon loved the way her dirty little mind worked.

"You want it slow?" Tripp asked.

Skylar smiled seductively. "Slow and sexy."

"As you wish." Tripp turned to Gideon. "Take off your glasses and kick off your shoes then come here."

Mouth dry, Gideon did as Tripp asked. When he neared the other man, Tripp surprised him by stepping back and turning Gideon until his back was toward Tripp and Gideon was facing Skylar. He could feel the other man's bulge pressing into his ass, which set off a new slew of sexual shivers racing across his spine. "What are you doing?"

"Giving the lady a show."

Tripp slipped his hands around Gideon's waist and took hold of the hem of his shirt. "Lift your arms," he ordered softly.

Gideon was helpless to disobey. When he raised his arms, Tripp swept his shirt off and tossed it to the floor. Instead of moving directly to his pants, Tripp brought his hands back to Gideon's waist and began to sway behind him, moving Gideon's hips along with his own to the rhythm of the beat.

Ever-so slowly Tripp began to rub his hand over Gideon's newly bared skin. The power of speech eluded Gideon. All he could do was feel. Closing his eyes, he surrendered himself to Tripp's tender touch. It was everything he'd ever wanted, hoped for and needed, and more than worth the wait.

"Is this slow enough for you, princess?"

"Oh yeah." Skylar's voice sounded as aroused as Gideon felt. "Maybe too slow."

"You want to see some goods?" Tripp's hand went to Gideon's waist and began to slowly ease down the band of his boxers.

"Yes."

"Let me see what I can arrange." Tripp slipped his hand in the front of Gideon's boxers and cupped his straining erection. Gideon caught his breath and trembled beneath the warm fingers tormenting him in the sweetest of ways. His cock, already hard and aching, begged for release. "Oh yes. You're going to want to see this."

"Tease." Her voice came out husky and her eyes bled through with need.

Gideon couldn't agree more.

"Isn't this what you wanted?" Tripp removed his hand and placed it on Gideon's hips. "Say pretty please if you want to see more."

Skylar licked her lips, her eyes riveted to Gideon's groin. "Please. Pretty please."

Gideon's head was swimming and he felt weak in the knees. He didn't know who Tripp was tormenting more—him or Skylar. But he didn't think it would hurt to add his own two cents to it. "Yes. Pretty please."

"Hmmm." Tripp lightly bit his shoulder. The dominant move made Gideon want to do whatever Tripp demanded. "You want out of these pants, baby?"

"Yes. God yes."

"Since the two of you asked so nicely." Tripp pushed Gideon's pants and boxers down at the same time, freeing Gideon's erection from its stifling confines. But it didn't remain free for long. Tripp gripped Gideon's cock in his hand and began to stroke him. "I think you're right, Skylar. Slow is so much better."

Tripp's uninhibited caresses were Gideon's undoing. His vow to remain aloof flew out the window under the onslaught of sensations.

"Gideon." Skylar's voice had him dragging his attention reluctantly away from Tripp's talented hand on his cock.

"Yes." The word was barely audible.

"Undress Tripp. But not slow. Not slow at all."

Chapter Eight

Tripp was utterly and completely amused at Skylar's abrupt about-face. "What happened to slow and sexy?"

"I don't think my blood pressure could handle any more teasing."

"Spoilsport."

"I'd say," Gideon spoke slowly, as if he were coming out of trance. "I was looking forward to testing the limits of Tripp's control."

Wow. Something told Tripp he wouldn't handle it as well as Gideon did. "I think Skylar has a very good point. Undress me quickly."

"Who's the spoilsport now?" she teased, coming to her feet. "Let's make this fun for everyone involved. For every item he takes off you, I'll take something off as well. Two for the price of one."

"Hmmm, sounds interesting." Gideon caught Tripp's stroking hand, forcing him to stop.

Pity. He was really enjoying making Gideon come undone. Just knowing that with a single touch he could make the normally sedate man his willing slave was power of the highest order.

"I hope so. I'll even up the ante. Feel free to go as slow or as fast as you want, but keep in mind, the longer you take to undress Tripp, the longer it will take for us to go further," Skylar teased with a hint of promise in her tone.

Tripp, intrigued, asked, "How much further are we talking?"

"I seem to recall you making a pseudo-promise of stuffing me full the other night. How about we put your plan into action?"

Gideon seemed pretty hip on the plan because he immediately turned toward Tripp and began to pull his sweater off. He wasn't sure if it was deliberate or not, but when Gideon removed the pullover, his fingers trailed up Tripp's abdomen and chest, causing Tripp to suck in his breath audibly. The garment was soon tossed to the side and in unison they both turned toward Skylar.

"Your turn, princess."

She smiled seductively and grabbed the hem of her jade green turtleneck and pulled it off in one fell swoop. Her breasts were covered in a provocative demi-cup bra that showed off all her assets.

"Bra too," Gideon urged huskily.

"He only took off one thing," she pointed out with an evil little grin.

But Gideon wouldn't be persuaded. Tripp knew he liked the other man for a reason. "He's bare on top so you need to be as well."

She pouted a bit but reached behind her and unhooked the bra, letting it fall from her body. Her breasts were flushed and the raspberry tips looked delicious enough to eat. "Check."

"I do believe it's our turn," Tripp urged, impatient to see all Skylar had to offer.

"Right you are. But first take off your shoes. Both of you." Acting quickly, Tripp and Skylar removed their shoes, neither one wanting to halt the play.

When they were done, Gideon stepped in front of Tripp and stared into his eyes. The lust and that shone there heated Tripp's inflamed passion even more. Gideon quickly pushed Tripp's trousers down over his hips, taking his briefs as well. Seeing the other man kneeling at his feet as Gideon pulled the pants down his legs had Tripp imagining all kinds of scenarios. He stepped out of the discarded clothing and kicked them away.

They didn't even need to ask this time. Skylar began shimmying out of her pants and panties, kicking them off within moments. Turning, she crawled to the middle of the bed and settled herself comfortably with her arms behind her for leverage and her legs curved at the knee.

She was so beautiful Tripp didn't know where to begin. It felt as if it had been a lifetime since he'd seen her this way instead of mere months. He felt like a randy schoolboy with his first girl, and when she rolled over onto her knees and presented her upturned cheeks to him, he almost expired on the spot. "Don't be shy. Tell me what you want."

"You buried in my pussy while Gideon fucks me in the ass."

"I love a woman who knows what she wants," Tripp teased. He dipped his finger into her snug sex and coated it with her sweet dew before moving up to the tight ring of her anus. "Do you take her here often?"

"As often as possible." Gideon grinned wickedly. "Lucky for me, it's possible very often."

"Lucky us," Tripp corrected, worming his finger deeper inside her.

"No, what's lucky for us is our sweet little princess comes, and comes hard from just anal penetration."

"She likes?"

"No, I love," Skylar purred, and thrust her bottom back, forcing his finger deeper within her warm passage.

"You're so fucking sexy. I could just eat you up," he growled. Tripp pulled his hand back, intending to lube a second finger to add to the first, but was stopped by Gideon's hand on his wrist.

"I do believe you've been assigned the front. The backseat is all mine."

"Selfish bastard," Tripp growled, reluctantly stepping back.

"There's always next time," Skylar promised seductively, rolling back on her bottom.

Next time. Now that was a phrase he could become used to. "I'm going to hold you to that." Tripp sat next to her and pulled her to him.

Skylar stationed a leg on either side of him and lowered her ass onto his lap. "Either you're very happy to see me, or I'm sitting on a log."

"Why can't it be both?" he teased.

As he hoped, she laughed, and he fell even deeper in love. Everything she was, everything she felt, was right there in her eyes for him to see. She was open and honest and so giving it made his heart ache. With love in his eyes, he cupped her face and kissed her with all the tenderness he felt. He loved her so much. Whether he deserved the second chance or not, he was grateful for it. Thankful for her and Gideon and the opportunity he now had to make it right once and for all.

He pulled back and whispered, "I love you."

"I love you too," she said just as soft and just as deep.

"Hey," Gideon interjected. "What am I, chopped liver?"

Skylar reached out to take his hand. "We love you too. Don't we, Tripp?"

"Yes, we do," he said sincerely. Tripp wanted this, wanted it so badly he was afraid of screwing it up. Not the actual sex part. That was easy. It was the aftercare that sent everything nose-diving into oblivion. "Very much."

"Fine then." Gideon nodded his head as if making a decision. "Proceed with the fucking."

"First condoms." Tripp would have loved nothing more than to thrust into her bareback, but it was safer for everyone concerned to do it this way. Until they were all tested. Then he would burn every condom in sight.

"Good thinking." Gideon rounded the bed and headed to the nightstand. He opened the drawer and dug around in it for a second before pulling out a box.

Skylar, on the other hand, kept herself busy driving Tripp insane with her mouth. The little vixen was grinding her wet pussy against his cock as she nibbled on his neck. "Condom. Now!" Tripp ordered. He wasn't sure how much more of her teasing he was going to be able to handle.

"I have it." Gideon came back to their side, latex in hand. "Skylar, rise up."

Tripp reached for the condom, but to his surprise, Gideon held it out of his reach. "I'll put it on you."

"Yo…okay." This was a first, but then again, Tripp was sure he would be experiencing a lifetime of firsts with the two of them.

Gideon grasped his cock, stroking him a few times. Tripp lifted his hips in reaction, their earlier jerk-off session still fresh in mind.

"Later," Gideon said with promise, giving the crown a little lick. He laughed at Tripp's moan, and then expertly placed the latex over the tip and rolled the condom into place.

"How's that?" Gideon asked as he gave a final stroke before standing and backing a few steps away.

A stroke that had Tripp fighting his need to come with everything inside him. The worst part was the bastard knew exactly what his touch was doing to him.

"Fuck, man." Tripp groaned. "You're killing me."

"You haven't felt anything yet," Skylar promised as she grasped his straining cock in her hand and lined it up with her moist opening. The feel of her heated sex against the tip of his cock was all the encouragement Tripp needed. He pressed his hips up as she slowly sank down, engulfing him in her warm sheath.

It took more than one thrust to sink him fully into her tight sex, but Tripp had no complaints, it was a hell of a descent. Skylar let out a low, deep-seated moan as she took his length. Her gaze stayed locked on his the entire time, connecting Tripp to her in the most intimate of ways.

"You feel so good, baby." His voice was rough, but his touch was gentle as he lifted her up then brought her down firmly, driving his cock to the hilt inside her. "So fucking good."

"So, so good," Skylar moaned. Her pussy clenched around his cock, causing him to cry out. He was one with her again. Inside his own personal nirvana, and it was heaven.

Tripp could have died buried deep inside her and he would have been a happy man. He was home. At last.

"You're going to have to use a bit more force with this one, Tripp," Gideon called out, dragging him back to the matter at hand. "During your absence I discovered our Skylar prefers a hint of pain with her loving."

Did she now?

"You don't say." His nails dug into her bottom as he worked her up and down his shaft. "Is this what she likes, Gideon?"

"Oh yeah." Gideon brought his hands around Skylar's front and took her beaded nipples between his fingers. "See how hard these little berries are? They only become this way when she's really turned-on."

"Is that right, baby?" He pumped his hips up in time with his words, fucking her harder, deeper than before.

"God yes." Skylar held on for dear life as he powered into her. "Just like that. Fuck me, Tripp, please. I need to come."

"No coming for you, baby, until Gideon's buried inside your tight little ass." The thought of the two of them fucking her, being buried inside her was making him insane with lust. Just knowing a thin membrane of skin would separate him from Gideon was something he couldn't even yet contemplate.

"Then fuck me, Gideon," Skylar begged, her voice filled with want and need. "Please don't make me wait."

A woman after his own heart. "You heard the lady, Gideon. Fuck her."

It took a second for her and Tripp to rearrange their bodies. They were in the same position, but farther up on the bed so there'd be plenty of room for all. Of course once she climbed back on his cock she just had to take it for another test drive.

The bed dipped as Gideon joined them. The feel of his hand stroking over her flank was nothing compared to his words.

"Lie forward," Gideon order huskily.

She did as he asked, excited beyond belief at what was to come. Skylar's body trembled as Gideon spread her cheeks apart. "What a pretty little pink star just begging for attention."

She felt on display for him, knowing he was looking at her in the most intimate of ways. One of his hard, thick fingers ran along her seam, touching her, stroking her, but not yet penetrating. The teasing only made her want it all the more. When he pulled his finger away, she was filled with disappointment, but it didn't last long because he moved even closer to her and touched her in a more intimate way than he ever had before.

"Ohhh…" she groaned. She had mentally readied herself for the brisk gel, but nothing could have equipped her for the warm flicker of Gideon's tongue. "God…what are you doing?"

Gideon rose up a bit to bite her lightly on her upturned cheek. "Preparing you."

If this was his idea of preparation, they were going to have to do this often. Skylar closed her eyes and gave herself up to the multiple sensations rocking her body. She was breathless with desire. Gideon's lapping at her rosette as Tripp was buried in her pussy—it was more than she could have ever imagined and yet just a prelude of what was to come.

"Fuck," Tripp groaned.

Startled, Skylar looked down at his pleasured-filled face. "What?"

"He's...he's toying with my balls...with his tongue. Fuck."

"Like it, do you?" Skylar rocked forward on his cock, enjoying the way his face reacted to the dual sensations.

"God do I."

Before she could comment again, Gideon's tongue was once again lapping at her back door.

If this felt anything like what Tripp had experienced, she could agree with his sentiments. Gideon wasn't just licking though. His wicked tongue pierced her rosette more than once during his preparation of her. She was soon rocking back and forth between them, causing Tripp to groan again in delight. Gideon gave one final swipe of his tongue and moved back.

"I think you're ready."

That was putting it lightly. "Hmm, more than."

She heard rather than saw him ready himself, and in less time than it took to imagine the act that was about to happen, he was behind her, sheathed and ready. She moaned aloud at the feel of his hard, slick cock pressing against her entrance. Her moan turned to a gasp as he pressed forward and the crown of his cock pressed past her barriers. Her muscles stretched to accept his large shaft.

"Jesus..." she moaned as she bowed her back and pressed her ass higher in the air. She knew she should stay still, but she just couldn't.

"Baby, don't move," Gideon gasped. "No matter how much I want to bury my cock in your ass, we're going to have to take this slow. Understand?"

"Yes." Skylar dug her fingers dug into Tripp's shoulders and held on for dear life as Gideon pushed slowly inside. They'd had anal sex countless times, but it was never like this, so intense she felt as if she'd split in two. An overwhelming sense of fullness overcame her and for a brief moment she wondered if she would be able to take them both. Biting her lip, she held as still as possible. She was grateful he took his time pressing into her channel, but it also felt as if he were extending the inevitable with his caution.

"Breathe, baby." Tripp rubbed his hand over her back.

Breathe. Hell, she could barely think. "I...I..."

"Maybe I should pull out." The words were grated, as if it took everything in Gideon to offer them.

"No." That was the last thing she wanted, especially since they were so close to fulfilling her fantasy. "Don't stop. Deeper. Please. Deeper."

"Are you sure?"

"Fuck! She's sure, man. Keep going."

Skylar couldn't have agreed or worded it any better. She wanted this. To be possessed by both of them at the same time, in this manner. No, wanted wasn't a strong enough word. She needed it. "Gideon, please. Fuck me."

He needed no further encouragement. With a guttural growl, he gripped her hips tight in his hands and seated himself fully inside her. His sudden move had them all crying out in pleasure.

"Fuck, man. She's tight," Gideon exclaimed in wonder.

"Almost too tight," Tripp added. He tightened his hold on her waist. "Skylar?"

She didn't answer. She couldn't. Skylar felt lightheaded. Filled. This was everything she'd dreamt of and yet so much more intense than she could have possibly fathomed.

"Say something, baby," Gideon spoke softly at her ear. His encouraging voice pulled her back from the headspace she'd slipped into. "Anything."

"Something, anything. I need..." She didn't know if she could say any more, but it wasn't necessary. He knew.

"Okay, baby, I'm going to move." Following his earlier command she held herself still, letting him control the pace. Gideon began to slowly fuck her ass. Each measured stroke caused an erotic chain reaction, forcing her pussy to glide up and down Tripp's cock.

Being filled by the two of them had been heavenly, but this sent her into outer space.

They fucked as if in tune with one another, one plunging as the other retreated. A steady, simple rhythm as choreographed as any ballroom dance, except wilder and dirtier. Skylar was unable to do anything except lie between the two of them and enjoy the wicked ride. Without a doubt, she knew it wouldn't be a long ride though. It felt way too good to last very long.

Skylar's body felt more alive now than it ever had before. It was as if all of her senses were hyperaware. She could feel the ebb and flow of their cocks inside her. Because they were separated by only a thin barrier, she experienced a level of sensation she never had before. The friction was so incredible she felt as if she might fly apart at the seams.

"This is so good it should be illegal," Gideon murmured, brushing his lips against her shoulder.

"It probably is," she agreed, losing herself in the moment. The way they were positioned forced her clit to rub against Tripp's cock, not that she needed the extra sensation to go over, but it was a welcome bonus. Her body quivered as her sensitive button was manipulated thrust after powerful thrust.

"I'm not going to...last much longer," Tripp gritted out through clenched teeth. He shoved his hips up, slamming into her from the bottom as Gideon powered into her from above.

It was a feeling Skylar echoed. Two cocks were so much better than one. "Don't stop. So close. So close."

"Come for me, baby." Tripp grunted, pumping into her with all his might.

With a savage growl, Gideon powered into her over and over, forcing her to ride the two of them at a backbreaking pace.

"God…yes…yes…" Skylar screamed as the strength of her orgasm stole through like a thief in the night. Her pussy clutched down on Tripp, which sent the groaning man over seconds before Gideon. Gideon's nails dug into her hips as he gave a final thrust, crying her name. His cries weren't the only sounds in the room.

"Yeah. Right there. Right there." Gideon's added encouragement and pleasure only increased her intensity. "Ahhh…"

Skylar sobbed as the intense climax robbed her of her will, her sense and her ability to do anything but to mutter, "I love you," over and over until the exhaustion overtook her body.

* * * * *

Gideon didn't want to open his eyes. Last night had gone so well he was afraid with morning's arrival denial and harsh words would come, and he didn't think he could take that again. Everything he'd ever hoped and dreamed for was in his grasp, and the idea it all could crumble at a single moment made him reluctant to face the day.

Despite all of Tripp's well-rehearsed words, Gideon was leery of what was to come. He wished he could be as all-forgiving as Skylar, but he just wasn't built that way. He needed proof, he needed time and he needed Tripp to show instead of tell. Unfortunately the only way he could find out if Tripp was a man of his word was to go on faith and open his eyes, but that was easier said than done.

Then again, Gideon wasn't a coward. And he wasn't in this alone. If Tripp was going to flip out again, it would be best if he did it while Skylar still slept. Gideon wasn't the only one wearing his heart on his sleeve for Tripp.

He was a man. He could do this. Opening his eyes, he blinked and looked around. His fears wouldn't be faced just yet. Both Skylar and Tripp were still asleep. Spooned behind her, Tripp looked peaceful. One hand lay under his head while the other cupped Skylar's breast. He'd always been a bit of a breast man.

Gideon reached out and brushed the hair out of her face. Even while she slept she had a small smile gracing her lips. They'd loved her long and hard last night to the point of exhaustion, but she reveled in every minute of it. Her happiness was paramount to him, even above his own, but at the same time he considered himself a guardian of sorts of her heart.

It was up to him to protect her as much as possible, even if it was from one of the men she loved. Gideon would never forgive himself if he allowed his passion to overrule his common sense and let Tripp hurt her again. One of them had to be strong. One of them had to play the part of bad guy, and there was no question in his mind exactly which one of them it would be.

As if sensing his intense stare, Tripp opened his eyes. Gideon braced himself for the look of revulsion he was sure to come, but to his surprise there was none. An easy smile played at the corner of Tripp's mouth as he rose on one arm.

"Morning," he said softly. Tripp leaned forward as if to kiss him, but Gideon pulled back. He wasn't ready for that.

In silent communication he glanced pointedly at Skylar then toward the door. Frowning, Tripp nodded his head and rose carefully from the bed, grabbing his boxers on the way out of the room. Vigilant not to disturb Skylar's slumber, Gideon eased out of the bed. After putting his glasses on, he silently made his way over to the bureau and pulled out a clean pair of shorts. He slipped them on then went into the living room where Tripp was waiting.

"Morning breath?"

Gideon frowned. "No—"

"Yeah, I didn't think so." Tripp ran his hands through his thrashed blond hair ruefully. He looked weary and completely different than he had just a few minutes earlier in bed. "You didn't do it, did you?"

"Do what?"

"Look in my eyes to see disgust or shame. My eyes were the first eyes you saw this morning and they were filled with the love and gratitude I said they would be, yet it still isn't enough for you, is it?"

Gideon realized the truth of his words. The last time they been together Tripp had been the one to pull away, but this morning it had been him who was unsure of where their future lay. With a heavy sigh, he sat down on the couch. Despite the way it might appear, he was tired of fighting.

Tripp crouched down in front of him and placed his hand on Gideon's thigh. Gideon looked away, suddenly uncomfortable. This was too close for comfort and felt far more intimate than anything they'd done in the last few days. Odd as it was, he could share Skylar with Tripp, but when it was just the two of them, he was lost. Especially right now when he didn't even have his anger to hold on to.

"You need to decide, Gideon. You either love me enough to try, or hate me enough to make me leave. Either way, the ball's in your court. But I think you know if I had a chance to do it all over again, I would." Tripp stood, obviously finished with everything he was going to say.

Gideon grabbed Tripp's hand to stop him from leaving. "Would you do everything differently?"

"No." A ghost of a smile flickered across his lips. "Not everything."

"Would you play the game again?"

"Yes, but I would have asked better questions so I wouldn't have ended up so drunk. What about you, would you have played?"

"Yes." Hell yes was more like it. Until that night he'd had no idea how he'd come out to his friends or be able to reveal his feeling to Tripp. Although the next morning was one of the worst in his lifetime, that night was one of the best.

"What would be some of the things you'd say?" Tripp asked.

"I'd say…I've never been as scared as I am right now. I never stopped loving you." Gideon rose and stood until he and Tripp were face-to-face. "And I'll never forgive myself if I let you walk out the door."

"I'm not going anywhere. Ever again."

He pulled Tripp into his arms. The other man moved willingly toward him and they hugged tight. There was nothing overtly sexual about the embrace, but it was almost the closest he'd felt to Tripp in a long, long time.

"I'll drink to that," Skylar said softly from the doorway. She stood there in one of Gideon's T-shirts, hair mussed, and if he wasn't mistaken, a slight sheen of moisture in her eyes. Of course he was sure if he asked her she would say they were tears of joy. The two men simultaneously held out their arms and she ran forward. They clasped her in their embrace. It felt so right, the three of them standing in the living room together. Almost as if he could imagine them like this in the years to come.

Gideon knew they had a long, bumpy road ahead of them. He forgave Tripp, truly he did, but forgiving and forgetting were two different things. Forgetting would take time, but for Tripp and Skylar, he had all the time in the world.

DOUBLE DARE
ಸಿ

Acknowledgement

☙

Dedicated to Liz, my heterosexual lifemate who took my three-year rule and threw it back in my face. I don't think I've ever told you how much I'm grateful for you doing that. Consider this a thank you and feel free to say you told me so.

Trademarks Acknowledgement

☙

The author acknowledges the trademarked status and trademark owners of the following wordmarks mentioned in this work of fiction:

Barbie and Ken: Mattel, Inc.

CSI: CBS Broadcasting Inc.

Finger-lickin' good: KFC Corporation

Hershey Kisses: Hershey Chocolate & Confectionery Corporation

Hopalong Cassidy: U. S. Television Office, Inc.

Juicy Couture: Travis Jeans, Inc.

Scrabble: Hasbro, Inc.

Sports Illustrated: Time Warner Inc.

Star Wars: Lucasfilm Entertainment Company Ltd.

The Matrix: Warner Bros. Entertainment, Inc.

Double Dare

Chapter One

If it was the last thing she did, Paige Reyes was going to kill Shane Oxley. She didn't care if it was his birthday. He was going down—by her hands. Thanks to her medical training and *CSI*, she knew many ways to hurt a man without leaving a hint of evidence and she couldn't wait to try out her newfound knowledge.

Revenge was sweeter than chocolate.

As if he could sense her homicidal thoughts, Shane glanced at her from across the room and smiled.

The bastard.

No, bastard was too good of a way to describe the cold-hearted blackmailer. Actually, the more she thought of it, the more Paige realized there wasn't a word in the English language that aptly described Shane. No word sick or twisted enough to rest upon his evil head. He was lower than low. The devil incarna—

"Something tells me you're not thinking happy birthday thoughts." The teasing words of Gideon Foley pulled her back from the abyss of her bloodthirsty fantasies.

"I'm sure I can somehow manage to carve happy birthday on his forehead before I dose him with gasoline," she said, turning her back on the object of her disdain to look into the kind gray eyes of her dear friend. As usual, the sable-haired man with his teasing ways managed to make her smile without even trying. "Tell me, Shakespeare, will you be my alibi?"

"Sadly, no."

"Damn." She snapped her fingers in mock outrage. "It was worth a try."

"Come on, squirt, it can't be all that bad. You wouldn't be here if it was."

That showed what he knew. The truth of the matter was, Paige wouldn't be here if she didn't love her brother Perry so much. If it weren't for him and the scholarship Shane's family sponsored, Paige would have told Shane exactly where he could put his birthday cake. But she wouldn't do anything to risk her brother's future and Shane knew it.

Which was why, no matter how much she might hate it, she had come to the little get-together. The one good thing about showing up to the party was the knowledge everyone would be here tonight. She couldn't remember the last time the seven of them were together, but they were all supposed to come tonight.

They were college friends who had managed to beat the odds and remain close long after they collected their diplomas. Seven oddballs who, by all rights, had nothing in common with one another on the surface, yet they somehow managed to forge a bond that outweighed all those differences. There was Bev Navarro, the Filipino brainiac of the group with the not-so-secret crush on Holden Lancaster, the party boy. And Skylar, the pretty, pretty princess who could never decide until recently whether she was in love with Gideon the poet, or Tripp Kowalski the jock. That left Shane, the self-appointed ringleader with more money than God, to round out the group.

So far Bev was the only one who hadn't arrived, but there was no doubt in Paige's mind everyone would eventually come, as decreed by Shane, for his party. He was the first one to turn thirty and in his annoying, controlling, highhanded manner, he demanded one night together. Just the old group — like old times. No dates. No excuses.

He'd been adamant about it being a gift-free event, which, in her case, was wise on his part. Paige sincerely doubted he wanted a bullet with his name engraved on it.

"Well..." Gideon persisted when she didn't immediately answer him.

"Well, what?" she asked, slightly confused by the question.

But if there was any confusion it was apparently only on her side because Gideon picked up right where he left off, deep in her business. "If it's so bad, why are you here?"

As much as she wanted to rail against the injustice of it all, Paige kept mum about the hows and whys. She didn't want their friends to have to pick a side, especially if there was an off chance they wouldn't take hers. "Let's just say I have my reasons."

"And are they all devious?"

"A good portion." She smiled. He knew her so well.

"Look, I don't know what Shane did. Despite my constant picking the last three years, you've yet to spill. And that's fine. We're all entitled to our little secrets, but you have to admit, if it weren't for him, none of us would even know one another."

Gideon had her there. Somehow or other Shane could be credited with being the man behind the curtain in all their friendships. If it weren't for him, she would have never met any of these people in the room with her now, and for that she was grateful. But just that. "Fine. In his entire miserable life he did one good thing."

"I'm sure he's done more than one."

"Really?" Paige tilted her head to the side and furrowed her brow. "Funny, but I can't think of anything else."

"Right..." Gideon peered at her in the quizzical way only he could, seeing directly through her bullshit, as usual. That was the problem with knowing someone for a decade, they saw past the lies and false pretenses. "Not a single thing?"

She didn't want to talk about this. Not even a little. "Subject change. Have you written anything lately?"

"Nice try, squirt, but no dice." Gideon reached out and pulled Paige against him, turning her around until she was facing Shane once more. "Look at him and tell me after all these years, the only thing you feel for him is hatred."

Shane was once more involved in a conversation with Holden, the host of this little shindig, allowing Paige to look at him unaware. It had been two years since she last saw Shane, but appearance wise he hadn't changed much. He was still as devastatingly handsome as he'd been when they first met in chemistry class. His thick black hair was a bit longer than it was back then, edging his strong jawline like a handcrafted picture frame. The big difference between the last time and now was he walked unassisted, something she knew he feared he'd never do again after his car accident four years ago.

Despite everything that had transpired between them, she couldn't stop the sense of pride that filled her at the sight of him standing tall and proud, unaided by a cane. Even back then she knew he would walk again. Shane was too bullheaded not to.

Then again, he was bullheaded about many things, which was why they were in the predicament they were in now. "I'll make you a deal, Shakespeare."

"Okay."

"If you let it go, I'll pretend I don't notice the way you're using Skylar as a shield to keep Tripp away."

Gideon's hands dropped from her arms, giving Paige the opportunity to face him again. Gone was the easygoing grin he'd been sprouting like wings earlier and in its place was the cool mask of indifference Paige had tried to perfect for tonight's festivities. His was better than hers though, making her wonder, and not for the first time, what was going on between him, Tripp and Skylar.

"I don't know what you're talking about."

"Of course you don't." She smiled in a sweet and mocking way. "And I'm going to let your little lie slide, just as you're going to let your question to me slide. Deal?"

"You're ruthless."

"See, now I've been saying the same thing for the last three years but do you think she'd listen to me?" Paige's smile slowly slid from her lips as Shane spoke in an amused tone from behind her. "Tell me, Gideon. What's your secret?"

"It's simple really," Paige said without turning around. "I don't hate him." And without saying another word, she bypassed Gideon and walked away, all without turning around to face the man who'd broken her heart. Maybe, just maybe, if she kept a wide-enough berth around him, she might survive the night with the remaining pieces of her heart intact.

It took everything out of Shane not to yank Paige back to him and throw her over his shoulder. The only thing stopping him from doing just that was the knowledge he wasn't walking out of this house alone. After months of plotting and planning, he was finally ready for her. And the little brat didn't have a clue it was coming.

"She doesn't really mean that," Gideon said.

"I know." She thought she did though, which was far more annoying. "Paige is just being Paige."

"That seemed a little stronger than her normally, umm…upfront self. Hate is a harsh word. I've never heard her say anything like that before."

"Then you don't know Paige the way I do."

"Lucky me," Gideon teased.

He didn't know the half of it. "If you say so." Shane offered the other man a carefree smile and walked away casually, all the while seething on the inside. The center of his palm tingled from his desire to lay his hand against the plump flesh of her bottom. If there was ever a person in need of a good sound spanking it was Paige.

She was a handful and she always had been. Of course that was also what attracted him to her. She was no wilting wallflower. Paige knew what she wanted and went after it, especially those things she cared the most about. Too bad he'd realized that after it was too late. On the other hand, he still had time to right his wrongs and he planned to do so tonight. Even if it meant making her hate him a little more before she admitted to loving him.

He walked over to the bar in the corner of the room and grabbed his drink from the table. All the while keeping Paige discreetly in his line of sight. The petite African-American was as beautiful as she was contrary. The new spiky, short hairstyle she sported flattered her oval face. It also added a few inches to her short frame, but it still didn't help the pint-sized terror out. What she lacked in height, however, she more than made up for with attitude.

When Shane first met Paige, he was a bit put-off by her abrasive manner. He was used to his wealth and looks getting him pretty much anything he desired, but the attributes he'd coasted on his entire life got him nowhere with the slim beauty. It wasn't until he started to give Paige attitude back that she even began to notice him, thus cementing their bickering relationship. It became a game to him, to infuriate her for fuck's sake, just to see if he could get a rise out of her. When she'd blow up, he'd win, if she was able to ignore him, she'd win. They were both so competitive that the malicious aspect of it soon faded away. Their transition from friend to frienemy was slow and shaky, but somewhere along the line the woman he loved to annoy became one of the closest friends he had.

She'd been one of the first faces he'd seen after his car accident. Paige worked in the hospital he was admitted to and, despite the rules and regulations, she had been inside the operating room with him, leaving only long enough to donate blood. The doctors refused to allow her to work on him, but she stayed anyway, just to watch over him she later said.

The fact they had downshifted so fast in their relationship from gurney guardian angel to words of hate bothered Shane more than he would ever admit. The worst part was he knew the demise in their relationship was his fault entirely. Since he was the one who put them in this situation, he was going to make sure he got them out of it as well. Whether Paige believed him or not, he loved her, and he refused to be without her for a moment longer.

He watched as the object of his thoughts stealthily made her way across the room. The second she moved away from him, she began to smile once more under what he could only assume was the largest cloud of delusion in the world. She might think she was a safe distance from him but she was wrong. Dead wrong.

He was aware of her every movement since she entered the house. Then again, there wasn't much about Paige Shane wasn't aware of. Just because she'd been avoiding him the last three years didn't mean he wasn't keeping tabs on her. He'd even gone as far as to hire a private detective to keep track of her whereabouts when she moved to Baltimore. If he couldn't be in her life on a day-to-day basis as he used to, he would be as knowledgeable about it as possible.

There was no doubt in his mind his actions were a tad out there, but he didn't regret his decisions regarding the matter for a second. If he hadn't been paying such close attention, he might have missed his opportunity with her. It was no surprise to him Perry was her Achilles' heel. The way she felt about her family was the same way some people felt about money. She'd even moved six hundred miles away to accept a job that paid more so she could help out with her brother's tuition. Medical school wasn't cheap. Not by a long shot. And Paige, like every other able-minded member of her immediate family, was doing all she could to help out the young man.

Shane was too. He arranged for Perry to receive a scholarship that would pretty much guarantee the young man a full ride, but it came with a string attached. And the string ran straight from Shane to Paige.

Using her brother was low, even for him, but Shane refused to apologize. He owed Paige too many of those already.

"Hey there, birthday boy." Bev interrupted his thoughts with her arrival, birthday candles in hand. As usual, the pretty brunette had a sunny smile on her face, but it seemed as if it was a little strained. It probably had a lot to do with the six-foot-tall radio jock staring a hole in her back. As far as Bev was concerned, Holden was pretty much up the same shit creek Shane was with Paige, and their buddy Tripp was with Gideon and Skylar, with none of the three having a paddle between them. "Are you ready for your spanking?"

"Hell yeah." Shane pulled her into his arms for a hug. "Damn, lady, you are looking good."

Bev laughed as she hugged him back before they parted. "You are such a flirt."

"That's what you love about me."

"So true." Bev glanced around the room, her gaze stuttering for a moment when it reached Holden before turning back to him. "I can't believe you pulled it off. Everyone is here."

"Was there ever any doubt?" Shane teased in a good-natured manner. "I only wish I thought of it earlier. We haven't all been together in quite some time."

"It's hard..." she hedged, making way for one of the many excuses everyone seemed to come up with over the years.

"No, we need to make the effort. We can't afford to let our friendships die out," Shane insisted. "At the end of the day, all we have is each other. I think somehow we all forgot that for a brief moment. We allowed petty differences to stand in the way of what really matters."

"And what's that?"

"That we love one another." Knowing what he did about their little group, Shane thought he had never uttered truer words. They needed each other. The tiny fractures in their group had made all their lives miserable, and it was time for it all to end. Tonight was the culmination of his hard work. He watched as Paige stood talking to Holden and realized it would soon be do or die. Thanks to him and the secret gifts he bought for the party, the stage was set. He could only hope everyone took advantage of the opportunity to mend their broken relationships. He knew he would.

"Are you ready for the cake?" Bev's question had him nodding. *Ready for my wishes too.*

"Oh yeah." He smiled. "Let's get the party started."

The sooner they lit the candles, the sooner he could get to the presents, and then the fun could really begin.

Chapter Two
೧೦

Regardless of her more-than-obvious disdain for the night's festivities, Paige reluctantly found herself joining in as the group sang *Happy Birthday* to Shane. Being the egomaniac he was, Shane stood in the place of honor at the head of the table, lapping up the attention like a cat laps cream. After the final note was bellowed, he blew out the candles amidst claps and wolf whistles.

Shane nodded his head regally, all the while gesturing with his hand for more, much to the apparent amusement of everyone else. From the way they were all acting, one might have thought he'd invented the cure for cancer instead of letting out some air.

The second the petty thought entered her mind, Paige forced it away. Not much longer, she reminded herself as she waited impatiently for him to the cut the cake. Their agreement stipulated she had to stay for an hour after the cake was cut. Then she was free to leave. As far as Paige was concerned, the hour started the second Shane picked up the knife to cut his cake. She only had fifty-eight and some change to go before she could walk out of Holden's house with her brother's scholarship in the bag.

The rowdy noise drifted into a dead silence as Bev began to pass out the cake. As bad luck would have it, Paige was seated to Shane's right, forcing her to be closer than she preferred to him. But she could deal with it. The night was almost over. The one thing making her feel marginally better was the fact she wasn't the only miserable person at the party tonight. As she looked around the table, it seemed as if everyone appeared a tad uncomfortable. In fact, she sensed a lot of weird undercurrents.

The undercurrents coming from Tripp, Skylar and Gideon was a no-brainer. During the course of their ten-year friendship, Paige had watched Skylar flit between the two men while dating mounds of others. In the past, it seemed as if the pretty blonde was never going to make up her mind about whom she wanted to be with. Then one day, out of the blue, she announced she was moving in with Gideon. From the way Tripp had been watching them all night Paige could sense he was none too pleased about the decision. The again, neither Skylar nor Gideon seemed all that happy either. They were their own twisted version of the Bermuda Triangle without a happy ending in sight.

With a begrudged look, Bev took her seat next to a grinning Holden and began to ignore the other man all over again. "So." Her words came out in a desperate rush. "What did you wish for?"

"Bev." Holden leaned toward her, eating up the space she managed to create for herself. "If he tells us what he wished for, he won't get it."

"You're going to wish you sat somewhere else if you don't move your hand."

Paige and Skylar shared a guilty look with one another. Bev had made the two of them promise not to leave her alone with Holden. And while technically she and Holden weren't by themselves, Paige knew Bev was closer than she wanted to be with him.

Two years ago, Bev took a page out of Paige's *Stupid Things to Do With Your Friends* manual and made out with Holden during a game of Seven Minutes in Heaven. Paige believed if things had ended after their allotted time, everything would have been fine. Unfortunately though, Holden made a grave error by telling Bev he hadn't really picked her name. And Bev being Bev, took his gesture as one of pity instead of one of unappeased lust and swore never to forgive him. From the way she'd been avoiding him ever since, Paige would say she was doing a damn good job.

From the way Bev squirmed in her chair, Paige could only suspect Holden was up to no good. Brat. He was no better than Shane. Perhaps it was time for her to step up and put an end to Bev's torture. The only question was, how could she do it without causing a scene or embarrassing Bev further?

"Where you going?" Holden asked in an innocent manner as Bev attempted to stand.

"Let go, you big bully."

"Actually," Shane said, interrupting before Paige could, "my wish was for all of us."

Curious as to where this was leading, Paige glanced over at Shane as Gideon spoke. "I hope it was for us to the win the lotto."

"Not exactly."

"Damn," Gideon said.

"Then what did you wish for?" Bev asked.

"In time all things will be answered." Shane rose from his seat. "I'll be right back. I have to go get the presents."

What the fuck! "Presents!" Paige couldn't stop her cry of outrage even if she wanted to. Shane had been adamant about her not bringing a present. Not that she really could have afforded a lavish gift, but she'd be damned if she was going to be the one person who didn't bring him anything. How pathetic did he think she was? "I thought you weren't accepting gifts this year. If you told me I didn't have to bring a present as some lame attempt to salvage my poor dignity or to preserve my pride, you needn't have bothered."

"The presents aren't for me, Paige. I brought them for everyone else." Shane smiled cruelly as he stared into her eyes. "And I assure you, little one, no one knows more about your pride than I."

Paige tilted her chin and met his icy cerulean gaze head-on. Fine, she was wrong, but she still refused to back down. She could be as stubborn as he was. Besides, it wasn't as if she were here of her volition. If he didn't like what she had to say, he could let her out of their deal and she would gladly walk away. A move he taught her three years ago. As if sensing her determination not to break first, Shane cursed under his breath and stormed out of the dining room.

"Pipe down, Paige," Skylar scolded. "It's the boy's birthday, for goodness sake. Retract the claws and cut him a little slack."

I'll cut him some slack, all right. "That's what's wrong with him now. Shane is so used to people treating him as if he were the crowned heir he doesn't know what to do when someone stands up to him."

"Are you willing to test your theory?" Shane dared as he entered the room once more with three gift bags of various colors and sizes.

"I should have never come." This was a mistake. A huge one. Paige tried to let go of her anger by keeping her end goal in mind. This was for Perry. Not Shane. He was just a means to an end.

"As if you had a choice. My threat wasn't an idle one."

His chilling reminder had her seething all over again. "Don't think I didn't realize that."

Fucking bast –

"So…" Tripp interrupted. "Should we all leave and come back at a better time?"

"No way. If we leave, I won't get my present." Skylar's teasing tone broke through the dark haze of Paige's fury.

"And it's all about you, isn't it, dollface?" Tripp's haunted eyes didn't quite match his mocking tone.

But if Skylar noticed she didn't let on. In her best pretty, pretty princess persona, Skylar tossed her hair over her shoulder. "Of course it is. Now gimme."

"Don't be greedy." Shane winked as he handed her a long orange bag. "You have to share."

"Who am I sharing it with?" Forever the girlie girl, Skylar glowed with pleasure at her unexpected gift.

"You're sharing with Tripp and Gideon."

Her smile quickly melted away as she cast a not-so-discreet glance between the two men with whom she had to share her present. Neither of them looked any happier than she did. And as horrible as it was, Paige felt a small measure of satisfaction at her friend's crestfallen expression. Everything was fine and good when Shane was meddling in her life, but now that the shoe was on the other foot, no one seemed amused. Somehow Paige doubted Skylar felt the need to cut Shane some slack now.

In the midst of her gloating, Gideon stood and walked to the liquor cabinet to refill his glass. When he faced the group once again, however, his face was wiped of all expression. His body language told another story entirely. He was not happy and she felt bad for him. Immediately she retracted her earlier thoughts. Just because she had to suffer with Shane's rudeness didn't mean her friends should have to. Shane should know it would hurt them to share anything with one another, even if it was something small enough to fit in a gift bag.

Before she could get herself worked up on their behalf, Gideon spoke, cutting through the tension in the room. "Shall we take this into the living room?"

Before agreeing, Paige glanced at her watch and smiled. Forty-four minutes to go. She'd play Shane's game for a little longer, if only to show him she could.

Shane waited until everyone was situated in the other room before he began. Tonight was a long time in the making and he didn't want anything to go wrong now. He looked around the room at his friends, recalling when he'd met each and every one of them. He realized most would be pissed at his gifts. In fact, he could already sense some growing resentment. Hopefully when all was said and done, everything would work out in the end and they'd be thanking him.

"On with the present-giving." He walked over to the love seat where Bev was sitting and handed her the small yellow bag. "You'll be sharing your present with Holden."

The smile Bev had been sporting immediately slipped away. Shane wanted to comfort her, or at least let her know he wasn't being cruel on purpose, but that would defeat his intention. Besides, Shane needed to save all his explanations for Paige. Speaking of which… "And last but not least," Shane walked across the room, stopping at the far wall where Paige was standing, looking disgruntled as hell, "for you, little one. You're sharing with…" Shane pretended to look around for an extra person before glancing back at her with mock amazement, "well, with me."

"Note the surprise on my face." To his irritation, Paige made no move to take the small purple bag. "I'll pass."

The hell she would. "I think not." He didn't come this far for things to fall apart now. "Take the bag, Paige."

When he didn't budge, she gave in and grabbed the bag from his hand. "There are over a thousand nerves in the human body, Shane, and you are on every last one of mine."

That wasn't all he planned to be on before the night was over. Just thinking of her sexy lithe body under his was enough to make him grin, which only seemed to annoy her further. Unable to resist irking her a little more, he winked at her before walking to the center of the room. He waited until everyone turned their attention his way before speaking again. "Everybody gather around with the co-owner or owners of your bags. It's time to play a little game."

No one said anything but the reluctance filling the room was more than obvious. Still, it couldn't be helped. They weren't going to fix their problems with avoidances and excuses. God knew they'd tried those slam, bang methods over the last few years to no avail.

The only one who seemed pleased with the turn of events was Holden, who, much to Bev's obvious annoyance, had joined her on the love seat. Shane thought it was fitting the two of them were on the love seat since they'd been head over heels with one another for as long as he could remember.

Unlike Holden though, Tripp was slower to move toward the couch where Gideon and Skylar were sitting stiffly. When he joined them, he stared straight ahead. He looked uncomfortable yet somehow right sitting with the two of them. Those three belonged together and it was time they all stopped fighting it.

Once his ducklings were all settled, Shane moved next to Paige, who was peering in her small bag as if expecting something to leap at her at any moment. So untrusting—not that he hadn't given her plenty of reasons to be. Just thinking about the many ways he fucked up in the past made him want to hurry through the night's festivities. The sooner they all fixed things, the better they all would be. "Now that everyone is in their place, feel free to open the bags."

"Yay!" With the delight of a child, Skylar opened their bag and pulled out a bottle of tequila. Her blonde brows shot up in surprise. "Exactly what type of game were you thinking of playing, Shane dear?"

"Yes," Paige held the keys to his family's cabin up for everyone to see. "What's going on here?"

"Hold up." Tripp frowned as he gestured over to Paige. "How come Paige has keys and all we have is booze? I don't want booze. I want keys too."

Before Shane could begin to explain, Gideon turned to Holden and Bev, who had yet to open their bag. "What did you guys get?"

Bev's face was a mask of confusion as she peered into the bag. "It's a stopwatch. I don't get it."

"Join the club," Skylar said, glancing back at Shane.

The motives for his desire for this little get-together were about to ring clear. "You all wanted to know what I wished for this year. Well, the answer lies within your hands."

"You wished for tequila?" Skylar questioned, still obviously confused.

"No, I wished for a do-over." Shane paused to look at Paige for a moment. It was imperative she listened and understood exactly what he was saying. "A do-over for us all."

And, man, did they need it. Every single person in this room was lying to themselves and each other about their true feelings, Shane included. The only difference between Shane and everyone else was he refused to waste another day without the person he loved.

Not only was Shane the self-proclaimed ringleader of their little group, but he was also the person everyone talked to. When Bev began to avoid Holden two years ago, it was he who Holden confided in. And a year ago, after Tripp, Skylar and Gideon made fireworks of their own at Tripp's Fourth of July party, it was to Shane who Tripp divulged the details of their drunken romp.

"What do you mean?" Gideon asked, drawing Shane's attention their way. "Why do you think we need a do-over?"

Why did they need a do-over? Shane wanted to hit Gideon for even asking. Seriously, was he the only person not drifting in the river of denial? "Because you're all unhappy. Let me rephrase that, we're all unhappy, and some of us are eaten up by guilt and regret."

"You? Guilt?" Paige's disbelief rang out loud and clear. "I don't believe it."

"Believe it." He had more reason to be guilty than anyone else in the room. "And I'm not the only one, am I?"

"I'm not," Gideon said, apparently still confused.

"No, you may not be." Shane nodded his head to Tripp, whose smug smile had disappeared. He didn't want to out his friends, but if no one was willing to fess up, he would do it for them. Lies and secrets were destroying them all. "But he is. Filled with it."

Skylar's gaze cut to Tripp. "What is he talking about?"

"I don't know." Tripp's words of denial rang false. "I need another drink."

Damn, Tripp was going to force his hand. Though it hurt Shane to do this to the other man, he knew he had no other choice. "Why don't you play another game of quarters while you're at it? Maybe this time you won't chicken out."

Skylar's gasp of shock was almost as palpable as Tripp's grimace of annoyance. "What I told you was spoken in confidence."

Also during a drinking binge, but Shane thought it best not to mention that. He'd already spilled enough of the man's secrets.

"You told him?" Gideon asked, standing as well. "You wouldn't talk to us about it, but you discussed it with him?"

"There was nothing to talk about."

"No?" Gideon's fist clenched and unclenched by his side. For a second Shane thought he might take a swing at the other guy, but at the last second Gideon controlled his temper. "You're right, Tripp. There is nothing to talk about. Now or ever again."

"Gideon?" Skylar reached out to him, the pain on her face heartbreaking. "You don't mean that."

"Yes, Skylar, I think I do."

"You don't, Gideon," Tripp said adamantly. "No more so than I meant what I said a year ago."

"You don't know dick, Tripp," Gideon ground out, his words full of fury.

But his anger didn't cause Tripp to back down. Not one little bit. "Which was part of the problem, wasn't it, ol' buddy?"

"Go to hell."

"I've been there all year." Tripp turned to face them again, sincerity now written across his face. "I could use a do-over. I'd be willing to play. What about you, Skylar?"

Skylar bit into her bottom lip and cast her gaze around the room nervously. If she was waiting for gasps of outrage, she was in the wrong room. Shane didn't care if Tripp and Gideon enjoyed catching and pitching. He just wanted his friends to be happy.

Skylar nodded in affirmation. "I would love a do-over. I'm more than willing to try again."

"Then goody for the both of you because I'm sure as hell not." Gideon's retreat was stopped by Tripp, who walked in front of the other man, blocking his exit. "Get out of my way, Tripp. You should be real good at that after the last several months."

"I don't want out of your way." His confession sounded raw, even to Shane.

"This time it isn't about you," Gideon said coldly as he brushed past Tripp and out the room.

So far his gifts weren't eliciting much of a positive reaction. But he wasn't willing to give up yet.

"It's not too late," Shane said to Tripp and Skylar. But his words weren't just for Tripp, they were for them all. "If you want to fix this, go after him and make it right. You only get one do-over, Tripp, don't mess it up this time."

Tripp turned to Skylar, who was watching him intently. "What do you think, dollface?"

"The same thing I thought a year ago. My feelings for the two of you haven't changed. I love you both, and I want to be with both of you."

That's what Shane was hoping to hear. One couple down, two to go.

Chapter Three

Good Lord! Eyes wide, Paige watched as Skylar and Tripp walked out of the room, hand in hand, as if nothing of importance had just occurred. What the hell had she missed in the last two years? Skylar was in for one hell of a phone call come tomorrow morning. In shock, she turned to look at Bev, who looked as confused as Paige felt. Good, at least she wasn't the only person in the dark.

"And then there were two couples," Shane said gleefully.

Paige tore her gaze away from Bev and stared in utter amazement at the obviously smiling man. *Is he fucking kidding?* There was no way in hell she was staying here to see what else he had up his twisted sleeve. Thirty minutes or not, she was out of there.

"Shall we move on to—"

Hell no! Paige held up her hand to block out his words. "I don't think so. They," she gestured with her hand in the direction the couple had walked out, "may not mind you putting their business all in the street, but I do."

Her words didn't appear to deter him at all. Shane turned and took a menacing step toward her. "Then come with me. You know what the key unlocks."

"Heartbreak and headaches, and thanks to you, I've already had plenty of both." Shane was delusional if he thought she was going anywhere near his cabin. Amazed at his audacity, Paige dropped the bag, keys and all on the floor, and walked over to the coffee table where she'd left her purse. "The only regret I have, Shane, is coming to your stupid party."

"Good." After picking up the keys, Shane stormed over to her. "That means you don't think the night in my cabin was a mistake. A night too good to be forgotten or regretted."

Fury filled her as he towered over her as if his very presence would force her to alter her decisions. The last couple of years must have clouded his memory because he truly forgot who he was dealing with. Paige couldn't be intimidated. Not by him. Not by anyone. "Goodbye, Shane."

"Think again, little one."

His impudence was infuriating. Without bothering to say goodbye to either Bev or Holden, Paige turned on her heels and stormed from the room. She was halfway down the hallway when Shane grabbed her arm and spun her around.

"Don't walk away from me."

"Are you kidding me?"

"Does it look as if I'm teasing?"

"No." She snatched her arm away and took a step away from him. "It looks like you've lost your ever-loving mind. Seriously, you're beyond crazy."

"The only thing I'm crazy about is you." Paige opened her mouth to blast him but nothing came out. She was too floored to come up with anything vile enough to say. "What? You don't believe me?"

"Of course I don't," she shouted. "Why would I believe anything you say ever again?"

"Honey, I know. If I could do it aga—"

"Do you know what type of fool I'd be to allow you within breathing space of me again? A huge one. Gigantic. Sorry, buddy, I'm not that girl. You had your chance and you blew it."

Paige forced herself to keep her hands by her sides and not ball them into fists and pound on his chest as she truly wanted. How dare he act so cavalier about something that at one time meant so much to her?

"I don't accept that," Shane insisted against all logic.

Paige tilted her head and spoke as if to a child. "You don't have a choice." Head held high, Paige turned around and walked out the house. The cold air was like a slap in the face, catching her off-guard for a second, as did the sight of Tripp and Skylar arguing in the front yard. Not wanting to interrupt them, she cut across the lawn out of their line of vision and headed for her car. Before she neared her vehicle though, she was grabbed around her waist from behind. Startled, she opened her mouth to scream, but was cut off by a large leather glove covering her mouth. "Ellllll—"

"Quiet, Paige," Shane whispered fiercely in her ear. "It's just me."

Did he think that eased her mind? "Fkng bstd, et g," she tried to speak while attempting to jerk from his gasp.

"Hush up."

Before she could protest further, he began to drag her away from her car. Her gaze darted to Skylar and Tripp, but they had entered their car and couldn't see her. She continued to struggle against Shane, although she realized the futility of her efforts. He was larger and stronger. The added element of surprise had completely taken her off-guard.

Wide-eyed with fury, she kicked out as he marched her across the street toward a limousine. When the driver's door opened, she thought she was saved for one brief moment. But the man stared straight ahead, as if he couldn't see a kidnapping going on right before his eyes. He held open the back door as if he were driving around a rich businessman. And in a way he was.

Once again Shane and his money had greased the wheels and made things happen. Too bad she was the one to suffer. Her only chance now would be when he tried to push her into the limo and she stopped her struggles for a moment, hoping to regain some of her strength.

"I'll explain everything soon. I promise." Shane's words held no meaning for her. She wasn't interested in his lame-ass explanations. His ass was going to be on its way to prison when she was done with him.

As they reached the car, he adjusted his grip on her and she pushed back against him in an attempt at escape. Attempt failed. Before she could even squeak out a scream he had her bundled into the limo. He quickly moved in after her, shutting the door behind him. The slamming of the door was like the slamming of a prison cell. She was trapped.

Instead of sitting across from her on the leather bench seat next to the driver's window, Shane sat next to her, which sent her shuffling over to the other side. She didn't want to be anywhere near him. "If you start this car…"

"You're going to do what?" He viewed her escape with mockery as he straightened his shirt. Her struggle had done a number on his outfit, forcing the normally suave-looking man to appear thrashed. "Damn, you're a wildcat."

His derision had her seeing red. "Bastard," she shouted as she kicked out at him. "Let me out of here."

Shane easily deflected her blow, grabbing her foot in the process. "Pipe down, Paige."

"Pipe down. Are you kidding me? You kidnapped me," she yelled. Yanking back her foot, she made a move to grab the door handle.

"Touch the handle and your brother can kiss his scholarship goodbye." When she eased away from the door, he gave a sharp nod of approval. "Good girl. If you happen to notice, the car isn't even turned on. All I want to do is talk. Then, after an allotted time, if you still feel the need to leave, I'll let you out."

"Who are you?" she questioned, confused. This cold man before her now in no way resembled the young man she knew.

"I'm the man who holds your brother's future in his hands."

For a moment she was too stunned to act. Shaking off the shock and lethargy infecting her, she sat up and regarded him defiantly. "Do you really hate me that much?"

The icy glare, which had shone so bright in his blue eyes mere seconds ago, seemed to defrost at her words. With a wary sigh Shane rubbed his hand over his face and let out a deep groan. When he dropped his hand away, he looked aged somehow. "I don't hate you at all," he said quietly.

Paige felt an uncontrollable urge to snort. These weren't exactly the actions of a person who cared. "You couldn't prove it by me."

"It's kind of hard to prove anything to someone who won't let you near them."

"Why would I?" she snapped, pushing herself back against the plush leather seat, as far away from him as she could.

"Because you missed me. Missed us."

"There was never an us."

He let lose a harsh crack of laughter that startled her. "I seem to recall quite vividly that there was."

"I think you're confusing sex with something else, Shane."

"It wasn't just sex."

"Keep telling yourself that."

"Fine." His mouth tightened. "Prove me wrong. If it was just sex and you feel absolutely nothing for me, come willingly with me to the cabin. I dare you."

His words brought back a rush of memories, some almost too painful to recall. "If I remember correctly, it was a game of Dare that landed me in this mess to begin with."

"You call it a mess. I call it the best weekend of my life."

*****
Three Years Ago

Shane was lucky to be alive, and if for one tiny second he forgot that little fact, someone, be it his parents, his doctors or his friends, was quick to remind him. The only thing though, Shane didn't exactly feel all that blessed, at least not all the time. Sometimes he straight-out cursed the fates for keeping him alive.

In fact, as he stared at the blank computer screen, he almost wished for death. Almost, and only because death had to be better than being forced to journal by his flower-power therapist. He didn't want to keep a diary and, frankly, was stumped at the reasoning behind this lame exercise. Besides, writing about emotions and shit was Gideon's job. His was to design buildings. And hopefully make it back to his old self.

Groaning, he took his fingers off the unused keyboard and rolled his neck in an attempt to release the tension gathered there. Talking about his feelings was something that had never come easily to him. Even if his therapist would be the only one to see what he wrote, Shane couldn't find it in himself to talk about what happened.

What was there to talk about, really? What was there to say he hadn't said before? This life-altering event that changed his world as he knew it happened not because of a drunk driver but because someone had simply fallen asleep while driving and crossed the center line, hitting his car head-on.

At first the doctors thought that on top of the crushed bones in both his legs he might be permanently paralyzed, but after the swelling went down, he'd been able to show some movement in his lower extremities, giving them hope he'd eventually recover. The other driver hadn't been so lucky, dying on impact, a sad fact Shane was still unable to talk about, despite how much everyone pressured him to do so.

For the life of him though, he couldn't figure out why anyone wanted him to. It wasn't as if he hadn't tried to proceed on with his life as if the car wreck had merely been a fender-bender and not the life-altering change it truly was. And because of that, he wanted to have as much normalcy in his life as possible.

Despite his parents' preference, he refused to move back home with them. He had his own place, with his own life before the accident and he would have one again. Fortunately his doctors agreed it was the best thing for him to resume life as he had before, not that he would have surrendered to his parents' will if the doctors hadn't. Love them as he did, they were a tad on the smothering side. Sometimes he wondered what was worse, parents who cared too much or ones who didn't care at all.

It had been over a year since he began rehabilitation and he was finally able to walk again. It wasn't easy, he still wasn't cruising on his own, but it was a start. A very, very good start.

"Hey, you."

Shane glanced over his shoulder toward the master bedroom door and spotted Paige, lounging in the doorframe. "Hey." Startled, he pushed away from the desk and turned his office chair around until he faced her. Talk about a surprise. The plan was to have his parents' cabin all to himself for the weekend. This was going to be his little retreat from his therapist and well-meaning family and friends. "How did you get in here?"

"Housekeeper let me in on her way out."

"Wow, remind me to fire her later."

"It'll have to wait until Monday. She said she was gone for the weekend."

"No worries. I'll remember."

Paige rolled her eyes. "Whatever. Leave the poor woman alone. She remembered me from the last time I was here."

"Is that right?"

"Yep. You know this probably wouldn't happen if you had more than one black friend." Shane shot her an aggravated look, to which she merely smiled. "I'm just saying."

"Well, don't." Shane always wondered exactly how he should respond to her little gibes about her being the lone black person in their group. The fact was, it was the God's honest truth. There was no way to argue with logic, or Paige for that matter, so instead he changed the subject. "What are you doing here, anyway?"

She walked all the way into the room and dropped her bulging gray backpack on the floor. "I'm here for the weekend."

"You are, are you?" Despite his gruff tone, he was happy to see her. Lord knew he didn't get to see her as much as he preferred since she began dating the four-eyed douche bag. He and Paige used to hang out a lot before that creature came along. Now she was apparently too busy making a new life for herself to have time to spend with the likes of him. Just thinking about it had his already sour mood turning morose. With the frame of mind he was in, he wasn't fit for company, even when it was with someone as sexy as she. "Why?"

"I pulled the short straw."

So his less-than-positive attitude of late hadn't been lost on his roommates. "I thought the suicide watch was over now that I can drag my sorry ass down the street, thanks to my old man's cane." No matter how lightly he tried to treat the matter, it still filled him with great pride. After months of nothing, there was finally something. He was walking again.

"It is. Now we've moved on to 'Shane is a pain but he's still our friend so we have to take turns keeping him company' watch. Since it's such a mouthful, we simplified it to A.S.S. duty."

"Ass?"

"Another Sucky Saturday," she explained, a deadpan expression on her lovely brown face.

He wasn't buying it though. "It's Friday."

"Then I'm early. But never fear." She wiggled a white plastic bag with blue writing on it in the air. "I brought movies. The best trilogy of all time."

"*Star Wars?*"

"Hell no." She frowned. "*The Matrix.*"

Was she mad? "That's just sacrilegious," he said as disgust filled him. He should kick her out for that comment alone. "What if I'm not really in the mood for movies or visitors?" He hadn't thought he was until she showed up, now Shane welcomed her company. But of course he couldn't admit it. That would be too much like right.

Not as if he needed to though, because, as usual, Paige didn't back down. "What makes you think you have a choice?"

"I don't?"

"Nope. I want to watch movies and I didn't want to do it home, alone. Plus, I'm too tired to drive back tonight, so unless you want to loan me Mommy's and Daddy's limo you're stuck with me. Deal with it."

"Alone." Paige hadn't been alone since she started seeing that accountant last fall. Hmm…was there trouble in paradise at last? "Why not call your pocket protector and have him come over to your place?"

"Jaffee," she said, stressing her boyfriend's name as she always did in a futile attempt to get him to address the other man properly. It wasn't going to happen.

"Whatever."

"He and I are taking a little break."

"Really?" Now this was news. "What happ—"

Paige held her hand up to silence him. "Nothing happened. It's not a permanent break. Just a small one. Weekend only. I just needed to pause for station identification."

"I don't know what that means," he said, confused as hell. "Is that like a black thing or something?"

"Yes, Shane. It's a black thing."

From her dry tone and the wry expression on her face, he could tell he was way off-track. "I was just asking."

"Well don't, and before you start, I don't want to talk about it." Paige brushed an errant strand of her shoulder-length hair behind her ear. "I just want to watch movies and veg in front of the TV."

"You can do that at your own house. Come on, admit it. You're here for something besides my big screen."

"You're right."

"I am?" Those were words he didn't hear often from her. "How so?"

"I'm here for you."

"Me?" This was getting better and better every second.

"Yes, if I was at home, I couldn't bother you, could I?" She seemed a little too happy about that prospect for his peace of mind.

Suddenly he wasn't feeling as pleased to see her. "What if I don't want to be bothered?"

Paige smirked, as if his wants didn't matter in the least to her. "Tough tittie."

"How did you even know I was here?"

"Tripp."

Fucking Tripp. Shane should have known better than to tell his roommate where he was going. "You know, most people who come to visit are invited and try to be civil."

"I'm not most people."

"Isn't that the truth?" he muttered under his breath. If she were most people, he could kick her out without a second thought. But she wasn't. She was Paige. And that meant more to him than it rightly should. Especially in light of her relationship status.

When it came to women, Shane prided himself on three things. He never made a promise he didn't keep. He never left them unsatisfied, and he never poached on another's man territory. Paige was the one person who made him want to rethink his third rule.

"Don't be a baby—you won't even know I'm here." Somehow Shane didn't quite believe her. "Besides, don't you think you're milking this accident just a bit? Stop with the moping already."

"Some would say I'm entitled to mope a bit, seeing as how I have been through hell in the last year."

"Those people would be stupid."

"Or they have eyes." He gestured to the red scars zigzagging up and down his legs, as if it somehow slipped her notice. Shane would have worn pants if he knew there was a chance someone would be stopping by. He hadn't exactly reached comfort level with his scars yet, but he wanted to drive home his point.

"Last time I checked, you were still rich, male and living in America. Even with your old-man stick, you have it better than half the population in our country. So get over yourself and be thankful for the things you have. Like me." She grinned and held her arms out wide as if putting herself on display.

Gee...I'm feeling better already." It was like arguing with the wall.

"Of course you are. I'm here." Shane snorted in lieu of commenting. Speaking would do him no good with Paige anyway. She was going to do whatever the hell she wanted. The accident didn't change the way she treated him one iota. She never let him get a word in edgewise before then, and she sure as hell didn't let him do it now. The most annoying part of that little fact was that as much as it annoyed him, it equally intrigued him. Where Paige was concerned, Shane's brain was as fucked up as his legs.

"You're sulking," she said, as if this too went unnoticed by him.

"You're bothersome." To his irritation, his comment made her smile, lighting up her pretty face in a way nothing else did.

"But you love me anyway."

"Like I love a rash," he grumbled.

"I'm going to take that as compliment."

"You do that, but I still think there's more going on here than you're letting on."

"And I think you're paranoid."

"But that doesn't mean I'm wrong." Shane grabbed the handle of his cane and rose to his feet. "Word to the wise, pretty lady. I'm on to you."

"Think what you want, Shane. You always do."

"Before the weekend ends I'll get the real reason out of you, Paige. I promise you that, and you know I always keep my promises."

"Whatever." Smirking, Paige bent over and picked up her bag. "I'm going to go put my stuff up in one of the guest rooms. I'll be back in a second."

"I'll be waiting." And not just for her. For answers, as well. Shane had a feeling whatever explanation for why she was here was a very important one indeed, and he wouldn't rest until he knew what it was.

Chapter Four

ಸು

"One more game of Scrabble?" Although her tone was innocent, Paige's grin was anything but. She couldn't help it. Some people were sore losers. She was an ungracious winner. She was competitive by nature and found it hard not to gloat when she won.

Shane was normally the same way, which made playing games with him all the more fun, especially tonight because she was kicking his ass. "I'll give you fifty points, right off the bat."

"Why, so you can throw it in my face that you won despite the fifty points?"

"Would I do that?"

"Yes, which is why I'm done playing." Shane rose from the table, not even attempting to help her put away the tiles and board. "Cheater."

Paige gasped. "I did not!"

"Oh please, using medical words is cheating."

It gave her an added advantage, but that was all. "Don't hate because I have a better vocabulary."

"Geek." He tossed the putdown over his shoulder as he slowly made his way from the dining room into the living room and over to the entertainment center. Although it was an open floor plan, the arrangement of the expensive yet tasteful furniture made the rooms appear separate even without walls, giving them a nice homey feeling. It also allowed her to keep an eye on the pouting man going through the DVDs.

"Sore loser," she tossed back before sticking her tongue out behind his back. "Hopalong Cassidy, get back here and help out. I'm not going to clean up after you. I'm not your maid."

"No one said you were," he said without turning around or coming back.

"Fine, be that way." If he wasn't going to contribute, neither was she. Two could play this sulking game. Paige rose from the table and walked over to the couch, which faced the television and sat down, curling her feet underneath her.

"I will."

Amused at his childishness, Paige watched Shane sulk with a small smile on her face. He was downright adorable when he pouted. The brat had always held a special place in her heart, and as big of a pain in the ass as he was, she knew she couldn't imagine her life without him in it. This weekend was their first chance to truly be alone since his accident and she wasn't going to waste their time together fighting, no matter how much fun it was. Because, after this weekend, she wouldn't have the opportunity again.

Or maybe she would. Paige still wasn't sure what to do. It shouldn't be this hard to accept a proposal of marriage, but for her it was. Her mother thought she was crazy, and part of Paige agreed wholeheartedly. But the other part of her knew the truth, which was sad truth of the matter was that although she loved Jaffee, she wasn't in love with him, or not enough to automatically say yes to him.

Paige hoped that time away from him and her pressuring family would help, but so far no luck. In fact, hanging out with Shane again had her feeling more confused than ever. She was having a really good time with him. Too good of a time for someone who was supposed to be considering marrying someone else. And to add insult to injury, her attraction to him was as strong as ever.

One would have thought, after all these years, she would have been over that by now, but one second alone with him brought all of her feelings back tenfold. Shane was the one man who wasn't intimidated by her. And the one she felt the most comfortable with. Yet he wasn't the man she was seeing, the one she was considering marrying, and that was the biggest problem she had with Jaffee's proposal. He wasn't Shane. It was one thing to date a man she didn't love, quite another to think about pledging her life to him forever.

With a heavy sigh, she pushed the troublesome thoughts from her mind and tried to concentrate on the moment at hand. "So what do you want to do now? Each other's hair and nails?"

"Oh, can we?" Shane mockingly asked before moving to the cabinet that housed DVDs like books, spines out. He stood silent for a moment and perused the shelf before letting out a disgusted sigh. "I've seen all of these at least twice."

"We could watch *The Mat*—"

"No," he cut her off in midsentence as he turned back to face her. "We can't. How many times have you seen those movies?"

"Three hundred and forty-seven for the first. Three hundred and—"

"Forget I asked." Shane picked up the remote control from the shelf and turned on the big screen television. He began to flip through a few channels for a second or two before letting out a loud sound of exasperation and turning the TV off. "I'm bored."

"Do you want to play another game?" Paige was beginning to feel as if she were sucking at her job. She'd come up this weekend to keep him company as much as she did to get some much-needed space from Jaffee, but from the looks of things, she wasn't doing such a good job with the former. Shane didn't look any happier than he had two days ago when she saw him at his place. "Any game. I'll let you pick."

"Any game?" Shane glanced over at her with a devilish look in his eyes.

The way he arched his eyebrow made her a tad nervous, but she would be a terrible candy striper if she let a little arch scare her away. "Any."

"How about," Shane walked over to the couch and sat next to her, "strip poker?"

"Sure, but we'd have to start off evenly matched," Paige nodded her head toward his dark gray sweat pants and light gray T-shirt. "How many items are you wearing?"

"Four. How many are you?"

Paige glanced down at her outfit. Shane wasn't the only one who'd changed before dinner. She'd nixed her jeans and T-shirt for a Juicy Couture hoodie, matching shorts and a pair of big thick socks. She was comfy and cute, two things she insisted on. "If socks count as one item."

"Yes."

"Then I have three."

"Three." Shane's brow furrowed in confusion.

"I'm not wearing a bra or any underwear."

"You're not..." His gaze shot to her covered breasts then back to her face in record speed.

"Nope. My boobs aren't all that big. I can go without one if I want." Paige was unashamed of her small breasts. There was nothing wrong with a full B-cup, at least not in her book.

"I think your breasts are just the right size." If she wasn't mistaken, she thought she could actually see a flush on his face. "I mean, for your height and everything. You're a small woman. Anything...overly large would be obscene."

"It seems as if you've given my breasts a lot of thought." Yep, he was definitely blushing. It was comical. Shane, the pussy hound of the dormvilles, as he was so lovingly called in college, was flushing at the mere mention of her breasts. Would wonders never cease? "Interesting."

"Just an observation."

"Uh-huh."

"You know what else I observed," he said, coming back strong. "You didn't bat an eye at the idea of playing strip poker."

"Of course not." It wasn't as if she had anything he hadn't seen before. To put it bluntly, Shane was a himbo. His sexual prowess was legendary and not even only in his own mind. Besides, she didn't plan on losing. Her pride wouldn't let her. Nor would her skills. "Why would I?"

"Because you have a man." His lips twisted into a cynical smile. "Or do you?"

"Of course I do." But she wouldn't for long if Jaffee knew she was considering playing such a risqué game with another man. Hell, if he even for a second suspected she was at the cabin alone with Shane he would blow a gasket. Personality wise, Jaffee was her complete opposite. He was more reserved and mellow, and they didn't exactly have the same taste in fun but they fit in other ways. Her mother always said he was the black Ken to her black Barbie, but her mother wasn't the one who would have to spend the rest of her life with him. A fact Paige was becoming more and more aware of. It wasn't something she wanted to chat with Shane about, however. "Jaffee has nothing to do with this."

"Doesn't he?" Shane was way too perceptive for her peace of mind, and too tenacious. Any other person would have let it go. But not him. No, he was going to keep at her until either she cracked or until she cracked his head wide open.

"No," she reiterated, cursing herself for ever mentioning Jaffee's name.

"Now isn't that interesting? Noteworthy, even."

Paige resisted the urge to roll her eyes. She really didn't want to get into this with him. Not today. Possibly not ever. "What part of 'I don't want to talk about this' didn't you understand?"

"The part where you didn't want to talk about it."

At least he was honest. "Why are you so nosy?"

"Why are you so hesitant to answer my question?" he challenged.

"Because it's none of your business."

Shane snorted with derision. "Since when has that ever mattered?"

"Since now."

"Oh, now we keep secrets." His voice held a vague hint of disapproval that made her shake her head in amusement.

What friendship has he been a part of all these years? "Please, Shane. We've always kept secrets."

"I don't keep anything from you."

"Liar." Of that, she was sure. "Everyone has secrets. Even you."

"If you think you know so much about me, Miss Smarty Pants, then tell me when I have ever been anything but open and honest with you?"

"I can't think of a 'for instance'. I just know you keep certain things to yourself. We all do."

"Then let's you and me start a brand new tradition. Nothing but the truth. From here on out."

"Uhh…I don't know if that's such a good idea." Not at all. Paige didn't think for an instant that the old adage of "the truth will set you free" was right at all. In fact, she thought it was bullshit of the highest order.

"Why not? Do you make it such a habit to lie and hide things that the mere thought of being a-hundred-percent honest gets you up in arms?"

"No, but I know you."

"And…"

"And to quote my boy Jack, 'You can't handle the truth.'"

"Think so, do you?"

Paige smirked. "Please. I know so."

"Then try me. I dare you."

"Dare." She quirked her eyebrow. "Sounds as if you're playing a game to me."

Shane shrugged his shoulders. "How about it? Truth or Dare, Paige. What do you say?"

"I say you're crazy."

"And I say you're chicken."

"Fuck you." There was no way in hell she could back down from a challenge, and the bastard knew it. "Fine, then. Let's play."

There was only one thing Shane hated more than losing and that was knowing someone was keeping something from him. It was ten times worse knowing Paige was the offender. It wasn't merely the fact she had a secret. It was that she didn't seem inclined at all to share it with him of all people. They had always been close, or at least he thought so, up until this moment. Even in a group of friends like theirs, people tended to pair off, and Shane had always thought Paige was the second pea in his pod. She was the one person he felt he could always talk to, and he would have sworn she felt the same.

The mere thought there was something going on with her he knew nothing about rubbed him the wrong way, especially knowing it had something to do with the dick she was dating. From the moment she introduced Jaffee to him, he hated the man on sight. The studious man had never stepped out of line with Shane, in fact he had never been anything but courteous, but that didn't stop Shane from disliking him with every fiber of his being.

She was too good for the likes of that guy, and the sooner they ended it, the better for all concerned. Especially for Shane, who wouldn't have to sit through one more group outing, watching Jaffee drape his arm around her shoulders, as if he had a right to touch her when Shane did not.

"So do you want to go first?" Paige nuzzled back into the couch and folded her legs underneath her.

"Sure." Unlike some people in the room, he had nothing to hide.

"Truth, Dare, Double Dare, Promise or Repeat."

"Excuse me?"

"Which one do you want? Truth, Dare, Double Dare, Promise or Repeat?"

"I get the first two, but I'm not so sure about the other three."

"Double Dare is the ultimate dare. With Promise, you have to promise something, like to loan me your car—"

"Sure, you can have what's left of it."

"And," she continued on as if he hadn't interrupted her, "Repeat means you have to repeat something I say, such as Shane is a big-ass titty baby."

"I'm not saying that." Not even on a dare. This was about telling the truth, after all.

"Then don't pick Repeat."

"Fine. I pick Truth."

"Pussy."

Shane smirked. "Truth is, I like it. That was easy." If she kept it up, this game was going to be over in seconds.

"No way."

"Oh, that wasn't your question."

Paige picked up a small pillow and hit him in the chest with it. "You know it wasn't. Now play fair."

"Fine. What's the question?"

"Have you ever fantasized about making love with someone in our group? If the answer is yes, who with?"

"That's two turns."

"No way."

"Yes way." Shane didn't mind answering the question, but he'd be damned if she'd cheat him. "Fair is fair."

"Fine. Let me reword my question." The glittering light of mirth in her eyes warned Shane of the trouble ahead but, as he said earlier, he wasn't afraid of a little truth. Besides, he knew Paige. She was too chickenshit to ask the good stuff. The stuff she may not like the answers to. In fact, he was counting on it. "Truthfully, who is the one person in our group you've fantasized about making love to?"

Maybe he was wrong about her after all because that was a pretty good question. One he didn't think she was really ready to hear in light of her current circumstances. "What makes you think I've fantasized?"

"Because we all have. Myself included."

"Really?" Hmm…now this was the stuff he wanted to hear.

"Yes. Now answer the question."

"Okay. Truthfully, I've fantasized about making love to Bev." Shane watched in peevish delight as Paige's smile began to dim. "And Skylar."

"Skylar too?"

"Yes."

"Why am I surprised?" Her once-twinkling eyes were now narrowed in irritation. Good. "You're a humongous horndog. You should really walk around with a sign that says 'Have cock, will travel'."

"Hey." Shane tried his best to look affronted by her accusation, but it was hard to pull off when all he really wanted to do was laugh. "You wanted me to be honest. I'm trying to do as you asked. You girls are like those potato chips, I can't pick just one. I'm sure I've had fantasies about you too on occasion."

As in every occasion he closed his eyes. Shane didn't know what it was about her he loved more, her feisty attitude or her sexy body. Both were pleasing in his eyes and surprisingly, both made him rock-hard.

"Wow. I'm lucky you've even had time in all these years to fit me in."

"I'm a busy guy."

"I guess." She didn't look too happy about it though. "Your turn."

"Okay. Truth or Dare."

"Dare."

"Now who's the pussy?"

"I don't think choosing Dare makes me a pussy at all. In fact, I think it's daring for me."

"Fine. I dare you to…" Shane paused as he tried to think of something good to say. Nothing came to mind.

"Well?"

"Gimme a second. This isn't easy." Not at all.

"Today."

"I dare you…" Since nothing good came to mind, Shane thought to suggest something there might be a slim chance she wouldn't do in order to push her into asking for a truth question. It was easier for him to think of something to ask her than it was for him to think of something to make her do. "To strip and do the hula."

He actually had her goggling at him. Score. "Dream on. Not going to happen."

"Why not? You were willing to undress at the turn of a card, why not now?"

"Because you're only picking this because you know I won't do it."

"Would I do that?" Not when he had the very good reason of wanting to see her naked because he found her cock-hardening attractive.

"Yes."

"I'm hurt you'd think that," he lied with a grin. He was more amused than anything else. "Come on, what's a little nudity between friends?"

Paige studied him for a few seconds more through narrowed eyes before she flashed a compliant grin. "You know what? You're right. Besides, it's not as if you haven't seen me naked before, anyway, right?"

"Wrong. I think that's something I might have remembered."

"Sure you have. That night we all went skinny-dipping at..." A funny little smile spilled out across her face. "Wait. That's right. You weren't there. It was just the three of us."

"Thee three of us, who?" Something told Shane she wasn't about to say Skylar and Bev.

"Gideon, Tripp and myself."

Damn, he hated it when he was right. "When the hell did this happen?" Shane wasn't sure what upset him more. Missing out on skinny-dipping with Paige, or the fact the other guys didn't.

"Awhile ago. It's not a big deal."

One more thing they had to disagree on. "Did anything else happen that night?"

"That night," Paige tilted her head to the side with a pondering look. "No."

That night. "Then what night?"

"You've already had your turn. Now do you want me to strip and hula or answer your question?"

Rock meet hard place. Shane couldn't shake the feeling Paige was fucking with him. What annoyed and upset him more though, was he couldn't say for certain she wasn't. He shouldn't care what she'd done with the other two. He knew there was nothing between them now. So why did all his logic not matter one iota? Fuck it. "Do the Truth."

"Are you sure?"

He was sure he was insane, but as much as he wanted to see her naked, he wanted an answer to his question more. "Are you trying to back out?"

"Never that." Paige met his challenging gaze in a bold and saucy manner. "But to be fair, according to the rules, it's up to me to decide which I want to pick. You're not allowed to switch them because you changed your mind about seeing me naked."

"The rules." He didn't want to hear about rules. He wanted to hear about whether or not she let Tripp or Gideon touch her. "Are you worried the Truth or Dare police might suddenly show up and fine us for not playing the correct way?"

"No, I simply don't think it's fair you're allowed to be all wishy-washy."

"Good Lord. I'll give you a take back in exchange for this one."

"Fine." Paige's pleased expression made Shane wonder what he'd agreed to, but before he could ask, she moved on. "Now what was your question again?"

"When, if ever, have you done something sexual with a member of our group?"

"Not counting the time Skylar and I kissed when she and I played this game with you and Tripp?"

Shane grinned at the memory. "No, not that time."

"A few times in college."

Shane's eyebrows flew up in surprise. A few times in college. As he repeated her words in his mind, his emotions zoomed past shocked and landed on fury with a vengeance.

College. Paige had fucked one of their friends. Oh, hell no.

Clenching his teeth, he fought hard not to lash out at her and demand answers and reparation. He could be reasonable about this. He was a man. Not an animal. After the last six months and everything it entailed, this would easy breezy. This was nothing compared to that. But why did he suddenly feel as if he were hurdling down a darkened road at a hundred miles per hour straight toward a brick wall?

Damn it all to hell. She was his. Not…not theirs. Taking a deep breath, Shane tried his best to calm down. It would do neither one of them any good if he blew up. Yet he wasn't going to sit idly by and just let her get away with this. He wanted answers. And he wanted them now. "Who?"

"Ah. Ah. Ah." Paige chided him, waving her finger as if she were scolding a wayward child. "You had your turn, now it's mine. Truth or Dare."

"Was it Tripp?"

"Why didn't you say Gideon?" Curiosity laced her voice.

"Why? Was it him?"

"I'm not saying if it was or not. I was merely curious as to why you immediately crossed him off the list."

"Don't change the subject. Answer my question. Now."

His command was met by her amused resolve. "Quid pro quo, Shane. You're going to have to wait your turn."

"Fine." He could wait, but before this night was over, he would have the answer he wanted, along with the name of the man he was going to kill.

Double Dare

Chapter Five
⁐

"So it's my turn, right?"

"Yes." His voice held no humor. Something told Paige he wasn't enjoying this little game as much as she was. "I pick Truth."

"Color me surprised," Paige retorted. "You know, we don't have to keep playing, Shane. We could always watch a movie or turn in."

"I said I pick Truth."

"I heard you. I just don't understand why you're so bitchy now."

"Keep fucking with me, Paige, and you'll find out."

"I'm not trying to fuck with you, Shane." It was just an added bonus of playing by the rules. "So Truth, huh? Okay. I have one for you."

"Ask it."

"Why don't you like Jaffee?"

"That's easy." Shane snorted derisively. "He's a dick."

Shane's comment was a little bit too much of "the pot calling the kettle black" in Paige's opinion. It wasn't as if her friend was known for his pleasing personality. But that was beside the point. "No, he isn't."

"Yes, he is. And the only dick I'm partial to is my own."

"Why do you think he's so bad? He's never done anything to you."

"Sounds to me as if you're asking another question."

"Piss off." Paige wasn't letting him off so easily. "Explain it to me. I really need to know."

Shane's brow furrowed. "Why?"

"Because it's important to me." On so many different levels. Maybe Shane had a reason to dislike Jaffee that would explain her hesitation to accept his proposal.

"How important?"

"Very." Paige was on the verge of vowing to spend the rest of her life with Jaffee. If something in the milk wasn't clean, she needed to know. "Did he ever do anything when I wasn't around? Have you ever caught him with another woman or flirting with Bev or Skylar?"

"He's still breathing, isn't he?"

"Yes." Paige wasn't exactly sure what he was getting at.

"Well, that answers your question. If I ever caught him doing you dirty, I'd kill him. End of story."

Paige cocked a brow, waiting for the punch line, but when Shane continued to stare at her, face solemn, eyes sincere, she felt herself melting a little on the inside. "You'd kill for me?"

"Hell, if you don't stop messing around and tell me who you fucked in college, I might kill you."

"I never slept with Tripp or Gideon." Shane's eyes widened and Paige could tell he had totally misunderstood what she meant. "Nor did I sleep with Bev or Skylar."

"Then what sexual thing were you talking about?"

"Like you, I fantasized about certain members in our group and sometimes those fantasizes led me to take," Paige cleared her throat, embarrassed by what she was going to admit, "matters into my own hands."

"Are we talking about solo satisfaction here?"

"We are."

A wicked smile danced over his lips. "Nice. Tell me more."

"No way." It was bad enough she had to admit to the bit she did.

"I could always dare you."

Paige crossed her arms over her chest. "And waste a perfectly good dare."

"Not too sure that would be a waste at all."

"Pervert." Paige shook her head and smiled at his total guyness. "Don't think I didn't notice though."

"What?"

"You never did answer my question. Why don't you like him?"

Shane groaned and leaned his head back on the couch and closed his eyes. "Let it go."

"No." Paige refused to be deterred. Reaching out, she covered his hand with hers and squeezed. "Tell me, Shane. Why?"

Shane opened his eyes and turned his head so he was looking at her. "Because he's not good enough for you. Not by far, and you deserve someone better."

As nice as that sounded, she couldn't believe it was so simple. "And that's the only reason you have?"

"I don't need another." His stubbornness was unbelievable.

"You're such a tyrant."

"I protect what's mine."

His words silenced her for a second, as did the stark truth that peered at her from his eyes. *His.* Despite how stupid and wrong she knew it was, Paige couldn't help but be affected by his possessive statement. Any more than she could help the sense of rightness she felt at his claim. But as much as she wanted to revel in his assertion, she couldn't. It would be the dumbest thing she ever did. Shane wasn't the type of man a girl could pin her hopes and dreams on. He was a love 'em and leave 'em kind of guy, and Paige wasn't built that way.

No, the more she thought about it, the more she realized the truth saying yes to Jaffee was the right thing to do. She had to keep her head on straight and stop thinking with her libido. "Last time I checked, Shane, I wasn't yours."

"Keep thinking that." From the smirk he shot her, she could tell he thought she was delusional.

"Okay, I am your friend, but I have to say, I don't recall you acting this way about any of the guys Bev or Skylar ever dated." Which was probably a good thing because she would have hated to have to kill either of her friends.

"And why do you think that is?" Shane turned his hand over under hers and began to gently caress her with his fingertips.

Paige pulled her hand back and crossed her arms over her breasts, trying hard not to let the implication of his words sink like lead into her subconscious. She didn't need another reason to second-guess Jaffee's proposal or another reason to hold on to her attraction to Shane. "Moving on," she said with a shaky laugh. "Since I answered your question about the sex thing, it's my turn again, right?"

"Yes."

"Truth or Dare."

"Dare."

"Really?" She was surprised he'd given in so easily.

"Yes."

"Okay. I dare you to…call Jaffee by his name." Paige laughed at his grimace. "Come on, you have to start sometime."

"No, I don't."

"Yes. You can't go the rest of our lives calling him my pocket protector."

"Then I'll call him something else." Shane tilted his head in thought. "What is the name of the nerdy kid from that show back in the day?"

"I have no idea what you're talking about."

"Come on. Yes, you do. The one with the suspenders and big glasses. Lived next door and was always breaking things."

"Urkel?"

"Yes. That's the one. That's who he reminds me of."

"Jaffee is not an Urkel. Take it back."

"No way. Your boyfriend has nerd written all over him."

"He does not. Take it back." Paige picked up the pillow once more and held it up in a threatening matter.

Shane glanced at the pillow then back at her with an unrepentant smirk on his face. "Not going to happen."

"Take it back." Paige rose to her knees and smacked Shane with the pillow. "Say it." She added another well-aimed blow for good measure.

"Okay. Okay." Shane held up his hand to ward off any further attacks. "I'll say it. Urkel." Acting quickly, Shane grabbed the pillow and moved it to his right hand and held it over the armrest, out of her reach.

"Gimme that."

"Come and get it."

She tried to lean over him, but his arm reach was much longer than hers. "That's my pillow, hand it over."

"Here you go." Shane held the pillow closer, as if he would do as she asked. Of course as soon as she moved to grab it, he laughed and pulled it away again. Finally getting mad, she scrambled over him, straddling his lap in her attempt to reach the pillow. He'd put his arm out behind him, making her lean forward. She realized her breasts were practically pressed into his face at this angle but she didn't care, she wasn't going to allow him this victory.

Shane, on the other hand, was as competitive as she, and just as her fingers brushed over the fabric he dropped the pillow from his grasp and it fell to the floor behind the couch. "Oops."

Laughing, she sat back and shook her head in defeat. "Damn it, if you can't win, no one can, is that it?"

"Exactly."

"Brat." Paige went to move off his lap but was stopped by Shane's hands on her hips, holding her in place.

"Where do you think you're going? Don't you know to the victor goes the spoil?" Shane hands slid from her hips to her ass then tightened his grip. "Give me my prize."

"Ha, ha, ha. Very funny."

"Who's joking?" Shane asked as he peered deep into her eyes.

Paige smile melted away as she met his heated gaze head-on. Suddenly she didn't feel like laughing. Swallowing hard, she tried to return them back to the subject at hand and the reason she'd put herself in this predicament in the first place.

"Say his name," she ordered in a husky tone, needing to put things back into perspective before she did something she'd regret. "I dared you. You have to do it."

"Baby." Shane reached up and gently brushed her wayward hair out of her face. The feel of his cool fingertips against her overheated skin made her tremble inside. "Not only am I not going to say Urkel's name, I'm going to do everything in my power to make you forget it."

She opened her mouth to speak, but words failed her. If there was anyone capable of making her forget Jaffee's name, it was Shane. And from the feel of his cock stiffening beneath her, she had a hunch he had the ability to make her forget her own name.

"Actually, that sounds like a better game to me. Make Paige forget Urkel's name."

That was a bad idea, all the way around. "If…if you're not going to say it that makes me the winner."

"You didn't win. I conceded and took a stance. A man has to have his limits."

"Well, when a man gets in the room I'll ask him about limits."

"Oh, never doubt, Paige. I'm still all man." Her pussy throbbed over the very proof of his words, begging her to take up the challenge he so expertly laid down. "Or do I need to prove it to you?"

"No." Nervous at the direction the conversation was going, Paige darted her tongue out to moisten her dry lips. "I...I can feel the proof for myself, which means one thing."

"What?"

"It's time for me to go to bed."

Shane released his hold on her. "Who's conceding now?" His voice was deep and husky and far too appealing for her piece of mind. She had to end this before she did something she'd regret or, more importantly, before she did something she wouldn't regret.

Paige moved off him and rose with shaky legs from the couch. Pasting a fake smile on her face, she looked at Shane and tried to put on the buddy-buddy cloak and pretend as if the last few minutes never happened. "Good night, Shane. It was fun beating your ass."

"You won tonight because I let you, tomorrow though, will be a different story."

"If you say so." She tried for cavalier, but it fell short by a mile. A fact that wasn't lost on Shane, who gave her a knowing look.

"No, baby. I know so."

*   *   *   *   *

Shane jerked awake, gasping for air and clinging to the sweat-soaked sheet as he tried to gather his bearings. Blindly he searched the nightstand for the remote that controlled the overhead light and fan. In his haste he knocked the glass of water he'd placed there before going to bed to the floor. The noise of shattering glass ricocheted through the room, an eerie reminder of the nightmare he'd escaped from seconds earlier.

"Fuck," he muttered as he continued with his search. Since the accident, he slept with a low-wattage light on, but last night he allowed his macho pride to keep him from turning it on, not wanting to seem like a baby in Paige's eyes.

Now, instead of feeling like a baby, he felt like an idiot sitting in the dark, afraid. He needed to get over this shit. Even now, as he flapped his hand around the nightstand like a fish out of water, he could feel panic rising inside him. Fucking nightmares, no, night terrors as his shrink called them, were taking over his life. He couldn't go a week without having at least one and it wasn't getting better.

Just as he was on the verge of a nervous breakdown, he touched the edge of the remote. The instant security he felt at the mere brush of his fingertips gave him the strength to lunge forward and grab the small rectangle. Pointing the box at the ceiling, he hit the bottom button as if it were the trigger for his old morphine drip, and let out a relieved sigh when light flooded the room.

Taking a deep breath then another, Shane tried his best to calm his racing heart. It took a few minutes to get himself back together, but the second he did, he vaulted over the foot of the bed and across the room, turning on the lamp at record speed. Once the room was duly lit, his heartbeat returned to normal.

Feeling as if he were the world's biggest pussy, Shane padded barefoot into the kitchen and retrieved the broom, dustpan and a roll of paper towels before disappearing back into the room to clean up his mess. It took a few minutes, but once he was done, he climbed into bed and tried to go back to sleep. It was a futile effort. He was far too worked up to simply drift off as he hoped.

The silence of the house began to get to him so he grabbed the other remote from the nightstand and turned on the TV. He had porno keyed up in the DVD player and, thinking a little sexual release would be the key to induce nature's own nightly coma, Shane hit play. He stole a quick glance at his open bedroom door and wondered for a brief second if he should get up and close the door. But then the movie came on and he pushed the thought right out of his head. Paige was more than likely asleep anyway.

Pushing the sheet past his lap, he reached his hand into the opening of his boxers and began to lightly touch his cock, which, unlike him, was still fast asleep. The movie, however, wasn't doing the job it was supposed to. The women were beautiful, but their golden blonde hair and overly large tits weren't working to stir him. He was more interested in a brunette firecracker with a smart-alec mouth and skin as smooth and dark as milk chocolate.

Closing his eyes, Shane replaced the plastic porn stars with images of Paige and just like that his cock began to stir to life. The mere thought of her, naked and spread for him, made his gut clench. Encouraged by the new direction of his arousing thoughts, Shane released his cock then shoved his boxers down his thighs and out of his way.

He licked the palm of his hand then grasped his cock and began to stroke himself to the image of Paige nude in his mind. Unlike Tripp and Gideon, he'd never had the opportunity to see her in anything more revealing than a bikini, but that didn't mean he hadn't imagined her in a lot less many, many times.

God, he wanted her. Had for more years than he'd care to admit. Even when he'd been with other women, she was always there in the back of his mind. The one he really wanted beneath him, over him, surrounding him with her sweet, heady scent as he powered into her, again and again.

He'd been such a fool not to make his move before, and now wasn't the time either, but he'd be damned if he didn't want to slake his lust with her. Once would do it. *Okay, who am I fooling?* At least a dozen times, but then he could walk away knowing he'd purged her from his soul. Eradicated the hold she held on him once and for all.

No one should have the power to seduce to the magnitude she did. Hell, it had taken everything out of him tonight to let her walk away. His cock had been so hard, almost as hard as it was now, from the second she moved over him.

It would have taken nothing but a moment for him to pull her sweats down and thrust his aching shaft deep within her. As small as she was on the outside, he'd be willing to bet she'd be likewise on the inside. He'd have to make sure she was excited enough so her tight little pussy could accommodate his long, thick shaft. Just the thought of sinking balls-deep inside her had his cock jerking in his hand.

"Fuck," he muttered, and squeezed the head of his cock, running his palm over the dripping slit then down his length, using his own juices for lube.

Shane picked up his tempo and felt the familiar tug on his testicles. He was so close. Close to spraying her pretty brown breasts with his hot, milky-white seed. He could imagine how she'd look beneath him, vulgar and wet with the evidence of his desire.

Or maybe instead of coming on her, he'd move up a bit and press the plum-shaped crown of his cock past her lips and into the warm haven of her mouth. He'd always been fascinated with her mouth, with the full plumpness of her mocha-tinged lips, the cotton candy pink of her tongue. Shane would happily give up his right nut for a chance to sink his cock balls-deep between those two precious lips.

Squeezing his eyes shut even tighter, he imagined Paige on her knees before him, mouth open to receive his dick. He groaned as he fantasized about Paige sucking him, tasting him, begging for his cum.

"Hmm…yeah…" His moans rivaled those of the woman faking on-screen, but he didn't care. Shane needed to come. No, what he needed was to fuck Paige, but that wasn't an option so he'd have to fuck his fist instead.

Oh, but if he could, he'd sink balls-deep inside her. He would do her so good she'd never give another man a second look, let alone a shot at a chance of slipping between her legs.

"Paige, Paige," His mind was flooded with images of her, not all sexual, some from memories past, but all of the one woman he couldn't stop thinking about. "Fuck."

Shane tightened his fist around his shaft and sped his strokes until his hand nearly became a blur. He imagined Paige under him, begging him to fuck her, telling him how good it was. Her pussy would clamp around his cock as he powered into her and she would be his. Finally.

That final thought had him soaring. Paige. His at last. Shane bit back a groan as he came, shooting stream after stream of creamy semen from his pulsating cock.

A sharp noise from the doorway drew his attention. Shane opened his eyes and turned his head, all the while stroking his still-spurting shaft. To his surprise, Paige stood in the open doorway, frozen, staring at his hand splashed with come, working his dick.

The shock of seeing her there, in living color, after vividly imagining her seconds earlier was surreal to say the least. "Paige. I—" he whispered, but it was too late. The sound of her name on his lips sent her scurrying back from where she came, but not before he noticed her nipples beaded underneath the short nightshirt. Shane wasn't sure how long she'd been there, but he was willing to bet it hadn't been for only a few seconds and he would put down double to nothing he hadn't been the only one who enjoyed his release. Now all he had to do was get her to admit it.

Chapter Six

☙

"Yeah. Yeah. I love you too." Laughing, Paige shook her head and hung up her cell phone. Even when she was feeling unsure about the world around her, all she had to do was make one phone call and she instantly felt better. It was a good thing, considering how her world had been spun on its axis last night.

God, just thinking about what she walked in on was enough to make her flesh warm anew. Never in her wildest dreams would she have ever imagined walking in on Shane masturbating. The image of him lying on his bed, cock in hand, was one that would stay with her forever. "Finger-lickin' good" didn't come close to describing the way she felt as she watched his cum come spurting out. It took everything in her to remain standing in the doorway and not slink over to him and replace his hand with her mo—

"Did you give Urkel my love too?"

Startled, Paige turned around to face a frowning Shane and placed her hands on her cheeks. She could feel her skin warm under his glare thanks to her wayward thoughts. "Christ," she said once she could get her heartbeat back under control. "You scared me."

"I'd be scared too if I had to say 'I love you' to him every morning," he grumbled as he limped into the kitchen, leaning heavily on his cane.

Under any other circumstances, Paige would have fired off a witty, cutting comment that would have left Shane crying in his cereal, but she was having a hard time doing anything other than staring at him. Shirtless and dressed only in jeans, he was quite a vision. His sable hair and chest were still damp from the shower she'd heard running a few minutes ago, leading her mind to travel down a road it need not venture. This is not good, not good. She was practically engaged, she shouldn't be having these thoughts.

"What?" Shane glanced down his body. "Did I leave my zipper open?"

"Uhh...no." Before she could do or say something stupid in regards to last night, Paige moved her hands from her face and returned her attention to the stove. She needed to stay busy to keep her mind and her hands off things that didn't concern her. "I was talking to my brother Perry, not Jaffee."

"Oh." Shane's voice had sounded completely annoyed until she mentioned her brother's name. "What's he up to?"

"The same." Paige toyed with the edge of the pancake with her spatula. "Driving my parents and his teachers crazy. He's been accepted to five different colleges but hasn't applied for a single scholarship. He'll be kicking it at the local community college, working at a burger joint, if he doesn't get his shit together soon."

"Give him time. Let him enjoy being a senior for a bit."

She flipped the pancake over once more to test the underside before scooping it up and placing it on the plate with the five she cooked earlier. "He's going to get to enjoy the perks of saying 'would you like fries with that' if he doesn't get on the ball. A good education is far too important to blow off because he wants to hang with his boys." After turning off the stove, she placed the skillet on the back burner before facing Shane again. "Anyway, enough about my knucklehead brother. Are you ready to eat? I made breakfast."

Shane glanced to the counter at the three platters brimming with breakfast goodies. "So I see." With a firm grip on his cane, he hobbled over to the counter and snagged a piece of bacon cooling on a paper-towel-covered plate. "Where did all this food come from?"

"Your refrigerator. Surprising. I know."

"I know that, brat," he said, nudging her with his arm, "but it wasn't in there prepared. What time did you wake up?"

It was more like what time did she give up the pretense of sleeping? "I didn't wake up that early," she hedged, not lying...exactly. "Besides. It's just eggs, bacon and pancakes. Simple fare for simple folks."

"It doesn't seem simple to me. Lord knows I couldn't have cooked all this without setting off the smoke alarm." Shane turned around and stole another piece of meat. "And I can't remember the last time I had pancakes."

"Well, don't get too excited. I didn't use Holden's famous recipe or anything," she teased, referring to the breakfast staple Holden made whenever the seven of them gathered together for a weekend getaway. "But I figured they would do."

"I'm sure they're much better than Holden's. I think the only reason they were famous to begin with was because it was the only thing he knew how to cook. Sort of like's Tripp's famous BBQ burgers or Skylar's famous menu drawer."

Paige laughed. Skylar didn't even attempt to cook. She could dial, though, with the best of them. "I guess we aren't all that original, but we do know how to have fun."

"True." Shane rested the cane against the counter and raised his hands high above his head, stretching his long, lanky frame. Despite knowing how wrong it was, Paige ran her gaze over his bare chest, taking in every newly formed scar, the wide planes of his pecs, the sexy little happy trail leading into his jeans. Six months working with a trainer had definitely done his body good. Everything inside her begged her to reach out and feel for herself just how good it all was.

"Thanks for making breakfast." Shane's voice brought her attention back to the here and now and away from the "don't think about it, don't talk about it".

"No problem. Besides, I figured it was the least I could do, considering how I did come up uninvited and all. And speaking of breakfast," she said with false pleasantries, "everything is done. Do you want to go throw on a shirt before we eat?" And then maybe she could concentrate on something besides how good he looked.

"Not especially."

"Okay." There went that diversion. Paige picked up the plate of bacon and handed it to him, forcing her gaze to stay at chin level or higher. "Take this and I'll bring the rest."

She'd put the game away and set the table earlier, leaving little left to do but fill the glasses with juice and bring the food out. Shane looked at her for a moment, as if he were going to say something, but then nodded and took the plate from her outstretched hand. She breathed a sigh of relief, hoping she had dodged a bullet. After setting the rest of the food out, Paige went back to the kitchen once more to retrieve a jug of orange juice from the refrigerator. With a carefree smile she didn't quite feel, she joined him at the table, filling both their glasses before setting the bottle down and taking her seat.

The easy conversation they shared in the kitchen dissipated once they were sitting across from one another, filling the room with tension so thick it was suffocating. Unable to meet Shane's gaze, Paige concentrated on loading her plate.

Picking up her fork, she toyed around with her eggs, not necessarily hungry but knowing she had to eat. Besides, if she ate, it would be a good excuse for why she couldn't talk. After getting a good scoop of food on her fork, she raised her head to look over at Shane to see how he was enjoying his breakfast. Unlike her, Shane hadn't made a single move toward the food. He sat quietly in front of her, hands crossed over his chest, staring straight at her with an amused expression on his face.

"What?"

"Truth or Dare."

She knew eventually they'd get back to this, she just hadn't expected it to be so soon. "We haven't even eaten yet."

Shane didn't waver for a second. "Truth or Dare."

Paige took a bite of her food and thought about her options. Basically, either way she went she was screwed, so she might as well put her big-girl panties on and deal with it. After swallowing her food, she took a dainty sip of her juice and went for it. "Truth."

"Are we ever going to talk about it?"

"It?" Paige looked everywhere but at Shane.

"Yes, it. My big it, even."

"Oh that."

"Yes. You walked in on me jerking off."

That was succinct. "What's there to talk about?"

"Oh, I don't know." Shane unfolded his arms and reached for the pancakes. He selected two before picking up the dish containing the eggs. "I can think of one or two things, can't you?"

Paige watched him fill his plate, feeling a bit trepidacious. She could see the trap, knew she was about to step right into its springy net, yet she could find no way around it. "Other than I'm sorry, not really."

"You're sorry?" He looked up and eyed her with speculation. "Why are you sorry?"

"You know, for interrupting your…" she paused to search for another word, "moment."

"Did it look as if my moment was ruined to you?"

Paige could feel her face warming again. "I guess not. Still, it had to have been a little embarrassing."

"No." He shrugged his shoulders then dug into his eggs with gusto, like a man who had everything right in his world. "Not really."

Now this she could not believe. Even Shane couldn't be this cavalier. "Seriously, you don't care in the slightest that I saw you being one with yourself?"

Shane set his fork down and shook his head in disgust. "Stop right there," he ordered. "You're a nurse, for goodness sake. Surely you know better words for masturbating."

"Talking dirty isn't a class they teach in nursing one-oh-one."

"Come on, do you actually say 'one with yourself' when you're masturbating?"

"Say it to who?" she asked amused. "It's not as if I'm going around announcing to everyone I'm about to touch myself."

"Well, what do you call it when you get yourself off for Urkel?"

"I don't call it anything because I don't do it in front of him."

"Never?"

"There's no need. He does it just fine for me." When they did it, that was. Which, of late, hadn't been often. "Just fine."

Displeasure marred Shane's brow. "As pleased as I am to hear the two of you are setting the sheets on fire," he replied in a biting, dry tone, "and believe me, I'm so pleased, I'm a bit disappointed to know you don't masturbate in front of him."

That made about as much sense as this conversation. "Why?"

"Because speaking as a guy, there is nothing hotter than watching a woman finger herself. Nothing. Don't you enjoy it when Urkel does it in front of you?"

"He...I..." Paige couldn't even imagine Jaffee in the same position she found Shane last night. She didn't want to. "We don't watch each other."

"You don't know what you're missing."

It was time to bring this topic to a close. "I'll have to take your word for it."

"Don't take my word for it. Didn't you enjoy watching me last night? I know you were there for more than the curtain call."

Just like that Paige felt herself tumbling down the rabbit hole. The trap was sprung, and she fell for it so easily it was out-and-out embarrassing. "I've already apologized for that. I should have left the second I realized what you were doing."

"But you didn't, did you?"

"No."

"Why?"

"Wow, this has been the longest Truth question ever." Paige picked up her glass with a shaky hand and raised it to her mouth. All of a sudden she was thirsty and desperate to find something to do with her tongue instead of flapping it. She chugged a good portion of her juice before setting the glass in front of her. "Okay, isn't it my turn now?"

"Can't hide forever, Paige."

"I can surely try." Paige took a deep breath. "Truth or Dare, Shane."

Shane watched Paige dance around the topic of last night like a prima ballerina. "I'm not sure if you should have a turn."

"Why?"

"Because I like this topic." He liked it a lot, in fact.

"Of course you do. Anything to embarrass me."

"Why are you embarrassed? It wasn't your body covered in semen."

"All righty, then." Paige rose from her seat. "I'm done."

Shane glanced at her full plate then back at her. "You've had one bite. Two tops."

"I'm not hungry." Paige grabbed her glass and headed for the kitchen. Acting fast, Shane pushed back his chair and reached out and grabbed her arm. "Hey."

He wasn't going to let her go so easily. "Hey, nothing." Shane moved back even more and pulled her to him, forcing her onto his lap. With one hand he took the glass away from her and with the other he anchored her to him.

It took everything out of him to keep his hand at her waist and not move it down to her bare legs. He didn't know what deity he had to thank for the sexy lavender short set she was wearing, but whoever it was, he owed them a statue in their honor. The color and the cut of her outfit highlighted not only her mouthwatering skin tone but her firm thighs and legs. The stretchy tank top was V-cut, teasing him with a peek at the gentle curves that lay beneath the soft cotton fabric. Damn, she looked good. He shouldn't be thinking of her in this manner. Instead, he tried to remind them both why they were here. Goading her, he asked, "Quitting already?"

"No. I told you. I'm done." She wiggled, trying to free herself, which was a wasted effort of both time and energy, but felt damn good against his denim-covered cock. "Let me up before you hurt yourself. I know your legs are bothering you this morning."

"My legs are fine." Pain was a friendly reminder he was still alive. Lord knows he had enough of it to know that. "Besides, you weigh like thirty pounds."

"Not hardly."

"I can barely feel you." Except for the one place where it counted most.

Paige glanced over her shoulder at him, her face immediately clouding over with concern. "That could be because of poor circulation. Let me look at your legs."

"Paige."

"Seriously, Shane." She gripped his hands and tugged. "I'm not playing around."

Shane smiled at her nurse voice. It was like a mom voice but less manipulative. "What'll you give me if I let you look?"

"A clean bill of health."

He snorted. "My doctor already gave me that."

"Then why not do it to give me peace of mind?"

Because he didn't want her seeing him as less than a man even though he felt that way a bit. Of course he couldn't tell her that. He'd die first. So instead, he deflected. As usual. "There's nothing for you to look at."

"Fine. I dare you to."

Shane couldn't help but chuckle. She was a determined little thing. "I didn't pick Dare."

"I'm picking it for you."

"I think you just want to get me out of my pants."

"Think what you want. Just drop them. Now. Or do you want to lose again?"

Shane released her instantly and watched as she rose to her feet. He knew a challenge when he heard one, and of course he couldn't let it slide. "I didn't lose last night." He felt the need to remind her as he took hold of the arm of the chair and used it as an aid to help him rise. "I let you win."

"Keep telling yourself that," she said in her condescending way before eyeing him with wary trepidation and obvious concern. "Do you need help?"

That was the last thing he needed. He wasn't an invalid, for Christ's sake. "No. I can do it. But brace yourself." Shane placed his hands on the button on his jeans. "It's not pretty."

"Somehow," Paige dropped to her knees in front of him, a position his stiffening shaft immediately welcomed, "I sincerely doubt it."

His cock picked a helluva time to jump up and say "hi", but it wasn't as if Paige hadn't already seen an eyeful last night anyway. With his gaze firmly centered on Paige, he unbuttoned and unzipped his pants. He watched her intently as she caught her breath when he pushed the denim down his hips and past his calves. When his jeans hit the floor, he tried to step out of them, but the material was too coarse for a smooth transition.

"I know you said you didn't want any help but..." Her gaze skated over his erection as she reached out to steady him. "Deal with it."

"Thanks."

"No problem." Paige sat back on her heels and stared for a long moment. He wondered what she was thinking but wasn't willing to break the silence to ask her. In what seemed almost timid at first, she reached out and traced the sharp remains of his multiple surgeries. His scars were puckered and deep red but healing nicely.

The doctors had told him in a few years they would fade away almost entirely, leaving behind just the memory and a slight permanent welt to remind him of his close brush with death. And if he were lucky, his mind would heal as rapidly. Nightmares aside, Shane still had more mental issues than *Sports Illustrated* magazine. His mind was brought back to the present as she gently probed at the zigzagging marks on his legs. "Nice."

"Glad you approve."

"I knew you would." Smiling, she spared him a quick glance before moving her hands around to the back of his legs. She lightly massaged his calves, as if trying to ease his pain, causing him to grow tense. The second she felt his discomfort she moved her hands and looked up at him again. "Am I hurting you?"

"No," he bit the word out. Pain was the last thing he was feeling. "You're not hurting me."

"You sure?"

Shane crossed his arms over his chest and willed his cock to behave. Despite his wayward thoughts from last night, he couldn't risk his dick acting out. It was one thing to fantasize about Paige and something entirely different to act on it. "Trust me. I've been in enough pain to recognize it by now."

"True." Paige rose to her feet, bringing his pants up with her. "Everything looks fine."

Shane took over when his jeans were mid-thigh and pulled them over his butt. He zipped up but left them unbuttoned. "That's because it is. I couldn't sleep, even after all that. I went out and swam. I might have overtaxed myself."

At his words, Paige frowned. "You shouldn't have swum alone. I would have gone with you."

That was news to him. "Really, because after the way you took off last night, I could have sworn you wanted to be as far from me as humanly possible. In fact, I was surprised to see you still here this morning. After you saw me and heard me, I was sure you'd be long gone." Which probably wouldn't have been a bad thing. As much as he wanted her, he was bad news right now. But later, oh later, she and he were going to have to have words.

"Heard." Paige licked her lips and looked away. "I didn't hear anything."

"Liar."

But he was going to let it slide. This time. He didn't want to start a fight. Not when he still had something important to tell her. Before she could try to escape once more, Shane reached out and took hold of her hand. "Thanks."

"For what?"

Hell, he didn't even know where to start. She had done so much for him, for so long, in numerous ways, that it seemed impossible to narrow it down to a single thing he was grateful for. "For being you?"

"Just doing my job."

Shane stepped back and ran his gaze down her less-than-professional outfit. "I don't see a little white dress."

"Nurses don't wear those anymore."

"And it's a shame." Since Paige seemed less like a flight risk now, Shane sat back down in his chair. He didn't release her though, instead he pulled her right back onto his lap, despite her laughing protest. "Speaking as someone who was surrounded by nurses almost twenty-four hours a day, cartoon character smocks are not the last thing a man wants to see before he meets his maker."

Laughing, Paige turned sideways on his lap, enabling them to see each other more clearly. "Leave it to you to think with your cock first, even when you were knocking on heaven's door."

"Trust me, I was nowhere near heaven."

"You're not as bad as you pretend to be." She flashed him a smirk.

"And you're not as good as you would like people to think you are."

"Oh please." She crossed her arms. "I'm so good."

"Good girls don't watch bad boys jerk off."

"Can't let it go, can you?"

"Nope." Shane wasn't sure why, but needling Paige was some of the most fun he'd had in a long time.

"You're such a child. When are you going to grow up?"

"Grow up?" Shane stuck his tongue out in disgust. "Who wants to do that?"

"Lots of people."

"Name one."

"Jaffee."

There she went again, bringing up the erection deflator. "You know, I think you enjoy saying his name to piss me off."

"Why would talking about my boyfriend piss you off?"

Shane sent her a leveled look. "Why wouldn't it? When are you guys going to break up already? You're really beginning to test my patience with him."

"We're not going to break up."

"Right."

"He asked me to marry him."

"Not funny."

"Wasn't meant to be."

Shane waited for her to crack a smile, but she didn't. She kept staring at him solemnly, as if he were the one who had lost his mind and not her. Finally reality smacked him in the back of the head. "You're not kidding?"

"No." Paige licked her lips, a telling action if ever there were. "He asked me on Wednesday."

"Tell me, Paige." Shane clenched his hands into fists in an effort to keep from shaking some sense into her. "Did he take it too badly when you laughed in his face?"

"I didn't laugh and before you ask, I didn't say no."

Shane could feel his blood pressure rising. "You can't marry him."

"Why not?"

Shane stared at her blankly. Was she serious? "Would you prefer the reasons alphabetically or numerically?"

"I'd prefer them to be real reasons and not just because you dislike him." Angry, Paige rose from his lap and moved away from him. Pivoting, she turned back to face him, hands on her hips. "It sucks that you don't like him, Shane, but it's not my problem."

"The hell it isn't. Tell the truth, Paige, you didn't come up here just for station identification, you came here to get away from him." Suddenly everything made sense. "You don't want to say yes and you're looking for the balls to say no."

"You don't know what you're talking about."

"I know someone about to marry the man of her dreams doesn't take a break so she can weigh the pros and cons of his proposal." Shane was feeling coldly furious. "And they definitely don't watch as another man jerks off."

"That was an accident."

"The stumbling in on me, sure. The staying and watching while I come, not so accidental. Admit it. You liked it, didn't you?"

She raised her chin and shook her hair back over her shoulders, meeting his unflinching glare head-on. "No."

Shane didn't let her obvious lie hold him back. He knew the truth, and he wouldn't be happy until she admitted it, to herself and to him. He'd been willing, more than willing, to let things simmer between them until he was in a better position to approach her, but her actions were forcing his hand. "Liar. Not only did you like it, you wanted to join me, didn't you?"

"No."

"And remove my hand to replace it with your own."

"No." Her voice grew louder and more desperate, but Shane would not relent. This was too important for him to back down now.

"Did you want to climb on top of me and sink your sweet cunt on my stiff cock?"

"Damn it. I said no. Stop asking me these crazy questions."

"I'll stop asking you when you start telling the truth, Paige." Shane rose to his feet, angrier than he'd ever remembered being before. Over the last year he'd learned as only one who'd experienced trial and suffering had that life wasn't fair. Nothing was driving home that point, however, as this madness taking place now. She couldn't marry him. She just couldn't. "Admit it. You wanted me last night. You wanted my hands on you and yours on me."

She shook her head as she backed away from him. "I'm done playing."

"Who's playing?" He'd never been more serious in his life.

"You are and I'm not going to indulge you a moment more. I have a man, Shane."

Shane snorted. "That's debatable."

"A good man," she continued as if he hadn't spoken, "and I'm not going to ruin it to give in to you."

"You mean give in to yourself, don't you?"

His accusation stopped her in her tracks. "You don't know anything."

"I know you don't want him the way you want me." And Jaffee could never want her as much as Shane did.

"You're a conceited ass." In her anger, she stepped toward him, ready to do battle once more. They were mere inches apart now, separated only by empty space and her rage.

"But I'm a truthful conceited ass," he admitted with no shame. "And you want me. Just as I want you." And it was time they both stopped denying it.

Chapter Seven

Paige stared at him with disbelief. She couldn't believe his bravado. Wait. This was Shane she was speaking about. Of course she could believe it. It was just so like him to toss out a relevant piece of information and expect her to act as he would, without any thought of the consequences. "I...I..." Paige shook her head, trying her best to process the madness swallowing her whole. "I have no words right now. None."

"You better come up with some and quick." He cocked his head and stared at her pointedly. "Admit it, Paige. Admit you want me."

She couldn't. She wouldn't. Not without a good fight. "What good would that do?"

"It would finally put it out there for us both to see. Then maybe we can stop avoiding the inevitable."

That wasn't a good enough reason for her. She'd been ignoring her feelings for him for a while now. Disregarding them for the ten minutes it would take to leave here now was a walk in the park compared to the last few years. "Nothing is inevitable, Shane, but death."

"I disagree."

He would, stubborn ass. "That's your prerogative."

"I never figured you for a coward."

Even though she knew he was only taunting her, his words raised her hackles just the same. "I'm not."

"You could have fooled the hell out of me," he snapped.

Annoyed, Paige took a step away from him, needing to put a little distance between the two of them before she did him harm. There was no one on this earth who could push her buttons so fast or so hard. "What do you want from me?"

"The truth would be a good start."

She'd teased him yesterday about his ability to handle the truth, when the fact of the matter was, she couldn't. "What good would it do to admit it? It won't change anything. I might want you, Shane, but I'm not going to act on it."

"Why the hell not?"

"Because I'm with Jaffee." And she was going to marry him. It was the right thing to do, even if it wasn't what she truly wanted to do.

Shane's mouth turned down in disgust. "Fuck him."

"Very mature."

"Right, because hiding behind him is real mature." His remarks hit a little too close to home for her. "Tell me this, Paige. If he's so real and if he's the man you want to marry, then how come you're here with me?"

"I'm asking myself the exact same thing." This was a mistake. She should have never come. Shaking her head, she turned and walked down the hallway to the bedroom where she'd spent the night. Unfortunately she wasn't the only one on the move. Shane was right behind her. He wasn't as fast as she was because of his cane, but he definitely put every step to good use and he cleared the doorway just as she plucked her backpack off the floor and set it onto the bed to pack.

The second he walked in Paige expected for them to pick up right where they left off. Instead, Shane merely leaned back against the wall and watched her through hooded eyes as she packed her meager belongings. The silent way he stared unnerved her. In her mind, Shane being quiet meant he was plotting, and Paige had a hard enough time dealing with him when he was working off the cuff.

Flustered, she placed her hands on her hips and faced him, unable to deal with the silence any longer. "What?"

Unlike her though, he didn't seem the slightest bit phased. "Running now?"

"I'm not running. I'm walking away." At a rapid speed, as if the hounds of hell were right behind her.

"Walking to what? To whom? You and I both know this thing with him will never work."

The calm, matter-of-fact way he spoke rubbed her the wrong way, mainly because she knew deep down he was right. But she would be damned if she admitted it. "I don't know any such thing."

"Then know this. You don't love him, Paige, and to be honest, I'm not too sure he loves you, either. Come on. You're smarter than this. Saying no is not only the right thing to do, it's the smart thing to do."

"What am I doing that's so stupid?" she replied in a sarcastic tone. "Considering marrying my boyfriend?"

"No, considering marrying someone you're not in love with."

"I do love him."

"But you're not in love with him." Shane pushed away from the door and slowly made his way across the room to her.

Refusing to budge, Paige raised her chin and met his determined gaze with her own.

She would not back down.

She would not cower.

"You're wrong." Her voice was strong, and even to her own ears her lie rang as truth. Maybe if she could convince him she would be able to do the same to herself later on.

"No, I'm not. Deep inside you know it." He reached her side and stared into her upturned face. "Damn it, Paige, don't do this. Don't make this mistake. You'll only end up regretting it."

"I thought you were my friend." Her voice quivered with frustration.

"I am," he said through gritted teeth.

"Then as my friend, you should be happy for me and congratulate me on my impending nuptials or whatever people do when someone shares this sort of good news with them."

Shane released his cane, reached out and curled his hand around her upper arm and pulled her to him. "Then let me speak as the man about to fuck you. You say yes to him and it will be the biggest mistake of your life." Bending his head, Shane captured her mouth and silenced her in the best way she could ever imagine. His tongue plunged into her mouth, demanding entry, not asking. Shane kissed her as if he had every right to, and her body responded in agreement.

Nothing this wrong had ever felt so right. She wasn't the type to cheat, never had before, and would have sworn she never would. But one taste of Shane's lips had her rethinking everything she'd ever held true.

His mouth devoured hers in a kiss so commanding and passionate it left her breathless and hungry for more. In all her years she'd never been so thoroughly made love to, all without removing a single stitch of clothing and never before had she felt as fucked as she did now. Paige knew she shouldn't be enjoying the taste of him as much as she was, but knowing had nothing to do with the reality of the moment. And it was a helluva moment.

Before she could lose her head entirely, Shane broke the kiss. Instead of releasing her though, he pulled back a bit and peered down at her with eyes filled with stubborn resolve. "You can despise me all you want, Paige, but if you go through with this, you'll hate yourself more."

"Yo-you think you know me so well." Her words were as stuttered as her breathing.

"Yes, I do." Shane tightened his hold on her. "And you know I do. That's what pisses you off so much, isn't it?"

"I'm not going to give you what you want."

"The hell you're not." Shane took his hands off her arms and wrapped them around her waist before taking her mouth under his once more. This time Paige was ready for him and waiting. She figured they could argue from now to doomsday or they could put their mouths to better use. She slipped her hands up his shoulders to wrap around his neck, pulling him closer to her as she surrendered to not only his wants but her own.

She welcomed his tongue inside her mouth and his hands on her body, especially as they made their way down her slender frame. When he reached her cotton shorts, he shoved them over her hips.

Frantic, she followed his lead, moving her hands between them to tug at his zipper and free his erection. Because neither of them were in a hurry to end their kiss it took twice as long as it should have for him to push her shorts past her thighs and for her to take his shaft in her hand.

His erection was thick and long and from the feel of him, not only was his cock impressive, his reputation was well-deserved. She stroked him feverishly as he ran his hands over her exposed flesh.

He brushed his hands over her ass, cupping the firm flesh.

They released one another and broke from the kiss long enough to push their garments to the floor and stepped out of them before coming together once more in a passionate embrace. Paige was still wearing her top, but that small fact didn't seem to bother either one of them. The important parts were bared and that was good enough for now.

Despite there being a perfectly good bed just inches away, Shane backed her against the wall. Gripping her, he raised her hips, causing her to automatically wrap her legs around his waist. The new position did something her morals did not. It caused Paige to push against him in an effort to be released. "Wait. Your legs."

"Fuck my legs," Shane ordered as he reached between their bodies to center his crown against her slick opening. "Tell me, God, please tell me you're on something."

"Yes." Paige was thankful one of them was thinking because Lord knows she wasn't.

"Good." And with that, Shane thrust inside her. There were no words of endearment, no passionate looks or even a warm-up period to get her wet and ready. She didn't need it. The fight had been foreplay enough.

Eyes closed, she held on tight as he began a frenzied rhythm, pumping himself in and out of her at a backbreaking pace. The intensity of his loving was so overwhelming she had to bite down on her lip to muffle her moans. Deep inside she'd always known they would end up together like this, but never did she think it would feel so damn good. Shane was everything she'd ever imagined and more. He took her with a fierce passion that damn near took her breath away.

"I...oh...mmm...I..." she moaned as she pushed down, meeting him thrust for thrust. She couldn't form a coherent sentence, but Shane seemed to get the gist of what she was saying.

"That's it, baby," he encouraged through gritted teeth. "Take my cock. Fuck me with your sweet pussy."

"God. Shane." Paige had never had someone talk dirty to her during sex, and it was amazing how erotic the words sounded pouring from Shane's lips. Then again, everything was better when it involved him, why did she even think sex would be different?

"Not his. Mine," he bit out savagely. "Mine."

Unable to argue with the truth, Paige wisely kept her mouth shut and tightened her arms around his neck. She leaned into the wall, using the sturdy structure as an anchor to hold her upright as Shane pushed into her, over and over. He blinded her to everything around her, making her focus on him and him alone.

As she climbed the steep hill to paradise, Shane rearranged his grip on her. He held her steadily against the wall with one hand as he moved the other between them to strum her engorged clit.

The new contact had her singing out with pleasure. "God...yes..."

"Like that, do you?"

"Yes. Don't stop. Donnnnnn—" she pleaded as her body raced closer and closer to her release. "Ohhh...mmmmm."

"Fuck yes." His voice had a frantic edge, and she could tell he was as close as she was. "Come for me."

As if she'd been waiting for those words, her body began to tremble with pleasure. Gripping him tighter, she cried his name as she came, her orgasm powering through her like a freight train. Her release was so intense it bordered on painful. "Fuuu... Shane..."

Her orgasm was the catalyst to his own. Gritting his teeth, Shane pumped his hips once more, burying his cock as deep inside her as he could go, and came, filling her with his creamy, hot seed.

"Fuck, fuck," he cursed as he trembled against her in the aftermath of his fierce climax.

Shane held himself inside her for a few seconds before slowly pulling out of her well-used body. After lowering her back to the floor, he released her and made his way to the bed. He dropped more than he sat, all the while breathing as if he'd run a marathon, which in essence, Paige had to admit, he practically had.

She also had to admit to a whole lot of other things. Things she wasn't so sure she was ready to face just yet. Had they really...had she? Her body trembled with aftershocks as her mind filled with the ramifications of their thoughtless actions. Wordlessly, she walked on shaky legs over to where her shorts lay on the floor. She was stopped by Shane, however, who reached out and grabbed her arm, pulling her to him.

"Stop it," Shane ordered in a harsh and demanding tone. "Stop feeling guilty. What we did wasn't wrong. You don't belong to him."

"No," she admitted to Shane, and finally to herself. "I don't."

"Then say it. Say who you belong to." Paige closed her eyes and pressed her lips together, unwilling to say the words that would give Shane the keys to her soul. But he would not be deterred. "Say it."

"I belong…" Opening her eyes, Paige peered down at him and focused her gaze on her irate lover. "To myself."

To her surprise, instead of becoming more upset, Shane laughed. "That's my girl. Fight me to the end."

As much as it would have pleased her to do so, Paige couldn't. The fight had gone out of her. At last.

* * * * *

Shane moaned in appreciation as he sank into the bubbling water of his parents' hot tub. His he-man act had really seemed like a good idea at the time. Now, two pain pills and a beer later, he wasn't so sure. His legs were sore as hell, but even despite the throbbing ache, Shane knew he'd do it again in a heartbeat.

Paige, on the other hand, didn't come off as feeling the same way. She seemed a little too shell-shocked for his peace of mind. And to his surprise and dismay, she'd insisted on showering alone. He'd asked her join him outside in the hot tub after her shower, thinking it best to give her a little space and time alone. He could tell by the wary look in her eyes Paige was still reeling. Truth be told, so was he. Although he'd wanted her for as long as he could remember, it was still a little heady to have his dream come to fruition.

But if he was only allowed to have one dream come to life, then this one was a hell of a good one. Even if he wasn't exactly proud of the way it went about. Sitting back in the hot tub, with his head leaning on the rim and his eyes closed, he thought back over the last hour and mentally kicked his own ass.

What the hell had he been thinking? Oh wait, that's right. He hadn't been. Because if he had, he would have never fucked Paige like that. She was his friend, one of his best friends, and she deserved better than a careless screw against the wall.

It wasn't as if he was sorry they made love, far from it, in fact. He just regretted the manner in which they did so. In his anger, he allowed his lust to overrule his common sense. In his haste to stop her from making the biggest mistake of her life, he'd taken her roughly, showing her no more affection than he would some girl he picked up in a bar. Paige deserved better than that.

Truth be told, she deserved better than he had to offer her, no matter which way Shane approached their problem. Yes, sex between the two of them had been as fucktastic as he'd always imagined it would be, but as of today, sex was all he could offer her. If Shane were forced to do an evaluation of his life and tally up the good versus the bad, he'd have to admit his cons would outweigh the pros.

It would be a year or so before he was done with his physical therapy and who knew how long he'd be in psychotherapy. Despite his degree, thanks to the accident he was unemployed. Sure he had money, but none of it was of his own making. He cared for Paige, loved her even, but as the old song went, what's love got to do with it?

Despite everything, he couldn't regret making love with her and hopefully changing her mind about Jaffee. True, Shane himself was nowhere good enough for her, but neither was that pocket protector. The difference was, Shane knew it, and he refused to allow Paige to settle for anything short of the world. Whether he liked it or not, he knew he had to put things back to the way they were before he messed things up entirely.

"Fuck," he muttered aloud, his mind fraught with confusion and uncertainty. What the hell was he going to do?

"Wow, don't you sound all post-coital tristesse? I thought that was my job."

Paige's voice startled him and woke him from his mental funk. Opening his eyes, Shane sat up and peered at Paige, who was standing next to the spa in a teal two-piece swimsuit. She fiddled with her dark hair, pinning it at the top of her head as she waited for his answer.

Instead of replying right away though, Shane took his time, drinking in her barely covered form. How in the world had he managed to keep his hands to himself all this time? More importantly, how was he going to manage keeping them off her after experiencing paradise in her arms? "Post-coital tristesse?"

"Uh-huh."

"Is that another one of your egghead words?"

"Sort of. It basically means to be sad after sex."

"Do you really think I could possibly be sad after having sex with you?" Shane stood and offered his hand to her.

"Actually," Paige took his hand and stepped carefully into the spa, hissing at the heat of the water as she sank into the warm tub. "I'm not quite sure what to think right now."

That was a feeling Shane was familiar with. "I see." He moved until he was across from her before sitting and leaning back against the backrest. She wasn't alone in her uncertainty. He was swimming in it. "Do you regret it?"

"Do you?" she fired back.

"Well," Shane hedged, just to annoy her a bit. "I regret not taking your shirt off so I could see your breasts."

Paige laughed at his comment. "They're just boobs."

Not to him, but they could argue about that later. "I also regret not lying down on the bed."

"I told you your legs would hurt. Do you need me to—"

"But most of all," he said, interrupting her before she went into nurse mode. "I regret not eating your pussy." Especially if it was his only chance to do so.

Paige opened her mouth to snap off another retort, but then closed it as his words sank in. He almost laughed at the stunned expression on her face. Who would have thunk it? His Paige. Speechless.

"Oh please, I beg of you," he teased, enjoying this side of his fighter. "Don't tell me that all this time, in order to get the last word with you, all I had to do was say something dirty?"

"I...ahh...of course not."

He didn't believe her for a second, but because he was such a nice guy he was going to let it go. For now. "What about you, what do you regret?"

"Nothing."

"Good to know." Shane smiled at her words. Her nothing meant something to him. He scooted over on the bench seat until he was sitting right next to her and took her hand in his. There was no reason they had to rush right back to being friends only. "So you enjoyed my less-than-impressive moves?"

"I wouldn't say they were less than impressive."

"Really?" He brought her hand out of the water and kissed her damp palm before lowering it back under the water and setting it on top of his rising erection. Unlike her, Shane hadn't put on a swimsuit. A fact he was very happy about now. "Because I would."

"Oh." Intrigue filled her voice and she took hold of his cock. "That seemed A-game material to me. I mean, I came."

"Yes, but only once."

"Once is good."

"That's the problem. I'm so much better than good." Shane leaned down and licked the shell of her ear.

"Mmm…Shane." Paige pulled her hand away. "We…we should probably talk."

"We will," he said as he took her hand in his once more and placed it back in its rightful place. His lap. He had to have her one more time. Just once, then they could talk. "Later."

"You're insatiable." She laughed. His cock had grown hard under her hand, giving her words credibility as nothing else could have.

"You say that as if it's a bad thing," he teased.

Paige began to slowly stroke his cock, holding his gaze all the while. From the heated look she was giving him, Shane could tell he wasn't the only one getting revved-up. "We're going to need a condom. Maybe even two."

The idea of fucking appealed to him, but the thought of sheathing up after riding her bare did not. "Why?" he asked confused. "I thought you said…"

"Yes, I am, but that was 'heat of the moment stupid me' talking. I'm a nurse. I should know better."

Shane frowned. "You worried your birth control won't be effective?" He hadn't thought about that. Frankly though, the idea of a little girl in the image of Paige didn't scare him. Even though it should have. He had nothing to offer Paige, let alone a baby. Hell, he could barely take care of himself these days. Yet knowing all that, Shane still loathed the idea of a condom.

"No, but kids aren't the only thing to worry about." She cocked her head. "You do have a reputation to live down."

Shane's brows shot up. She was worried…about him? Removing her hand from his cock, he reached out for her and pulled her onto his lap so she was facing him. "I'm clean. I swear it. I would never do anything to put you in harm's way."

Paige gave him a smile. "I know you wouldn't."

"I haven't gone bareback since high school and I've been tested since then. Many times," he said, wanting to assure her in every way possible. "And again after the blood transfusion, but that was for my own piece of mind."

"Shane," Paige laid her finger across his lips to silence him. "I believe you. I'm clean too, I just…well, you know you?"

Shane pulled back so he could speak. "I can't change my past, but I can own up to it. I've never been a choirboy, but I don't have a death wish, either. More important though, I would never do anything to hurt you."

Paige sighed and looked away. A move that upset Shane more than he ever thought possible. Reaching out, he took her chin in his hand and turned her face back to his. "Do you trust I would never hurt you?"

"Never…is a big word."

"Never," he assured her with emphasis. "Hurt you. Tell me you believe me."

She opened her mouth then closed it and nodded. "I believe you."

"Tell me you want me."

"Needy much?"

He was where she was concerned. "Stubborn little minx." He reached behind her and attacked the strings to her top. "Going to make me work for it, aren't you?"

"Hell yes. Things come too easily to you as it is."

"You didn't," he reminded her as he freed the strings at the center of her back before moving on to the ones at the back of her neck.

"Didn't know you wanted me."

"I did. Right from the start. It's always been you."

"You sure hid behind a lot of girls."

"But I'm not hiding now." The knot gave, causing the teal top to drop into the bubbling water, followed quite closely by Shane's gaze, which zeroed in on the sexiest brown morsels he'd ever seen. "Looks as if I'm not the only one done hiding."

The sight of her breasts made him suddenly want to travel back in time. These were breasts to be worshipped, held in wonder. Not something to be discounted lightly. They were pert and round, and from the looks of things, they'd fill his hands quite nicely without spilling out. And if that wasn't cock-hardening wonderful enough, both breasts were topped with the smallest areolas he'd ever seen. Her nipples themselves were like dark chocolate Hershey Kisses, peaked out, begging to be touched.

"They're just as I knew they would be." Shane bent forward and laved one of her nipples with his tongue before sitting back up and smiling. "Perfect."

"Not too small?" she moaned, arching into his touch.

"Not at all." And to show her how perfect he thought they were, he lowered his head once more and covered a nipple with his mouth as he cupped her other breast.

He teased one bite-sized nipple with his fingers as he suckled the other in his mouth, dragging moans of approval from Paige. Her breasts might not have been as big as those of his last few dates, but they seemed more sensitive. From the moans she was making, and the way her hand gripped the back of his head, Shane was willing to bet he could make her come from using his mouth on her tits alone.

He was going to try that out. Soon. But not today. Today he had to get back inside her wet warmth or go mad from lack of trying. Reluctantly he pulled his mouth away from his new favorite tongue-resting place. "I want to fuck you again." Even though he knew it was wrong, he couldn't help it.

Paige undulated on his lap, rubbing her still-bikini-covered pussy over his erection. "I could tell."

"Know what I can tell? You have way too many clothes on."

"Just this one tiny thing?"

"If you want to keep this one tiny thing intact, take it off. Or I'll take it off for you."

Laughing, Paige pushed off him and moved to the center of the spa where she pushed her bottoms off before climbing back on his lap. "Happy now? I'm now naked."

"Happy doesn't come close to describing it." Shane gripped her hips, pulling her tight against him. Damn, she felt good. Too good. And before he lost what little sanity he had left, there was something he needed to ask. "Do you want me to go grab a condom?" He hadn't really given her a choice before, but he would this time. Shane didn't believe in making the same mistake twice.

To his immense pleasure though, she shook her head as she took his cock in hand. "I trust you and I don't want there to be anything between us when you come inside me."

"Careful what you ask for or I might just come before I get inside you. I'm a man out on the ledge here, woman."

"Then let's see what I can do to send you over." She took him in slowly, teasing them both with her unhurried downward descent. Just when he thought he'd go mad with longing, she seated herself fully, engulfing his cock in her sweet sex. The heat surrounding his pussy-covered shaft rivaled that of the water splashing about around them. And even though he knew it wasn't true, he felt as if it'd been an eternity since he had last been in her welcoming depths.

Damn, she was tight. It took almost an act of God to work her up and down his shaft. At this rate, he'd have to fuck her at least twice a day to get her body accustomed to his width and length. That was a chore Shane was more than willing to take on.

Even with the water as an added lube, it still didn't give him much in the help department. Shane could only wonder if her pussy was this taut, how her ass would be. He was willing to bet she'd never been taken back there, something he'd have to rectify and soon. But for now he had a pussy to accommodate.

The water, already splashing about, grew tidal-wave deadly as they began to move against one another. The bubbling spa didn't necessarily create an ideal spot to make with the loving, but it didn't hurt, either. Of course with the heat they were generating, plus that coming up from the hot water, Shane was sure he'd eventually pass out. It would be entirely worth it, if he was able to get her off just before he slipped into a heat-induced coma.

For the first few minutes Shane allowed Paige to set the rhythm and just sat back and watched her ride on his dick. Her pretty little breasts beckoned for him to come back for another taste of their sweet, dark flesh, but he held back, knowing there would be time for that later. For right now he was simply going to concentrate on sinking his cock deep inside her, again and again. He closed his eyes, letting the sensations wash over him, the feeling of her riding him, the touch of her hand on his neck. All those little things were beginning to get to him, however.

Unable to give up complete power, Shane gripped her hips and worked her up and down his cock, controlling the movements and her release. His new approach didn't win him accolades from Paige, who apparently was under the mistaken impression it was she who was in charge. When she tried to speed up, he tightened his grip on her and slowed her down, never letting her go any faster or any slower than he decreed. After a few minutes of his loving, she gripped her hand in his hair and pulled. "Bastard."

"Yeah, but you love it. Don't you." He thrust his hips upward as he pulled her firmly down on him, causing her ass to smack against his lap. "Love me taking over and making you work for it. Love me making your pussy mine."

"Yes, but I hate you," she gasped, rising once more to repeat their demented dance.

"I can live with that." He began to rock her faster and harder, causing her to dig her fingernails in his shoulders to hold on as he sped up his thrusts. "That's it, baby. Fuck my cock with your juicy pussy. I can't get enough of it. Enough of you."

"Shane...ohhhh." Throwing her head back, she let out a cock-tingling cry of pleasure as she came. Her body trembled as she undulated her hips, fucking him through her orgasm as if striving for another.

If that was her goal, Shane was just the man to help her achieve it. "Come for me. Flood my cock with your sweet dew," he ordered as he continued to drive his cock into her as she sank down.

"Yes. Yes. Yes" Her cries were barely audible over the roar of his own. After a while, Shane lost the ability to make any sound whatsoever. He sped up her thrusts, feeling his own orgasm approaching at a ball-breaking rapid speed. Despite that, he held out until she came again before succumbing to the pleasure himself.

Exhausted, Shane collapsed against the backrest of the spa with Paige sprawled across him, head on his shoulders, arms lying limply by their sides. If he wasn't so damn tired himself, he might have laughed. But he could barely work up the energy to blink.

Once he was finally able to breathe without feeling as if his lungs were on fire, he spoke. "Fuck."

Paige raised her head off his shoulder and peered up at him with a sleepy little look in her eyes. "What?"

"Once again," he grumbled, "you managed to withhold your pussy from my mouth."

"Sorry," she said with a smile that didn't look the least bit repentant. "I was too busy riding your cock to think about moving up a few inches to ride your lips."

"Then think about it next time. Sheesh. What's a man have to do to eat some pussy in this house?"

"Try fucking me in a bed."

"Oh," he said as if the mere thought had never occurred to him. A bed. What was that all about? "Now there's an idea with merit."

"But feed me first. A girl has to keep her energy up around you."

"I'll make you a deal. I'll feed you then you feed me."

She stuck out her lower lip and lowered her gaze as she grumbled. "If I must."

"Oh trust me. You must." And the sooner the better—for the both of them. If they only had tonight, he was going to make sure it was the best night of both their lives.

Chapter Eight

"Let me ask you something."

Paige rolled over onto her side, away from the flickering fireplace she'd been staring into absentmindedly and faced Shane, who was studying her intently. Lazily, she propped her head up on her hand and ran her gaze down her lover, grinning when she spotted his thickening cock. It had been over twelve hours since their first sexual encounter and just minutes since their last, and somehow he still had the energy to speak. They had made love half a dozen times in so many positions and ways that even the back of her knees were sore, and yet he was still lounging about with a semi, as if the other six times had only been appetizers.

He and his cock were her new heroes.

"The answer is no. I'm tired. My pussy needs a break." Though she was sure with the right motivation she could be properly convinced otherwise.

Shane chuckled softly. "Pay no mind to the man below the bellybutton. Despite his rousing interest, that's not what I was talking about."

"Oh. Then…ask away."

"Where do you see this going?"

"This what?"

"Us."

"Wow." He considered them an us. Smiling, Paige felt her heart swell with joy. For so long she'd protected her heart from him, fearing he'd hurt her, only to find out she couldn't be further from the truth. Feeling all kinds of good, she reached her hand out and ran her fingers lightly across his cheek. "Isn't that my question as the girl?"

"Normally yes, but before things went too far, I thought we should talk about it."

"Went too far?" Good mood gone. Feeling a little bit too exposed now, Paige sat up and reached for her shirt lying only a few inches away and slipped it on. "What do you mean 'too far'?"

"You know I care about you. Right?"

"Yes." This conversation was quickly going downhill. And the faster it rolled, the more clothes she felt the need to put on. With nervous hands she grabbed her shorts, stepped into them and then rose to her feet, pulling them up her legs as she did.

"And I still want to see you." Shane rose painstakingly slow to his feet but bypassed his sweats to go straight to her side.

"I would hope so," she said with a little shaky little laugh.

"But I don't think it's a very good idea if we do. See one another, I mean."

Her stomach knotted and for a moment, she feared she'd be sick. "Excuse me?"

"I have a lot things going on with me, Paige. Things I need to deal with."

"And seeing me would complicate that?" Paige stared at him, her body cold, her heart pounding so hard she was sure it would burst from her chest at any moment. Was she dreaming? Was this all some chlorine-induced nightmare, or was Shane really saying what she thought he said?

"Complicate is not the right word." He ran his hand through his dark hair in obvious frustration. "I'm not saying this right."

Paige disagreed. She thought he was saying it right, but just in case he needed another word, she had a few for him. "How's 'fuck it up for you', then?"

"You're getting upset for no reason."

"No, I think I have a very good reason." Every emotion rained down on her as she fought with all her might to remain standing. She felt disillusioned, hurt and angry, but most of all she felt stupid for believing she could ever mean anything to him. "Tell me something, Shane. Was this like the world's longest one-night stand or what?"

"Of course not."

"Then what is it?"

"I can't be in a relationship right now."

"But you can fuck me and ensure I mess up any chance I have of having a relationship with someone else?"

"Someone else like who, Jaffee?" He spat the other man's name out as if it were distasteful.

"Oh, I see you can say his name now."

"And I see you're trying to run right back into his arms." Shane crossed his arms over his chest and his lips twisted into a cynical smile. "Tell me, Paige, would he be so quick to give you a ring if he knew you spent almost the entire weekend riding my cock?"

No. He. Didn't. "Oh my God. I can't believe you. I can't believe what you made me do."

"Whoa." Shane jerked back as if she'd slapped him. "Let's get one thing straight, Paige. I didn't make you do anything. You wanted me as much as I wanted you."

"It wasn't just sex I wanted, Shane." She shook her head, the regret she hadn't experienced before now filling her so full she felt as if she were drowning in it. "Fuck. I knew this was going to happen. I knew it was going to happen, but I let myself believe your bullshit and lies."

Without giving him a chance to respond, Paige tore from the room, barreling down the hall until she reached the guest room. With wide eyes, she scanned the room, looking for any and every trace of her brief trip to hell. Single-mindedly she gathered her clothing and dumped it on the bed before storming over to the closet and yanking the door open to retrieve her backpack and slip on her shoes. By the time she made it back to the bed, Shane was standing in the doorway, dressed now in sweatpants and accompanied by his cane.

"I never lied to you."

She could tell by his sincere tone he really believed what he was saying. Well, that made one of them. "Maybe not with your words but most definitely with your deeds," she said as she began to stuff her backpack. "I can't believe I hurt a good man for you."

"Good," Shane scoffed. "Face it, Paige, there's nothing good about him or evil about me. You're just mad because I made you face up to something you've been waiting to deny for too long."

"What's that?"

"That you're not in love with him."

"Wow. Gee. Thanks a lot for that. Don't I feel loads betters? You saved me. Now I guess instead of having a bad relationship, I have no relationship."

"I'm not saying no to a relationship, Paige. I'm just saying not now. I have to get my shit together before and be good for myself before I'm ever good for you."

"Which one of us is in denial, Shane? You'll never be good enough for me."

His blue eyes sharpened with anger. "Honey, I'm the best thing that could ever happen to you."

"Well, your best isn't good enough." She was a fool, a fool who needed to wise up, and quick. "You know what the worst part is? I have no one to blame but myself."

"Why does there have to be blame at all?"

Paige yanked one of her shirts from the bed and jumbled it into a ball before tossing it in her backpack. "Because assigning blame assigns responsibility. So I blame myself and give myself the responsibility to make it right."

"And how do you plan on doing that?"

"By getting the hell out of here and never speaking to you again."

"How the hell would that solve anything?" Shane looked as if he could barely speak his jaw was so tight.

"For a start, it would go a long way to make me feel better."

"This isn't just about you, Paige." He stepped forward as if he were going to grab her, but his hands remained at his sides.

"Right, just how it wasn't only about you until you climbed up on your pedestal and made it that way."

"I. Didn't," he said, in a firm, unwavering tone.

"The hell you didn't. You're a selfish asshole and you don't care what happens to anyone else as along as you get your way."

"That's not true."

"The hell it isn't." It was sad how things seemed so clear in hindsight. "You didn't want me to marry Jaffee so instead you fucked me."

"Oh please." His curt voice lashed out at her. "You're not a victim in this, Paige. I didn't force you. You wanted me too. You admitted you didn't love him."

Her cheeks burned with resentment and humiliation. Leave it to Shane to remind her of her own idiocy. "Fat lot of good it did me. This is what I get for changing horses midstream. I...I need to talk to Jaffee."

"And tell him what?" His chiding tone made her angry. "You don't love him. You can't marry him. Even you wouldn't go that far to get back at me."

"Everything isn't about you. He's a good man. He'd forgive me."

"Why on God's green earth would you want him to? You keep hiding behind this saintly person when the sad truth of the matter is the only reason you want to be with him is because he allows you to control the entire relationship. And to you that makes him perfect, but that's not perfection. It's stupidity."

"You would know," she retorted with cold sarcasm.

"I do." His face hardened until she barely recognized him. "You can't control me, Paige. I'm my own flawed person. I don't fall in line with the rest of these bootlickers you date. I won't toe the line. I tend to be a bit of a dick and do not-so-nice things sometimes, but I'm also the same man who was inside you just moments ago, making you scream."

"And you're the same one who just managed to break my heart." Paige clapped her hands together repeatedly in a slow, condescending way. "Kudos to you and your many multiple personalities. I hope you all rot in hell."

"You're scared and running, Paige."

"Funny, Shane, I was thinking the exact same thing about you." No longer caring if she gathered all of her stuff, Paige zipped her backpack and slung one of the straps over her shoulder. "Bye, Shane. Thanks for…thanks for nothing."

"Don't go to him," he urged. "He won't make you happy."

"Yes, well, he can't make me unhappy. Thanks to you, no one else can or will again."

"Don't do this," he ordered. "I just need time."

"Take all the time you want, and when you get everything hunky-dory, forget you ever knew my name." Weariness filled her body and she had the sudden urge to crawl into a bed and pull the covers over her head. For the next month or two. "Goodbye."

For a moment she thought he wouldn't let her pass, but then to her surprise he stepped back into the hallway, giving her the room to leave. "This isn't goodbye. Far from it, Paige."

Shane could argue all he wanted. She was done fighting with him. Hell, she was done with him in general.

* * * * *

Present Day

Things weren't exactly going as planned. Although he hadn't for a second thought she'd give in to his charms so easily, he also didn't think she'd fight him tooth and nail. God, this was a disaster of titanic portions. All he wanted was to talk to her. To explain to her all the things he'd meant to say and try to take back all the things he did say. Yes, it was true he hoped his friends would reconcile as well, but nothing was more important to him than smoothing things out with Paige. Nothing.

"What do you say? If you come willingly with me to the cabin so we can talk, I'll make sure your brother receives the scholarship. Do we have a deal?"

"Do I have a choice?"

"You always have a choice." That was a lesson he learned the hard way when he made the wrong one. "It's just not always one of your liking." Shane reached over and took hold of the door handle. "Are you staying or going?"

"I hate you."

Shane flinched. No matter how many times she declared her feelings, it didn't get easier to hear. "That wasn't what I asked you."

Paige narrowed her eyes. "Staying."

Shane sat back in his seat. "Excellent." Acting as if her decision hadn't held him in knots, he casually lowered the privacy glass. "To the cabin, Morris."

"Yes sir," the driver replied, as if every day he took part in kidnappings.

Paige's snort of derision was loud enough to shake the car.

This ought to be good. "What?" he asked as he raised the glass.

"Yes sir," she parroted in a poor imitation of Morris' voice. "Is there anything your money doesn't buy?"

"Since I bought you for the price of a scholarship, I'd have to say no." Even as the words slipped out, Shane knew it was the wrong thing to say. Before their fallout three years ago, he wouldn't have thought twice about taking her to task for giving him shit about his wealth. It was how they'd been with one another. Each giving as good as they received. But now everything seemed to have a double meaning, an extra blow landed with every word. Shane couldn't help but wonder, even if he was able to explain things to her satisfaction, would they ever get back to the way they were? "That was a joke, you know?"

"Wasn't funny."

He sort of figured that out by the lack of laughter on her part. "Or maybe you can't remember how to laugh anymore."

"And if that's the case, I wonder who's to blame?"

"The first half I'll take full responsibility for."

"That's mighty white of you."

"The second half," he continued on through clenched teeth as if she'd never interrupted him, "is all your doing."

If he wanted to garnish her attention, it seemed he'd finally succeeded. Eyes wide, she stared at him as if he'd grown two heads. "How do you figure?"

"If you would have given me an opportunity to explain myself, we wouldn't be here today."

She frowned. "You know, you have a really twisted view of reality."

"That doesn't mean it's wrong."

"Do you even understand the concept of right and wrong?"

"Do you understand the concept of forgiveness?" he immediately countered.

"I understand it. I just don't practice it."

And he was living proof of that. "Tell me something I don't know."

"You're an asshole."

"No, I knew that." A small smile flickered across her lips before it slipped away. But it didn't matter. He saw it. "You know it's okay to let your guard down with me."

"Since when?"

"Since forever."

Paige grimaced. "You have a funny way of showing it."

"Not really, I just think your view is slightly askew."

"You fuck me, kick me to the curb, blackmail me and then kidnap me." Her voice was heavy with sarcasm and self-righteousness. Never before did Shane want to kiss her silent more. "I think my vision is fine."

"When you put it that way," Shane wasn't above mentioning his faults but things weren't as black and white as she wanted to believe, "I don't come off in the best of lights."

"Is there any other way to put it?"

Well, since she wanted to know. "Yes. I did it for you. All of it for you, and if you weren't so damn stubborn you'd realize that."

"When are you going to realize that all you're doing is pissing me off more than I already was?"

"Is that even possible?" he questioned.

"Before you called me with your list of demands, I would have said no."

Maybe he shouldn't have called, and instead just showed up and kidnapped her straight from her house. Somehow, though, Shane didn't think it would have gone any easier on him if he had. "Do you plan on fighting with me the entire way to the cabin?"

"Will it do me any good?"

"No," he admitted. She could argue until she was blue in the face and he would not waver from his plan.

"Then no." Paige crossed her arms and shot him a look of distaste. "I'll save my energy until we get there. That way I'll be all nice and relaxed while I kill you."

"Do you really want me dead?"

Paige turned her head to peer out her window.

Her silence was answer enough. Chuckling, Shane reached out and patted her leg, leaving his hand there for shits and giggles when he was done. "That's what I thought."

Paige pushed his hand away. "Don't touch me."

"Before this weekend is over, I'll be touching more than your leg."

"In your dreams."

Since all his dreams of late had revolved around her, Shane couldn't deny it. Instead he opened a side compartment, extracted two magazines and offered one to Paige. "Want one, it's a long drive?"

Paige glanced at the periodical before turning her attention back to the window.

"We could always play a game. Twenty Questions. I Spy." Paige clenched her hand, an action that caused Shane to smile. Oh yes, he could become used to this again. "The license plate game is always a win—"

"For Pete's sake." She snatched the magazine from his hand. "Happy now?"

"No, but it's a start," he said with a smile. "It's a start."

Chapter Nine

"Wake up, baby. We're here."

Wake up? When did she fall asleep? Drowsy, Paige lifted her head from the too-comfortable yet familiar place on Shane's shoulder and looked around. The interior of the limousine was still as dark as sin, but the same couldn't be said for the cabin outside her door. Geez, they were there. When did that happen? Somewhere along the two-hour route, Paige had fallen asleep on Shane, making the drive seem to pass in a blink of an eye. "You too sleepy to walk? I can carry you?"

His offer was a cruel wake-up call. Paige jerked away from him. The less he touched her and vice versa, the better. "No. I can walk."

"Pity."

Before she could formulate a reply, her door was opened from the outside. "Ma'am."

"Thank you," she automatically said to her kidnapper's accomplice as she stepped out. Good manners were a curse and a blessing.

"You're welcome," Morris said before closing the door behind her. "Tomorrow, sir?"

"Yes," Shane replied, already out and at her side. He moved so fast Paige couldn't help but wonder if he'd hurried in fear of her fleeing. If that was the case, his haste was in vain.

She was pissed but she wasn't stupid enough to try to escape into the woods to get away from him. If she'd learned anything from horror flicks, the black chick was always the first to die.

"After you?" Shane gestured with his hand toward the front door.

"Whatever," she muttered under her breath as she hurried up the path to the front door. Silently she waited for him to unlock the cabin before storming in the lit house. Ready to do battle, Paige attacked the second they entered, not even waiting for Shane to close the door before she started in on him. "So we're here. You wanted to talk. Let's talk."

Unfortunately though, Shane didn't seem as in a hurry to get things over and done with as she was. Instead of giving in to her fit, he calmly closed the door and locked it before heading into the living room, leaving Paige no choice but to follow him or hang out in front of the door like a big loser.

"Well," she asked once they were in the other room. "Get to it."

"Actually, all I really want to do is go to bed."

Bed! Hell no, Shane had seriously lost his damn mind. "If you think I'm fucking you, you're crazy."

"I do think that, but I don't think it will happen tonight."

The confidence of his tone only infuriated her more. "I love my brother but I'm not whoring myself out for him."

"I don't expect you to. You can stay in the guest room. It's already made up for you."

"Oh." His forethought took some of the wind out of her sails.

"Despite what you might think, or how you've interpreted my actions, all I really want to do is talk. Morris is heading to town. I've instructed him to come back tomorrow. If you want to go back then, I won't stand in your way."

The calm, cool, logical manner in which he spoke was such a contradiction to his behavior earlier, Paige was a bit taken aback at first. It couldn't be that easy, could it? "And Perry?"

"Scholarship is his. He'll be getting a personal phone call from the chairman of the Foundation Committee first thing Monday morning. You have my word on it."

"Thank you," she replied, stiff-lipped. Despite the manner in which he went about it, Paige couldn't help but be grateful for his help regarding the scholarship. She knew without him Perry wouldn't have even been a blip on the committee's radar as a candidate.

In the last few years her family had bent over backward to make sure her brother's tuition was paid without Perry having to take a job in order to allow him to concentrate on school full-time. The money he would receive would go a long way to ease a lot of the pressure their parents had been under.

"You're welcome," Shane said with a small smile. "Would you like me to show you to your room?"

"I think I can remember the way."

Shane shrugged as if she were being astute and leaned back against the couch. "Okay then."

His lack of sarcasm bothered her. She didn't want him to be reasonable. She wanted to fight. It was so much easier to hold on to her anger when they did that. "There is one small problem though. I don't have any clothes or any bath things here."

"Check the closet and drawers. There should be something—"

Jealousy quickly reared its ugly head. "I'm not wearing your whore's castoffs."

"You wouldn't be. Other than my parents stopping by a few times during the last three years, there hasn't been anyone here since you. In fact, last weekend was the first time I've stepped foot in here since our weekend together."

"Then how..."

"Everything in there was bought for you."

"How did you even know I would agree to come here?"

"Because I know you."

"At one time I thought I knew you too."

"You did. You do."

"Right. Since I'm too tired to try to Houdini my way out of here, I'm going to go to bed."

"Are you hungry? I had the refrigerator stocked. I can make a couple of sandwiches. Nothing too fancy, just something to tide us over until morning."

Now that he mentioned it, she was a little famished. But doubts still plagued her. "Are you going to slip something in it?"

"Yes," he drawled sarcastically. "Meat, mayo and mustard. If you're lucky, tomatoes too."

His mockery appeased her. It was good to know he hadn't planned on being anyone other than himself this weekend. Smartass Shane she could hold her own with, this apologetic, sincere dude she had no defense built up for. "Hold the mayo and make the tomatoes happen."

"Aye-aye, Captain." His smart-alec salute reminded her so much of how they once were with each other that it was almost painful to see. Even though she thought it was easier to deal with him when he was this way, it still hurt.

"I'm going to shower. I'll be back."

"Okay." His easy acquiescence was beginning to grate on her nerves. "If you need me to wash your back, just call out."

"I'll call you all right," she muttered to herself as she headed down the hall to the guest room. As he'd said, the bedroom was equipped with a few items of clothing, eerily close enough in her size she could wear them quite comfortably. The bath was stocked as well, with unopened bottles of shampoo, conditioner, shower gel and a bath scrunchie, all arranged hotel style in a basket on the sink.

Everything looked so inviting she was almost tempted to steal the fluffy cream bathrobe on the back of the door.

Shaking her head at the weirdness of it all, she started the shower and began to strip off her clothes. She had no idea why she agreed to be a party to her own kidnapping. In her rationalization, she told herself it was only for her brother. But truly, in her heart of hearts, she didn't really know if she believed Shane would have followed through with his threat.

No matter how ruthlessly he acted, she knew he was aware of the pressure her parents had been under. Even though she hadn't spoken to him, other than snide comments in passing over the last few years, she had talked with her friends about her woes. Their conversations had more than likely been leaked back to him, allowing him to help her in this sick and twisted way.

Wait. Was she making excuses for him? "God," she cursed aloud as she slipped the plastic shower cap on her head. It had only been a few hours and Stockholm syndrome was already kicking in.

Irritated with herself and the situation at hand, Paige pulled back the shower curtain and stepped into the steaming cubicle. Closing her eyes, she let the warm water wash over her. As much as she hated to admit it to herself, she wanted to hear what Shane had to say. After three years, she needed to understand why he'd left her brokenhearted. Maybe then she could finally move on.

Listening didn't mean forgiving, however. That she was something she wasn't sure she could do, ever.

* * * * *

After months of plotting and planning, the moment he'd been waiting for had finally arrived, and Shane was nervous as hell. This was it. His one and only shot and he couldn't blow it. Not again. As it was now, it was going to take a miracle to get Paige to hear him out, let alone forgive him. This opportunity was a one-time-only type of thing, so he had to have his game on and get it right or risk spending the rest of his life without the woman he loved. He'd barely survived the last three years sans Paige, he didn't think he could make it another three years.

"Need any help?"

Shane closed the lid on the potato salad container with a snap of his wrist. "No. I'm all done." He shot her a smile he didn't quite feel as he took the plastic bowl to the refrigerator. After closing the door, he looked over at Paige and drank in the sight of her.

She was wearing a pink and brown pajama short set he picked out for her, something similar to sleep outfits he'd seen her wear in the past and from the looks of it, it seemed to fit. With the exception of her new haircut, she hadn't changed much in the last few years. She was still as beautiful to him as she was the first day he'd met her.

From her relaxed stance and stress-free demeanor, he'd have to say the shower did her some good. She didn't remotely look like the same hot-tempered, irritated woman he'd arrived with. Maybe there was hope for them yet. "Feel better?"

"Are you still holding me here against my will?"

"Yes."

"Then no, I'm not."

"Fine." Or maybe his expectations were a tad high. It was just a shower, after all. "Let me rephrase. Did you have a nice shower?"

"Yes. If your parents ever decide to go into the bed-and-breakfast business, let me know. I'll be glad to write them a letter of recommendation."

At least she was pleased about something. "I'll be sure to let them know."

"By the way, should I even ask how you knew what size clothes to buy?"

"Hmm...no." There was a lot about Paige he knew that if it came out would make him a prime candidate for a police lineup. "It's better not to think about it."

"I had a sinking feeling that might be the case."

Shane walked back to the counter, picked up her plate and handed it to her. "Here you go, madam, your mayo-free, untainted sandwich is ready."

Her lips twitched as if she were holding back her laughter. "Thank you."

"It's the least I could do." Paige opened her mouth to reply, but Shane cut her off at the path. "No smartass comment necessary."

"Ahhh...am I hurting your feelings with all my cynicism and derision?"

"If you weren't cynical you wouldn't be you." He handed her one of the glasses of soda he fixed earlier before grabbing his own sandwich and drink and heading out to the table.

"Too true," she replied as she followed suit and walked out of the kitchen.

"And if I weren't plotting to control everything around me, I wouldn't be me."

"Amen."

Without saying another word they each took their seats, the exact same ones they used the last time they were together. A fact Shane was wise enough to keep to himself.

He waited a few minutes for them both to become settled before he spoke again. "With knowing me the way you do, why were you so surprised by what I went through to get you here?"

"It wasn't the kidnapping or even the blackmail that surprised me."

"Then what?"

"The fact you still care. You're like a dog with a bone. Let it go already. I mean, seriously, you got what you wanted, let's move on."

"What exactly is it you think I wanted from you?"

"Sex."

"You're wrong." Shane picked up his soda and took a drink.

"Really, because I distinctly remember you trying to chafe the hell out of my pussy three years ago."

Oh shit! His soda skyrocketed on the wings of his laughter, back up his throat and out his nose, thanks to her crude yet funny comment. Shane quickly moved his hand in front of his mouth to try to spare the table and his guest. "Fuck," he chuckled as he picked up his napkin to clean first his hand then his mouth. "That was mean."

"Thanks," she said, seemingly cheered by his statement.

"You seem in better spirits."

"You know," she cocked her head to the side and nodded, "I am."

As much as that pleased him, he couldn't help but be a tad wary. "Why?"

"Because I can either spend the rest of the night plotting the many different ways to kill you or I can just do my time and wait for my ride home and away from you."

"There's a third option I believe you're missing."

"Which is?"

"You could try listening to what I have to say." Shane shot her a mocking look. "You know, the complete opposite of what you did last time you were here?"

"Just like last time, I doubt there is anything you have to say I want to hear."

"Want, probably not, but need to, yes."

"Shane, do you honestly think anything you have to say is going to make a bit of difference?"

"I have to believe it will."

"Then you're more delusional than I thought." Paige picked up her sandwich and took a bite.

"I'm not delusional."

"What do you call it?"

"Dedicated," he said with a smile before picking up his own sandwich and diving in. After a few minutes they began to converse a bit, Paige loosening up as the time wore on. It was just as it used to be, almost. "I have a question for you."

She shrugged as if she didn't have a care in the world. "This is your hostage situation, ask your question."

He hated to go there since they were sort of getting along, but there was something he had to know. "What happened with Urkel?"

"Urkel, are you serious?" The disbelief on her face was laughable. "After all this time, can't you at least say his name?"

"Fine, Jaffee. Whatever." Three years later it still grated on Shane to say the other man's name. He could never get over knowing the other man touched his Paige, made love to her, and for a time had a right to call her his. "What happened with the two of you?" The answer to that riddle was one thing his money couldn't buy. "It's apparent you didn't say yes, so what did you say?"

Paige took a drink before answering. "The truth."

Shane raised an eyebrow at that shocking bit of news. "Really?"

"Well, not the part that involved you and me of course."

"Then what other truth was there?" Shane picked up his glass, feeling a bit smug. "Other than the part about you not loving him, that is?"

"I didn't say that, either." She set her drink back on the table with a loud clank. "I simply told him I couldn't say yes."

Her answer wasn't nearly good enough. "Did he ask why?"

"I don't really want to go into this with you."

"I can't imagine why." To be honest, he didn't care what pathetic excuse she gave Jaffee for ending things. He was just pleased she did.

"I'm sure you can't, but I'm not telling."

"What if I ask nicely?"

"I'd tell you to get used to disappointment."

There was a word he was pretty done with. "I've already had my share of it. Three years worth."

"Oh please," she said with a roll of her eyes. "You should thank me for leaving that day."

Was she mad? "Thank you?" His hand tightened around his glass. "I assure you, gratitude is the last thing I felt that morning. Or the day after. Or the day after that." Or the many, many days that followed. In fact, the only thing Shane had been grateful for in the last few years was the opening Perry gave him to get Paige back.

"It should have been. I gave you the best of both worlds, sex with no strings attached."

"All the while robbing me of one my best friends and the woman I love in the process."

Paige didn't even let his declaration set in before she stood. "What do you know about love?"

"More than you think," he said, coming to his feet as well. If she wanted to, they could talk about this right now and put everything out in the open once and for all.

"I sincer—" Paige took a deep breath and held out her hand to stop him from speaking. "No. I'm done for tonight. We can play this game tomorrow. I'm going to bed."

"One would think after three years your legs would be awful tired from all the running you're doing."

"Good night, Shane."

He watched her walk from the room without a backward glance. Damn it, as much as he wanted to talk to her, he knew this discussion in the vein it was going wasn't helping at all. He could only hope the morning brought cooler heads.

Chapter Ten

After tossing and turning for the last hour, Paige threw back the covers and headed down the dark hall into the kitchen for a drink. The conversation from earlier in the night was still pounding through her brain. As was the feeling of rightness she felt from being with him again. Without even trying, they had quickly fallen back into their old banter before reality reared its ugly head. They weren't friends. They couldn't be. Paige wouldn't allow herself to be stupid enough to fall for him again.

Again was probably not the most accurate word, seeing how she never really got over him. Yes, she'd been hurt by his actions and pissed off by his behavior, but the truth of the matter was she never stopped caring for him. She wished she could have, wished she could have walked way from him as easily as she'd been able to walk way from Jaffee. That, of course, was telling in itself.

God, what a mess she was.

Heavy-hearted, Paige made her way into the kitchen and over to the refrigerator. Nighttime snacking had become her mistress, but since her treadmill wasn't here to counter the effects of her unhealthy lover, Paige settled on a bottle of water.

She was just making her way back toward her bedroom when she heard a low moan. Frowning, Paige turned her head and stared down the hallway toward Shane's room. For a moment she thought she imagined it, but then the sound came again, and before she could stop herself she booked it down the hall to his room.

Unlike last time, his was door was closed. Holding her breath, Paige stood very still and listened to see if she could pick up any telltale noises. Other than the sound of what she could only describe as someone in distress, nothing could be heard. Softly, in case she was interrupting his alone time again, she knocked on the wooden frame. When she didn't get a response, she turned the handle and opened the door and peeked in, making sure she was as inconspicuous as possible.

Thanks to a small lamp sitting in the corner of the room, there was enough light for her to see Shane. And what she saw didn't mimic any form of masturbation she'd ever witnessed. The covers were disheveled and Shane was tossing and turning like a buoy on the sea. His eyes were pinched closed, his face was a mask of terror, and he appeared as if he were in the throes of a nightmare.

Pushing their petty differences aside, Paige moved toward the bed and quietly called out his name. When he once again didn't respond, she reached out and touched his shoulder, giving him a gentle nudge. Fast as lightning, Shane instantly awoke and jackknifed into a sitting position. Eyes wide, he grabbed hold of her arm and held tight.

"Ow...Shane." Paige could tell that from the hazed-over expression in his blue eyes he wasn't coherent enough to realize what he was doing. "Shane, it's just me. Paige. It's okay. You're okay."

"Paige..."

"Yes. You were having a nightmare, but it's over now."

Saying her name seemed to do the trick for Shane and he instantly released his hold of her. His breathing was erratic but he appeared more clear-headed and focused now. "Did I hurt you?"

"No." Paige had worked the emergency room far too many times to be brought asunder by a strong grip. "I'm fine. What about you?"

"Peachy," he murmured as he ran his hand shakily through his tousled hair. With a heavy sigh, he reached over to the bedside table and clicked a button, flooding the bedroom in warm ambient light. "Did I wake you?"

"No, I—"

"Christ," he muttered before she could finish what she was saying. "Why won't this shit stop already?"

"Stop?" Lowering herself onto the bed, Paige peered at him warily. "You're still dreaming about the accident?"

"Unfortunately, yes."

Her eyes widened as she stared at him in shock. She hadn't known. She wondered if anyone did. "Have you talked to someone about it?"

Shane let out a harsh laugh. "Sometimes I think it's all I ever talk to anyone about."

Paige wasn't sure who "anyone" was, but she knew it hadn't been her. "Do you have them all the time?" She couldn't even imagine reliving the accident again and again.

"No, thank God. Just when I'm really tired or stress—" Shane abruptly stopped speaking and looked away. "I'm sorry I bothered you."

"You didn't." But her conscience was beginning to. As a nurse, she should have realized what he was going through, instead she'd merely chalked up his bad moods to his slow recovery, never imagining it was something more. "I thought…" Paige paused and licked her dry lips before continuing. "I thought you were doing okay after the accident. You never said anything about nightmares or having problems sleeping."

"I kept a lot of things to myself at the beginning."

"Why?" But even as she asked the question, she knew the answer. Shane was the rock. The glue that held everyone together and he took his role very serious, even to the detriment of himself apparently.

"Everyone was already worried enough about me. My parents practically aged overnight and my friends were taking turns helping me take a leak. Adding one more thing to the list of worries seemed a tad bit selfish to me."

"Instead you kept it to yourself and bottled it up inside." She shook her head in disappointment.

"No, I talked to my therapist about it."

She waited for him to continue but he didn't until she insisted on the matter. "And…"

"And," Shane scooted back in the bed until he was leaning against the headboard, "he said, 'and this too shall pass'."

"But it didn't." And quite frankly she was shocked at the thought he'd been suffering this long.

"It's…" he paused as if searching for the right word, "lessened."

"I see…" Not really seeing at all. If this was the downsized version, she would hate to see the supersized one.

"I told you I had issues I needed to work through."

She remembered the conversation well but figured his issues had more to do with commitment phobia than some sort of posttraumatic stress. "I have to say this isn't exactly what I thought you meant."

"Would it have mattered?"

It would have, but it did no good to reflect on something she had no power to control. "I can't rewrite the past."

"No, you're too busy living in it."

Damn it, why did he have to constantly push her buttons? Annoyed at the new direction the conversation was heading, Paige stood. "And this is where I say goodnight."

Before she could make good her escape though, Shane reached and took her hand in his. The surprising gentleness of his touch was like the sun after a rainy day. "I wasn't trying to pick another fight."

She believed him, she really did, but that only made things harder on her. She had to stay strong. She had to. "You know what they say, 'if it looks like a fight and sounds like a fight...'"

"That's the real problem, Paige, fighting is what the two of us do best." Shane ran his gaze over her. "Or should I say the second thing we do best."

"You'll have to be satisfied with the silver because you don't stand a chance at the gold." Despite the way her body was warming at the simplest of touches from him.

"Since you've been gone I've been settling for a lot less than silver." Shane cocked his head to the side and grinned. "I'm not sure if it even counts as a mineral, now that I think about it."

Irritated, Paige yanked her hand from him. "Sad to hear the chicks you've been banging lately haven't measured up." Okay, she wasn't really sad, but she didn't want to hear about the other women he'd slept with, either.

"Banging." His brow furrowed in confusion before realization seemed to hit him and he gave a little half smile. "I haven't been with anyone since you and I were together last."

His words hit her like a ton of bricks. Was he serious? The mere concept was so un-Shane-esque it blew her mind. "You haven't been with anyone in three years?"

"Yes." He met her gaze head-on in an unflinching fashion that left little doubt to the authenticity of his words.

"Why?"

"When I told you I wasn't in shape to be with anyone, I wasn't just spouting off bad breakup lines. It was the truth. Besides, I only wanted you, Paige. No one else would do." Sincerity laced his every word. "Should I take it from your deer-in-the-headlights stare you can't say the same?" Even though his words were jesting, he looked anything but amused.

"The same?" She could but she would never give him the satisfaction of knowing the truth. He and his enormous ego would take it the wrong way and make it about him instead of making it about her and the lack of decent men she'd met over the years. "That's none of your business."

Instead of putting him in his place as she'd hoped, her comment made him smile. "Looks as if you can."

"Why do you say that?"

"Because if you had slept with someone you would have thrown it in my face just because you could."

What troubled her most was it sounded just like her, and she couldn't tell what bothered her more, the fact she was the kind of person who would do that or the fact he knew she was. "Goodnight…Shane."

"Goodnight, Paige," he said with a smile too smug for words. "Thanks for waking me. I'll see you in the morning."

As she left the room, she somehow felt as if Shane now held the upper hand, and she didn't like the feeling one bit.

* * * * *

Paige came out of the bedroom as Shane was placing the baskets of muffins on the table. Knowing Paige was an early riser, he'd set his alarm to wake him at six thirty just so he'd have time to make her breakfast. It hadn't been easy to get up when the alarm had gone off. Falling back to sleep after having a nightmare was never an easy thing, but Paige's presence last night made it all the more difficult.

Three years ago he'd let her go because he needed time to heal. He'd finally thought he was ready to be the man she needed him to be only to have a frickin' nightmare. All the vulnerability returned tenfold, to the point where he wondered if he'd ever be healed enough.

In some ways he didn't think he'd ever be a hundred percent again, but this time he had the common sense to know the right thing to do. And that wasn't to push the person he loved most in the world away.

If last night's little episode had warmed her heart toward him in any way, Paige was doing a good job of keeping it to herself. Although she was less antagonistic during breakfast, she was far from engaged. Instead she was politely civil, a trait that in no way resembled the woman he knew and loved. By the time they were through eating, Shane was ready to bang his head against the wall.

"What time is Morris coming?" It was the first iota of conversation she'd initiated, but unfortunately for him it was in no way one he wanted to discuss.

Annoyed, Shane pushed his plate away. "Still in a hurry to leave?"

"Did you think I wouldn't be?"

"I was hoping." Sighing, he stood and walked around the table to her chair and pulled it out for her so she could rise. He waited until she was standing before he placed his hand on her lower back. "Let's continue this in the living room." If they were going to fight, they might as well do it in a more comfortable setting. One where there were less sharp, pointy instruments within her reach.

"Fine." Her posture was stiff, but she allowed him to lead her in the sitting area before she broke away from him and sat in the plush chair cattycorner to the couch. She appeared indifferent, as if his words would be negligible at best. "Let's get this over with."

Gritting his teeth, Shane tried his best to temper his rising frustration. Over the course of their estrangement he'd thought of little else but mending the broken bridge between them. He had speeches on top of speeches planned, reasons and explanations by the tons, yet now that she was in front of him, he could only think of one thing to say. "I should tan your ass."

"What the hell." Affronted, Paige sprang to her feet. Gone was her blank stare and in its place was one that could have killed him on the spot. She was pissed, but anything was better than the vacant disinterested persona she'd worn like a new wardrobe only seconds earlier. "Tan my ass?"

"And good," he said with a firm nod. "Man, my hand is tingling at the mere thought."

"The only one who should be hit around here is you. In case you've forgotten, you're the one who was in the wrong, not me."

"Right," he scoffed. "Me. Just me. And your yell-first, listen-second routine had nothing to do with it? You were so quick to leave you never gave me a chance to explain."

"Because there was no explanation."

"Yes, there was, but you were too stubborn to listen. With you, Paige, there is no gray, only black-and-white. Right or wrong. With you, sins are either forgivable or, as in this case may be, unforgivable."

"Of course it's unforgivable. I can't believe you want me to make this easy for you. I mean, easier than giving in to your blackmail and demands."

"You know what? Yes, yes I do." If he was going to dream, he might as well dream big. "Make this easy. I won't tell anyone. It will be our little secret."

"You know what they say, two can keep a secret," Paige took a menacing step forward, "if one is dead."

"What are you so afraid of, Paige?" he asked as he took a step as well. "Giving in to me, or giving in to yourself?"

She pressed her lips together and shook her head, refusing to answer. But he wasn't in the mood to allow her to escape him so easily. "No, Paige, I think you owe me this."

"I owe you?" She took another step forward. "Think again, buddy. I don't owe you anything."

"Tell me, damn it. Tell me what it is you're afraid of."

"I can't do this again. I never expected hearts and roses from you three years ago. But I didn't think you'd throw me out the door, either."

Her take on the situation was vastly different from his. "I wasn't the one running. That was you."

"Not true. You might have been sitting here calmly, giving me all the reasons you couldn't be with me, but it was running away, plain and simple."

"I was being smart. I was no good for you then." Shane ran a hand through his hair. "It didn't mean I didn't care. It was the exact opposite. I cared too much. Still do."

"What you failed to realize is I would have stuck by you through all that stupid shit. I would have been at your side."

Her words raised his spirits. "Because you loved me, right? Because you still love me, even now."

Biting her lower lip, she looked away. "I'm not saying that."

But she wasn't denying it, either. "You don't have to. I knew the second you left I had made the biggest mistake of my life."

Raw hurt glittered in her eyes as she turned to face to him once more. "And now you expect me to do the same and let you in my life again?"

"Giving us a chance won't be a mistake."

"You can't know that." She shook her head regretfully.

"Just as you can't know it will." Unable to hold back any longer, Shane reached out to her and brushed his fingers over her warm, soft cheek. "Being without you these last three years was like losing a part of myself. I missed you more than I could ever say."

"Of course you did. There was no one around to check your ego at the door."

"True," he said with a small smile. "But there was also no one around who could make me feel like I was ten feet tall with just a glance. No one to make me want to be a better man. No one to care for me, care about me the way you do. You took my heart when you left, Paige, but you can keep it if I can have yours." Shane slid his hand around to cup the back of her head and pull her into him for a kiss. Paige's eyes widened but she didn't resist, going with the flow of things and moving closer to him until their lips were aligned.

And just as Shane began to move in to sample the sweet essence of her once more, the doorbell rang. Startled, he jerked back and swung his head toward the front door. Confusion filled him for a split second before reality kicked in. Fuck, Morris was early.

Paige stiffened and took a hesitant step backward, breaking his hold on her. Cursing to himself, Shane turned to her once more, only to be met by the haunted look returning to her eyes again. "Looks as if game time is over."

"Doesn't have to be. I can send him away."

"And what kind of fool would that make me if I agreed?"

The same kind he was for pursuing her when there was barely a glimmer of hope. "One in love."

"Shane, I...I can't."

"You know what I can't do? I can't let you walk away again. I can't stop thinking of you, can't stop loving you." Shane closed his eyes briefly before opening them and staring at her intently. "I can't live without you."

"Please."

"Tell me you don't think of me. Tell me you don't want me even though I hurt you. And I did. I know I did. But I'm here now, asking you to give me a second change. Give us a second chance. Don't go."

"I do still care about you and maybe if you'd told me everything, then things could have been different. But too much time has passed, too many things have happened. I can't..."

"Can't or won't?"

The doorbell rang again. "I need time."

There was no doubt in his mind if he let her walk out the door she would find a reason, any reason to never walk back in it again. Fear pumped through his veins as images of another day without her rushed through his mind. He couldn't do it again. He couldn't let her go. "I love you, Paige."

"Don't." Tears welled in her eyes, and she shook her head sadly before turning and heading for the door with him right behind her.

This was one time he would not concede, nor would he lose. "I love you," he said, this time louder and more insistent. "Stay with me." His fingers tingled with the need to reach out and pull her to him.

Instead of replying, she opened the door. Morris, who was waiting on the other side, stepped back to let her exit. "Hello, sir. Ma'am, are you ready to depart?"

"No," Shane said at the same time Paige said, "Yes."

"Okay." The other man's normally neutral expression broke for the first time since Shane had known him. He seemed unsure about what to do, taking a step backward. "Ummm... Sir?"

But Shane didn't care about Morris' uncertainty. All he cared about was Paige's. Even though she'd rushed to leave the room, she hadn't made a move to step outside, a sign Shane couldn't help but see as something good. "Paige."

"You hurt me." Her words were barely above a whisper.

The desolation in her voice was causing his heart to break in two. "I know, baby, and as God is my witness, I'll never do that again."

Her hand clenched around the doorknob, and he could practically see her struggle to remain with him. He knew everything he was asking went against the very grain of her soul, but it didn't stop him from asking, or hoping.

"How can I believe you?"

"You'll have to trust me, even though my past actions would give you case not to."

"Please don't ask this of me." Her voice cracked under the weight of her words.

"I'm not asking. I'm challenging you to do what you've always done."

"What's that?"

"Take me on. You never let me get away with anything before and you never backed down, no matter how big the odds against you winning were. So don't do it now. Play with me, Paige. Winner takes all." Shane was putting all his hopes and dreams in this one moment of decision. "I dare you to stay. I dare you to try. I dare you to love me." Shane waited and he hoped, and when Paige closed the door, he thanked the good Lord for an undeserved but well-appreciated second chance.

Chapter Eleven

Paige took a deep breath and stared at the wood grain of the door, wondering if she'd made the biggest mistake of her life. She was being a fool in love. Her feelings were something she still had barely admitted to herself, let alone Shane. Her only hope was that she wasn't taking this chance in vain. "I'm scared."

"Don't be scared, baby. Just love me." Shane reached out and turned her around and the instant she saw his face, she knew she made the right decision.

"I do. I love you so much." Without saying another word, she went into his embrace and burrowed into him. Here, with him, was where she belonged. He wrapped his arms around her and held her tight to him.

"God…baby." His voice trembled but his hold was steady, like him. "I love you. I love you." He murmured the phrase repeatedly until it was coming as fluently as the rise and fall of his chest. After a few seconds, the declarations drifted off, but the feeling of completeness stayed with her.

He loved her, just as she loved him and because of that, everything else could and would be worked out in time. Closing her eyes, she squeezed him to her. "Three dares in a row. I'm…I'm surprise you didn't double dare me."

Chuckling, Shane pulled back and rested his forehead against hers. "That was going to be my next move if this didn't work."

"What makes you think it did?" she teased. Just because she'd decided to stay and give it a go, didn't mean she was going to make things too easy for him. Paige didn't want him to start thinking he had the upper hand after all.

"Because you're still here." His logic was going to be the singular downfall to her great "make him squirm" plan.

"Maybe I just forgot my purse." Paige released her hold on him and stepped back.

"I know exactly where you left it."

"Where?"

"My bed." The corner of his lips turned upward. "Need help looking for it?"

Paige laughed softly. "One of us needs help, all right. And I think it's you."

"I know it's me." Teasing done, he lovingly ran his thumb on the underside of her chin before tilting her face up to his. The amusement fled from his gaze as gratitude poured in. "Damn, baby. I thought I lost you there for a second."

"I thought you did too," she admitted. "For a second there it was touch-and-go. I wasn't sure if I should stay or leave with Morris. Oh my God, Morris." Paige pulled away and looked back at the door. "I slammed the door in his face. After he drove all this way." She couldn't see his shadow anymore but that didn't mean he wasn't still out there. "Should we tell him I'm staying?"

"Don't worry, I think he figured it out."

"Jesus." She was so embarrassed. Shaking her head, she turned back to face an amused-looking Shane.

"It's okay. I'll slip him a bonus and apology later. Right now the only person I want to think about is you."

Since there was nothing she could do about Morris, Paige decided to concentrate on the matter at hand. "And I want to think about the many ways I'm going to make you pay for being such a jerk to me."

"Pay?"

"Yes. If you think about it," she said in a rational tone, "it's the only thing that could possibly work. I have a whole list of ways to make you earn your way back into my good graces. First, we can start off with a little sexual slavery."

"Sounds like a plan to me. Although," his forehead crinkled with confusion as he peered down at her, "I'm little perplexed about one thing."

"What?"

"How is you being my slave going to make me pay?"

It took her a second to get his joke, and when she did, she snorted. Damn, she walked right into that one. "Your slave." Paige slapped her hand against his chest in poor retribution as he laughed. "I think not."

"Maybe we can take turns," he said with a hopeful grin.

Turns. Now he was talking. "Do I get to go first?"

"And second and maybe third too."

His image-provoking words had her knees trembling and her pussy flooding with cream. "That's very magnanimous of you."

"I'm a giver. Let me prove it."

"What?" Paige looked around the living room. "Here? Again?"

"No, I was thinking of the bedroom to save wear and tear on my knees and your back."

Licking her lips, Paige reached out and cupped his denim-covered cock. "What makes you think it's me who's going to be on my back?"

"Honey, I'm game either way."

As was she.

Hand in hand, the two of them walked into his bedroom. Once there, they separated and faced off. Even though she hadn't admitted it, like him, it had been three long years since she made love. Paige wasn't sure if she could remember what went where anymore.

"Where did my magpie go?" Shane cocked a brow. "Having regrets already?"

"No." Far from it. "I'm a little out of practice. I hear it's supposed to be like riding a bicycle or something."

"More like a unicycle," he teased gently before turning somber. "All kidding aside, I'm as nervous as you are. But we're in this together and we have three years to make up for. Let's start one night at a time."

"I like the sound of that."

"From here on out. You and me."

"You and me." The words had barely passed her lips when he lowered his mouth and covered her lips with his own. And just like that, she was home. His tongue danced across her own as he kissed her senseless. Moaning she grabbed on to his shirt and held on tight, reveling in the powerful way he took command of her. She missed this closeness with him, even though they'd only had one night together.

Wanting—no needing—more than his lips, Paige broke away from his too-tempting mouth and took hold of the hem of his shirt and began to pull it up. Catching on, Shane took over and yanked his shirt over his head before tossing it carelessly over his shoulder.

Paige ran her gaze hungrily over his bare chest. His pecs were definitely larger than the last time they were together. "Somebody has been working out." She stroked her hands over his muscular chest. "I can't believe how hard and ripped you are."

"That's not the only part of me that's hard."

"Prove it." Grabbing the loop of his jeans, she walked backward to the bed, pulling him with her. When the back of her knees hit the edge of the mattress, she sat down and with her eyes on the prize, unbuckled his pants before carefully lowering the zipper over his bulging erection. Antsy to touch him, she pushed his jeans open and moved his boxers out of the way, causing his cock to spring out of its tight confinement. "Looks as if you were telling the truth."

"You know, looks can be deceiving. I think you should go in for a closer inspection."

"I couldn't agree more." Paige reached out and took his cock in hand, lovingly stroking him for a few seconds before leaning forward and running her tongue across his pre-cum-slicked crown.

The small taste of him made her hungry for more and she greedily took him deep into her mouth. His salty essence marinated her senses as she familiarized herself with him once more. Three years ago she'd only had a brief sample of his heady flavor, this time she wanted to make a meal out of him.

"Fuck, baby." Shane's heated words were all the approval she needed to swallow as much of his length as she could before working her way back up his shaft then down again.

Getting into the swing of things, she began to use her hand along with her mouth to pleasure him, stroking and sucking him at the same time.

"God, your mouth feels good." With a guttural groan Shane slipped his hand around the back of her head and began to set a rhythm all his own. His excitement made her own rise to heights unseen and her pussy began to weep from the pleasure of it all. And just as she began to speed up, Shane gripped her hair in his hand and pulled her off and away from his cock. "Stop, baby, before I come in your mouth."

Paige licked her swollen lips as she continued to stroke him and looked at him, desperate to have him inside her once more. "I don't mind."

"I do. Damn." Shane's breathing was as erratic as her own. Stepping back, he kicked off his shoes then shoved his pants down to the floor. "Strip now. I have to get at that cunt."

Sweeter words had never been spoken. Mad with desire, Paige rose to her feet and quickly undressed. As soon as she was done, Shane picked her up and laid her out on the bed. He climbed on the bed with her and settled himself between her parted legs. "My turn." Shane ran his fingers over creamed-covered nether lips. "Lucky, lucky me."

To Paige's immense delight, Shane buried his face between her legs and thrust his tongue deep into the depths of her sex. As if he were a man on a mission, he teased and lapped at her until she thought she'd go out of her mind with pleasure.

Shane was one of those people who excelled at many things. Lucky for her, eating women out was one of them. He knew exactly what to do to drive her wild and he wasted no time in bringing her to the brink with subtle twists and licks of his tongue. And just when she thought she couldn't stand a second more of his oral loving, he added his fingers to the mix. Dipping two digits into her sopping-wet pussy, he stroked and stretched her in the sweetest of ways.

Before she could become used to the feel of him inside her once more, he withdrew his dew-slicked fingers from her core. He moved them to her rosette where he pressed against it gently, all the while still feasting on her. Paige moaned and moved into his touch, loving of the feel of him against her puckered hole.

He pushed harder until his finger popped through the resistant ring and sank knuckle-deep inside her.

"Shane." She gasped his name as he moved slowly in and out of her ass. She had never had anal sex before but Shane was quickly making her long to experience the taboo thrill.

"Gonna come for me, baby?" Shane added a second finger into her tight hole and twisted it as he pumped it back and forth. "Gonna come from me fingering your sexy ass?"

"Yes." And how. Moaning, she buried her fingers in his thick, dark hair and pressed him harder against her. "Yes, God, yes," she cried as her body bucked with pleasure.

"Then show me, baby. Show me how much my dirty girl enjoys having her backdoor fucked." Before she could speak,

Shane covered her clit with his lips and sucked hard on the sensitive nub.

The unexpected pleasure was one too many to her overheated body, and with a soul-shattering cry she came, screaming his name in the process. Wrung out from her intense climax, Paige released her hold on him and dropped her hands to the bed. Despite her exhaustion, Shane was far from done with her. As she trembled in the aftermath of her orgasm, he moved up and positioned his cock against her wet slit. "Damn, baby, you make my cock so hard. Do I need to use anything?"

She was still on birth control and like Shane she hadn't been with anyone since they were last together. "Just your cock in my pussy."

"That I can do." And with that Shane thrust forward, sinking his cock in her with one fell stroke. The welcome invasion made her catch her breath. Notwithstanding their glorious foreplay, it had still been three years since she'd last had sex. It took her pussy a second or two to catch up with the rest of her, which was raring for him to fuck her silly.

Thankfully, Shane was wise enough to give her a few seconds to adjust to his girth and length before he began to move, but when he did, it was miraculous. He knew her as no other man did, which made being with him all the better. They fit together, not just physically but mentally, and it made the loving between them so much more than mere sex. It was love.

Neither muttered a coherent word as he thrust into her over and over. Paige couldn't say why on his part, but on hers it was because she was too busy feeling, enjoying the way he moved inside her. Closing her eyes, she gripped his sides and welcomed him even deeper inside her.

"Baby," he groaned, his first word since entering her. "Been too long. You feel good, so damn good." His hips pumped faster and faster, pushing Paige into the mattress with every thrust. "Your tight cunt is going to be the death of me."

"As if...as if I'd let you slip away that easy."

"Don't worry," he said, never wavering from his steady thrusts, "the only place I'm going is balls-deep inside you." As if to prove his point, Shane slid his hand between their bodies, stroking her clit in tune to the tempo of their loving.

The added stimulation was almost more than she could handle. Wrapping her legs around his waist, Paige held on to him as he spun her world on its axis. Blinded by pleasure, she could do nothing more than hold on with all her might and enjoy the ride of a lifetime.

And what a ride it was. Shane powered into her continuously, pounding into her body as Paige undulated beneath him. "Yes. Yes. Don't stop, please. Please, oh, oh." The words tumbled from her lips, a tangled web of jumbled nonsensical sounds that became their own personal soundtrack.

Just when Paige thought she was incapable of lasting a second longer, Shane squeezed her clit between his fingers and sent her soaring. Her release sent him tumbling over the edge right after her. He pumped faster and faster inside her until he too came, flooding her pussy with his come. Exhausted and worn down to the nub, she released her death grip on him and dropped her legs to the bed. After a few seconds, he pulled from her tender body and collapsed on the bed next to her on his back.

"You know," he said once he was able to get his breathing back under control. "If make-up sex continues to be so appealing, I won't have any incentive to improve my bad behavior."

Laughing, Paige rolled over onto her side so she was facing him and propped her arm up under her head. "If I know you—"

"And you do."

"You have no need to worry on that front. I see lots of make-up sex in our future."

"But you see a future, right?" Smiling, he brushed the back of his hand against her cheek in a gentle caress.

Paige leaned into his touch. "Yes."

Shane slid his hand around the back of her neck and gently pulled her to him, lightly brushing his lips across hers. "Then that's good enough for me."

For once, Paige couldn't have agreed with him more.

* * * * *

One Year Later

"I can tell by the silly look on your face, you're much too pleased with yourself."

Shane stilled his expression and glanced at his fiancé. "I have no idea what you're talking about."

"Liar." Paige smirked at him. "Come on, admit it. You're freaking eating this up, aren't you?"

"What?" he tried again, this denial no better than the one before.

"This." Paige gestured to the small party gathered together in honor of his birthday once more. "Everyone. You're pleased as punch."

Who wouldn't be? Shane looked around the room and grinned. If he had to say so himself, he'd done good. His birthday wish from last year not only changed his life, but those of the people he cared the most about. His friends.

Bev, who a year ago refused to be in the same room with Holden, was sitting in a large oversized chair with Holden perched next to her on the arm. He toyed absentmindedly with a strand of her dark brown hair as he listened to Tripp regale his latest locker-room tale.

And Tripp, who for years had idiotically passed on a chance of happiness with Gideon and Skylar, was now sitting on the couch across from Holden and Bev with Gideon on one side and Skylar on the other. From the way Tripp's hand was on the back of Gideon's neck, and the way Skylar was curled into Tripp's side with her head on his shoulder, Shane could tell the three of them were growing even closer as time went by. Tripp appeared happier than Shane could ever remember the other man looking, and he sincerely doubted it had anything to do with the new contract he signed and more to do with the two people who were flanking him.

"Uh-huh." Paige's amused voice drew his attention back to her. "Just as I thought. You're loving it."

"Look, woman," Shane growled as he pulled her into his arms, "can't a man enjoy his party and the people he loves without his woman giving him hell?"

"Not if the man is you and the woman is me." She grinned. "I'm always going to give you hell. You might as well get used to it." Paige raised her left hand and wiggled the engagement ring that had once belonged to his grandmother at him. "You're in this for life."

"Now you tell me," he said with a laugh although, truthfully, Paige knew how much it meant to him to have her in his life and how thankful he was to have her.

"Seriously though, you did a phenomenal job here, you know that, right?"

"Nah, fate had a hand in this," he said modestly.

"But it took you to make it all come together." Paige wrapped her arms around his waist.

"I might have put the wheels in motion, but what happened here was..." Words seemed to escape him. As much as he'd hoped and prayed his friends would find their true loves, he never knew it would have worked out so well. But what happened with him and Paige was beyond his wildest expectations. Her faith and love in him had brought about so much healing in his life he'd never be able to express to her how important she was to him.

"I know, baby." Her hand stroked over his back. "Miraculous I think is the word you're looking for."

It wasn't the word he was thinking but it would definitely do. Because, honestly, it had been nothing short of a miracle they had all found each other only to fall in love with one another and begin to work their way to a happily ever after now.

"Hey, Shane, when are we eating cake?"

He looked over at Bev. "Whenever you're ready."

"I'm ready now." Bev stood and glanced down at Holden. "Want to help me?"

"No," Holden rose and held his hand out to her. "But I'll do it anyway."

"That's all that matters." She laughed as she took his hand and walked into the kitchen. Shane watched them leave with a smile on his face. Little did Bev know the next event they'd be celebrating would be her engagement party. Before dinner, Holden had pulled him and Paige aside to show them the platinum ring he'd picked out for the pretty Filipino woman. And if Paige's squeal of delight was anything to go by, Bev was going to be extremely pleased.

"Are we receiving presents from you again this year?" Skylar asked eagerly as she joined him and Paige in the dining room.

"Greedy much?" Tripp teased, coming up behind her. "Didn't you get enough last year?" He reached around and caressed her barely distended belly.

Shane wasn't sure exactly who the father was, and from what he gathered, neither did Skylar, Tripp or Gideon. Nor did they care.

Skylar placed her hand over his. "More than enough."

Just at that moment the lights were lowered and Bev and Holden returned to the room. Bev was holding a large cake full of lit candles. "Happy birthday to you," she began to sing.

The others joined in, singing off-key as usual, as Bev brought the cake into the dining room and placed it on the table. Once the horrible and barely legible song was over, Bev gestured for him to come closer to the table. "Come on, birthday boy, time to make your wish."

With his arm around Paige, Shane walked over to the table and glanced down at the candle-heavy cake. He wasn't sure what to wish for since he had everything he wanted right here.

"Come on already, make your wish," Gideon encouraged. "We want to eat sometime tonight."

Shane looked around the room once again at all his friends before releasing Paige and leaning forward. Closing his eyes, he blew out the flames while making the only wish he possibly could—that they would all stay as happy as they were now from here on out.

At the sound of everyone clapping, Shane opened his eyes and stood back up. "Good job, old man," Paige teased. "All out on the first try. This means you're going to get exactly what you wished for."

"Of course I will." Shane would settle for nothing less. Now all his dreams had come true, he'd never let them go.

Also by Lena Matthews

eBooks:
Ellora's Cavemen: Dreams of the Oasis IV (*anthology*)
Friends with Benefits *with Maggie Casper*
Full Exposure *with Evangeline Anderson*
Georgia Peach
Maverick's Black Cat *with Maggie Casper*
Myth of Moonlight *with Liz Andrews*
Shadow of Moonlight *with Liz Andrews*
Stud Muffin Wanted
When Angels Fall

Print Books:
Ellora's Cavemen: Dreams of the Oasis IV (*anthology*)
Good Girl Seeks Bad Rider (Pocket)
Maverick's Black Cat *with Maggie Casper*
Myths and Shadows *with Liz Andrews*
Tempting Treats (*anthology*)

About the Author

℘

Lena Matthews spends her days dreaming about handsome heroes and her nights with her own personal hero. Married to her college sweetheart, she is the proud mother of an extremely smart toddler, three evil dogs, and a mess of ants that she can't seem to get rid of.

When not writing, she can be found reading, watching movies, lifting up the cushions on the couch to look for batteries for the remote control and plotting different ways to bring Buffy back on the air.

Lena welcomes comments from readers. You can find her website and email address on her author bio page at www.ellorascave.com.

Tell Us What You Think

We appreciate hearing reader opinions about our books. You can email us at Comments@EllorasCave.com.

Why an electronic book?

We live in the Information Age—an exciting time in the history of human civilization, in which technology rules supreme and continues to progress in leaps and bounds every minute of every day. For a multitude of reasons, more and more avid literary fans are opting to purchase e-books instead of paper books. The question from those not yet initiated into the world of electronic reading is simply: *Why?*

1. *Price.* An electronic title at Ellora's Cave Publishing and Cerridwen Press runs anywhere from 40% to 75% less than the cover price of the exact same title in paperback format. Why? Basic mathematics and cost. It is less expensive to publish an e-book (no paper and printing, no warehousing and shipping) than it is to publish a paperback, so the savings are passed along to the consumer.
2. *Space.* Running out of room in your house for your books? That is one worry you will never have with electronic books. For a low one-time cost, you can purchase a handheld device specifically designed for e-reading. Many e-readers have large, convenient screens for viewing. Better yet, hundreds of titles can be stored within your new library—on a single microchip. There are a variety of e-readers from different manufacturers. You can also read e-books on your PC or laptop computer. (Please note that Ellora's Cave does not endorse any specific brands.

You can check our websites at www.ellorascave.com or www.cerridwenpress.com for information we make available to new consumers.)

3. *Mobility.* Because your new e-library consists of only a microchip within a small, easily transportable e-reader, your entire cache of books can be taken with you wherever you go.
4. *Personal Viewing Preferences.* Are the words you are currently reading too small? Too large? Too… ANNOYING? Paperback books cannot be modified according to personal preferences, but e-books can.
5. *Instant Gratification.* Is it the middle of the night and all the bookstores near you are closed? Are you tired of waiting days, sometimes weeks, for bookstores to ship the novels you bought? Ellora's Cave Publishing sells instantaneous downloads twenty-four hours a day, seven days a week, every day of the year. Our webstore is never closed. Our e-book delivery system is 100% automated, meaning your order is filled as soon as you pay for it.

Those are a few of the top reasons why electronic books are replacing paperbacks for many avid readers.

As always, Ellora's Cave and Cerridwen Press welcome your questions and comments. We invite you to email us at Comments@ellorascave.com or write to us directly at Ellora's Cave Publishing Inc., 1056 Home Avenue, Akron, OH 44310-3502.

COMING TO A BOOKSTORE NEAR YOU!

ELLORA'S CAVE

Bestselling Authors Tour

UPDATES AVAILABLE AT
WWW.EllorasCave.COM

Cerridwen, the Celtic Goddess of wisdom, was the muse who brought inspiration to storytellers and those in the creative arts. Cerridwen Press encompasses the best and most innovative stories in all genres of today's fiction. Visit our site and discover the newest titles by talented authors who still get inspired - much like the ancient storytellers did, once upon a time.

Cerridwen Press
www.cerridwenpress.com

Discover for yourself why readers can't get enough of the multiple award-winning publisher

Ellora's Cave.

Whether you prefer e-books or paperbacks,

be sure to visit EC on the web at
www.ellorascave.com

for an erotic reading experience that will leave you breathless.

Made in the USA
Lexington, KY
16 October 2010